DANCE OF DEATH

Lieutenant Paul Bourne raised his head above the thick rice stubble that bordered the stream bed and felt the breath catch in his throat. The moonlight glimmered off so many Viet Cong rifle barrels that the field on the far side looked like a parade ground. There were three long lines of at least two hundred soldiers wearing camouflaged uniforms and another column of Viet Cong moving along the tree line.

Bourne glanced behind and signaled to his team of commandos at the edge of the stream bed. Then he turned back and pulled the trigger of his submachine gun. The men behind him opened up a moment later, and the chatter of Browning automatic rifles, carbines and M-79 grenade launchers produced a weird musical background for the enemy soldiers as they performed a macabre dance on the moonlit streamside stage with the help of the bullets striking their bodies. The first rank was decimated before the Viet Cong could unshoulder their weapons. The second rank wavered, and suddenly a trumpet could be heard above the din of battle. They're pulling back, Bourne thought.

But he knew it wouldn't be long before they returned.

THE WORLD-AT-WAR SERIES
by Lawrence Cortesi

COUNTDOWN TO PARIS (1548, $3.25)
Having stormed the beaches of Normandy, every GI had one dream: to liberate Paris from the Nazis. Trapping the enemy in the Falaise Pocket, the Allies would shatter the powerful German 7th Army Group, opening the way for the . . . COUNTDOWN TO PARIS.

GATEWAY TO VICTORY (1496, $3.25)
After Leyte, the U.S. Navy was at the threshold of Japan's Pacific Empire. With his legendary cunning, Admiral Halsey devised a brilliant plan to deal a crippling blow in the South China Sea to Japan's military might.

ROMMEL'S LAST STAND (1415, $3.25)
In April of 1943 the Nazis attempted a daring airlift of supplies to a desperate Rommel in North Africa. But the Allies were lying in wait for one of the most astonishing and bloody air victories of the war.

LAST BRIDGE TO VICTORY (1393, $3.25)
Nazi troops had blown every bridge on the Rhine, stalling Eisenhower's drive for victory. In one final blood-soaked battle, the fanatic resistance of the Nazis would test the courage of every American soldier.

PACIFIC SIEGE (1363, $3.25)
If the Allies failed to hold New Guinea, the entire Pacific would fall to the Japanese juggernaut. For six brutal months they drenched the New Guinea jungles with their blood, hoping to live to see the end of the . . . PACIFIC SIEGE.

THE BATTLE FOR MANILA (1334, $3.25)
A Japanese commander's decision—against orders—to defend Manila to the death led to the most brutal combat of the entire Pacific campaign. A living hell that was . . . THE BATTLE FOR MANILA.

Available wherever paperbacks are sold, or order direct from the Publisher. Send cover price plus 50¢ per copy for mailing and handling to Zebra Books, Dept. 1742, 475 Park Avenue South, New York, N.Y. 10016. DO NOT SEND CASH.

EAGLES CRY BLOOD

A NOVEL OF THE VIETNAM WAR BY

DONALD E. ZLOTNIK

ZEBRA BOOKS
KENSINGTON PUBLISHING CORP.

ZEBRA BOOKS

are published by

Kensington Publishing Corp.
475 Park Avenue South
New York, NY 10016

First printing: January 1986

Printed in the United States of America

BOOK ONE

Chapter 1

The rain beat down hard against the female spider monkey's face, making her instinctively lick the water accumulating around her mouth. She sat curled up in the nook of the giant mahogany tree holding her week-old baby tightly against her chest and making a worried clicking sound that made her infant shift his position against her warm breast and snuggle even closer to the secure sound of her heartbeat. The young mother wasn't afraid of the loud sound coming from the rain but of the large green boa constrictor she had sighted only moments before the heavy monsoon storm had appeared above her tree. The large snake was too slow-moving to catch her when she could see it, but the solid sheet of water obstructed her view and was making her very nervous.

The monsoon stopped as suddenly as it had started, leaving the shiny leaves dripping tons of water down to the ground. She reached up to push the branch in front of her to one side as she tried locating the green monster. A loud noise below her on the animal path drew her attention away from her search. She saw the human fall down and regain his feet by grabbing ahold of a clump of young bamboo. The soft whimper from her baby brought her attention back to her perch on the tree limb just in time for her to see the ten-foot tree boa coil the front half of its body for a strike. She bared her fangs and screamed at the tree villain, jumping off the limb and reaching out for a serendipitously-located branch that bent under her weight like a fishing rod and then sprang back, hitting the snake when its load was released.

Paul looked up in the large tree and saw the snake, but could only hear the screaming mother scold the boa as she scampered for safety through the trees. He stopped on the trail, breathing hard as his body fought for oxygen from the difficult climb up the trail from the valley floor below. The noise of gear rattling against metal and high-strung voices clattering to each other through the thick undergrowth reached his trained ears where he stood exhausted and dripping wet. He looked up the hill, trying to locate the only other remaining survivor from the North Vietnamese ambush, but he couldn't see ten feet up the trail.

A loud voice called down the trail from only a few feet below him and was answered by one of the enemy's comrades farther down the path. Paul whirled around too fast on the mud and felt himself falling down on the trail. He felt the air escape from his lungs and wondered to himself if he had the strength left to draw it back into his body. Finger-wide rivulets of brown colored water created by the recent monsoon downpour rushed past his cheek, forming up with more of its kind into a decent jungle stream in the valley. Releasing a pain-filled groan, Paul rolled over onto his stomach and pressed his mouth against one of the brown runnels; he sucked the cool water mixed with mud into his dehydrated body.

The three other members from his reconnaissance team had been killed down in the valley in a well-executed North Vietnamese ambush just minutes before, and Paul had escaped, covering his teammate's trail up the hill. The North Vietnamese had screwed up when they had stopped to strip the Americans of their watches and clothes. The barbaric act had given the two survivors time to gain a respectable lead on the enemy patrol.

Paul knew that he couldn't stay ahead of the enemy soldiers too much longer if he kept Bill on the trail—and breaking through the thick jungle growth lining the path would be impossible considering his condition and the wounds Bill was suffering from the ambush. Paul had to find a good hiding place and hope that the Vietnamese would either pass them by in their haste or allow him to conduct a counterambush.

Paul listened to the NVA calling to each other as they followed the mud spoor. He started climbing again using both his hands and feet to claw up the hillside. The fresh monsoon mud clung to the sides and bottoms on his green mesh jungle boots, building up layers on top of each other until the weight became so heavy that the mud broke its hold against the hard rubber soles and fell off in huge chunks that made it easy for the enemy trackers to follow his trail.

Bill staggered twenty meters ahead of Paul on the trail. He was falling regularly and was regaining his feet by using the reserve strength only those who are fighting against certain death can muster from somewhere inside their innersouls. A field of small boulders and slabs of vine-covered rocks replaced the mud on the trail for the next hundred meters of the gradual incline leading to the top of the ridge and a possible helicopter extraction. Bill struggled over the slippery rocks and collapsed along the side of the animal path, too exhausted to move any farther.

Paul found Bill on the trail and stopped to see if his partner was dead. He leaned over the man's chest and could hear a faint heartbeat. Paul sighed. He knew that he couldn't carry him. The voices coming up the trail gave Paul the strength he was searching for, and he grabbed his buddy by his web gear and pulled him off the trail into a thick stand of bamboo. The thin strip of thick vegetation that separated them from the path sprang back into its haphazard pattern as soon as Paul had passed through, making it difficult for the trackers to spot the exit off the trail by the Americans. Using all of his strength, Paul dragged Bill over to the bombed-down tree and tucked him against the rotting, sweet-smelling wood. He scooped up handfuls of the brown bamboo leaves and covered Bill with a two-foot-thick layer of camouflage before he took up a defensive position near his hidden buddy.

The first powerful strike created so much instant pain that Paul bit through his lower lip rather than release the scream that had rushed up through his throat from his lungs. Blood seeped between his teeth and covered the taste buds on his tongue. Pain flashed up his leg in violent ripples, forcing him to involuntarily tense his leg muscles tight as a stone. The huge, four-inch-long black jungle scorpion spread its legs on his camouflaged trouser leg and curled its tail for a second strike. Paul slowly shoved the warm barrel of his CAR-15 submachine gun over until he poked the monster, forcing it back into its hiding place under the loose tree bark.

Bill moaned.

Paul pushed the heel of his dirty hand against his friend's mouth; any sound that they made now would cause their instant deaths at the hands of the enemy patrol. Paul knew that the North Vietnamese wouldn't take an American paratrooper prisoner.

The enemy patrol passed their location and paused on the trail twenty-five meters past their hiding place. Paul kept his hand pressed against Bill's mouth and held his own breath in order to partially control the pain that was wracking his own body. For the first time in his life Paul wanted to die and end his suffering. A loud command reached Paul through the thick brush and the patrol moved on. Paul kept glancing at the spot on the tree trunk where the scorpion had scurried, and then he looked up at the wall of green vegetation bordering the trail. He didn't know what he feared most: the NVA or the black monster returning to sting him again.

A light machine gun broke the jungle silence to the left of Paul's hiding place, sending a troop of monkeys chattering through the trees. Bill jerked upright and then lay back on the leaves when he heard the cyclic sound. Paul reached over and pulled his delirious buddy back down behind the protective rotting tree. A growing roar of rifle fire joined the machine gun, forming a death symphony that was interrupted occasionally by the loud boom of exploding grenades that gave a base melody to the battle sounds and changed the tempo. Paul's trained ear separated the different modulations coming from the different types of weapons. The NVA patrol had walked into one of the companies from Paul's battalion.

The slapping sounds of Ho Chi Minh sandals impacting against the mud path alerted Paul to the retreating enemy soldiers approaching his hiding place on the trail, and his warrior's instincts surfaced through his pain. The trained reconnaissance man pushed Bill aside and forced his pain-wracked body to stand up.

Bill felt the wet leaves brushing his face as Paul scooped more leaves over the top of his head. The wounded soldier could see his partner standing above him favoring one leg. He watched as Paul staggered over to the trail and took up a crouch, placing the steel butt of his CAR-15 against his upper thigh and waiting.

Paul's leg began to throb and shake from the poison the scorpion had delivered to his flesh. He started to remove his finger from the trigger and reach for the wound when a running khaki-clad North Vietnamese slid around the curve just up the trail. Paul could plainly see the red enamel star centered on the man's sun helmet and the sweat covering the tanned yellow face just as he squeezed the steel trigger. The short burst sent the enemy soldier dancing backward against the rain-washed dark green leaves. Paul stepped out onto the center of the trail and looked both ways. He saw a pair of NVA break out of the jungle onto the trail fifty meters below him, and he sent a volley of death pellets across their backs.

A scattering of armor piercing bullets bounced off the packed mud on the trail around Paul. He shifted the muzzle of his weapon in the direction the rounds had come from and squeezed the trigger on his compact submachine gun, sending the enemy soldier to join his comrades in the happy rice bowl of the afterlife. Paul's CAR-15 made a familiar popping sound that told his alert ears that the magazine was empty and the bolt locked in its rear position. He didn't look down at the weapon as he reached over and ejected the empty magazine and removed a full one from his ammo pouch surrounding his waist.

The sound of a breaking branch reached him as he crouched reloading his machine gun. Paul's useless CAR-15 automatically swung around following his eyes. The brush parted and the shiny sweat-covered face of a black soldier smiled through the jungle growth at the recon man.

Bill drove the borrowed dark-blue AC Ford Cobra

with time-conditioned skill along the familiar graceful curves on California's Highway 1. The ride down from the Malibu beach to Los Angeles International Airport was a short drive by California standards, but beautiful with the expensive ocean beach houses lining the right side of the road and the golden hills touching the highway on the left as he headed south down the black strip of asphalt.

Lieutenant Bourne took off his green beret and rolled the coveted piece of green cloth up before he tucked it under his leg when Bill accelerated the powerful convertible along one of the rare stretches of road. The speedometer registered a hundred and twenty-five miles an hour before Bill eased up on the pedal and tapped the brakes. Paul relaxed his head against the leather seat and allowed the salt air to slap his hair from side to side. Paul forced his mind back to the present, leaving the battles that the two of them had fought locked in the secret chambers of his most guarded thoughts.

The two weeks Paul had spent with Bill in his canyon cabin were well worth the special effort that he had taken to spend some time with his old war buddy. They had gone down to the beach every day to surf, and they had spent their nights at parties with the local girls. The relaxing time Paul had spent on the beach had removed most of the tension that had been beaten into his senses from the hellish six months he had spent at the Army's Infantry Officer's Candidate School. Paul had developed an instant love for Malibu and its free-living people. He could understand why his friend had chosen the beach sands as the place he wanted to live after his stint in the war.

The blue car's nose dipped slightly when Bill down-shifted the oversized engine. The Cobra obeyed and shot forward around the curve when Bill's hand automatically shifted back to fourth and his foot softly massaged the accelerator. Topanga Canyon road signs flashed past the duo without being read. Lieutenant Bourne turned on his seat to see if Bill's mind was still with him in the car or was riding a wave on some beach.

"I have to stop and get some gas." Bill turned into an Exxon station where a group of bikers had stopped to gas up and buy beer.

Paul shifted uneasily, expecting trouble. One of the bikers pointed at the car and grinned, showing all of the rotten teeth in the front of his mouth.

"Man, that's a car!" The Levi-jacketed man reached into his back pocket and removed a pint of vodka. He held the bottle to his lips and drained a third of the contents before he stopped.

Bill nodded his head at the mass of chrome and waxed machines and spoke to Paul. "They spend a lot of time on their bikes and do a lot of dope, but they pretty much leave people alone." Bill jumped over the door and slipped down on the warm seat.

"You take care of that car, honey!" a cute blonde attached to the rear seat of one of the bikes spoke just as Bill popped the clutch and left the gas station.

Bill had told Paul earlier that there weren't more than a dozen AC Cobras in California, and with all of the attention the car had been getting, Paul believed him. A lot of very good-looking women had paid Bill's price for a ride with him in the beautiful hand-finished car. Bill slowed the car down when they reached the outskirts around Santa Monica pier. Surfers were hot-dogging around the pilings with the ever-present seagulls crying down to the fishermen on the point of the pier for morsels of fish bait. Bourne relaxed again when Bill stopped for a red light at the intersection of Santa Monica Boulevard and Highway 1.

"Man, I sure don't envy you going back there." Bill spoke to Paul, but had his attention on two very good-looking women who sat smiling at him from one of the park benches. Bill locked their exact location in his mind for his return trip back to his cabin from the airport. Bill ran his fingers through the tangles of his thick ocean-bleached hair and gave the girls a slow wink. Since he had returned from Vietnam, he felt that it was his duty to service every girl in California, and his solid build and good looks definitely made the task an easy one.

"Hell, it's a way of making a living." Bourne closed his eyes.

Bill and Paul had first met in Vietnam Ranger training, and had served together as enlisted scouts for a year, sharing some very tough times running reconnaissance missions for the 173d Airborne Brigade. The mutual spilling of blood and sharing of the horrors found in war had welded an unbreakable friendship between the two men of the kind that could only be understood by other combat soldiers.

"Personally, I'd rather stay here screwing a few good-looking ladies and surfing during the day." Bill accented each word. "You know I'll hide you if you want to stay. . . . Hell, they'll never find you back in the canyon, and my fellow growers will blow away any strangers messing around their gardens."

Paul smiled a rejection of his friend's offer. He didn't like Bill's heavy use of marijuana but he understood the offer that was written between his friend's words. The year they had spent together in Vietnam had almost ruined the beautiful, free-spirited surfer boy from California. There had been too much killing on both sides that had placed a heavily barred door in Bill's brain that he was constantly fighting to keep locked. Bill played the free-spirit game with him, but Bourne knew his friend better than to fall for the exterior mold being presented to the civilian world. His friend's carefree attitude masked a very sensitive soul that had been scorched by the very fires of hell.

The AC Cobra burnt rubber turning into the main entrance of the Los Angeles International Airport, skidding slightly when Bill tapped the gas pedal with the wheels still turned hard to the right. Passenger heads turned as the dark blue car pulled to a rough stop in front of the V.I.P. entrance.

"I'll let you out here. You deserve first-rate treatment for wanting to go back there again." Bill's laugh was forced out between his teeth. He could feel that old feeling of not ever seeing a friend again enter his stomach and move to the muscles surrounding his heart.

A uniformed attendant started walking toward the sports car, giving Bill just the distraction that he needed. He scooted up and sat on the top edge of his low seat and waved at the approaching man.

"Get the hell away from us!" The evil look in Bill's eyes was worse than the spoken warning and the man stopped near the doors.

"Thanks for the lift, brother." Bourne locked fingers with Bill over the low windshield. "Later, here!" Paul's throat tightened and he choked on the last word.

"Yeah, I'd go with you to the planes, but you know . . . those foxes back there need some looking after before some sly devil coaxes them into his apartment." Bill slid back down onto his seat and gunned the oversized engine. "Besides, I haven't dressed for the occasion!" Bill glanced down at his faded pair of yellow surfing shorts, the only item of clothing he was wearing.

Lieutenant Bourne grabbed his small traveling bag off the back seat of the car and stepped back away from the curb, allowing the AC Cobra to scream away leaving the smell of burnt rubber lingering next to the cement curb. Bill didn't look back. He assumed that he would see people again, and that sentimental goodbyes were therefore a waste of time. Paul fixed the angle of his green beret before he entered the airport building. Los Angeles International was always a show in itself with all of the movie stars, hippies, and weirdly dressed left-wing religious groups parading down the long hallways and constantly entertaining the other passengers between their flights. Paul went straight over to the debarkation gates and entered his waiting aircraft through the accordion tunnel attached to the stainless steel fuselage. He found an empty seat in the back near the rear toilets and slid in next to the window. Paul had received a lot of hostile stares when he had walked through the long airport corridors to his airplane. A Green Beret uniform wasn't well liked by the hippies, and the American middle class was beginning to turn from the government's support of the unpopular war as the years passed. Paul pressed his lips tightly together and shook his head. He hadn't started the war, but he knew that he wasn't going to run over to Canada and hide until it was over with, either. His kids wouldn't have to hold their heads in shame when they were asked what their daddy had done in the war. He had fought. The Canada runners would always be a part of any society and they would return after the war to breed other little runners who would either hide behind their mothers' skirts or verbalize the wrongs of the world when it came their turns to defend the nation.

A man wearing a wide-brimmed leather hat took the aisle seat in the same row where Paul was sitting looking out the window at the men loading baggage onto the plane. Paul placed his travel bag on the seat between them in order to prevent an over-talkative hippie from joining the man in the leather hat. Paul had heard enough of the left-wingers spewing forth their one-sided garbage about the immoral aspects of the war. Paul bit his lips as he thought. A soldier obeyed orders and he was a soldier, couldn't they see that? It was the politicians who should be yelled at if the people really wanted to stop the war, not the poor soldier who *died* for their mistakes.

The man sitting near Paul glanced at him and nodded his head. Paul didn't return the friendly greeting, but instead removed a magazine from the rack on the seatback in front of him and feigned reading an article on the South Sea Islands.

The aircraft was in flight for almost an hour before the man, who was still wearing the leather hat, turned in his seat and spoke to Paul.

"You going up to San Fran?"

"Oakland." Paul made his answer purposefully short.

"You a soldier?"

"Yes, I'm with the 5th Special Forces Group out of Vietnam." Paul glanced at the man, closing his eye halfway.

The man ignored the threatening glare. "I'm with Sunstorm. It's a new rock group." The young singer was trying really hard to strike up a conversation. "We just had an audition in the Los Angeles Columbia Studios. Man, we made it big!" Pride filled the singer's voice.

Paul looked over at the beaming man and saw the joy coming from his eyes. "I'm glad for you." Paul smiled.

The aspirant rock star and the seasoned warrior talked about their stays in California and the good times they both had had in Los Angeles. The conversation was interrupted when the lights above the cockpit door flashed on, announcing for the passengers to stop smoking and fasten their seatbelts.

"Quick trip," the singer commented as he pulled his leather-bound pad out of his jacket pocket and wrote something on one of the pages.

Paul left the plane as soon as the door was opened by an attractive stewardess, and headed for one of the nearby restrooms where he could adjust his tailored uniform and wash his face before he caught a taxi for the Oakland Military Terminal on the other side of the bay.

He soaped his face and was rinsing with cold water when he heard the singer's voice behind him. The first thought that passed through Paul's mind was that the man was trying to hustle him.

"Here . . ." The singer pushed a folded piece of paper into Paul's rear pants pocket. "Take this, and I hope you have a good time in San Francisco."

Paul dried his face and looked around the empty room. He reached back, removed the folded piece of paper, and opened it. The heavy lines created by a felt-tip pen spelled out the figure of one thousand dollars.

Lieutenant Bourne whispered under his breath. "The guilt-ridden son of a bitch!" He started tearing the check but then stopped, returning the green paper back to his pocket.

Paul left the restroom and walked over to a nearby bookstand and bought a box of envelopes and a stamp. He wrote a short note to Bill on the back of the check, telling him to have a good time on him if the check didn't bounce. Paul shoved the white envelope into the mail drop outside the bookstore and forgot about the singer and the money.

The black taxicab took Paul from the civilian airport over to the Oakland Army Terminal on the far side of the city. The entrance to the facility was packed with troops unloading from the line of buses. Paul could just about tell from what part of the country they were assembling from by the uniforms they wore: tan short-sleeved khakis were worn by troops coming from the southern states and dress greens were worn by soldiers arriving from Fort Ord and the northern posts. Paul paused under the familiar arches leading into the busy terminal, acknowledging the fact that he had passed this way before. He then turned sideways and squeezed through the crowded doors, smelling the odor of too many people packed together in one place. Paul walked quickly around the stacks of duffle bags toward the 24-hour snackbar and found all the tables filled with troops killing time as they waited for their flight numbers to be called out over the intercom system. Paul bought a Styrofoam cup of black coffee and walked over to a large bookstand across from the snackbar. He felt an old fear starting to creep up his throat, drying the tissue as it groped for his tongue. His eyes flashed over the title of the books but his mind failed to absorb the brightly printed words.

Burned . . . black . . . smell . . . gag . . . charred . . . bodies . . . *Help!!! Help!!!* napalm . . . machine guns . . . *Run!!!No! . . . stay . . . Stop the noise! . . . Fight! Kill!!!* . . . Must kill! . . . aim . . . *Damn you! Aim your gun!*

A crystal-clear picture formed in front of Paul's open staring eyes. He could see his own face pushed against decomposing bamboo leaves with his own sweat working as a glue for the small pieces of yellow, dry, dead leaves stuck to his face.

"Aim! Get your face off the ground!" Paul thought that he was screaming but the words were barely audible. The Vietnamese soldier's face that had replaced his own blurred and then disappeared amongst the books.

"What did you say?" a soldier standing next to Paul asked, bringing him back to the air terminal. Paul ignored the man and fought with his own emotions, trying to gain control of his fear. He reached up and removed a random paperback from the rack and thumbed through the pages without looking. He had been through this emotional nightmare before, and knew that the only way to handle the terrible demasculating force was to face it head on, just like he had faced his first parachute jump.

Lieutenant Bourne didn't like losing control of his emotions, and he always worked very hard preplanning all of his actions so that he wouldn't have any unwanted surprises and could reflect total control in front of his subordinates. Paul had won the Leadership Award and a good reputation from his Officer Candidate School classmates for his ability to function under extreme pressure. Paul's eyes focused again and he read the title of the book he had been randomly flipping through: *My Ten Years Living in a Gay Community.*

His face flushed bright red, Paul quickly glanced around to see if anyone had been watching him and then placed the paperback in the rack behind another title. Paul quickly took a western novel from the shelf and paid the old woman operating the cash register for the book.

The waiting room was half full of soldiers either faking sleep or boastfully telling each other stories of their conquests over beautiful women while they were on their thirty-day leaves. Paul found an empty seat and turned the pages of his novel as if he were reading, but his thoughts had returned to Vietnam and the fear was repeating its effort to creep back into his mind and gain control over his body. Paul made a great mental effort and again vanquished his old foe back to the hindmost chambers of his subconscious mind.

A voice echoed metallically around the huge vaulted waiting room from the loud speaker system calling off a list of flight numbers, which gave Paul a chance to concentrate on something else. He heard his flight number called next to last and stood up fixing his gig line. Paul glanced around at the hundreds of milling soldiers who were locating their baggage that they were carrying on the plane with them. All of the men were suffering from the pre-Vietnam jitters, and were using any excuse they could find to occupy their hands by keeping busy adjusting satchels and straps. There were no mothers and fathers in the large halls to soften the blow of getting on the planes that would separate some of them permanently from their loved ones.

The lines in front of the locked gates grew rapidly. Everyone had gotten in their flight lines too early, and the men began shuffling and trying to strike up small talk in order to hide their growing fears.

A small group of signal corps soldiers were laughing in the back of one line and pointing at a young paratrooper who was totally disoriented and visibly lost in his personal fear. The young blond soldier stood stiff-backed, staring out in front of his place in line, unable to hear the taunts coming from the black soldiers. Paul pushed his way through the pack of black signal corps soldiers and placed his arm over the boy's shoulder. The stare Paul flashed at the noncombatants shut them up.

"Hey, trooper. Do you have your boarding pass ready?" Bourne tried to break through the young paratrooper's fear and gain his attention. The young warrior was too far into his own fear of the unknown to respond to the lieutenant's question. The youth reminded Paul of the first man in a jump school stick, standing in the open doorway twelve hundred and fifty feet above the surface of the earth, waiting for the red light attached to the doorframe to go out and the green light to flash on. Only remote control of the man's nervous system kept him on his feet.

Paul snapped his elbow in the jumper's side.

"Paratrooper! Which unit are you going to join in Vietnam?"

The young man continued looking through Paul but found an answer in the part of his brain that was still functioning and returning to reality. "The 173d Airborne, sir!"

"You're lucky! That's one of the finest units over there." Paul looked at the group of grinning black signalmen. "It's made up of some damn fine fighting men." The lieutenant grinned. "Not everyone *fights* in Vietnam."

The black group who had been picking on the lone paratrooper turned their backs on the lieutenant. The young paratrooper's eyes slowly focused, showing that the teenager had returned to the outside world from his inner self. Embarrassment replaced the boy's fear.

"I'm . . . I'm sorry, sir. I was thinking about something else. Were you talking to me?" The fear lines in the youth's face relaxed and a handsome grin took its place.

"I was just saying, we should have a good flight if the weather stays this nice." Lieutenant Bourne smiled a knowing comrade's grin at the young soldier. "Hang in there. We're all in the same boat, paratrooper!"

The young trooper's eyes thanked Lieutenant Bourne.

A pair of air force sergeants opened the gates and let the waiting army men board their leased commercial aircraft. There was another air force sergeant seating the soldiers when Paul and the young paratrooper stepped through the small airliner's doorway. The sergeant was filling the aircraft from back to front, disregarding the wishes of the soldiers. The young paratrooper cut in front of an indifferent black soldier wearing a First Cavalry shoulder patch and took the empty seat next to Lieutenant Bourne.

"I'm Pfc. O'Toole, sir." The young man shook hands with the lieutenant. "Have you been over to 'Nam before?"

"Yes. I went over with the 173d when I was seventeen years old. That was before they changed the regulations to a person having to reach their eighteenth birthday before they could be shipped." Both men smiled as Bourne added, "I ran recon."

"I just turned eighteen in jump school." The trooper's face lit up. "My Dad was a Ranger during World War Two." Pride filled the young voice. "I think that I'll volunteer for recon, too."

The two soldiers talked about different recon techniques during half of the flight to Vietnam. Paul wondered if he had been so energetic the first time that he had gone to war, deciding that he had probably matched the young man's enthusiasm.

Lieutenant Bourne placed the paper-cased pillow behind his head and slipped off into his own private world of thoughts for the remainder of the trip. The young paratrooper stuck to Paul during the unloading at the refueling stops like chocolate on a preteen's fingers. The flight was smooth and fast, taking less than twenty hours to travel from Oakland to Bien Hoa. Lieutenant Bourne's eyes wandered over the faces of the young soldiers who were standing in the crowded aisle getting their personal gear ready to debark the aircraft. He wondered how many of them would be riding in the under-belly baggage compartment on the return trip home. Paul forced his mind to transfer over to more pleasant thoughts.

"Officers, go over to the main processing building for your in-briefings. . . . Enlisted men, follow your guides to the open air veranda!" The personnel sergeant had his hands hooked in his belt as he stood filling the center aisle of the airliner. He was at least forty pounds overweight and the sweat stains on his khaki shirt reached down to touch the black belt surrounding his ample waist. "Before any of you leave the aircraft I must inform you about a few combat precautions." The sergeant paused in the middle of his memorized speech for effect. "First . . . in the event we receive any incoming rocket or mortar fire as we debark the aircraft . . . do not panic! Follow your guides and they will lead you to safety in the bomb shelters."

A captain standing against the bulkhead in the rear of the airplane raised his arm to gain the sergeant's attention.

"Yes, Captain?" The sergeant's voice was bold.

"When was the last time this airfield received *any* enemy fire?"

The sergeant paused in answering the officer and looked down the row of scared young faces that were looking at him filled with fear of the unknown. "That's not the point, Captain. It's the policy here to inform newly arriving personnel about mortar and rocket attacks . . ." The personnel sergeant knew that he had lost the effect he had wanted with the questioning remark from the officer and gave up his attempt trying to scare the new men. "All right, let's debark!"

"Don't let fats scare you guys!" the captain yelled so that everyone on the plane could hear him. "There are people waiting outside for you guys to get off and they want to see you step off the plane scared shitless!"

"Not us, Captain!" A roar filled the confined space in

the plane as the men grabbed their gear and growled defiantly at the departing sergeant.

The long line of new troops wearing wrinkled khaki uniforms followed their guides dressed in camouflaged jungle fatigues to the covered briefing areas. A loud cheer rippled through a group of soldiers who were waiting behind a nearby cyclone fence for the airplane to empty so they could board it for their return trip home after a long twelve months in Vietnam. Lieutenant Bourne smiled as he walked past the fence and ignored the good-natured catcalls. He acknowledged their earned privilege to harass the replacements, who in turn would harass the newcomers arriving a year from now when they left. Paul's eyes caught Pfc. O'Toole staring at him from the first row of soldiers under the enlisted men's veranda. He smiled and gave the young paratrooper a thumbs-up sign, and received a smile in return that spread out over the teenager's face into a confident grin.

"Morning, sir." A soldier wearing an impeccable tiger-suit touched Lieutenant Bourne on his shoulder. "You don't have to process in with the rest of the leg officers at Camp Alpha. We have our own processing section at the downtown B-Team." The sergeant looked around at the group of newly arrived senior enlisted men and officers. "Are there any more Special Forces people on the plane, sir?"

"No, I'm the only one." Lieutenant Bourne followed the sergeant to a jeep parked next to the air terminal building and threw his baggage on the back seat while the sergeant unlocked the chain that secured the steering wheel. "We'll do all of your in-processing for you while you're at the B-Team. It's one of the benefits of being a Green Beret." The sergeant looked over his shoulder and pulled the jeep out in the congested traffic passing in front of the terminal.

The familiar smells of nuc-mom, freshly turned earth, and burning wood that was particular to the orient—and specially of Vietnam—reached Paul's nostrils the instant they left the area filled by the exhaust fumes from the aircraft.

"Watch your arm as we go along the streets, sir. The little kids sometimes tear watches off your arm if they think that they can get away with it in heavy traffic." The sergeant expertly wove the jeep through the unpatterned Saigon traffic.

"I've been through here before." Paul's right arm was lying across his lap.

The sergeant turned the jeep onto a long cement driveway that led up to a heavy wrought-iron gate. They waited while an old Nung warrior swung the right half of the beautiful forged gate open to allow the Special Forces jeep to enter the old French villa.

"Morning, Nhu!" The sergeant's voice reflected the respect that he felt for the old man, who smiled a betelnut grin in a return greeting. "He's one of the meanest warriors in his tribe!" The sergeant twisted on his seat so that he could face Paul. "He killed over two hundred Viet-Minh during the war between the French and the communists. The French decorated him six times for bravery."

The old man waved them through the gate as he slowly checked the wheel wells of the jeep for attached plastic explosives. Paul noticed that the villa grounds were superbly kept up. The flower beds were in bloom along the long brick walkways and the sidewalks were swept clean.

"You keep this place up pretty good." Lieutenant Bourne reached in back of the jeep for his gear.

"Nhu's wife and young sons work in the kitchen and the yard. You can see that they take a lot of pride in this villa."

The inside of the building was cleaner than the patios. Paul followed the sergeant down the long cool hallway to the large single room assigned to new officers and placed his gear on an empty bed.

"The XO wants to see you as soon as you're ready, sir." The sergeant showed Paul the closed door down the hall marked Executive Officer.

Paul put his bags under the bed and brushed his hair back out of his eyes before he went over and knocked on the door. He entered when he heard a voice from the other side tell him to come in.

"Morning, sir." Paul saluted the young-looking major occupying the chair behind the wide wooden desk.

The major stood up and waved for Paul to take a seat. "Glad that you could join us, Lieutenant." He reached over a stack of personnel folders and shook hands with Paul.

"Thanks, sir. This is a really nice set-up you all have here." Paul glanced around the paneled room.

"We're proud of our operation. We try and make the processing of our personnel as pleasant as possible." The major paused and released a grin. "Don't get any ideas about us cadre hiding here away from the war." The major flashed a frown, at the same time holding his smile. "In order to get a job here in Saigon, all of us had to serve at least a year in the field and then extend for another six months for duty here."

"What camp did you run out of, sir?"

"I didn't. I worked with the III Corps Mike Force." The major looked at the lieutenant to see if he recognized the name and continued when Paul nodded. "We had a lot of action along the Cambodian border last year." The major crossed his legs over the corner of his desk and changed the subject without warning. "The way things work around here is that we do all of the in-processing for you. The reason being, we don't want the personnel people at Camp Alpha to even see you."

A frown crossed Paul's forehead.

The major nodded his head and continued. "The personnel people at Camp Alpha just love for Special Forces people to come through . . . especially Green Beret medics. There isn't a leg unit in the country that wouldn't give ten of their pill pushers for just *one* Green Beret-trained medic. The divisions were bribing the personnel clerks, and last year they ripped off damn near every Special Forces man coming into the country."

Lieutenant Bourne shrugged his shoulders. "I don't blame them for doing that if they could get away with it. Everyone needs good medics. I wish we had a couple of them when I served with the 173d."

"Agreed, but we can't afford to take sixty-five weeks to train just one trooper and have some other unit get him. Actually, it pisses the man off more than it does us." The young major paused and lit up a fresh Kool cigarette.

"Do I still have to go to Nha Trang after I leave here?"

"It all depends. If you settle on an assignment we can ship you right out of here to your B-Team." The major butted the half-smoked cigarette.

"We want you to enjoy your stay here. The meal hours are posted on the door in your room. You get up in the morning when you want to, so that you can let your body adjust to the jet lag. The only catch here is that you can't leave the compound for any reason until we've finished processing you. The people over at Camp Alpha are pissed that we've stopped their little games, and they're waiting for the smallest incident to occur downtown so they can close this shop." The major stood up, signaling that the interview was over. Lieutenant Bourne was astute enough to realize that the relaxed conversation was designed to check him out so that the major could recommend his assignment to higher headquarters. The Special Forces units tried to assign their people to teams in which they would fit in with the other men.

The first couple of days at the B-Team were enjoyable. Paul had used the time to adjust his body to the new hours and reduce the effects of the jet lag coming from the states. He had drawn his initial issue of tiger-striped fatigues and had a few modifications made on the pockets. He laid one set of the fatigues out on his cot and showered before going down to the B-Team's bar to watch the nightly poker game. The men who arrived at the B-Team from the outlying A-sites were the main reason why Paul went to the bar and sat for hours, listening to the war stories these men told that gave him the latest information on enemy tactics and equipment. Paul had gathered from the conversations over the past two days that the camps attached to B-24 up in II Corps were the hottest fighting spots currently, with the I Corps sites coming in a close second. The bulk of the conversations from the men returning from I Corps concerned the high death rate among their officers. It seemed that the NVA were making a concerted effort to kill as many Green Beret officers as they could. Paul sipped from his bourbon and listened.

"Lieutenant Bourne!" The B-Team executive officer beckoned for Paul to join him at his table.

Paul sensed that he was about to get his assignment. The major smiled as the lieutenant approached. "Are you ready to leave tomorrow?"

"Anytime! Tonight is fine with me." Bourne sat on the edge of the chair and crossed his hands in front of his chest on the tabletop.

"We received a telephone call today from group headquarters concerning your assignment." The major waved for one of the bargirls to wait on him. "You have a choice, based mostly on your prior recon experience. You can go to one of the Greek Projects . . ." The major gave Paul a few seconds to think about what he had offered before continuing, ". . . or you can go to A-253 at Duc Co." He took the drink off the tray and covered the twitching in the corner of his mouth by taking a sip.

"Where's Duc Co?"

"B-24 . . . By Kontum up in II Corps." The major averted his eyes from the lieutenant and acted as if he was interested in the poker game going on around the table near his. "B-24 has three active A-Teams: Duc Co, Plei Me, and Plei Djereng. All of them short officers and all of them under attack."

Lieutenant Bourne inhaled a quiet breath. "Well . . . I came here to kill commies . . ." His voice deepened. "I'll take B-24." Lieutenant Bourne didn't feel as brave as his facial expressions reflected.

"Good!" The major stood up and drained his glass.

Paul went back to the bar table he had been sitting at and ordered another double bourbon. The major left the bar and went to his office. The desk lamp was the only light burning in the small room. He didn't feel good about what he had done, and he was forced to rationalize that Lieutenant Bourne had a better chance of surviving the siege around Duc Co than some fresh lieutenant from the States who didn't have any combat experience. The major picked up the telephone and placed his first call of the day to headquarters in Nha Trang.

Chapter 2

The emotional upheaval created over going to his first operational A-Camp had settled in the bottom of Lieutenant Bourne's stomach, making him feel like he wanted to vomit.

The briefings that he had received from the B-Team operations officers had projected a very bleak scene for the Duc Co Special Forces camp, which was just beginning to recover from a North Vietnamese siege that had lasted 167 days. The NVA soldiers had pressured both Duc Co and Plei Me Special Forces camps, and had also attacked the famous First Cavalry Division, giving that unit a black eye, but destroying itself in the process.

The Ia-Drang Valley, which was composed of a series of rolling hills and freshwater streams twenty thousand meters wide and thirty thousand meters long, was wedged between the two Special Forces A-Camps located on the Vietnamese side of the border and ended in the west against the Cambodian mountains. Paul had been briefed by the operations officer that Duc Co was one of the hottest camps in Vietnam. A shiver slipped down Paul's neck as the thought registered. What a way to start a new tour of duty, especially after the officer had told him that the six prior executive officers at Duc Co had been either killed or seriously wounded in action. Lieutenant Bourne rationalized away the briefings when he thought about how staff officers enjoyed scaring the hell out of young lieutenants with their office-generated war stories.

Paul Bourne lifted his gray B-4 bag off the bench outside the headquarters building and walked down the narrow red laterite road that served as the central thoroughfare for the B-Team base camp. He saw a UH-1C Iroquois gunship with the familiar Special Forces crest painted on its nose parked on a PSP pad near the outer perimeter and walked toward the dark green helicopter.

"Hey, Lieutenant!" The voice came from the top of a five-man fighting bunker. "Are you the officer who needs a ride out to Duc Co?"

Paul spoke up to the unseen man on top of the sandbags. "Yes, I was supposed to meet the crew here at noon."

"We're running a little late. The door gunners had a problem reloading the gun pods and then our pilot decided that he wanted to eat in the mess hall before we left." A hand reached down over the edge of the bunker and waved for Paul to join him. "You might as well hop up here and get some sun. . . . It'll probably be another hour before we leave."

Paul crawled up the sloping side of the sandbag fortress leaving his B-4 bag on the ground below. The helicopter copilot was lying stripped to his waist on his Nomex fatigue jacket. His eyes were closed.

"This sun is about to burn my ass up!" The aviator wiggled his shoulders against the hot sandbags. "But I have to get a decent suntan and get rid of this damn RAMF look."

"What in the hell is a RAMF?"

"A rear area mother fucker. They're the ones who

always eat good, never go out on patrols, and always terrorize the new personnel arriving in-country with their fucking second hand war stories!"

A grin crossed MacKey's face and he opened his eyes to challenge Bourne's stare. "I know what you're thinking, Lieutenant—but I fly gunships and there ain't *nothing* rear area about that!"

"No offense, but I wasn't thinking about that. How old are you?"

The very young-looking face tried to crunch up in an unnatural frown. "I'm nineteen . . . I can hold my own!"

"Damn, you don't look a day over fifteen!"

MacKey's eyes narrowed into aggressive slits. He shook his head in order to remove the strands of silver-blond hair that were sticking to his sweaty forehead. "So you're going to Duc Co?" The change of subject was also welcomed by Paul. He had taken a liking to the surly attitude of the young aviator and didn't want to drive away a possible new friend. The young copilot continued talking.

"We've just returned from your A-Camp this morning." He tossed his head toward the parked UH-1C Iroquois. "Our gunners are replacing the rocket pods and 7.62 ammo that we shot up. Duc Co is one hell of a hot camp to fly into; in fact, only gunships are allowed to enter the Ia Drang Valley A0." MacKey smiled a full-toothed grin. "I don't envy your ass one bit, Lieutenant. There's a lot of land to hump through over there that's crawling with NVA."

"Yeah, I've been told . . ." Paul looked over the dark green hills toward the west from his perch on top of the bunker. "Where are you from back in the states?"

"California . . . The Countyline, if you've ever been around L.A."

"No shit! I was just on leave back at Malibu . . . I

surfed up at the Countyline a couple of times."

"California is the only place for me. A person really don't appreciate just how nice it can be until they leave it. I'm going to round up a few young things when I get back there and fuck for ten days straight!" MacKey's hand automatically rubbed his crotch.

"Let's crank her up!" the voice came from down the road toward the main buildings.

"He's back early." MacKey grabbed his shirt and jumped down off the bunker. "We'll have to get together sometime for a few beers and swap some surfing stories."

Paul picked up his B-4 bag off the ground and followed the copilot toward the aircraft. "Sounds good. I should be able to make it back here in a few months."

Lieutenant Bourne hopped onto the nylon mesh seat and locked his safety belt around his waist in one smooth motion. The helicopter rose above the steel landing pad with a cloud of red dust billowing out from the edges of the PSP. The helicopter tilted forward slightly, and began to roar over the grass plain that surrounded the B-Camp, headed toward the highland jungle to the west. Occasionally the bare ground would be revealed through the dark layer of green trees where a two-thousand-pound bomb had rearranged the setting that nature had carefully organized.

Paul leaned out the open side door and felt the rapidly moving air flowing around the helicopter push the skin on his face back tight against his cheekbones, causing a flow of water to be released from his eyes and run alongside of his head to end up hiding behind his ears. Paul was totally absorbed by the beauty of the highland jungle and the feeling of freedom the helicopter provided. The aircraft dipped and swerved like a soaring eagle, trying not to establish a pattern that unseen NVA gunners down in the jungle below could lock their sights onto. Paul wished that he could fly. A hand reached out from behind the butterfly mechanism of the door gunner's M-60 machine gun and grabbed Paul's shoulder. The door gunner was shaking his head sideways and pointing at the chopper pilot, who was using sign language to tell Paul to put on the intercom headset that was lying on the passenger seat. Lieutenant Bourne obeyed and leaned back inside the aircraft.

"It's not a smart idea to lean out over the skids like that, even if you have a safety belt on," the pilot's voice snapped and crackled over the intercom system.

Paul pushed the black switch attached to the headset cord. "Sorry." He leaned over the seat to return the headset back to its hook with his eyes looking down at the steel floor of the helicopter. The worn gray steel plating had seen some heavy use in the past and was in need of a new paint job.

One . . . two . . . three holes appeared in the floor leaving the edges curled around them.

The helicopter shuttered violently. Paul looked up from the floor and saw the Plexiglas in front of MacKey shatter and the copilot's head drop down against his left shoulder and then flop around with the movement of the aircraft. The pilot was trying to break the sight lock of the NVA gunner by using evasive maneuvers. Blood covered the radio console located between the two aviator seats.

"Shoot, damn you!" the pilot's voice screamed over the intercom. Immediately the two door gunners started firing their machine guns wildly down at the jungle floor. They were shooting at invisible targets, trying to pacify the pilot's anger over taking the hits. The area from which they had received the fire was miles behind them within seconds.

"Lieutenant! Get up here and see what's wrong with

MacKey!"

Lieutenant Bourne unbuckled his safety strap from around his waist and crawled forward on the bucking floor toward the copilot's armored seat. He grabbed the edge of the high-back chair and looked over it. A single .51-caliber round had ricocheted off the front of MacKey's chest armor and exited through the roof of the helicopter. Another round had punched through the floor between MacKey's feet and hit him just under the front edge of his chicken plate. The seat between the young copilot's legs contained a thick pool of blood. The copilot's mouth sagged open below the dark visor of his helmet. He was dead.

Paul pushed the intercom button and reached for the copilot's wrist with his free hand, still hoping to find a pulse. "He's dead or in a very bad way."

"Christ, I hope not! This was his first day flying in Vietnam." The pilot's voice broke over the airway. "Hold his head, Lieutenant, we're almost at Duc Co's runway."

Paul looked through the shattered Plexiglas and saw the red laterite strip that had been cut out of the jungle.

"Red Fox Alpha . . . Charlie Delta Bravo Seven . . . We're in trouble . . . I'm going to try and bring her down on the far end of your runway away from your fuel pods . . ." The helicopter shuddered its full length when the pilot changed the pitch in the rotor blade.

"Roger, Bravo Seven . . . We have a medic standing by." The mature voicing coming over the radio from the A-Camp was calm, and emitted a level of confidence that only long days of combat could develop.

The helicopter jerked violently to the left when the pilot tried holding it in a hover. Paul grabbed for the copilot's safety strap and got blood on his shirt sleeve. Five feet off the gound, the engine whined loudly and stalled.

Paul was pushed down to his knees on the steel floor with his mouth striking the back of the copilot's armored chair. Blood seeped between Paul's teeth.

A jeep left the A-Camp through the main gates that faced the runway and raced down the strip with a huge cloud of red dust boiling up behind the rear wheels. There wasn't even a faint breeze to blow the dust cloud off the runway, and it settled back down where it had been kicked up.

Paul jumped down from the passenger compartment of the helicopter and opened MacKey's door. A voice came from behind Paul's back.

"Let me help you with him."

Paul and the team medic unstrapped MacKey from the seat and pulled him out of the aircraft onto a waiting canvas stretcher. The medic quickly removed the aviator's helmet and felt for a pulse on the bloody side of MacKey's neck. Paul stared into the unseeing eyes. The young pilot's hair was matted with splotches of red blood and looked macabrely beautiful with the sun bouncing flecks of light off the silver-blond hair that had accented the youth's aqua-blue eyes. The medic unstrapped the chicken plate and opened MacKey's shirt to check for wounds. He found only a large bruise and pulled the aviator's pants down below his hips.

"He caught one against his chest armor, but the one that killed him hit his groin and came out of his lower back." The medic pointed to a black mark on MacKey's chest. "That one probably knocked him out."

"Oh, shit!" Tears ran down the pilot's cheeks and appeared below the black sunshield of his helmet, still lowered, that covered the upper portion of his face. "He's just a kid!" But death had reached out when it was ready, and the age and dreams of the youth hadn't

mattered.

"Come on, sir." The medic took ahold of the shaking pilot's arm. "Let's go up to the teamhouse and have a couple shots of booze."

The medic supported the pilot and helped him into the vehicle, leaving Paul with MacKey and the helicopter door gunners. Reality was slowly replacing the excitement and unwrapping the protective cloak from around Paul's emotions. The body lay on the stretcher at his feet and the helicopter with its skin punched full of bullet holes remained parked twenty feet away. This wasn't a little-boy's pretend war game, and MacKey wasn't going to suddenly jump up to run off to hide again. Paul could hear the two door gunners talking off their excitement. He removed his tiger-striped shirt and laid it over MacKey's face. Paul hauled his B-4 bag out of the chopper and flipped it over his head, carrying it on his back like a paratrooper carried a used parachute.

A very beat-up three-quarter-ton truck pulled through the narrow gate and turned onto the runway, headed toward Paul who had started walking back to the camp. The truck stopped just past Paul,—the driver had pressed down on the squeaky brakes but the vehicle had continued traveling past the lieutenant—a sergeant stuck his head out of the passenger's compartment. *"Get in!"*

"I'll walk. Go pick up the door gunners and the body." Paul used his head to point toward the helicopter and kept on walking along the edge of the runway with the barrel of his submachine gun bouncing against his leg.

The dark green mountains in the foreground framed a multicolored sky in appropriate grandeur in front of Paul. He slowed his pace and watched a bright shaft of light escape from behind a cloud bank and send its rays through a break in the mountains.

"Take the kid . . . God . . . Please?"

The shaft of light blinked off behind the clouds and a film of water covered the lieutenant's eyes.

Lieutenant Bourne walked toward the main gate, blinking back the tears so that the Montagnard guards wouldn't see him crying. He walked under a hand-painted sign nailed to a post next to the gate that read: HOMESTEAD LAND AVAILABLE—INQUIRE WITHIN. Paul continued walking along the rutted road leading through the center of the sprawling camp. He picked out an American dressed in a tiger-striped set of fatigues and standing next to a waist-high pile of sandbags, and changed his course toward him. The man had a half-smoked cigar sticking between his teeth.

"I'm Captain Pellam . . . I run this place." The captain nodded at Paul's bare chest. "Are you some kind of fucking hippie? Or is it you just don't want to bother wearing a complete military uniform?"

Paul looked at the senior officer allowing the disgust he felt for the man's comment to show in his face. "I left my jacket over the copilot's body out on the runway."

"I heard about the chopper taking some rounds but wasn't informed that anyone had been zapped." The captain shrugged his shoulders. "How does it feel being shot at?" He tried grinning around the cigar stub in his mouth.

Paul looked slowly at Pellam who had remained leaning up against the sandbags. Paul pressed his lips tightly together for a few seconds before he risked speaking. "Shitty, sir . . . real shitty!"

Captain Pellam sensed that the new lieutenant had a backbone and changed the line of conversation. "Come on, I'll buy you a drink." The captain led the way down the dark hallway that ran through the center of the building to the rear area set aside for a bar and recreation area. The helicopter pilot was slouched down in one of the bamboo chairs with a full glass of bourbon gripped in his fist. Pellam went behind the bar and poured Paul half a glass of Jim Beam and threw two ice cubes on top of the liquid.

"Thanks, sir." Paul tipped the glass toward the captain and then tilted his head back until the ice cubes clicked against his teeth.

"Damn, man!" Pellam's voice reflected a mild concern. "Go light with the booze! There's a war still going on around here!" He looked hard at the lieutenant trying to decipher from the man's face if he had a heavy boozer on his hands.

Paul didn't answer the captain and poured himself another tall shot of bourbon, then sat in a chair near the pilot.

"We'll be eating supper soon . . ." Pellam spoke to no one in particular, then glanced at the pilot. "You'll have to spend the night with us. We can't find a shit-hook pilot who'll fly in here at night to lift out the Huey."

The pilot failed to hear the captain as he slipped deeper into his drunken stupor, letting the glass in his hand slip down to the mat-covered floor. The booze sloshed around the edge of the glass but didn't spill out.

Paul left the teamhouse through the rear door in the kitchen. The sunset was gone and a very dark night had taken its place in the sky. Paul felt with one hand for the row of sandbags that surrounded the frame longhouse until he located the barrier and hopped up on top of the still-warm bags, spilling a portion of his drink in the process. The night birds and animals on the other side of the compound's barbed-wire defensive screen called to each other as Paul sat listening to the old familiar sounds. The kitchen door opened and closed, allowing a short flash of light to escape along with a sharp smell of cooked food that lingered on the black night air for a few seconds before the breeze brushed it away. A dark figure moved toward Paul in the dim moonglow.

"Hello, sir. I'm Sergeant Mills, the team medic. We met out on the runway earlier."

Lieutenant Bourne reached out in the dark and felt around until he touched the front of the sergeant's jacket. He found the medic's hand and shook using a firm grip.

"I'm your new XO, I guess."

"Whenever you're ready to go inside, I'll show you to your room." Sergeant Mills leaned up against the cloth sandbags and waited for the lieutenant to answer.

"Yeah . . . just give me a few more minutes. I'm trying to get my stuff together."

"Today your first time under fire?"

"No. I spent a year running recon with the 173d just about a year ago when I was an enlisted man . . ." Paul rambled on, ". . . I forgot just how shitty this war really is . . . ."

"Gotcha covered, Lieutenant." Mills started to go back inside the teamhouse. "You coming?"

Paul slid off the sandbags. "Why the fuck not."

"Was the copilot a friend of yours?" Mills didn't turn around when he asked the question, but continued walking down the hallway.

"Not really. We met right before we took off from the B-Team pad."

Mills stopped in front of a closed door at the far-left corner of the long teamhouse. "The captain wants you at this end. He lives down by the kitchen." Mills nodded back down the hallway. "That way there's an officer at each end of the building just in case we get mortared—we won't lose both of you with one round."

Paul's gear had been placed on the cot in the room.

He thanked Mills and excused himself. He wanted to be alone for awhile. Sergeant Mills understood. Paul stretched out on the narrow cot and laced his hands behind his head. The early morning hours arrived before he slept.

Lieutenant Bourne awoke to the muffled sound of pots and pans rattling in the kitchen. The morning sun had not yet appeared over the eastern hills. Paul felt the hunger in his stomach before he opened his eyes. He stood up fully dressed from the night before and strapped his leather pistol belt around his waist. Paul walked down the hall combing his hair with his fingers. He could see the lights burning in the kitchen. A Vietnamese was setting the table from an officer's wooden field mess kit and turned to face the lieutenant when he entered the room.

"Ah . . . Lieu-ten-ant!" The man's smile was more of a permanent part of his face than a genuine greeting. "I am Lu-Van-Prong. The cook. Everyone call me Mister P."

"Hello, Mister P. Who's the pretty woman behind you?"

"That Missus P." He laughed and his wife blushed a light pink color. "You want breakfast now, Lieu-ten-ant?"

"Please, lots of it. I'm starved!" Paul sat on a wooden stool near the window screen. It was still shuttered, but he could smell the fresh air seeping into the room from outside. "You have powdered eggs, Mister P?"

"No sweat. Have plenty. You drink coffee. Me done plenty soon." The cook shuffled out of the kitchen area back to the cooking shed attached to the side of the teamhouse.

Paul walked over to the big chrome coffeepot that

Missus P had just placed on the counter and poured himself a metal mess cup full. The morning sun was breaking through the mist that hung over the camp during the night. Sergeant Mills entered the kitchen freshly shaved and showered.

"Morning, sir." Mills poured himself a cup of black coffee.

"Morning, Sergeant Mills." Paul sipped from the hot edge of the coffee cup. "Has the chopper pilot left yet?"

"No, he's due to leave early this morning just as soon as a rescue chopper can make it here." Mills nodded at two more sergeants who Paul hadn't seen before, and took a seat across from the lieutenant. "He's taking the kid's death real hard. He's blaming himself for the shoot-up . . . feels that he could have avoided the trap somehow. I finally had to give him a couple of tranquilizers last night on top of the booze that he drank."

"It's always harder to take it when a guy is young and has a lot to live for."

Mister P entered the room carrying a tray piled high with powdered eggs and thick slabs of fried Spam. Mills removed large helpings off the community tray onto his own steel plate and handed the tray over to Paul.

Sergeant Booker, who was the A-Team's intelligence NCO, sat next to the medic, ignoring the new lieutenant.

"Hey, Mills," Booker forked a large chunk of Spam into his mouth and continued talking, "I saw some bamboo birds in the draw outside of the camp late yesterday. You want to go after them this morning?"

"Sure!" Mills laid his fork down against his plate and reached for his coffee cup. "Let's go right after breakfast before they leave their nesting site."

"Bamboo birds?" Paul smiled and raised his eyebrows.

"Yes, sir. We call them bamboo birds, but they're more like pheasant, except the meat is sweeter. Damn fine eating." Mills looked up from his almost-empty plate. "Care to join us?"

"I'd like to, but I think Captain Pellam will probably want to talk to me the first thing this morning."

"No problem. He pulled the graveyard shift on radio watch this morning and won't be up until this afternoon." Mills stood up holding his coffee cup in his hand.

"Sure, I think I'll tag along. It'll give me a chance to see the area defense around the camp."

Mills drained the last of his coffee from the cup and set the cup down on the table. "We hunt the birds with twelve-gauge shotguns, using double-ought buckshot. Regular birdshot is very hard to find in Vietnam."

"I like the idea of using double-ought buckshot just in case we run into some hostile natives." Sergeant Booker pushed his chair back away from the table and grinned at the new lieutenant.

Sergeant Mills knocked lightly on Paul's closed door. "Ready, sir?"

Paul reached back from his plywood dresser and opened the door for the sergeant. "If you brought a shotgun for me. I forgot to ask you to find me one."

Mills held up his arm. "So happens that I do." He handed Paul a riot shotgun with a folding bayonet attached to its barrel and a claymore-mine bag, full of loose shotgun shells.

Paul picked his pistol belt up off the cot and pulled it around his waist, adjusting the holster that contained his prized Smith and Wesson 9mm pistol. He patted the sheath containing his custom-made Randall knife, sliding the leather case to a comfortable position on his left side. "Let's go."

A jeep with a .30-caliber light machine gun mounted on the hood was parked in front of the teamhouse with six Montagnards dressed in full battle gear sitting on the fenders, waiting for the hunters to emerge from the teamhouse. Paul looked at Mills with his question written on his face.

"They're coming along for the ride." Mills smiled. "I might end up getting my ass blown away in this fucking war, but it won't be because I'm stupid." Sergeant Mills nodded at a trail leading away from camp. "The officer that you're replacing was killed walking down there by four NVA soldiers, not three hundred meters from the main gate. Would you believe in the middle of the afternoon?" Mills pointed toward a Montagnard village sprawled over the side of a nearby hill. "He was walking over there to talk to the village elders about damming up that stream over there and making a fish pond and a waterfall where the villagers could bathe. They caught him on the trail talking to a couple Montagnard kids who worked for us in the camp. The gooks killed all three of them." Mills pointed up to the camp water tower. "The guard up there saw it all happen and killed two of the NVA with the .50 caliber before they could get away."

"Let's go!" Sergeant Booker slammed the screen door open and interrupted the conversation. The senior NCO hopped onto the passenger seat and beckoned for the other two Americans to join him.

Mills shook his head over the master sergeant's disregard for the lieutenant's rank. "Oh . . . by the way . . . We don't have any good hunting dogs, so we all take turns being the hound." Mills grinned. "The birds nest in the top of the bamboo, so someone has to walk through the draw to flush them out." Mills leaned up against the hood of the jeep and drummed his fingers against the steel fender. "I was the dog last time, Sergeant Booker . . . It's your turn today."

"Shit!" Booker glared at the lieutenant and then slapped him on his shoulder. "I guess we should let the lieutenant enjoy his first hunt."

The jeep bounced along the rutted road that circled the perimeter of the large A-Camp. Sergeant Mills stopped the jeep and pointed toward a draw filled with interwoven shoots of bamboo, growing from finger-sized poles to the diameter of a grown man's thigh.

"There's going to be some tough walking down there for the dawgg!" Mills drawled out the words, mimicking Booker's southern accent.

"Screw you, *Buck* Sergeant!" Booker retorted gruffly over his shoulder and slung his shotgun across his back, wiggling his shoulders until the weapon was centered between his shoulder blades.

"Sir, you walk on this side of the ravine that's closest to camp and I'll jog over to the far side." He pointed with the barrel of his shotgun. "Stay a little behind Booker when he gets down on the bottom; that way you can keep an eye on his location and shoot around him when we kick up the birds."

"Mills, if you shoot my ass . . ." Sergeant Booker started to climb down the side of the steep gorge and slipped on the thin layer of dew that covered the elephant grass. He slid down to the bottom, creating a matted chute that entered the heavy bamboo thicket.

Paul moved to the high ground bordering the edge of the ravine and took up a Vietnamese squat. He waited for Sergeant Mills to get over to the other side of the wide ditch, at the same time watching Sergeant Booker struggle with the tangled undergrowth that snatched at the older man's feet with every step that he took. The ravine was about two hundred meters long and thirty meters wide at its broadest point. Paul figured the bamboo stood, on average, a foot over Booker's head with islands of fifty-foot clumps growing sporadically along the length of the cut. He made a mental note to talk to Captain Pellam about placing some booby traps in the gully so that the NVA couldn't use it to their advantage during an attack on the camp. Lieutenant Bourne looked back over his shoulder at the parked jeep. The Montagnards had dismounted and were lying in a row against the shady side of the vehicle.

"Damn! This stuff is thick!" Booker's voice floated up through the tangle of clicking bamboo poles to where Paul stood with his shotgun resting on his hip. "Are you guys ready up there?"

"Ready!" Mills answered from his side of the ravine.

Paul kept close track of Sergeant Booker's slow progress by watching the tips of the bamboo sway as the sergeant pushed his way through the mass of interwoven stalks.

Two birds spooked fifteen meters in front of the human dog.

"Mine!" Mills fired as he yelled.

Pow! Pow!

The birds stopped their forward flight and crashed down in the waist-high elephant grass.

"A double!" Sergeant Mills ran toward the spot where the birds had disappeared in the grass.

Lieutenant Bourne slowly lowered his shotgun from the ready position against his shoulder. He hadn't fired for fear of hitting Mills. Paul dropped down on his calves and watched while the team medic retrieved his brace of birds. The lieutenant's eyes automatically scanned the tops of the bamboo and along the edges of the ravine, mostly from professional instinct. Paul's eyes stopped roving and locked on an object about twenty meters farther down the ravine and fifteen meters to the right of Sergeant Booker.

"Hey, Lieutenant! I'm coming up out of this shit for a break on your side!" Booker started moving again toward Paul's side of the ravine, but was having difficulty traveling in a straight line and wandered toward the object Paul had been staring at.

A black shape rose slowly a foot above the tops of the bamboo. Slowly the shape started to expand and sway gently from side to side. Sergeant Mills stood up from his kneeling position and held the two birds high up in the air so that Paul could see them, but the lieutenant's attention was riveted on the swaying object. Booker abruptly changed directions, and when the black object turned to face the moving threat now heading directly toward it, Paul could see the cream-colored underbelly of the giant king cobra glistening in the morning light.

Cobra!" Paul raised his shotgun to his shoulder and yelled the warning down to Booker. "He's right in front of you! Stop moving!"

The cobra started swaying slowly, flicking out its tongue, trying to sense the distance of the warm-blooded invader in its territory.

Pow! Pow! Pow!

Buckshot whizzed through the air inches above Paul's head. Sergeant Booker was shooting wildly in the bamboo. Paul dropped down into a crouch and placed the front sight bead on the center of the cobra's expanded hood.

Three more shots cracked in the morning air. The snake thrashed against the bamboo causing the stalks to click together in a musical melody. Sergeant Booker broke through the bamboo tangle on the edge of the ravine as if the strong bamboo poles had been magically transformed into soft Kentucky bluegrass. Sweat covered the sergeant's face and functioned as glue for the tiny pieces of yellow and green bamboo leaves clinging to his cheeks and neck like small leeches.

"Damn! I almost pissed my pants!" Booker's eyes glanced down to check his crotch just in case he had. "Where's that damn thing at?"

"Over there." Paul pointed with the barrel of his shotgun. "It's dying."

"How in the hell did you see it from here?" Booker's head kept turning as he checked the area around them.

"It hooded at least a foot above the bamboo tops. I couldn't miss seeing it."

"A foot? Do you realize how long that bastard has to be in order to raise up that high?" Booker gasped. "A cobra can only raise one-third of its body off the ground!"

"What are you shooting at over there!" Sergeant Mills held his two birds above his head so that Booker could see them.

"Killed a cobra!" Booker waved at Mills to join them. "Come on around to this side!"

It took Sergeant Mills five minutes to walk around to where Paul and Booker stood watching the bamboo stalks moving below them in the ravine.

"I'm going down there and get that snake. I want to put its head in formaldehyde." Mills dropped his brace of birds down next to Booker's boots.

"*You* can go after that sucker by yourself!" Booker sat down in the grass.

"I'll help." Paul slipped down the side of the ravine behind Mills, who was following Booker's trail through the thicket. The two soldiers moved with extreme caution when they neared the place they thought the snake was located.

"Thosedamnthingstravelinpairs!" Booker had transferred himself over to the hood of the jeep, and was calling to them through cupped hands.

Lieutenant Bourne paused for a second when he recalled reading somewhere in an animal encyclopedia something about cobras mating for life. He pushed the bamboo aside in front of him using the barrel of the shotgun. He had moved about ten meters through the thick growth when he saw part of a black coil interwoven in the base of the bamboo, about a foot off the ground. Paul pointed the shotgun and fired. The shape twitched from the impact of the pellets, but displayed no motor movement. Paul carefully reached down, ready to jump backward if the deadly creature showed any signs of life, and wrapped his fingers over the still-warm body of the reptile.

"Found it!" Paul released his hold on the cobra. "Come over here and help, but be careful until we find its head."

Sergeant Mills crashed through the clicking stalks until he neared Paul. The head of the snake soon appeared at the medic's feet, hidden in a knot of coils.

"I found its head!"

"Good! Let's work from your end." The nearness of Paul's voice startled the medic.

Paul and Mills worked for over twenty minutes unwinding the snake's tangled and twisted body from the stalks of young bamboo.

Sergeant Booker reluctantly left the false safety the hood of the jeep provided and went over to the edge of the ravine to help Paul and Sergeant Mills.

"This damn thing is slippery as snail slime! Ugghhh!" Booker gingerly took a hold of the shiny black reptile and tugged.

Sergeant Mills scrambled up the side of the gorge and helped Booker heave the snake up on the bank. Paul followed close behind the medic.

"The dew really makes the skin shine." Mills ran his hand along the coils.

"That is one beautiful and deadly bastard!" Paul rested the butt of his shotgun against his right hip and scanned the area around them just in case there was a mate nearby.

"Let's get it in the back of the jeep and take it to my clinic in camp. I want to measure it and get the head preserved before it starts to decay." Mills glanced up from the snake at Paul. "By the way, Lieutenant, that was some damn fine shooting."

"Thanks." Paul hopped in the jeep, avoiding any further praise.

"I owe you one, Lieutenant. You saved my ass back there." Booker looked over at Paul out of the corner of his eye with a great deal more respect than he had shown before they had left for the hunt.

"Let's get out of here." Mills placed his shotgun across his knees. He sat in the back of the jeep with the snake piled up between his legs. "Watch out for its mate." He smiled as he looked at Booker, who wasn't going to recover from this hunt for quite a while.

The Montagnards jogged behind the jeep, jabbering in their local dialect to each other and pointing at the traditional enemy of the mountain people. The small Montagnard warriors refused to ride in the jeep with the snake, fearing that the spirit of the reptile would possess them.

Sergeant Booker guided the vehicle around the worst ruts in the perimeter road, but still managed to bounce the snake and passengers around in the jeep.

In front of the teamhouse, Mills unloaded his brace of birds first, hanging them over a steel post that supported the pile of sandbags by the door. Paul and Mills pulled the cobra out of the back of the jeep. The beautiful snake was coated in a red layer of dust the instant it touched the ground.

Sergeant Mills used one of his steel medical tapes to measure the snake. The king cobra stretched out at nineteen feet, seven and a half inches. A full grown man could lose his fist in the snake's mouth. A group of Montagnard children were drawn up to their natural foe with wide-open eyes. At least one child from the village every year would end up as a victim to a cobra bite.

"I bet quite a few stray camp rats have lost their lives to that creature!" Captain Pellam joined the group that was standing around the cobra. "He's probably been hanging around Duc Co since it was built."

"Tell me about it!" Booker's fear of the snake was temporarily placed aside. "He almost had *my* ass for breakfast, but thanks to the lieutenant, the snake is dead instead of me."

Pellam glanced over at his new XO and nodded his head in approval.

"Maybe we can roast the snake for supper." Mills joked as he tied the snake's head to an engineer post and prepared to remove the skin. "We can invite those artillery officers down the road to come for supper."

The other team members laughed while the captain thought for a second and then spoke. "I just might do that, Mills . . . They would shit!"

Chapter 3

Sergeant Mills had cured and nailed the king cobra skin to the wall behind the teamhouse bar. The effect made the skin look even longer than its nearly twenty feet. The rest of the bar's decor was very masculine, with Montagnard hand-forged knifes and crossbows hanging from the rafters.

Lieutenant Bourne sat in one of the bamboo chairs near the screened window cleaning his CAR-15 submachine gun. The bright sunlight filtered through the rattan-covered window, making a checkered pattern on the floor at Paul's feet. Sergeant Mills entered the room through the kitchen entrance, wearing a sweat-soaked drive-on rag around his forehead to keep the sweat from running into his eyes. The camouflaged tiger-stripe jacket he wore was completely saturated with his body sweat.

"Days like today make you wish for the monsoon rains." Mills opened the small white Japanese-built refrigerator and removed a cold can of beer from the stacked shelf. He pulled the tab and kicked the door shut at the same time. "Want one, sir?"

"No thanks . . ." Paul pushed in the locking pin with his thumb and tested to see if the breech was closed firmly on his CAR-15. "I have to go over to the Montagnard village and see the chief."

"Let me finish this beer and I'll go with you. The headman's youngest wife has a severe case of intestinal worms and she's seven months pregnant with her first child."

Bourne finished rubbing in the fine coat of oil on his weapon, using the palm of his hand. He picked his thirty-round magazine off the floor and checked the edges for any wear, and after finding none pushed the clip into the weapon's receptacle and then wiggled it to insure that it had locked firmly in place. Paul stood up and slung the submachine gun upside down over his shoulder, hooking the front site blade behind his pistol holster.

"Ready?"

"Yes, sir. I just have to stop in my room for a minute and grab my shotgun and medical kitbag."

The two men stepped out into the hot sun and instantly felt the heat against the back of their jackets. The distinct sound of a helicopter rotor blade could be heard coming from the east side of camp. Both men automatically turned their heads and looked in the clear sky for the aircraft.

"Sounds like the captain is returning from the B-Team early today." Sergeant Mills squinted his eyes to protect them from the bright glare as he scanned the sky above the treetops for the chopper.

"I'll go get the jeep and we can meet him on the runway. The Ol' man told me last night that we might be having some special company when he returned." Paul jogged over to the sandbag enclosure and slipped behind the wheel of the jeep.

He stopped in front of the teamhouse just long enough for Mills to throw his medical kit onto the rear seat and hop in next to him. They arrived on the airstrip just as a silver helicopter appeared low over the treetops at the far end of the long runway. The aircraft drew closer and Paul could read the large letters that had been painted on the removable doors: *Air America.*

"Looks as if the captain has hitched a ride with a civilian contractor, sir."

The blades of the helicopter were turning slowly when Paul pulled the jeep up next to it—after he had waited a couple of minutes for the traditional red dust cloud to take its place back on the runway. Captain Pellam exited the left door, which was nearest to the jeep. A tall thin man wearing a lightweight two-piece suit, penny loafers, and mirrored sunglasses stepped around the front of the parked aircraft. Paul noticed a slight, almost undetectable bulge under the man's left armpit. He had a very good tailor. The man walked straight to the jeep and extended his hand to shake with Paul.

"LeBlonde." His voice sounded as if his vocal cords had been sandpapered.

"Lieutenant Bourne . . . and this is our team medic . . . Sergeant Mills." Paul shook the older man's hand and nodded at the sergeant.

LeBlonde changed his hard gaze back to the helicopter and watched two men unload a heavy-looking aluminum box. The men strained from the weight of the cargo they were moving and bent forward trying to gain leverage, causing the Swedish K submachine guns strung over their shoulders to slip forward and hit the metal box.

LeBlonde returned his attention back to Sergeant Mills. "I know quite a bit about you." LeBlonde adjusted his sunglasses. "You graduated first in your Special Forces medical class and your brother died last year from an overdose of heroin." The last sentence was tacked onto the first, catching Mills off guard.

"I didn't catch what you said that you did for a living . . . *Mister* LeBlonde." The tone of Mills's voice reflected the anger he was containing and stated that he didn't want the conversation to continue concerning his family.

"Mister LeBlonde will tell you both what's going on here later, when we get up to the teamhouse. Right now, let's get our asses out of this damn heat!" Captain Pellam looked more nervous than hot.

"They'll find out soon enough . . ." LeBlonde lowered his glasses and looked down his nose at Sergeant Mills. "I'm a field agent for the Counter Intellegence Agency . . . the CIA."

Bourne and Mills had already figured out on their own that he was an agency man the second they had laid eyes on him and his buddies struggling with the aluminum box. What they hadn't figured out was what they wanted with them and the Duc Co Special Forces Camp.

"Oh really?" Sergeant Mills clicked his tongue and opened his eyes wide, similar to those of a child looking through a candy store window.

"Your bodyguards can ride in the back of the jeep if there's enough room." Captain Pellam slid over to the far side of the narrow rear seat leaving room for only one of the men who had arrived with the senior agent, so one of the bodyguards took a seat on the hood of the jeep. The man kept changing positions as the heat penetrated through the seat of his thin civilian pants.

LeBlonde smiled and looked at Paul. "We know that you've just spent some time near Malibu, California, and you have a good friend back there who's growing marijuana back in Topanga Canyon."

Paul interrupted the agent's speech. "Look . . . I'm sure you people know a lot about what I've done and *haven't* done . . . it's really obvious that you make it your business sticking your fuckin' noses where they don't belong! I don't appreciate you flapping your gums here in front of everybody what I consider rather *private* information!" Paul's eyes flashed silver, reflecting the anger that had rapidly built up behind them.

"Just a damn minute, Lieutenant!" Captain Pellam spoke. "Mister LeBlonde has a military rating equivalent to a Brigadier General! Show some respect!"

"Then he should *act* like one." Paul placed his attention on his driving and ignored LeBlonde the rest of the drive to the teamhouse. The brakes created the only sound when they stopped in front of the high sandbag wall surrounding the makeshift showers.

Captain Pellam was the first one to jump from the vehicle and led the way for LeBlonde's entourage. "Sergeant Mills . . . help the men put away their gear and then join us in the bar." Pellam spoke over his shoulder as he disappeared down the breeze-cooled corridor that split the teamhouse. Paul brought up the rear of the group, watching LeBlonde closely as he entered through the doorway. There was no doubt the intellegence agent was a professional and probably one of the best that the CIA had to offer.

The group that had gathered around the kitchen table was hand-picked: Captain Pellam, Sergeant Mills, Lieutenant Bourne, and LeBlonde—all had taken seats along the back wall with the agent's bodyguards taking up positions at the entrances to the room. Paul took a sip from his cold Shasta orange. Of all the different kinds of canned soda peddled in Vietnam, Shasta orange was the only one that tasted good when it was warm.

"We only have time to go over this one time, so please pay close attention . . ." LeBlonde took up a comfortable position leaning against the homemade china cabinet that dominated the kitchen area and separated the bar from the eating section. He reached up to his face and removed his sunglasses. Everyone in the room, including Lieutenant Bourne, stared at the agent's eyes. One was blue and the other was a dark green. LeBlonde continued talking, knowing exactly what kind of effect he was having on his audience. "For the time being, consider everything discussed in this room as top-secret information." He paused. "As this special operation becomes known, I'll let you know what you can put in your letters to your mothers." The dry attempt at humor didn't get any reaction from his listeners. LeBlonde caught Bourne's hard stare and grinned. "I think the lieutenant's interested in my eye." The grin left his face. "The green eye is glass . . . I lost the real one in the Congo when I was on a special assignment . . . for the State Department . . ." LeBlonde kept looking at Paul, who had shifted his attention to the label on his Shasta can. "They were starting to dig out my other eye with a stainless-steel spoon when some of my friends dropped in and interrupted their fun. We convinced them that their conduct wasn't condoned in the civilized world." The room became midnight quiet. LeBlonde grinned and stared at Paul out of the corner of his good eye. The agent took a deep breath and continued his briefing. "I have to leave Duc Co shortly and meet nearby with an ex-Viet Cong leader who is willing to trade us some information." LeBlonde crossed his arms. "So! What do we want with you two?" He pointed at Paul and Sergeant Mills at the same time using both of his hands, and then leaned over to look out the screened window. His head brushed the plastic-coated grids, disturbing two fat green flies who had been in the middle of propagating their maggot-producing species.

The hum from their wings was the only sound in the room as the group of soldiers waited for the special agent to continue talking. "I have information that MACV Headquarters gathered late last year concerning a large increase of heroin trafficking to American troops in-country since the late summer of '67. . . . What concerns the brass the most is that our troops can now buy refined heroin on the streets of Saigon—cheaper than it costs to manufacture it. Certain senior South Vietnamese generals have had the market cornered on drug sales and prostitution since the beginning of the American build-up in the South." LeBlonde looked over at Mills and half-closed his eyes before he spoke again. "We feel that the communists have entered the drug market."

"How do you figure that?" Mills interrupted.

"Because . . . the South Vietnamese generals don't have a reason to lower drug prices. Don't forget, they control the market and they're profit oriented . . . they've had good teachers." A genuine smile cracked at the corner of his mouth and quickly disappeared. "Only the communists would have something to gain by lowering the price and raising the availability of heroin to American troops. The Agency has contacted the Asian warlords who have control of the growing and shipping of the raw opium coming from the Golden Triangle around Burma, Thailand, and Laos. We have also confirmed that the North Vietnamese—along with their Chinese advisors—are buying all of the opium base that they can get their hands on and are paying top dollar for it."

Lieutenant Bourne and Sergeant Mills leaned forward on their seats as their interest in the subject was whetted from the agent's conversation. Captain Pellam was glancing out the window like a trapped animal.

LeBlonde took his time lighting a skinny, dark

brown cigar that he had removed from a case hidden inside his jacket. He inhaled the first smoke deep into his lungs and held it there before releasing it as a blue jet stream between his teeth. Paul understood why the agent's voice was so rough. LeBlonde took another deep drag and exhaled, followed by a series of deep coughs, before he continued. "With Laos and Burma neutral nations, a large military force crossing their borders would cause a very big political incident. I think all of us remember what happened when U.S. forces crossed into North Korea." LeBlonde's eyes swept the room and found everyone watching him. "The communists have rapidly gained control over all the big poppy growers in the Golden Triangle, either with bribes or assassinations of key people. It's the latter reason that has caused the warlords to cooperate with us . . . but, of course, in secret."

"*Shit!*" Mills couldn't contain himself any longer and the word sprang from between his clenched teeth. "You telling us that our fucking *allies* are the main suppliers of drugs to American troops!"

"You've put that problem together rather well . . . but you must remember before you come down too hard on anyone that the South Vietnamese generals are using capitalistic principles that have been taught to them by members of the West . . . *and* there are American pilots who are flying the heroin into this country from Thailand . . . *and* you can't sell a product if you don't have any customers. . . ."

Lieutenant Bourne's mind wandered as LeBlonde talked to Mills. He recalled his first tour of duty in Vietnam serving with paratroopers out of the 173d Airborne. The opium-smoking North Vietnamese had always gotten their asses kicked when they met the highly disciplined Americans. Giap had changed all of that by executing field commanders and soldiers who abused drugs in his combat units. Now the communist fighters were nearly drug free—and the Americans were the ones resorting to drugs for their courage.

"After all of that background talk, you two are probably trying to figure out what we want from you." LeBlonde's voice became even deeper as he reached down to lift the lid from an aluminum box that hadn't received much attention on the floor next to his foot. He removed what looked like a roll of silver dollars and broke the paper cover against the edge of the table, allowing the double-eagle gold pieces to spill out. LeBlonde flipped a coin to Paul and Mills. "Keep them as souvenirs." He stacked the remaining coins in a neat pile, still looking down at the dull yellow-colored coins as he spoke. "We would like you to meet a special envoy of warlords and buy this year's opium harvest from them with the coins in that box." He nodded down at the open container.

"What's my part in this?" Captain Pellam's voice sounded like that of a prepubescent boy compared to LeBlonde's.

"Sorry, Captain . . . there's not a part in this play for you . . ." He tapped his cigar against the side of the table in order to knock off the cold gray ash and relight the stub. "We only want to borrow a couple of your men . . . I realize that will bother you somewhat . . ." LeBlonde reached inside of his jacket, " . . . but I have a letter here from General—"

"That's all right. . . ." Pellam raised his hand to stop LeBlonde from producing what he had concealed in his jacket pocket.

"You sure?"

"I trust you . . ." Pellam was just glad that he hadn't been asked to join the duo from his team.

"Well, I hope you can keep what you've heard to yourself, Captain Pellam. . . . You can imagine what will happen to these two young men if the South Vietnamese generals even suspected that we knew what was going on . . ." LeBlonde's eyes crossed slightly looking at the cigar he clenched between his yellow front teeth. He puffed hard to help his lighter start the tobacco burning again. "So don't tell anyone about this meeting—including your colonel . . ."

"But—"

"No damn buts! Especially your colonel!" LeBlonde smiled. "He has too much contact with Vietnamese. . . ."

"Well, thanks a fucking lot!" Mills's voice carried an angry tone, but Bourne could tell that the sergeant was leading the agent on.

LeBlonde's eyes left Pellam and cruised over to the sergeant. "We could have found a dozen glory grabbers in Nha Trang and had them kissing our asses for a chance at this mission." LeBlonde flicked his tongue against his teeth trying to dislodge a piece of tobacco. "Consider it an honor that you've been *selected*."

"I've had a couple of missions that didn't pay as well as this one." Paul rubbed his thumb over the face of the gold piece he held in his hand.

"The pay for a lieutenant going on this mission is exactly the same as for one working in the Saigon post exchange." LeBlonde's lip twitched. "If I didn't already know that you possessed an extraordinary sense of integrity, I would have been insulted by that remark you just made, Lieutenant."

Paul smiled, showing his teeth. He had to give LeBlonde credit for doing his homework. The opportunity to steal large sums of money from camp funds had presented itself almost daily, and he had been accused by other A-Camp executive officers as being too strait-laced during monthly money payroll pick-ups, when he would turn in accurate accounts for the money he had spent the previous month. A lot of civilian contractors were running huge profit-making black market operations, and in some instances were actually selling American arms to the Viet Cong agents that worked near the docks in Saigon and Nha Trang. Paul could point at a lot of sergeants and officers at Fort Bragg, North Carolina, who lived in huge homes that had been bought with *schwarz-geld*, but the owners claimed that they had inherited money. Paul was honest and that was the way he was going to stay, regardless of the temptation.

LeBlonde was staring at Paul when the lieutenant's eyes refocused on the people in the room with him.

"Are you going to join us again, Lieutenant?" The agent wasn't trying to be sarcastic.

"Where and how is the exchange going to take place? How far do we have to haul these gold coins?" Paul was ready and wanted to get on with the details of the mission.

"Why do we have to even use gold coins—paper money would be easier to backpack," Mills joined in with his own question to the agent. "Hey! Why are all of these coins dated the same?" He shoved the pile of gold double-eagles out over the table.

"*Hold it!*" LeBlonde frowned. He realized that the two men had accepted the mission in their own fashion, but they were asking too many questions that needed answering in a more sterile setting. "Only two answers: First, we are using gold coins because the warlords don't trust paper money; secondly, they are all dated the same because we had a special batch run off for us by the Denver mint." LeBlonde glanced from Mills to Bourne, "The mission orientation briefings start tomorrow. . . . Your meeting with the warlords will take place seven days from today."

"Where is the meeting going to take place?" A

puzzled look appeared on Paul's face that couldn't be ignored by the special agent.

"The Tri-border area . . ."

"You mean the Laos-South Vietnam-Cambodia intersection?"

"Nope."

"*Holy shit!*" Mills voice cracked, "not the fuckin' North Vietnamese intersection—there's five fuckin' enemy divisions up there!"

"Bingo! Young man—the warlords are taking one hell of a big risk bringing their opium down that far south. They're going to bluff their way by telling them that they have to deliver to PAVAN Southern Headquarters. Some of their men will be dressed as NVA officers. . . . enough said!" LeBlonde realized that he was telling too much, but he was as excited about the mission as the two young Green Berets.

"Why don't you get some of those super SOG recon men up in Da Nang to handle this mission for you. Hell, that's their area." Sergeant Mills had made a good point.

"Like I told you before, Sergeant, you have a special qualification that we need: your hate for drug dealers." LeBlonde assumed his professional expression. "Tomorrow, the two of you will be taken to Da Nang and briefed." The agent stood up straight, and unbuttoned the second button on his jacket, and adjusted his holster. "Bring only your personal articles with you; everything else will be supplied by Command and Control North." LeBlonde nodded to his bodyguards and turned back to Paul. "Oh—I forgot to tell you that the mission is voluntary."

"Gotcha. . . ." Bourne knew as well as LeBlonde did that he couldn't say no. "I'll have to think about it and let you know in the morning."

Sergeant Mills grinned at the lieutenant. "That's

ditto for me too, Mister LeBlonde."

"Shit, I must be getting soft in my old age," LeBlonde frowned, "I'm beginning to like you two clowns!"

Lieutenant Bourne and Sergeant Mills started laughing at the obvious effort it took for LeBlonde to keep from smiling.

Lieutenant Bourne ate very little during supper, and then went to his room early to change into clean, sweat-free clothes for the night. Duc Co didn't very often allow the luxury of sleeping in shorts or naked. Rarely would a night pass when the North Vietnamese failed to mortar or send an infantry probe against the camp. The enemy would leave Duc Co alone only after a big fight, and even then it would only be for a couple of days. Duc Co's strategic position straddled the Ia Drang Valley, which was a natural invasion route into Vietnam through Cambodia, and had been used over the centuries by Chinese hordes. The NVA could easily leave their bases in Cambodia, travel the short three thousand meters to Duc Co, and return to their sanctuary before daylight.

Paul slipped through the back door of the teamhouse wearing only a cut-off pair of black Vietnamese peasant pants and his pistol belt, which held his 9mm pistol and his Randall knife. He walked slowly in the dark, feeling for the row of sandbags that surrounded the structure. When he felt the cool burlap bags he climbed up to the top row and took a seat.

A cool breeze coming from Cambodia blew against his face. Paul felt the hair on the side of his head brush against the top of his ears. His mind left him on the sandbag wall and traveled over space to Malibu, California . . .

He was walking on the beach towards the familiar outline of Point Dume against the skyline. Salt spray filled his nostrils as bubbling ocean waves rubbed against his ankles. Paul looked back down the stretch of beach and saw a young boy trotting toward him. He had been aware of the kid for the past five minutes. Paul changed his attention to the top of the cliff that bordered the ocean to his right side and saw his girlfriend, Linda, standing on the very edge of the rocks high above him. They had both been invited to a beach party and she had decided to stay up on the cliff while he went for a run along the beach. Paul smiled as he watched her spread her tanned arms up over her head mimicking the famous pose of the statue called Victory. Linda always allowed her imagination to carry her into many make-believe worlds, which was one of the reasons why Paul loved her so much. She was never boring and was very capable of entertaining herself.

Paul loved Linda more than anything on Earth. He thought that he had caught her eye, and he waved as she turned her head slightly and stared out across the open ocean. Paul slowly started climbing the steep path back to the cliff-top surfer party, avoiding patches of ice plants. Paul slipped a little on the rocks and glanced back down at the sandy beach. The boy who had been behind him was looking up the surfer's path at something above Paul.

Linda had sprung from the edge of the cliff, executing a beautiful swan dive. She landed with a soft thud on the sand two hundred feet below. Paul leapt from the perch he was standing on and hit the sand running toward her, leaving only his toe prints to mark his path.

Linda's body released itself from all earthly attachments by marking the dry sand around her with a spreading wet spot that originated from her crotch as the muscles that controlled her bladder relaxed. Paul was witnessing his first encounter of a human death, not a staged movie death for a television plot but the death of someone whom he had loved without any restraints.

Paul's ears recorded voices rolling over the edge of the cliff far above him with one soprano rising and separating from the other. "Hey, guys! The dumb bitch jumped!" The words echoed over the water and faded. "Shit! This electric wine sure is heavy stuff!" A face appeared over the cliff edge. "Hey, bitch! Next time *ask* what you're drinking!" Giggles from many throats followed the youth's last statement down to the beach.

Paul had heard about electric wine before. Some really strung out surfers would lace wine with LSD-25. It would give one hell of a shock to those who drank even a small amount of it. Sharp pieces of rock cut through the palms of his hands as he climbed straight up the side of the cliff, causing blood to form into paths on the undersides of his arms and begin to coagulate in his underarm body hair.

The fingers of Paul's right hand wrapped over the top edge of the rocky cliff.

The blood streaking over his body, and the hate outlining his face, terrorized the party group on the cliff top into nonmovement—like a rabbit confronted by a huge snake. Paul's eyes focused on a five-foot-long piece of dry driftwood that had been placed near the edge of the fire the stoned surfers were sitting around. Paul picked up the wood and swung the club until there were no more targets remaining upright. He limped over to the spot on the cliff where Linda had been standing only a few minutes earlier and dropped his chin down against his chest. A small group of beachcombers and joggers had begun gathering in a tight circle around Linda's body. The boy who had been behind Paul on the beach had removed his windbreaker and was placing the bright orange jacket over her upper body. Paul jerked his eyes away from the death scene and rested them on the rolling water that spread out before him. The first of many tears escaped from a corner of his eye. A scream formed somewhere in his lower diaphragm and raced up his throat bursting out between his teeth. The people on the beach shivered and looked up to search for the origin of the horrible man-scream.

The surfers around Point Dume and Topanga Beach still talk about Paul Bourne around their night fires and no one uses the clifftop for parties anymore. And electric wine lost its popularity for good that summer at Malibu.

Lieutenant Bourne shifted position on his sandbag perch. The newly formed tear leaving his eye was pushed back into his sideburn by the wind coming from Cambodia. Paul stayed sitting on the comfortable sandbag ledge until the cool morning sun began to show its light through the treetops on the ridge east of camp. Paul slipped down and walked quietly through the kitchen and down the hallway to his room. He stretched out on his canvas cot and folded his arms behind his head. Sleep still wouldn't come. Morning would bring the return of LeBlonde and he would accept the mission.

The sound of muffled footsteps against the cement floor in the hall alerted Paul and his hand slipped down to his pistol. A light tap echoed in the room followed by Mills's soft whisper: "Sir, are you up yet?"

"Yeah, I'll meet you in the kitchen for breakfast." Paul reached for his shaving gear on the wooden ledge above his bed as he stood up and went into the shower room attached to the rear of the teamhouse. He brushed the nightly accumulation of dead bugs from the ledge below the mirror and placed his shaving gear on the shelf that had been painted an infantry blue by the first A-Team in the camp. When Paul joined Sergeant Mills at the breakfast table he was feeling wide awake.

"Have trouble sleeping last night?" Mills smiled, knowing most people couldn't sleep very well when they were waiting to go out on a mission. "I couldn't sleep very much myself. Maybe this mission will give me a chance to get even with dope pushers."

"Where are you from, back in the States?" Paul changed the subject. He sensed that the conversation could get very heavy, and he wanted to avoid talking about anything that would take his mind off the upcoming mission.

"A small town in Michigan. You wouldn't have heard of it—most of the people living around there are part-time farmers. We live on a farm near Bridgeport, just outside of Saginaw. Dad's got a job with General Motors at their steering-gear plant during the night shift and he farms during the day. The poor guy works his ass off. The family was starting to do a lot better until my little brother got involved in his high school's drug cult."

Mr. P brought Sergeant Mills a plate piled high with mounds of fried rice and powdered eggs surrounded by three thick slices of fried Spam.

Paul cocked his head to one side, trying to recognize the sound he heard coming from the east side of the camp. "What's that?"

"You got me, Lieutenant," Mills talked around a

mouthful of food, "It sounds like a jet coming in." He leaned back in his chair so that he could look out the screened window that faced the 3400-foot runway the First Cavalry Division engineers had built for the Special Forces Camp during the invasion of the Ia Drang Valley. A Lear jet's wheels touched down on the laterite runway and the aircraft raced ahead of a large red dust cloud.

"You're right. A jet just touched down."

Mister LeBlonde was standing on the top step of the aircraft waiting for them when the two Special Forces soldiers pulled up next to the jet in the camp's beat-up jeep.

"You all ready to leave?"

"Hell, no . . . We have to go back and get our stuff. We weren't expecting you so early . . ." Paul felt like a fool being caught unprepared.

Sergeant Mills threw the gear shift in reverse and spun the wheels, throwing a small cloud of dust against the silver aircraft. They covered the distance back to the camp in near-record time. Paul was jumping out of the front seat before the dull green vehicle came to a complete stop and entered the teamhouse ten feet ahead of Mills. Paul strapped his NVA ammunition pouch against his chest and balanced his CAR-15 in the palm of his hand, hefting it slightly to see if he had a full magazine in it. Mills tapped on his door as he raced back down the hallway to the still-running jeep. Captain Pellam watched through the cracks in the bamboo shade covering his window. He wanted to join his men, but a deep sense of self-preservation told him that any mission chosen by the CIA was too dangerous. He felt ashamed, and was glad he was standing in the dark where he couldn't be seen.

The Lear jet had turned around on the runway and was ready for takeoff when Bourne and Mills hopped out of the jeep onto the lowered steps.

"Buckle up. I want to get off this runway before an NVA forward observer can get our range and call in some mortar fire on us. My boss would never forgive me if I lost his plane!"

"You have a boss?" Innocence covered Mills's face. LeBlonde grinned a cockeyed smile and whispered something under his breath.

Lieutenant Bourne settled into the plush jetliner seat and turned his head toward the seat his sergeant was stretching out on. "This is the only way to travel around this country: air-conditioning, stereo, and a built-in bar." It was obvious that the airplane belonged to a senior member of the intellegence community. And since the agency had a well-established reputation of taking care of its executives who produced successful programs, the luxury raised the odds somewhat that Paul had a chance to return from the mission alive.

A helicopter or a C-130 cargo plane would have taken a couple of hours flying to the northern city, but the jet made the flight in forty-two minutes. When they landed, two army jeeps pulled up on the tarmac and parked close to the jet. The vehicles were painted a dull, flat black, with a Command and Control skull crest hand-painted in six-inch patterns below the windshields on the front panels. The two drivers were wearing neat tiger-striped fatigues with black jungle hats that had been modified by shortening the wide brims.

"Let's move." LeBlonde glanced down the runway to see if anyone was paying too much attention to their arrival. He deplaned carrying his leather briefcase, followed by his two bodyguards who struggled with the box containing the gold coins. Paul and Mills slipped into the rear seat of the first jeep, leaving the front seat vacant for LeBlonde.

The route to the Command and Control North Headquarters was mostly along South Vietnam's national Highway One numbered the same as California's Highway One. The similarity of both Highways running north and south along the coast and both roads touching waters that formed the Pacific Ocean, coupled with the fact that Paul had recently traveled both routes made the drive seem uncanny to the point of sending a shiver down Paul's spine. There was a high probability that some of the blue-green water touching the Vietnam coast had also touched the beach at Malibu.

"Hey, check out those guys!" Mills pointed to a team of U.S. Navy SEALS dressed in wetsuits who were checking out the underwater supports of the main bridge leading out of Da Nang. Navy SEALS had a reputation for being a very tough group of men. U.S. Army Special Forces had teamed up many times with SEAL units to conduct clandestine operations. Paul had gone through HALO School with three SEALS and respected their grit, especially when they had to parachute from thirty thousand feet at night and then traverse a swamp as a final test for the difficult course. Lieutenant Bourne raised his hand as they passed the working SEALS. One of the black-clad divers looked up and waved back.

The jeeps left the road and pulled up in front of a main gate that was locked. Access to the secret compound was strictly controlled with high cyclone fences dividing the areas so that an outsider could go only where he had business. The gate guard made everyone dismount while a second guard, who was located inside a well-fortified machine gun bunker, called the headquarters. A third guard circled the jeeps carrying a long pole with a mirror attached to it. The device resembled the tool dentists used when they checked for cavities. The guard stopped at each wheel well and checked carefully for hidden explosives.

"They do this all of the time?" Lieutenant Bourne looked over at his escort who had driven the jeep.

"Yes, sir. The local Viet Cong are very good at sneaking up to a vehicle in heavy traffic and attaching satchel charges under the fenders. SOG vehicles are prime targets. Last month a Viet Cong slipped a hand grenade into a jeep gas tank. The safety handle had been wrapped with plastic electrical tape. It took about twenty minutes for the plastic to dissolve in the gas and release the handle. The explosion killed everyone in the jeep, plus eight bystanders." The soldier pointed at his jeep. "We have padlocks on all of our gas caps now."

Paul nodded his head. He was very impressed with everything that he had seen so far, and made a mental note of the special Green Beret unit.

The two jeeps were joined by another black vehicle, which carried a captain from the headquarters who acted as their escort. The small convoy stopped in front of a small building that was located in the center of the camp and surrounded by a fifteen-foot barbed-wire fence and a half-dozen layers of concertina wire strung out at the base and along the top of the fence. A solid wooden fence eight feet tall was between the cyclone fence and the building, preventing any visual entry into the classified area. The only entrance was where the jeeps had stopped. Mister LeBlonde led the way past an armed gate guard and through a solid steel door.

"This will be your home for awhile. You'll learn everything concerning your mission right here. The next time that you'll leave this building will be for your insertion. I'll be back on your last day of training to brief you on your final instructions. I recommend that you pay very close attention to your instructors—

they're some of the best in the business." LeBlonde turned on his heels and left the room without waiting for a reply.

The special isolation building contained everything they needed for a comfortable stay. One of the drivers gave Paul and Mills a tour of the facility. It was constructed out of reinforced cement, and had tile floors and air-conditioning. The floor plans included separate bedrooms for up to seven team members, kitchen, showers, operations room, equipment storage areas, and a very well-done recreation room with attached sun deck. Paul was again very impressed with the efficiency of the CCN people.

The next six days in the isolation building were well spent. Paul and Mills were shown how to operate some of the most modern military equipment in the world. They would be carrying a radio, smaller than a hand-held walkie-talkie, which could send and receive messages over ten miles.

A special team arrived at the isolation building on the morning of the last day before they would be inserted, and dyed Paul's hair a dark brown. Mills needed only a touch-up to darken the sun-bleached portions of his naturally brown hair. They had been issued authentic North Vietnamese Army uniforms that fit both of them perfectly. Paul was standing in front of a full-length mirror adjusting his leather belt when Mr. LeBlonde's image appeared behind him in the mirror.

"Well, it looks like the pair of you are just about ready to go to work." LeBlonde adjusted his sunglasses. "One more minor preparation and you'll be ready for tonight. Both of you go in the shower room and strip down. Mister Thaler here has one last touch for your make-up." LeBlonde recognized the small man standing next to him by placing his arm over his shoulder.

Paul looked over at Mills and shrugged his shoulders in puzzlement as he started undressing on the shower bench. Paul tried reviewing everything they had gone over during the past six days and couldn't think of anything they had missed. The instructors and briefers had been so thorough during the mission preparation that they had even included pills to constipate both of them during the mission phase, which was only supposed to last a few days. The small man entered the shower room carrying a leather suitcase and a wash basin. He placed both items on the bench and opened the suitcase. He removed a plastic package that contained a dark yellow powder and emptied a portion of the package into the basin. Thaler pushed his wire-rimmed glasses against his forehead using the back of his hand as he prepared a concoction of powder and warm water. He wore a pair of rubber gloves to prevent the dye from staining his hands.

"Gentlemen, please use these sponges and apply this special dye to your private areas. I'll do the rest of your bodies because shading is very important, especially around your eyes." The small man caught their quizzical looks and added, "You may feel that these precautions aren't necessary, but we don't leave anything to chance if we can help it. If you have to urinate we want *everything* to look oriental."

"I realize you people are very thorough, but my height will give me away before the color of my cock will," Paul grinned.

"There are tall North Vietnamese . . . Lieutenant." Thaler's voice reflected his contempt for the lieutenant's comment. "Of course, if they get too close, then you'll probably have to use these." The little man reached back into his suitcase and held up two Hi-Standard .22-caliber pistols that had been equipped with silencers.

Mills took one of the handguns and rubbed the soft leather holster between his fingers. "Sir, if we don't make it on this mission it's because *we* screwed up. These people really have their shit together!"

Mister Thaler looked up at Mills without moving his head. "Thank you, Sergeant Mills." Thaler finished applying the dye to Paul and stepped back to look at his completed work. The man nodded his head in self-satisfaction and then reached out and dabbed a little more dye against Paul's right thigh. "Before I leave, Lieutenant, Mister Le Blonde asked me to inform you that you're to memorize all of the data in the instruction packets you received yesterday. You'll only be allowed to take the coded maps with you on your mission." Thaler repacked his suitcase with the precision of an artist. "Oh . . . please lay out in the sun for an hour or so to ensure the dye dries completely before you dress."

Lieutenant Bourne stepped in front of the mirror after Thaler had left the building. His first glance shocked him. He *looked* like a North Vietnamese. Thaler had worked the dye around his eyes to give them a slanted effect and around his cheekbones to set them out from his face. The special dye had changed the tone of his skin to sun-tanned oriental.

Paul stepped out on the wooden patio deck behind the cement building and felt the heat against the sole of his bare feet. The deck was surrounded by an eight-foot wooden fence that provided privacy so that he could lay in the sun nude. He could hear the surf crashing against the beach on the other side of the fence and he felt very lonely and scared. Lying in the sun and thinking about Malibu and then the mission was too much for him. He sat up and reached for his CAR-15 submachine gun. Paul busied himself checking the working mechanism for wear and cleanliness.

Slowly his mind left the sound of the surf and locked in on preparing for the mission. He was well aware of the importance of the proper functioning of the first magazine of ammunition for his submachine gun. Paul removed each round and cleaned it by hand using a soft dry cloth. Sergeant Mills pulled up a chair next to Paul and dismantled his shotgun. Paul could see his hands shaking slightly when he pulled the weapon apart. He looked down at his own hands and saw the same slight shaking. They were both suffering from pre-mission jitters that he knew would go away once they were actually inserted in the area of operation. Right now, though, there wasn't enough to keep them busy and there was too much time to think about what might go wrong.

The sun slipped behind the wooden fence, causing a long shadow to reach out and touch Paul's bare toes. He stood and walked over to the open door and stopped. The front door to the isolation building had opened and closed, signaling visitors.

"We're back here!" Mills bent forward in his seat. He placed his assembled shotgun across his naked lap.

LeBlonde stepped around Paul onto the patio. The agent was wearing a well-tailored white walking suit. "Lieutenant, would you mind getting some clothes for you and the sergeant? I want to introduce you to the rest of your team." LeBlonde beckoned with his hand and three Meo tribesmen stepped forward onto the patio from the main building corridor. Paul stepped around them and went into the supply ready room, where he removed a pair of pants for him and Mills. He returned to the group in a matter of seconds and threw his partner a pair of the folded NVA trousers.

LeBlonde had waited until Paul had returned before talking. "All of these men speak excellent English, French, and dialects of North Vietnamese. They will be going with you during your insertion and will stay with you for the execution of your mission. Mauk will be your pointman and will be the spokesman for your team if you should encounter any NVA trail watchers." LeBlonde placed his hand on the next man's shoulder. "Tru is an expert in silent killing . . . He'll remove the trail watchers for you. Pra-Teup is your stay-behind man in the event you have to run. He was raised in the area that you're going into and can easily walk himself out." LeBlonde smiled. "All of these men have been briefed on the mission and will help you carry in the gold coins to the warlords."

"I was wondering how we were going to get the loot there and the opium back here," Paul spoke to LeBlonde with Mills nodding his head in agreement.

LeBlonde reached into a cardboard box he had been holding under his right arm and removed two cans that resembled spray paint containers. "These contain a chemical solution that will take care of the opium base for you so that you won't have to carry it out." LeBlonde flipped a can to both Americans. "The compound inside those cans has been blended back in our Stateside lab, and will react to the acid base of the opium and destroy the drug. I want you to use this test kit . . ." LeBlonde held up a leather carrying case, "to check each brick of opium to ensure it's real, and then line up the bricks in stacks of five and sprinkle on the powder. I want a picture taken of the piles of opium with the 35mm provided in your packs. Destroy the camera and bring back only the film. By the way, a little of the powder goes a long way, so you don't have to put a lot on the stacks of opium-base bricks." LeBlonde lit a fresh cigar and looked over the burning tobacco at Paul. "We've had a small setback, but I think you can handle it. We can't extract you from your mission area—you'll have to walk out to the Special Forces camp at Lang Vei." He looked over at Mills for a reaction and then back at Paul.

Lieutenant Bourne packed the canister of powder and the test kit into his rucksack. "You and your people have done an excellent job preparing us for this mission and I want you to know that we appreciate it." Paul held his hand out for LeBlonde to shake.

The agent took the offered hand and grabbed the lieutenant around the shoulder with his free arm. LeBlonde was showing emotion.

Four sleek Cobra gunships lined the oceanside of the PSP helipad and two Huey slicks were parked in the center. The black stepvan stopped between the two passenger choppers and the rear doors flew open. What looked like a North Vietnamese squad exited the vehicle and scrambled into the waiting American helicopters. One of the door gunners did a double take when he saw the team. He had been told not to be alarmed over who they were transporting, but the NVA-looking Special Forces team had caught him off guard. The pilot's voice coming over the intercom system calmed the young soldier. Paul slid backward onto the steel deck of the slick, leaving his rucksack on. He sat in a crossed-leg position and smiled over at the door gunner.

The thick jungle was abnormally quiet once the helicopters had dropped off the special team and disappeared almost instantly from sight. Paul ran toward the protective shelter of a bamboo thicket, followed closely by his team. The men zigzagged around the low branches and vanished in the dark foliage. Paul dropped down on one knee and removed his lensatic compass from its nylon case attached to his shoulder harness. He shot an azimuth and touched Mauk on his shoulder, nodded, and pointed in the direction he wanted to go. The team automatically took their assigned places in the short battle column behind the pointman. Very few words would be spoken; hand signals would be used until they reached the pre-arranged meeting spot in the jungle three days away. Mauk slid through the undergrowth like one of the wild animals it concealed. The farther they moved away from the insertion site, the more the jungle began to regain its normal sounds.

The next forty-eight hours of travel produced very little action for the team, with the exception of two small North Vietnamese patrols that had passed them on a hidden jungle trail that led south. The enemy soldiers had talked in loud voices, which told Paul that they felt secure and didn't suspect any danger.

Lieutenant Bourne halted his team and checked his map to make sure they were at the right location. Huge boulders covered with jungle vines and small plants dominated the clearing. Paul nodded reassuringly to Mills and motioned for the team to travel in a spiraling circle around the spacious clearing where they were to meet the warlords. Paul had pushed his team hard through the jungle so that they would arrive a whole day early at the site. He wanted to ensure that his team was the first party at the meeting place, in order to guard against an ambush or betrayal. There was the possibility that the warlords would kill the special American team and take the money. The NVA would be blamed for the act, and they could sell the opium base at a premium price to the South Vietnamese generals. Paul wasn't going to take that chance. A small freshwater stream appeared near the far edge of the clearing and Paul led his team up it for a few hundred meters before he raised his hand to halt. A natural pile of vine-covered boulders had forced the stream to change directions, but also made a natural landmark. Paul removed his rucksack and took out the small packets of gold coins. The rest of his team followed his lead and stacked their gold next to Paul's. The Special Forces lieutenant used hand signals to tell Mills to take the team back downstream while he hid the gold coins in a crevice of the rock formation. Paul constantly kept an eye out for cobras while he worked in the natural hunting grounds of the deadly snakes.

Dusk was beginning to change the jungle undergrowth when Paul rejoined his waiting team from a different direction than they had taken from the rock formation. He selected locations in the jungle surrounding the rendezvous site for his team to take up hiding places, and helped camouflage each of them so that they blended perfectly with the jungle setting. Paul was impressed with the Meo tribesmen, who had blended perfectly with Paul and Mills as a team. They had worked together as if they had trained as a team for months instead of just a few days. Paul finished camouflaging Sergeant Mills, and then found himself a nice open spot in the clearing next to a flat rock where all of his men had a clear view of him. Paul leaned his back against a small boulder and waited.

Morning broke quickly through the jungle once it had decided to make its appearance. The hours had passed slowly for Paul during the very long night of waiting in the nearly-total darkness of the nighttime jungle. He had taken three amphetamine tablets from his pill vial in order to stay awake. A hunting tiger had coughed earlier in the evening from the far side of the clearing, which had kept him alert until the very early morning hours.

A troop of monkeys passed through the tree tops around noon and stopped to feed two hundred meters south of Paul's position. Around mid-afternoon, the troop leader paused in the act of turning over a rock and sounded a warning to his females. The clearing emptied of scrambling monkeys as they scurried for safety in the tall trees. The jungle quieted to the north of Paul's position, alerting him. Paul placed his thumb on the selector switch of his CAR-15 and waited as the jungle around him stopped making its natural sounds. The insects on the edge of the clearing were the last to become quiet as the circle of silence closed in around him. The warlords had arrived in exactly the manner Paul had guessed they would, coming from all directions at the same time. Paul eased the air out between his teeth in silent relief for having had the foresight to hide his team and bury the gold coins. A quick movement caught his eye near Mills's position, and then fifty armed men appeared simultaneously in the clearing surrounding Paul's rocky location. The band carried weapons covering a dozen different countries—from American Thompson submachine guns to French MAT-49's and Russian AK-47's. Paul even saw a Swedish K over the shoulder of one of the rear guards. He hated to think of the ammunition resupply problems that warlords had. Paul's combat eye quickly noticed that the men carrying the American and French weapons held the guns as if the feel was uncomfortable. Paul stepped down from his low rock ledge with his CAR-15 off-safety and pointed down slightly at the ground, just enough to be polite, but ready. A tall Frenchman stepped out from his concealed position at the edge of the jungle catching Paul slightly off-guard. The Frenchman smiled, using only half of his mouth.

"You have come here alone? Yes?" He glanced around the clearing as if he were waiting for men to emerge from under the rocks.

"I come here alone, no." Paul returned the Frenchman's half-smile.

"Where are your people?" The tall man kept glancing around the clearing past his own men.

"I'll conduct whatever business there is between us . . . alone." Paul's mind began receiving danger signals from many different sources.

"You are too untrusting for one so . . . young." The man looked deeply into Paul's eyes, trying to size him up quickly. "We must trade quickly or the People's Army will come here."

"Where's the cargo?" The comment made by the Frenchman that referred to the North Vietnamese as the People's Army had alerted Paul to be on guard.

The Frenchman allowed a small chuckle to slip through his lips. "The opium base is here . . ." He raised his hand and a portion of the jungle parted, letting a packtrain pass into the clearing. Sixteen horses were visible within a few minutes. "You take the opium and give me the ten million dollars promised us." He nodded to one of his lieutenants and then looked back at Paul. "I hope you have followed our instructions and bundled the hundred-dollar bills in twenty-thousand-dollar packets."

Lieutenant Bourne's suspicions were confirmed. He didn't know what had happened to the warlords, but he knew that someone had probably paid with their life to set the Frenchman up. "First, have your men unload the horses and place the opium bricks in rows five high . . . and I'll take you to the money."

The Frenchman shrugged his shoulders and smiled,

mostly to himself. He spoke in fluent Vietnamese to the men standing near the horses and they began unloading their cargo. Paul walked back to the rock formation that he had been hiding near and recovered from his rucksack the test kit and the canisters LeBlonde had given him. The black opium bricks had been laid out in long lines next to the horses as he had requested when he returned. Paul spot-checked different bricks to ensure they were opium base and then, quickly, before the Frenchman realized what was going on, he opened one of the canisters with the blade of his Randall knife and walked back down the line sprinkling the powder on the opium. Paul remembered as he was walking fast what LeBlonde had said about a little of the stuff going a long way.

Bourne stopped in front of the Frenchman and grinned. "I have your money hidden back in the jungle . . . if you're ready." He watched the expression on the European's face when smoke started on the tops of the piles in little wisps and then turned into columns as the chemical reaction destroyed the opium. The muscles around the Frenchman's mouth tightened when he realized what Paul had done.

"Why did you do that!"

"It's mine . . . right?" Bourne raised the barrel slightly on his CAR-15, expecting trouble to start. "I can't take it with me . . . so I destroyed it. Come on and get your money." Paul turned on his heels and started walking toward the jungle. If they were going to kill him it would be after the Frenchman got his money. He couldn't afford to lose both the opium and the money or the North Vietnamese would kill him. Paul could almost feel the eyes burning against his back with hate.

"Are you coming?"

The Frenchman nodded to one of his bodyguards

and started after Paul. The lieutenant noticed before he turned back around that the Frenchman had slipped the safety off his AK-47. Paul stopped near a huge tree when they were halfway to where the money had been stashed.

"I've got a bad case of dysentery. . . . I'll be right back . . ." Paul didn't wait for a reply and reached for his belt buckle as he left the trail.

Laughter followed Paul into the jungle when the Frenchman translated what he had said to the bodyguard. Paul pulled his .22-caliber silenced pistol from its hidden holster and quietly slipped around the far side of the tree trunk. The bodyguard was squatting ten feet up the trail from the Frenchman. Paul shot him in the back of the head and watched as the guard slumped down. The Frenchman's eyes were riveted to the spot of the jungle where Paul had disappeared. The lieutenant stepped out from his hiding place with his pistol leveled at the enemy's surprised face.

"If you touch your rifle . . . you're one dead commie!" Paul reached out and grabbed the folding-stock AK-47 the Frenchman had rested on the trail next to him and threw it out into the jungle. The pistol in the holster at the man's side followed his rifle seconds later.

Paul pushed against the communist leader's back. "Move!"

The pace the lieutenant set down the trail had the Frenchman gasping for breath in a matter of minutes. Paul grabbed the man's collar to stop him and then pushed him into a thicket. The enemy fell down on the bamboo leaves and gasped for breath. It was obvious he wasn't a field soldier.

"What happened to the warlords who were supposed to meet me."

"How . . . how . . . did you know about me?"

"Only a fucking commie would ever refer to the

NVA as the People's Army. . . . that was your first fuck-up . . ." Paul leveled the pistol in his hand at the man's left eye. "Answer my fucking question!"

"Please . . . they forced me to help them. . . . After the French Army was defeated and my outpost was captured . . . I *had* to help them or die!" The Frenchman's voice carried a whining tone but failed to convince Paul of his sincerity. "I've been waiting for a chance to escape from them! Now that you have liberated me, I can tell you Americans many things about the NVA!" Paul moved the tip of his silencer against the Frenchman's ear. "Please!" The man was scared and knew that his life was in jeopardy.

"How many men did you bring with you?" Paul listened to the jungle sounds around him.

"We were supposed to meet up with you and get the money and then ki—I mean, capture, your unit. The opium was supposed to have been returned. You know they will kill me for allowing you to destroy it." The Frenchman had been talking so fast that he had to pause to breathe.

"Who are *they*?"

"General Ho Van Duc. He is the one who tortured the information about this meeting from the warlords."

Lieutenant Bourne was glad that one of the warlords had taken his revenge by giving the North Vietnamese general bad information. "You still haven't answered my question—How many soldiers did you bring with you?"

"I brought one of my companies . . . 120 men . . . The remainder of the battalion is bivouacked two thousand meters away." The Frenchman nodded his head in the direction of his unit.

Paul had extracted enough information from the NVA battalion commander to make a run for the border with the majority of the enemy unit to his west.

Paul hoped that his team members had observed enough at the rendezvous site to make it to one of their prearranged assembly points.

The soft hiss was the only noise coming from the pistol when Paul pulled the trigger. The copper-coated bullet entered behind the Frenchman's left ear and came out of his right eye socket. Paul searched the man's clothes and removed his wallet and some folded papers from a side pocket. He placed the end of his pistol up against the Frenchman's heart and fired three more shots as a *coup de grace*.

The sun had set when Lieutenant Bourne stopped for his first break since leaving the dead Frenchman. He was headed for Co Roc Mountain, which he had designated as the last assembly area for his team in the event that any of them became separated from the main body. Paul scanned the jungle from his prone position, trying to find a suitable tree in which to spend the night. He forced himself to stand on his exhausted legs and continued heading west. He spotted the perfect tree just as the last rays of light filtered through the thick growth. The tree had a big fork twenty feet off the ground, which would hold him with room to spare. Paul slung his CAR-15 over his back and climbed the tree trunk using small branches for footholds. He removed his rucksack and wedged it in the fork of the tree for a backrest. Leaves had filled part of the hollow formed by the joining of the two huge branches, making a natural mattress that needed only to be checked for snakes and scorpions before being used.

Paul placed his CAR-15 against the tree and stretched out in his nest. He took a deep breath and relaxed, allowing his eyes to wander down to the base of the tree and lock on the face of a huge tiger that was looking up at him. There wasn't a sound from either of them as Paul realized that the tiger had been stalking him. The two natural adversaries stared at each other for a long minute, both of them knowing that Paul was safe in the tree nest and had the advantage. The tiger emitted a low rumbling sound from deep in his throat and vanished into the shadows. Paul blinked his eyes and leaned forward from his perch. He wondered if his eyes had been playing tricks on him, but he was too tired to think much about the subject before he fell asleep.

A loud pathetic scream woke Paul with a start that almost had him falling out of the tree. The tiger had made a kill, probably a small forest deer. Paul pulled the piece of green cloth tape off the crystal of his watch and read the luminous hands—fifteen minutes after three. He replaced the tape and felt with his hand in the total darkness for the side pocket on his rucksack. He removed the canteen and a small vial of salt tablets. Paul's whole body ached from the severe workout he had had the day before, trying to break through the thick undergrowth of the jungle. He needed salt or his legs would cramp up. Paul replaced his canteen and lay back wide awake, and started plotting the new day's course of action. He figured he would reach Co Roc Mountain sometime during the late afternoon if he got an early start and didn't run into too many thickets of new bamboo. He planned on waiting at Co Roc for a half day to see if the rest of his team would show up, and then strike out on his own for the Lang Vei Special Forces Camp. The NVA would surely have patrols searching the jungle for him by morning and would probably be using tracker dogs. Paul grinned when he thought about the big tiger that had been tracking him. It would be funny when the dogs hit the cat's spoor.

Daylight crept through the jungle canopy in fine slivers of soft light. Paul checked the ground carefully before he lowered himself nervously to the jungle floor.

The kill the tiger had made during the night should have satisfied the animal's hunger, but Paul was still very cautious just in case the cat's lair was nearby and it decided he was encroaching. The fear of the beast's tracking him without his slightest awareness the day before was fresh in Paul's mind. He had to remain very alert traveling alone in the jungle. Fear had its good point, especially in keeping survival senses working at peak levels.

Lieutenant Bourne maintained a steady course toward Co Roc all morning. He traveled slower than the day before, stopping often to listen to the jungle. The sun was tilting toward the west when Paul reached the western base of the prominent terrain feature. The mountain had a sheer cliff face on its eastern side, but the western slope was a gradual incline covered with open rocky patches and fields of elephant grass. Paul slowed his pace, the extra pull of the slope against his legs telling him that he was getting very tired. Paul moved through the eight-foot-high grass and low shrubs, carefully, in a half-circle to the southernmost edge of the mountain that touched the river. He spotted a small strip of welcome shade between the cliff front and the shallow river, and edged around the rocks, watching out for snakes as he angled toward the natural crevice.

"You must really be getting old, Lieutenant."

Paul's breath caught in his throat. He turned quickly, bringing his CAR-15 up, and came full face with Sergeant Mills, who was perched up on a rock next to the cliff.

"How in the hell . . .?" Paul had been caught cold. The rest of his team appeared in the shadows when his eyes adjusted to the lower light. All of them were wearing impish grins.

"Remember Pra Teup?" Mills maintained his grin.

"He moves as well at night as he does in the daylight." Mills beckoned for Paul to join him in the shadows. "Shit! I thought that I was a hot recon man. These three guys gave me lessons traveling through the jungle at night that I'm *still* wondering about."

The Meo tribesmen beamed over the American's compliment.

Mauk spoke, "You are a very good also . . . Much better than NVA soldiers."

"We had better stop talking so much or the whole world will know where we're at." The voices of his men seemed unnaturally loud to Paul after the solitude of the jungle, yet everyone had been whispering.

"No sweat, Lieutenant. We've checked the area pretty good." Mills pointed up the cliff wall. "The NVA have a lookout position about three clicks away. The rest of the area is clean."

Paul stood up from the squatting position he had taken in the shade. "We had better start moving toward Lang Vei . . . it's not far from here and we can cross the river in the shadow from the mountain."

"You must go alone," Mauk pointed in the direction of the Special Forces A-Camp. "We are going north to join up with our people." The Meo tribesman was speaking for the three of them. LeBlonde had used Paul's mission as a ruse to insert a special agent team.

"I hope we will meet again." Paul shook hands with each of the men. His eyes reflected the fellowship he felt for the mountain tribesmen.

The two parties disappeared along the river edge going in opposite directions. Paul paused after a few meters next to a natural ford across the knee-deep river. The shadow from the mountain wasn't dark enough for the crossing, so the two recon men took up hiding positions in the rocks until nightfall.

The cool river water reached a little past Paul's

knees. They had waited seven hours to make the five-minute river crossing. Paul crawled through the thick underbrush lining the Vietnamese side of the river, followed by Mills.

Mills crawled up next to Paul and cupped his hand next to the lieutenant's ear. "Hear them?"

Paul listened, and heard the dogs baying about fifteen hundred meters away. Paul knew that the jungle was famous for distorting sound and fooling the listener.

"Let's move," Paul bent over low to the ground so that he could see the outline of the trees and thickets in the moonlight. A hundred meters from the riverbank Paul stepped out into a large field of elephant grass as high as his shoulders. He paused and waited for Mills to catch up.

"What luck," Paul whispered in his sergeant's ear. Hand signals didn't work at night, so whispering was necessary. Mills shot an azimuth with his wrist compass and pointed the direction in which they needed to travel to reach the American camp.

The elephant grass covered the rolling hills for eight thousand meters, making travel easy for the two men. Paul picked up a shallow gully and followed it until he reached the end. Twenty meters to his front was the French-built Highway Nine, shimmering in the bright moonlight. Paul moved parallel with the east-west road, headed east toward the A-Camp and safety. He slowed his pace even though he wanted to go faster, because they were still dressed as NVA soldiers and he didn't want to run into a night ambush from the camp. Three hours later they spotted the night lights of the A-Camp. Paul knelt in the grass and pointed to a ridge running two hundred meters from the front gate. He decided that he would risk crawling close to the safety of the American position. He wanted to be in close enough to be protected from the camp's periodic harassment fire from their 4.2-inch mortars, but far enough out so that they wouldn't be detected by the perimeter guards. Paul knew the next couple of hours would be spent crawling on his stomach, but it was the only way they could approach the A-Camp dressed as enemy soldiers and not be shot on sight. First light brought movement around the sandbag bunkers that surrounded the camp as the guards changed for breakfast. The sun was almost directly over their heads when Paul tapped Mills's leg with his boot to alert him and then stood up, leaving his CAR-15 lying in the grass.

"*Cheiu-hoi! Cheiu-hoi!*" Paul yelled the NVA surrender at the top of his lungs and stood waiting. The main gate flew open ten minutes later and two tall Americans followed by five well-armed Vietnamese walked cautiously toward Paul. The group paused a few feet outside the gate fearing an NVA ambush. One of the Vietnamese called out to Paul.

"*I'm an American soldier!*" Paul could see the shock on the Americans' faces. The two Special Forces soldiers called for him to advance at the same time. The effect almost made Paul laugh. "*I have one more American with me! He's lying in the grass and will get up now!*" Mills stood slowly with his hands held above his head. The two recon men walked to the dirt road that led into the camp, then headed toward the waiting group.

"*Damn!* They *are* Americans!"

"I'm Lieutenant Paul Bourne and this is Sergeant Mills." Paul kept his hands held high as he spoke, waiting for the rifles to be lowered by the camp guards.

"Well, I'll be a son of a bitch! They're Americans dressed as gooks!" The shorter of the two Americans stepped forward holding out his hand. "Get your hands down . . . shit."

The Vietnamese, who didn't fully understand what

was going on, kept their weapons pointed at the two recon men.

"I'm Captain Blackmore and this is my XO, Lieutenant Jeb Hall." The captain turned toward the open gate. "Let's get the hell out of the sun and have a cold can of beer."

"Sounds good to me, but first, let us go back and get our gear. We didn't want to approach your camp carrying weapons."

"That was one of your better ideas. . . . The guards would have opened fire as soon as they saw you." Blackmore stopped walking. "Where did you leave it?"

"Back there next to the road."

Small-arms fire cracked over Paul's head. The group dropped to the ground and crawled back through the gate toward the safety of the fighting bunkers. The camp's .50-caliber heavy machine gun answered the NVA rifle fire with its deep-sounding thuds. Paul was glad that they had made their move when they had or the enemy patrol would have gotten too close and they would have been trapped in a crossfire from the camp and the NVA. The range of the .50-caliber forced the NVA to evacuate their positions and run for cover, chased by exploding mortar shells from the camp defenses.

Paul relaxed in the cool room and sipped from his cold beer. Mills had drank three Shasta strawberry sodas before Paul downed his first beer.

"Where are you all coming from?" The team captain had played the proper host, but was now ready for some answers. "Those NVA were tracking you, weren't they?"

"Yes," Paul pulled the tab on his second beer and then handed the captain a small card with a coded message written on it. "Sir, would you have your radioman send this message for me?"

"Sure. . . ." The captain paused and turned back around to face Paul in his chair, "but stick around. I want some questions answered."

"Believe me, captain, we're not planning on going anywhere soon!" Mills crossed his legs and took a drink from his soda as the captain left the room.

"Mills, you did a super job out there," Paul had rested his head against the back of his chair and sat with his eyes closed. He could almost feel the tension leaving his body.

"Bullshit! I didn't do a damn thing except run. I'll tell you, Lieutenant . . . I thought your shit was going to be spread all over that clearing back there when ze ol' Frenchie appeared with his pack. I could have warned you but a couple of minutes after you had left the clearing with the Frenchman, his people took off back into the jungle. That's how we got out of there so fast. We went north and then headed straight east until we hit Co Roc."

"That bastard commie was working as a battalion commander for the NVA—" Paul stopped talking as the captain returned to the room.

"They're sending a fucking Lear jet to pick you up!" This is unbelievable!" The team commander shook his head from side to side. "We have to leave now if we're going to make it in time."

Paul kept his beer and followed the captain out of the front door of the teamhouse to the waiting jeep that had his rucksack and CAR-15 on the back seat next to Mills's gear. One of the other team members had driven out to where they had left it and picked it up for them. The captain drove them to the waiting helicopter and stopped. Paul could see the jealous look on the man's face as they shook hands.

"Thanks for your hospitality and for getting our stuff for us . . . I owe you one."

The captain nodded his head in acknowledgement and tried smiling.

The Lear jet touched down on the Marine runway twenty minutes after Paul and Mills had arrived in the Special Forces jeep at the Khe Shan encampment. The Marines watching the men in the jeep were confused at what looked like NVA soldiers shaking hands with the familiar Green Berets. A Marine full colonel pulled up in his jeep and tried waving down the jet as it was taking off. Captain Blackmore stopped him. Paul could see the bewildered expression on the colonel's face through the porthole in the airplane as they raced past the parked jeeps during takeoff. LeBlonde stopped next to Paul's seat after they had gained cruising altitude.

"I guess I don't have to offer you any booze." He glanced at the beer Paul was holding in his hand. "We'll talk when we get back to CCN Headquarters. Enjoy your trip." LeBlonde patted Paul's shoulder and left for his seat near the rear of the plane.

They entered the isolation building from the black step van that had transported them from the airfield. Paul led the way into the strange-looking yet familiar surroundings. It had only been a few days since they had left the rooms he was walking through, yet Paul felt the time span had been much greater. The fresh air-conditioned rooms reminded Paul how rotten he smelled.

"I sure could use a shower and some clean clothes," Paul glanced over at LeBlonde.

"Sure, but first I need some preliminary information from you, and then we'll leave you alone so that you can get the dye off and cleaned up." LeBlonde turned on the tape recorder that was on the table in the room. "Lieutenant Bourne, you're first. Begin with the helicopter's touchdown on the landing zone and tell us everything . . . terrain features . . . colors . . . sounds . . . everything that you can remember," LeBlonde looked over at Sergeant Mills. "Feel free to interrupt anytime you feel that you can add more detail." The agent motioned for Paul to start talking. Paul talked for two hours, stopping only for LeBlonde to change tapes on the recorder. Paul finished and rubbed his eyes with the backs of his hands. He was tired and wanted a hot shower.

"Let me see those papers you mentioned that you found on the Frenchman." LeBlonde tried to control the excitement he was feeling but his voice gave him away.

Paul reached down into the tie pocket of his rucksack and handed LeBlonde the wallet and small bundle of papers. LeBlonde checked the wallet first. He thumbed through the photographs and stopped at an NVA identification card.

"Jean-Paul LaTruseau . . . Colonel LaTruseau!" LeBlonde waved the wallet at Paul. "*Damn!*" Do you know who this character is?"

"Was." Paul corrected the agent and shrugged his shoulders.

LeBlonde moved closer to Paul's chair and placed his hand on the lieutenant's arm to hold his attention. "Are you *sure*, I mean really sure, that you killed him?"

"Yes. The bullet went through his head and I put three more into his heart just to make *sure*. I didn't want him telling any of his friends which way I went." Paul frowned. "Why? Would you have rather me brought him back here?"

"*Ha!*" LeBlonde slapped his leg. "*If* you could have done that!"

Paul's eyes flashed at the agent's comment as if he were being insulted.

"Oh . . . nothing against you, Lieutenant . . ." LeBlonde smiled. "The NVA would have sacrificed *two* divisions of troops to have taken him back if you had captured him alive."

"What makes him so damn valuable?" Mills raised his eyebrows and looked at Paul.

"LaTruseau was the one who betrayed the French garrison at Dien Bien Phu during the Indo-China War. Since then he has been working as a double agent and has been causing a great deal of trouble. Hell—one of his capers was to infiltrate the MACV Headquarters in Saigon."

"Did he?"

"Not only did he, but he walked out of the building with a copy of the monthly operations plan for the whole of South Vietnam! Talk about some very embarrassed general officers!" LeBlonde tapped the wallet against his leg and pushed his lower lip out in deep thought. "We've been trying to have him assassinated for years, and we've lost quite a few very good men in the process." LeBlonde threw his head back and grinned. "And damn if you don't just walk in there and put a bullet through his head!"

Paul smiled, showing his teeth around a devilish grin. "Do I get a happy face, teacher?"

"You're damn right you get a happy face—and maybe a gold star next to it!" LeBlonde jumped to his feet. "All right! Both of you get cleaned up. I have to make a few quick telephone calls." LeBlonde left the room waving the wallet and mumbling to himself, "Shit! This is better than invading Hanoi!"

The two men raced each other undressing and ran for the showers, leaving their filthy clothes next to the chairs they had been sitting in. Paul turned on the shower and stuck his foot under the water to test how hot it was.

LeBlonde stuck his head in the shower room entrance. "Lieutenant Bourne, don't forget to draw a map showing where you hid those gold coins." The agent winked and pulled his head back out of the doorway before Paul could answer.

Paul stepped under the welcome shower smiling. LeBlonde didn't miss a trick.

Mills yelled over to Paul over the shower noise. "Hey, Lieutenant, let's pick up a couple of whores and a few bottles of whiskey and get some beach time down by the ocean."

"Sounds good to me!" Paul yelled back over the steel divider to his teammate.

The night had passed too quickly, and Paul felt an unwanted pressure in his stomach when the Lear jet took off and pulled up to gain altitude. He was still drunk. He had stayed up all night next to the ocean drinking and listening to the waves lap against the sand. It had been a very good night spent with the girl the CCN people had slipped in past the guards for him. Mills had taken up a position with his woman about fifty meters away, and the two of them hadn't seen each other all night.

The familiar battered camp jeep was waiting next to the Duc Co runway when they touched down. A feeling of coming home ironically passed through Paul's mind. He smiled to himself, thinking how little it took to please him.

Mills hopped over the back of the jeep and took a seat next to his gear. Paul slid in on the passenger seat next to the driver.

"Well, Sergeant James, how are things on the home

front?" Paul asked to the camp's new communications sergeant, who had driven out to pick them up.

"Not worth a shit, sir!" The sergeant kept his eyes on the red laterite road winding through the center of the camp.

"What's going on?" Mills leaned forward on his seat.

"Captain Tong and Pellam are at it again. Tong's drunk or stoned . . . one or the other." The jeep pulled to a jerky stop in front of the teamhouse and waited for the Vietnamese soldier to allow them to pass. Paul noticed immediately that there weren't any of the familiar Montagnard guards, only Vietnamese in the camp. Paul picked up his gear and CAR-15 and walked slowly toward the screen door. Captain Pellam, followed by Tong, stepped out of the teamhouse.

"*Damn it, Tong! I'm sick of your bullshit!*" Pellam was yelling at the Vietnamese commander, only inches from the man's face.

Tong pointed his finger at Pellam's face and yelled back. "You will have respect for me!"

Lieutenant Bourne glanced around the open area surrounding the American teamhouse and noticed that there was a crowd gathering of armed Vietnamese soldiers. Over two hundred men were standing in loose groups around the building, including Tong's special bodyguards.

Paul stepped forward to stop the public argument between the two commanders. Paul was a good friend of the Vietnamese commander. He touched the Vietnamese on his shoulder to gain attention. "Sir, let's go over to your house and talk."

The small Vietnamese turned and recognized the lieutenant with a friendly grin. "Lieutenant Bourne! Welcome back to Duc Co!" Paul had given Tong a respectable way out of the confrontation with Pellam, and the Vietnamese was taking it.

"*Get the hell out of here, Lieutenant!*" Pellam's voice cut into the conversation, filled with sarcasm.

"Captain, you are a fool." Tong's voice carried a razor-edge threat with it.

Captain Tong's head snapped back from the force of the slap landing on his cheek. A shiver went down Paul's spine. The camp became absolutely quiet. Captain Tong stood straight-backed, facing Pellam. Slowly the Vietnamese commander turned away from the American captain and faced his troops. The handprint was turning a deep red on his cheek. The embarrassed leader walked slowly across the open ground, taking long strides until he reached the door of his quarters. He turned around slowly and glared back in the direction of the American teamhouse. The company officers from the Vietnamese units followed their leader into his headquarters.

"He's going to cause us some grief for that slap, Captain," Paul shook his head in disbelief over what had just occurred.

"You let me handle that little son of a bitch!"

Paul glanced over at Mills and detected the deep concern the sergeant had over the incident. Trouble would come, that was for sure.

Sergeant Mills went over to his medical bunker to check on his patients and get some aspirin for the pounding headache he had from the booze he had drunk the night before.

Paul hung his gear up on the wooden pegs in his room. He felt hungry and went into the kitchen to find a snack of some kind before supper. Pellam was sitting in the bar pouring himself a half glass of whiskey. Paul made himself two Spam sandwiches and took them with him outside to eat. The only troops he could see were a few American artillerymen working on the howitzers in their compound outside the Special Forces camp. When he had finished eating he went back to his room and lay down on his bunk. He closed his eyes and fell asleep almost instantly.

For better or worse, Paul was home at Duc Co again.

Chapter 4

Lieutenant Bourne opened his eyes slowly. He listened in the darkness for any sound that would tell him what had pulled him from his shallow sleep. A shiver flickered along his spine and spread out over his scalp from the base of his neck. Two voices filtered through the bamboo matting of his wall facing the hallway. The sounds were coming from somewhere near the kitchen. Paul slid out of his bed and started toward the door. A strong intuitive urge to put on his battle gear nagged him. He shunned the impulse and slowly moved across the room in the dark. He stopped near the doorway and returned to the pegs on the wall where he had hung his battle gear.

Paul whispered to himself, "I'm going to look like a total ass if there's nothing wrong out there." He slipped his BAR belt, which contained thirty-two magazines of ammunition for his CAR-15, around his waist and stepped out into the hall.

The far end of the kitchen revealed Captain Tong standing naked under a bare light bulb waving a cocked .45-caliber pistol. Tong was talking in a deep, slow, and deliberate tone of voice to someone who stood out of sight from Paul's hallway position.

"You have insulted me . . . *No more! Son of a mutant pig!*"

"Tong, go back to bed . . . You've drank too fucking much booze!" Pellam's voice sounded tired. "I'm getting sick of your constantly being drunk."

"Do you think you can slap my face in front of my soldiers and live?"

Lieutenant Bourne dropped down into a low crouch in the unlit hallway. He knew Tong couldn't see him, because the single burning lightbulb in the kitchen was between Tong and Pellam. Captain Tong's hand was gripping the handle of the .45 so tightly that the blood vessels in the small man's forearm looked like rope cords. Foam began appearing at the corner of the Vietnamese commander's mouth when he opened and closed his lips without speaking. Paul was sure the man had taken opium before coming over to the teamhouse.

"You will die tonight . . . I die, too! See—I have removed my clothes so my journey through the world of the dead will be swift." Tong's mouth twisted from the hate he was feeling toward the American. "You, Pellam, shall die with your brains spread out on the floor! And then I am going to cut off the hand that insulted me!"

Captain Pellam stepped away from the wall to where Paul could see part of his shoulder and his face. Sweat was forming on the American commander's upper lip, revealing the fear that was beginning to gather in the pit of his stomach.

Paul heard a muffled grating sound that came through the tightly woven matting that served as material for the walls of the teamhouse. A loud click followed the first noise. Paul's mind tried deciphering the sound. It was too long to have been a rifle bolt sliding forward . . . *damn*! The bastards were setting up a .50-caliber heavy machine gun at the east entrance to the teamhouse.

Paul had missed most of the conversation between

Pellam and Captain Tong. The young lieutenant tried figuring a way out of the pending predicament. His eyes began scanning the walls and roof beams with the intensity of a wild animal that had been caged. The four-foot-high wall of sandbags surrounding the teamhouse would protect them from small arms and shrapnel, but the large slugs from the .50-caliber machine gun could eventually knock a hole through anything, given enough ammunition and time. Paul removed a magazine from his BAR belt and shucked eight rounds into his hand. He slid the magazine into his shirt and moved pantherlike down the dark hall. Paul carefully opened each room door that he passed and threw a round of ammunition at each of the sleeping men. The moonlight seeping through the windows revealed Paul in full battle dress to the other A-Team members. The men didn't need to be told that there was trouble.

Paul eased down against the exit door at the east end of the building and squatted with his back touching the matting. He tuned his ears to the outside sounds.

". . . and now, you American pig . . . *you die*!"

Paul caught the last words of Tong's threat and looked up in time to see the Vietnamese leader point the pistol directly at Pellam's fear-filled face. Paul reacted. He tore a hand grenade from his webbing and pulled out the safety pin, using his boot to push open the door, and pitched the live grenade underhand over the sand bags. The lieutenant's movements were fluid as he stretched out on the concrete floor, slipping the safety off his CAR-15 submachine gun and guiding the barrel up to Tong's bare chest. The sounds of the .45-caliber pistol, the automatic weapon's chattering, and the hand-grenade explosion all meshed together. Red spots appeared across Tong's flesh. The man's arm locked and a flash appeared around the muzzle of the pistol. Pellam's body twisted around from the impact of the .45 round smashing into his left hand. Paul's eyes focused on the brightly burning bare bulb in the kitchen and shot it out with a short burst from his weapon.

Darkness engulfed the building. The whole sequence had lasted less than five seconds, yet the action in Paul's mind seemed to have lasted for minutes.

The quiet pause between the last round fired from Paul's submachine gun and the first volley of fire from Tong's supporters was long enough for the other Americans to get out of their rooms and into the kitchen area with Captain Pellam.

Paul crawled along the rough cement floor down the long hallway toward the rear exit. He figured that they would be smart enough to have another automatic weapon covering the rear of the teamhouse. Paul twisted his body around the corner of the kitchen wall seconds ahead of a stream of red tracers that occupied the space he had recently filled on the hallway floor. The sight seemed strange to Paul—there wasn't any sound, just red streaks flashing down the corridor—and then the roar of the machine gun filled the room. He heard a scream come from where Sergeant Hellman had been crawling near the bar. Four more machine guns opened fire, accompanied by many rifles. The air three feet above Paul's head was laced with ever-changing patterns of red and black. A signal raced along Paul's spine to his brain. Pain flashed along his nervous system announcing that he had been hit. Paul reached instinctively for the Saint Christopher medal on its chain around his neck and placed the silver token between his teeth.

"Damn it! I'm not going to die! I'm not going to die crawling on my belly . . . not like this!" Paul's voice was drowned out from the sound of the weapons firing outside the teamhouse.

"Lieutenant Bourne! I'm hit! I'm hit!" Pellam's voice rose above the noise. *"HELP ME!"*

A lull replaced the roar.

"Over here, sir." Paul waved. "By the wall."

The Vietnamese outside the house heard the American voices and opened fire with a greater intensity. The area below the sandbags began to glow a pale pink from the tens of thousands of tracers.

Pellam continued screaming for help. *"Come here, Lieutenant . . . I'm hit bad!"*

Paul could feel the blood spreading along his side as he crawled along the cold cement floor leaving a trail of his own body fluid like a slug would leave on garden bricks. Paul reached out in the quasi-darkness and felt a boot.

"That you, sir?" Paul rasped the words around the Saint Christopher medal he still carried in his mouth. "Where are you hit?"

"Shit! The wrist . . . damn the pain!" Pellam had his injured hand placed between his knees and was lying on his side.

The artillery battery located two hundred meters south of the A-Camp began firing illumination rounds over the team house so they could see what was going on inside of the Special Forces compound. Paul could see clearly from the additional light a red line below Pellam's Rolex watch where the .45-caliber round had grazed him.

"Lieutenant Bourne, I'm hurting too bad to get the team safely out of here. You have to get the men to the bunkers." Pellam was rambling. "Or somewhere . . . just out of here!"

Paul tried grinning, but lost the desire. "Yes, sir, I'll do my best." He sounded more confident than he felt. How was he going to get the team through the Vietnamese surrounding the teamhouse without being killed? Paul's thoughts danced between quitting and fighting, and then he remembered the field telephone located in the corner of the kitchen. The telephone had been installed by the artillery unit so that they could check friendly troop locations before they fired their nightly harassment high-explosive rounds. Paul had started crawling toward the phone when an ear-shattering explosion pushed his face against the cement floor. The Vietnamese soldiers surrounding the teamhouse were rolling hand grenades off the tin roof. Paul pulled the telephone off the window ledge and turned the hand crank, hoping that the instrument hadn't been shot. A voice at the other end answered.

"Camp? Is this the Special Forces camp?" The voice rose into a scream. "What in the hell is going on over there! Give me a damn report!"

Uncontrollable anger entered Paul for the first time that evening. "A report! They're trying to kill us and you want a fucking report! You dumb ass! Send some of your infantry guards up here to get the Viets off our ass!"

"Who's trying to kill you?"

"Our counterparts . . . and you had better send some help soon or you can change 'trying to kill' to just plain 'killed.' " Paul held the telephone that represented safety close to his mouth with both hands.

"Hold on. I have got to clear this with my higher headquarters before I do anything."

Lieutenant Bourne's temper removed itself from all reasoning. "*Get a clearance? We need help now! You damn fool! Now!*"

The voice on the other end of the line changed its tone. "This is Captain Neeb speaking . . . Who in the hell am I talking to?"

"Second Lieutenant Paul Bourne." Paul sucked in

some air between his teeth to ease the pain coming from his side. "One person who doesn't have much time to lie around bullshitting . . . *Sir!*"

"Listen, Lieutenant! Don't get smart with me! I have to get some facts before I go calling my higher and have an ass made out of me." Captain Neeb was having difficulty making a decision. He didn't know what to do. No one had told him what to do in a situation like this. He was expecting the Special Forces camp to help him out in an emergency, not vice-versa. The situation had the potential of ruining his very promising career, and he wasn't about to make any mistakes.

"Hey, Captain!" Paul yelled into the handset. "Are you still there?"

Neeb heard the lieutenant but didn't answer.

"Forget the help . . . but listen to me, punk! We're going to fight our way out of here to your position and then, son of a bitch! I'm personally going to kick your chicken-shit ass!" Paul heard a voice screaming over the receiver as he reached up to replace it in its cradle.

". . . court-marshal you . . ."

"Is he sending any help?" Pellam groaned out the words.

"He's rounding up a relief force now, sir." Paul lied. He didn't want to upset his captain. The American unit had washed their hands of the matter, and it would only be a matter of a few minutes with the Vietnamese lobbing grenades through the holes they had made in the roof before one of the olive-drab explosives would find the kitchen area.

Lieutenant Bourne oriented himself back to the action surrounding the teamhouse. The firing seemed to have died down a little. The roof of the house looked like a giant screen. Paul unhooked two hand grenades from his web gear and pulled the first pin, counting to three before throwing it through one of the larger holes in the roof. He followed the first grenade with the second one.

"We might as well fight back and kill as many of these bastards as we can before they get us," Paul said to himself. "I never thought that I would be greasing our allies." The thought made Paul chuckle in a Vincent Price accent.

The other team members saw what Paul was doing and started throwing grenades through the holes in the roof above their positions. The onslaught of grenades coming from the Americans stopped all of the small-arms firing from the outside. The night became quiet. Paul heard the motor from an armored personnel carrier far on the other side of the camp cough and then roar to life. The sound increased in volume as if Lieutenant Bourne was turning up the speakers on a stereo headset until it was the only sound in the world. The side of the teamhouse shook and then collapsed, revealing the rear end of an olive-drab armored personnel carrier. The steel tailgate was lowered by the man concealed inside the fighting vehicle. Sparks flashed when the gate touched the cement floor, and the vehicle jerked backward another foot into the building. The weapons carrier's two mounted machine guns discharged a steady stream of death into the surrounding bunkers and buildings.

"All right, men—move it!" Pellam came out of his shell of pain as soon as he saw the American armored vehicle. *"Move it!"*

Two of the team members slipped out from under the kitchen table and joined Pellam, who had taken up a position by the fighting vehicle.

"Where are the rest?" Pellam's command voice lost part of its composure. "Lieutenant Bourne! Get your ass over here!"

Paul heard his captain's voice coming through what

seemed like a long steel tunnel. He tried to get up on his feet but nothing would respond to his mental command. Bourne's mind was working separately from his rebelling body. He lay on the cold cement floor and thought about death. He felt hands grabbing him by his boots and the rough cement grating against his cheek as he was dragged into the back of the APC.

"Get the hell out of here!" Pellam screamed, holding his wounded wrist. "We've got all the dead on board!"

The APC raced back toward the safety of the artillery camp with its machine guns chanting a death song to anyone foolish enough to raise their heads to listen. The armored personnel carrier entered the artillery position, through the same hole in the fence that it had made earlier. The driver pulled back on the left stick, locking one of the steel-capped tracks, causing the vehicle to spin around and brake to a rocking standstill. Paul heard the engine stop and thought the vehicle had been hit, but the driver had turned off the huge diesel engine. Pellam's voice reached Paul's ears in the back of the vehicle, and he tried moving his hands, but they were weighted down with the dead body of one of his team mates. Captain Neeb's high-pitched voice echoed against the steel walls of the carrier.

"Hey, Pellam! Where's that smart-assed lieutenant of yours?" Neeb waved his finger at Pellam. "I'm going to see that his young ass is court-marshalled personally!"

"He's dead."

The APC driver had left his vehicle and was standing by the lowered tailgate talking to his executive officer.

"Pfc. Caudwell, you know the ole man is going to have a piece of your ass for taking off like that without his permission."

"Sir, I couldn't just sit there and watch fellow Americans get slaughtered without trying to help." The young soldier tapped against the side of the vehicle's track with his boot.

"Well, stand by. The ole man will want to see you after he's done talking to Captain Pellam." The artillery lieutenant left and joined the captains who were standing next to the fortified command bunker. Pfc. Caudwell turned and looked back into his vehicle at the seven American bodies lying in a pool of drying blood. Tears appeared at the corner of the young man's eyes and broke free, leaving a trail in the red dust covering his face.

Lieutenant Bourne's eyes opened. He was looking directly into the young soldier's gaze. "I heard you talking . . . thanks for saving us . . . buddy."

The private first class turned and yelled at the three officers. "*Hey the lieutenant's still alive!*"

The two artillerymen carried Paul on a canvas stretcher to the edge of the helipad and lowered him gently to the ground.

"Sir, I'm going to put a poncho over you to keep the dust out of your wounds when the chopper lands," the taller of the two men said.

"Sure, just don't slip me into a body bag. . . ." Paul closed his eyes trying to control the pain coursing through him.

"No sweat, Lieutenant. We aren't about to do that. Man! You sure kicked a lot of ass at the A-Camp. I mean, there's at least eighty dead gooks up there!" The short soldier was speaking from the foot of the stretcher. "You're sure one mean bastard! Sorry, sir . . . What I mean is that you've been hit four times and your captain's only got a—"

The tall soldier placed his hand on his partner's arm

to get him to stop talking. He shook his head and nodded down at the lieutenant, who was in obvious pain.

Paul's words eased out between the irregular wavelets of severe pain. "Is . . . is . . . are the rest of my team all right?"

The short soldier looked down at the red clay dust covering his boots. "They're all dead except for you and three others. . . ." The soldier changed his focal point from his boots up to the sky pretending he was looking for the med-evac.

A long pause ensued, and then Paul released the words that were causing another pain, but this time located in his heart. "All of them? . . . *All?*"

"Lie still or you'll start bleeding again," the taller man's voice quavered. "Where in the hell is that chopper?"

The low-pitched sound of the med-evac helicopter's blades could be heard in the quiet predawn morning. The air was cool in Paul's lungs when he took in short breaths. A large breath caused pain to engulf his whole body, so he breathed gingerly, stopping frequently when red sparks flashed in front of his eyes. Paul turned his head to one side and was suddenly very much aware of the smell of new canvas. For some unknown reason, the odor had a soothing effect on him. It conjured up thoughts of security and comforting hands. He felt the tears form and simply let them fall and dampen the rough material under his cheek.

Paul's lips trembled and then the words formed: "Six Americans dead . . . Eighty Vietnamese . . . and all because of one pissy ass slap on the face! Damn! Damn! Damn!"

Chapter 5

A clean, antiseptic smell registered in Lieutenant Bourne's nostrils. Paul told his eyes to open and they fluttered before responding to his mental command. The bright sunlight shining through the open screened windows forced his eyelids to snap shut. Paul sent a message down to his legs querying them for information. A message returned through his nervous system, written in pain that was caused by the slight movement of his muscles. He moved his fingers. They worked. He tried hard to identify his location without the aid of his sight. His brain began to collate information he was receiving through smell and touch, and by rehashing the events that he could remember before he was med-evac'ed from Duc Co. He could recall being wounded and flown out of his A-Camp on the steel floor of a helicopter. He shivered, recalling the extreme changes in the temperature when the helicopter had changed altitudes during its flight. Paul reasoned that he must be lying in a hospital bed somewhere near Pleiku. Before he could attempt opening his eyes again a voice reached him from across the room.

"I hope you don't mind sharing this room . . . sharing this room . . . sharing this room. . . ." The booming voice echoed in Paul's mind.

"Where am I?" Lieutenant Bourne's voice sounded

to him as if he were screaming and he lowered it halfway through his sentence.

"Ah! The proverbial question coming from the awakening wounded soldier!" The other man in the room pushed his call button as he spoke. "You'll have to speak louder so I can hear you."

A bright-eyed doctor who was followed closely by a nurse entered through the thin wooden door and walked straight over to Paul's bedside.

"Well, how are we feeling? Better? Good!" The voice sounded as if it were a tape recording, not really wanting an answer to its questions.

Paul cracked his eyes open slowly and fought the urge to close them. He began blinking rapidly so that he could focus on the doctor's face. It took a minute before he could see anything clearly. "Feeling better than what?" He turned his head away from the light source to ease the pain in his eyes.

The doctor didn't answer and talked with the nurse. Paul's mind only grasped bits and pieces of the conversation as he drifted between consciousness and nothingness. He felt someone take ahold of his arm with cold fingers, and then felt a slight prick as the needle found his vein.

"His head should clear up in a few minutes." The nurse was speaking to the doctor as she left the room.

Paul could feel the physical awareness rapidly spread throughout his whole body. A dull pain was coming from several locations. His mind started working faster as the medicine reached his brain. Finally, the drug had removed the steel straps from his mind. Lieutenant Bourne turned his head on the pillow in the direction from which the voice had spoken to him earlier.

"They have it down to a fine art, don't they? I mean, putting you under and then bringing you back with drugs. A person could almost enjoy the process . . ." A soldier was sitting in an upright position across the aisle from Paul. The sheet was tucked neatly under him where his legs should have been. One of his arms was missing from his shoulder. "I'm Lieutenant Beusenal from the Third Herd."

Paul looked over at the foot of Beusenal's bunk and saw the 173d Airborne's shoulder patch attached to the bed frame in a metal holder.

"How long have you been with Special Forces?"

"How do you know I'm SF?" Paul tried scooting up on his pillow, but stopped when a fire-hot streak of pain shot up his side.

Beusenal ignored the pain on Paul's face and spoke. "They place a shoulder patch on everyone's bed so the visiting commanders can locate their troops."

"Ummm . . . how long have I been under?" Paul's eyes roved around the stark hospital room.

"You've been in this room since early this morning." The lieutenant used his remaining arm to adjust his body position. "I think you were in the recovery room for a couple of hours after they worked on you. . . . Looks like you did all right, I mean everything is still there."

"Thanks. I guess I was lucky." Paul turned his head and moved his arm up slowly so that he could reach the call button. He pushed the red switch and waited for the nurse.

"Well, you're looking a lot better." The doctor had answered the call. He spoke in a self-defensive monotone. The doctor was treating soldiers who were wounded in a war that he hated. "Nurse, prepare him for a check-up while I look at Lieutenant Beusenal."

Paul felt embarrassed when the nurse pulled the sheet back, exposing his bandaged body that was otherwise naked. The embarrassment left Paul when he thought of what could have happened to his genitals. He was glad that they were still there. Paul's eyes roved over the nurse's face. She had a pert turned-up nose with beautiful gray-green eyes, which seemed to absorb energy from anything they looked at and return the electrical shine to targets of her choosing. She sensed Paul's embarrassment.

"Don't feel shy. I've been taking care of you for the past three days in the intensive care unit." Her eyes wandered down to Paul's generously endowed sex organs.

"You might have been looking at me for three days, but I haven't had the opportunity to look back."

She blushed. "You soldiers are all alike! Doctor, this *animal* is ready!"

A burst of laughter came from Beusenal. "I'll have to remember that line!"

Paul looked at Beusenal. He couldn't figure out how the man could be so happy with both of his legs and an arm gone. Maybe the laughter was fake. The nurse took Paul's attention from the amputee when she yanked a bandage off his side.

"They're healing very nicely. "You're a lucky man. We've taken twenty-six pieces of shrapnel and two bullets out of you. A couple of them were lodged in critical areas. Very lucky! Your aorta has been bruised, but we think it will heal without any serious complications." The doctor repeated himself. "You're a very lucky young man!"

Paul glanced at Beusenal out of the corner of his eye. He felt very guilty. The doctor followed Paul's glance and realized his error. "Of course, complications can set in. . . ." It was too late. The damage had been done to Beusenal.

Paul chanced a glance at his roommate after the medical team had left their room. The man's defenses were all down and grief was cut in deep lines across his face.

"I'm sorry." Paul couldn't think of nothing else to say.

Lieutenant Beusenal didn't answer. He closed his eyes and turned his head, trying to feign sleep.

Only the soft nightlights above the beds were burning when Paul was woken by the muffled sound of someone releasing a soul-searing anguish into a pillow. Paul pushed the switch attached to the side of his bed to raise his body so that he could see across the aisle from him.

"Is there anything that I can do?" Paul spoke softly in the half-light. There was no answer.

He waited.

"Hell! I'm just feeling sorry for myself. You know I wanted to get married . . . have a couple of kids . . . . that sort of dumb thing . . ." The voice was barely audible above the sound of the ceiling fan. "Who would want to marry me now?"

Paul fought to find a suitable answer. Nothing came.

"I really shouldn't sit here and cry like a fucking baby! So *many* others died . . . so damn many!" The voice choked back the sobs.

"What happened?" Paul's war wounds and his occupancy of a hospital bed gave him the right to ask that question without seeming pushy. A half-hour passed. Paul waited patiently.

"We were patrolling as a team—Alpha and Charlie Companies. We had just finished searching the mountain range east of Dak To when our company commander gave the order over his radio to head back down the mountain slope to the brigade's base camp. Alpha Company, Second Battalion—that was my company—was in the lead ahead of Charlie Company, who brought up the rear three thousand meters behind us." There was a long pause while Beusenal thought about something that he didn't want to share with Paul. "Hell—we could see Dak To airstrip below us! Even the general's tent. We weren't four thousand meters from the center of the base camp."

A loud moan coming from down the hall interrupted the lieutenant.

"The captain called the platoon leaders over the radio and said that the last platoon getting into camp wouldn't get any beer. We knew that he was bullshitting, but we enjoyed the challenge anyway. The real threat was not getting any water for showers. You know how fast they run out of water when three hundred men all want to shower at the same time." Beusenal paused again in his story, and thought for a long time about something that was extremely painful for him to talk about. "Then we did something really stupid. It didn't seem so at the time, but *man* was it dumb! They wouldn't allow us to enter the base camp with any tear gas once a case had been broken open. You know how they were afraid that we'd frag some asshole rear-area officer or something . . . well, we pulled the pins on our tear-gas grenades and dropped all of our powdered tear gas along the trail as we hustled downhill. I can remember someone saying that we had better hold up on the tear gas because Charlie Company was following. Everyone started laughing over what Charlie Company would do when they hit our tear gas ambush. I mean, it was funny at the time . . . but *dumb! Do you understand*?"

Paul nodded his head in agreement, allowing Beusenal to continue telling his story.

"I was a lieutenant . . . shit, I should have *tried* stopping them, but shit, who would have listened to me? Anyway, we started to run down the hill ahead of the tear gas. The wind was pushing the gas down trail—except for the powdered stuff, which stayed on the trail. The First Platoon was about three hundred meters ahead of us. I was next . . ."

The soft creaking coming from the fan filled the room as Beusenal stopped talking. A nurse walking down the hallways stopped a half-dozen doors away and pushed open a closed door to check on a patient. Paul waited.

"All hell broke loose . . ." The words were spoken so softly that Paul had to strain to hear. "I mean the world came alive! I was told later that a North Vietnamese battalion was trying to sneak around the big Dak To base camp and that the first platoon ran right into it. Do you remember the cowboy movies we'd seen when we were kids, where the buffalo would stampede over a cliff and because of the momentum they would just tumble over the edge?"

Paul remained silent.

"Well . . . that was us . . . we just couldn't stop in time. The whole First Platoon didn't last three minutes. The way they were strung out. . . . The NVA had it easy." Beusenal paused again and wandered somewhere in his own personal world. Fifteen minutes passed before he spoke again. "I had enough time to stop my platoon and form a half-assed battle line. We held them for about ten minutes but then they outflanked us. Christ! There were hundreds of them! Like fucking ants! We pulled back to the Third Platoon, and then all of us pulled back into the Heavy-Weapons Platoon. We lost a lot of men. We found out later that a lot of them had been cut off from us, and had been individually killed by the NVA. They weren't taking any prisoners . . . yet."

Beusenal sighed.

"What remained of the company formed up on a

small ledge about a hundred meters wide and covered with bamboo and underbrush. We couldn't see shit. Man, we killed hundreds of those cocksuckers."

Beusenal drifted off into a world of a mentally relived terror that was reflected to Paul on the man's face. He blinked a few dozen times in rapid succession and then spoke.

"Charlie Company couldn't get to us because of that goddamn tear gas! They had to break new trail through the jungle. They tried . . . I know they tried. . . ." His voice rose to a near-hysterical pitch. "We held them most of the afternoon. They broke through a couple of times, but we pushed them back out of our perimeter. They were fighting for their lives, too. If they didn't stay in close contact with us, they knew we would call in artillery on them. The base camp still fired our artillery at them—direct fire . . . but all of a sudden the artillery fire stopped . . . it just stopped. . . . That's when we really got our asses kicked." Beusenal turned his head and looked out the window. When he spoke again the sentences were fragmented. ". . . I wonder why . . . I shot one in the face. . . . Oh! . . . I can't stand to hear the screaming . . . oh shit . . . I tried . . . really. . . ."

"Tough fight." Paul felt that he had to say something. He had actually felt the intensity of the battle through Beusenal's words. He hoped the lieutenant had released some of the horrible anguish by telling the story to him. He looked over and saw that Beusenal had his eyes closed. Paul lowered his bed and tried to find sleep. He reviewed the horror of Beusenal's story for over an hour in the darkness of the room.

"Thanks, Bourne." Beusenal had also remained awake.

"Get some rest, buddy."

The rattle from the breakfast trays being unloaded in the hall brought Paul from his sound sleep. He was feeling hungry before he even opened his eyes. He thought it was a good sign that he was healing. Paul raised his bed and glanced over to see if Beusenal was going to eat.

The room was filled with bright sunlight that accented the dark red stain covering half of Beusenal's white hospital sheet. The lieutenant's head was turned toward Paul. The man's eyes were open.

Paul reached up for his call button and pushed. Seconds passed as he stared at Beusenal's black face. He pushed the button again. Paul yelled for a nurse and threw his sheet aside, dropping his legs over the edge of the bed. His bare feet felt the cold cement floor just before a sharp pain caused his vision to become interlaced with bright blue flashes. He stood up, grabbing for the nearby nightstand for support. His unused muscles rebelled but he forced them to obey. Paul fell against the side of Beusenal's bed and saw the razor-sharp scalpel lying on the paratrooper lieutenant's chest with his remaining hand lying across his lap cut at the wrist. Beusenal had held the scalpel between his teeth and cut lengthwise down his wrist.

Paul pushed himself away from the blood-soaked bed. He noticed that he had some of Beusenal's blood on his shoulder from where he had fallen against the bed; he tried to wipe it off with his hand, but only succeeded in spreading the thick blood over his chest. Paul stumbled on weak legs, ignoring the pain, toward the door. He grabbed for the handle as he fell, with his body weight opening the door. A nurse carrying an armload of empty breakfast trays saw him and the blood and dropped her cargo. She ran toward him and dropped down to his side.

Paul opened his eyes and whispered a single word,

"Beusenal. . . ." before he passed out.

Paul awoke in a different room. A nurse was sitting next to his bed reading from a romance novel. She was the same nurse who had talked to him the day before. He stared at her for five minutes before she looked up and smiled.

"You're awake." She lay the book on her lap. "You Special Forces types seem to catch all of the bad luck."

"Seems that way, doesn't it?" Paul continued staring at the nurse. Her dark brown hair was pulled back into a bun. She was beautiful sitting there in the soft light coming from the window.

"Well, the Lord only gives a person as much as they can handle. That's what Granny used to tell us when we were little."

"Maybe not. . . ." Lieutenant Bourne wasn't being sarcastic.

"I hope you can. . . . I really do." The nurse was really trying.

Paul smiled. "Maybe Beusenal took the best way out for himself. I'm not talking about being a triple amputee. . . . I'm talking about what he was carrying around in his soul. . . ." Paul smiled again to reassure the nurse that he was all right.

She returned his smile. "I have to go and tell the hospital chaplain that you're awake." She gave Paul a sly grin. "We don't want a repeat of what happened last night." She didn't tell Paul the terrible pain she had felt when she had seen him covered with blood lying in the hall. She had at first thought that he had been the one who had committed suicide, not Beusenal, when she had answered the distress call from the nurse's station.

"You don't have to worry about me—" Paul stopped and kept the next thought to himself. He was so damn tired of seeing death and the effects it had on other people that he sometimes wished that he would take a hit and get it over with—quickly. Just over with. He turned his head to the only outside view visible to him from his hospital bed. A brightly feathered parrot sat preening itself on a limb of a shade tree at window level. A fine-linked chain was attached around one of the bird's legs and the tree branch. Someone had intentionally placed the bird there for the patients to watch.

"Handsome, isn't he?" Paul had failed to hear the chaplain's approach. "Some of the nurses pitched in and bought a bunch of them to liven up the inner courtyard. I think it was a good idea."

"Who was the nurse that was just here?"

"Captain MacReal." The chaplain took a seat in the chair next to Paul's bed. "She's been working in this hospital for three years now—it seems that they can't force her to leave. She's one of those really dedicated types who everyone likes." He accented the word everyone.

"Yes, she seems to care." Paul turned to look at his visitor and was mildly surprised. The chaplain's voice did not fit his physical description. He looked like a choirboy. Paul supressed a chuckle. "They sent you here to console me?"

A smile crept over the black-suited man's face that couldn't be penetrated with harsh words. He was in his element and had total control. The chaplain's smile was a very formidable weapon.

"True. They sent me here to console you." The joking tone in his voice eased the tension and brought a laugh from Paul.

"Don't worry yourself about me. I can handle anything." Paul glanced out the window at the parrot cracking a sunflower seed.

"I really believe that you can. Did you know Lieutenant Beusenal well?"

"No, I just met him here in the hospital. He told me last night . . . before he . . . what happened to his company. It wasn't very nice."

"Yes, I know. We kept a great deal from him. He was the sole survivor from his company. A hundred and ten men died." The chaplain's eyes were locked on Paul, trying to detect any sign that the story had had a demoralizing effect beyond the normal shock of hearing that an American unit had been wiped out.

Paul turned his head. "All of them?"

"Yes. When we brought Beusenal here we didn't think that he would make it. I was called in for his last rites. He talked constantly while he was under sedation. I agree with you—it wasn't very nice what happened. Especially when the North Vietnamese were policing the battlefield and Beusenal could hear them executing the young Americans they found hiding in the bamboo thickets. One young paratrooper in particular stuck in Beusenal's mind. He was a young man who had run out of ammunition, and when the NVA had located the position where he had crawled to, they called out for him to surrender. He told them to get fucked. They bayoneted him. Lieutenant Beusenal kept repeating that part of the story." The chaplain kept watching Paul to see if he was going too far. "Between you and I, maybe what Beusenal had done was the best thing for him. I don't condone suicide, but that boy was carrying a great burden that he couldn't deal with at all. The Catholic Church and the Lord will forgive him, I think, for what he has done to himself."

"Maybe, Chaplain . . . maybe. . . ." Paul closed his eyes to signal that he wanted to be left alone.

"Lieutenant Bourne?" The chaplain stood to leave. "You'll be going to Japan in a few days and then back to the States. Hang in there, OK?"

"No sweat, Chaplain," Paul had other ideas. "I'm going to stay right here in Vietnam. I can heal just as fast here as anywhere."

The sun was warm against Paul's cheek as he lay stretched out and comfortable on the deck chair. He had been transferred to a hospital located on the South China Sea in order to recuperate from his wounds after he had refused to be taken to Japan. That had been a long hassle, but he had finally convinced his doctors that he could heal just fine in Vietnam. The hospital at Da Nang was a compromise. Three weeks of lying in the healing sun next to the sea was the very best medicine Paul could have gotten. The scars covering his body had turned a dark purple and had completely healed. He was building his muscle tone back slowly, and figured that he would be ready to go back to work in a week or so.

"I hope that you're not planning on spending the rest of your life in this resort hospital!"

Paul looked up over his shoulder to locate the voice talking to him and recognized his Special Forces group commander. He tried getting up and was pushed back down by the colonel. "Stay sitting."

Paul relaxed again on his lounge chair.

"How are you doing, young man?" The colonel took up a seat across from Paul.

"Fine, Colonel, just fine. I should be out of here in a week. Maybe less." Paul flexed his muscles. "I'm looking forward to humping those hills again in the highlands."

"I don't plan on sending you back there." The colonel paused in order to gauge Paul's reaction to his comment. "We've replaced your whole team at Duc Co.

There are no hard feelings against the way that you handled things there, but part of the bargain with the LLDB called for both teams—American *and* Vietnamese Special Forces—being replaced."

"Sounds fair. At least it'll give the camp a new start." Paul looked straight at the old colonel. "What are your plans for me?"

"Well, you were supposed to have gone back to the States. Pellam has been sent to an American unit where he won't have trouble working with the troops. His life wouldn't be worth a monkey's fart if he stayed in SF. I plan on moving you to my operations shop in Nha Trang." The colonel immediately saw the hurt that was reflected in Paul's eyes and added, "But we might be able to work out something in the future, depending on how well your wounds heal."

"I've heard, sir, that they're going to be building a new A-Camp in the delta region next spring after the monsoons are over." Paul was trying to get out of the rear-area assignment before the colonel had firmly set his mind on it. "I sure would like a chance at the executive officer's slot—if it's still open." Paul already knew that the slot hadn't been filled yet.

"Damn it! If a new camp was going to be built, it would still be in secret planning stages. I know better than to ask you how you found out about it." The colonel's fake anger hadn't ruffled Paul's composure. "We'll see about it, Lieutenant. You had better get off your ass and start doing some push-ups if you want to try for that job." The colonel turned to the captain who had accompanied him but hadn't entered the conversation. "Do you have the lieutenant's awards?"

"Yes, sir." The tall captain handed two blue leather boxes to the colonel.

"Lieutenant Bourne. I've heard that you saved your team members lives up at Duc Co and turned what could have been a very nasty defeat into a victory . . ." The colonel popped open one of the boxes and removed a Silver Star medal and pinned it on Paul's striped hospital pajamas. He added a Purple Heart medal next to the red, white, and blue ribbon before Paul could speak.

Lieutenant Bourne thought about Beusenal and looked up at the colonel from his awards. "Sir, I can't accept these. I didn't earn them. We were fighting with our allies, not the enemy." Paul's eyes pleaded with the colonel.

"You're wrong, Lieutenant. I'm not supposed to let this information get out, but we found out during our investigation that Captain Tong's recon platoon were all Viet Cong who had been infiltrating Duc Co for years. They are the ones who pushed Tong into attacking you and destroying the camp. They damn near made it!" The colonel patted Paul's shoulder. "So you did fight the enemy. Quiet! We don't want that leaking out into the wrong circles. You can imagine what that would do to the morale of all the other A-Camps? Hell, I wouldn't be able to get ten volunteers in the whole country to man them."

"Thanks, sir," Paul touched the Silver Star, "but I still don't feel like I've earned this."

"Believe me, boy! You've earned it." The colonel shook hands with Paul as he stood up to depart. "I'll remember your request and will see what I can do about it." He winked at Paul.

The colonel waited until he was out of hearing range from Paul before he spoke to his captain. "I couldn't count the damn glory grabbers who would have kissed my ass for those awards."

The captain looked down at the cement walkway and nodded his head in agreement.

Paul unpinned the decorations and placed them

back in their boxes on the tan velour lining. He still felt very guilty. There was no way that he could compare his Purple Heart with Lieutenant Beusenal's. Both awards had been given for exactly the same reasons, receiving wounds in combat, yet Beusenal had forfeited parts of his body and had been recognized with exactly the same medal. Paul thought about different levels of the Purple Heart for soldiers as he sat looking out over the dark blue, angry-colored water.

"A penny for your thoughts?"

Paul knew he had heard the voice somewhere before and turned his head against the back of the wicker chair. His face came within inches of Captain MacReal's. She had approached quietly behind him while he was lost in thought.

"Hi!" Paul was genuinely glad to see her again. He needed to be with someone who wasn't going to talk about war. "I'm glad to see you. When did you arrive up here in Da Nang? Are you just visiting or have you been transferred?" Paul blushed. He was asking too many questions.

"One of my best friends works here in intensive care."

Paul's smile dropped slightly at the curled corners, but enough to be caught by the nurse. "*She* and I went through nursing school together, oh, a million years ago . . ."

Paul's smile instantly regained its joyful curve and they both laughed.

"Well, I'm glad *she* is working here; in fact, I was just thinking about you this morning." Paul placed the blue boxes that he was still holding on a small wicker table next to him. "Pull up a seat and stay for awhile. How long do you have to spend here?"

"I planned on leaving the day after tomorrow, but it probably will be sooner because Sue is being sent up to a Marine forward hospital for a few weeks. It seems there's a big battle raging next to the DMZ and they need more doctors and nurses to help out." She glanced down at Paul's partially exposed chest. "I see you're healing very well."

"Yes, ocean air seems to be my best medicine." Both of them looked out over the rolling water and watched the Vietnamese fishermen maneuver their bull boats against the currents. A sense of peacefulness passed between the two of them.

"Where are you from, back in the States?"

"Malibu—a little north of the actual city." Paul looked from the water to the woman and knew that he wanted to take her to bed. He squelched a chuckle. "What's your first name?"

"Natasha." She smiled as she sensed Paul's need. "How's that for a combination: a Russian first name and a Scottish surname." She threw her head back and shook the loose hair free from her shoulders. The brisk breeze coming off the sea fluttered the ends, making them look like long waving fingers.

"Say, Natasha, I've been given privileges to leave the hospital for a couple of hours a day. How about having dinner with me downtown. I know a real good French restaurant that's located right on the docks. I promise you, it's the best seafood in Asia!"

"I'd love to, Paul."

He caught a look coming from deep within her that told him that she wanted to go out with him very much. She needed to escape from the broken bodies she dealt with daily as much as Paul needed to be with someone who wasn't going to talk about their last big fight.

"Say, about eight?"

"Ummmm-huh . . ." Natasha's attention was on a school of dolphins that were passing by close to shore.

"I'm staying in Sue's quarters. Room number five; it's upstairs in the corner." Natasha stood and smoothed out her uniform. "I'll be expecting you around eight, then. You had better get some rest. I don't want to be back here at nine!" She flipped her hair and bounced away across the cement patio. She paused near the steps on the far side of the long deck and looked back at the watching soldier. She waved, then disappeared behind the sea wall. Paul's heart felt as if it would explode in his chest. She had accepted his offer without any hesitation!

Natasha felt very guilty as she walked briskly back toward Sue's quarters. She had known that Sue wasn't going to be in Da Nang, and had used her friend's name as an excuse. Natasha smiled and looked out across the sea. She had loved him from the very first time that she had seen him lying broken and bleeding on the blood-soaked green canvas stretcher as they had unloaded him from the med-evac helicopter. All of her life she had heard nurse's stories about falling in love with patients, and had always thought that the nurses didn't have any self control. She had always believed that a good nurse did not get emotionally involved with just one of her charges. Well, it had happened to her with the force of a sledgehammer against her heart. She loved Paul with an almost-mad passion that made her blush just thinking about what she would like to do. The first three days he had been in intensive care, she had used all of her spare time, including her breaks, to be with him. She had examined every line on his face as he had lain sleeping, and when she changed his bandages she had massaged his unworked muscles, not to help him heal better, but as an excuse to touch him. It wasn't by accident that Natasha had appeared in Da Nang where Paul had been reassigned. She had nearly cried herself sick when Paul had left her hospital, and she had known that she would have to see him at least once more to find out just how he felt about her. Actually, she really didn't care—she would make him love her.

Paul rushed down the hallway to his friend's ward. The civilian contractor was lying on his bed reading the latest issue of *Playboy* magazine. He had been in the hospital for three weeks recuperating from a bout of malaria.

"Hey, Chuck! Can I use one of your walking suits and your CJ tonight?" Paul's words rolled together.

"Whoaaaa . . . slow down, big fella! What in the hell has gotten into you?" Chuck placed his open magazine down on his chest.

"Man! I've got a date with the most beautiful woman in the world!" Paul slapped his palms down on the man's cot. "Man, I mean a *dinner* date!" Paul picked the magazine off Chuck's chest and closed it.

"Give me my damn book!"

Paul tapped the man's chest with the rolled up *Playboy*. "First! Do I get to use your jeep?"

"Yes! Damn it! Give me my book!"

"And one of your suits?"

"Yes, now give it to me, Paul, I was reading a good story!"

"Sure you were," Paul grinned, and tossed the book back to his friend. "That rise under your sheet agrees with you."

"Fuck you!" Chuck laughed, but adjusted his sheet so the bulge wasn't so noticeable. "Your date's a good looker, huh?"

"Need you ask?" Paul opened the closet door and slid his hand over the half-dozen suits hanging there. "I hope one of these fits me."

"Should, we're about the same size. Try the cream-colored one—it will go with your suntan."

Paul removed the suit from the closet and laid it on the foot of Chuck's bed. He slipped out of the hospital robe and pajamas and into the suit pants. A near-perfect fit.

"The keys to the jeep are on the dresser." Chuck placed his attention back to the centerfold.

"Thanks, Chuck!" Paul pulled the door shut behind him.

Lieutenant Bourne felt very uncomfortable wearing civilian clothes. He adjusted the pistol that he was carrying in a shoulder holster under his jacket before starting up the steps of the nurses' quarters. He found the door marked five without any problems, and paused a second before knocking.

"Come in, Paul!"

The door eased open with little effort when he pushed down on the latch. He took a deep breath when he saw Natasha. She was wearing a beautiful black dress that clung to where it should and rolled over those parts of her body that required accenting.

Natasha saw the effect of the dress on Paul's face.

"I bought this dress when I was on R & R. I was going to save it for when I got back to the States, but since this is a special evening for me I thought I'd wear it. Do you like it?"

"Do I!"

"Come on, Paul. We had better leave now." Natasha had followed Paul's bedroom eyes to the cot, and she didn't need an interpreter to tell her what was on his mind.

They drove through the downtown area of Da Nang and past the quiet marketplace. The restaurant was located on a small peninusla overlooking the busy harbor. A German hospital ship was berthed less than two hundred yards away from the front doors of the very impressive-looking French-owned establishment, with all of the lights burning on its decks.

The Eurasian maître d' met them at the door and asked if they wished to dine inside in the main dining room or out on the garden patio. Paul looked over at Natasha, waiting for her to make the decision.

"Outside, please; I like the water and the stars."

Paul was glad that she wanted to eat outside, where he could keep an eye on the jeep.

The maître d' spoke with a heavy French accent in a passable English. "Miseuir u' Dame, do you wish for a apertif?"

"Yes, please, and some red wine."

The maîre d' nodded, and waved for a garçon to assist at the table. Natasha looked around the tastefully decorated patio at the well-dressed Vietnamese crowd sprinkled with a few Americans and French civilians. "I didn't think a restaurant this fine was left in Vietnam."

"Like it?" Paul smiled across the dimly lit table. Natasha nodded happily as she watched the color of Paul's eyes change in the flickering candles.

The garçon arrived carrying a bottle of red wine imported from France and two glasses that sparkled in the starlight. Paul and Natasha touched glasses and hearts in the reflected moonlight from the river. The spell broke softly with the arrival of a young garçon carrying a tray of special hors d'oeuvre. The small boy placed the tray between the two guests and smiled, backing away from the table. Natasha sipped from her wine and touched a slice of black egg with the fork.

"What is this?"

"Century eggs. They're a delicacy here in the far east," Paul placed two slices on his side dish and answered her quizzical look with a bite. "They're really very good. They bury the eggs underground for one hundred days."

"Oh, maybe later . . ." Natasha laid down her fork and picked up her safe wine glass.

"Come on, try it! Very good and expensive when you can find them."

Natasha wrinkled her nose and took a single slice from the tray, looking for the smallest one. She nibbled at the delicacy and then smiled her approval. It tasted very good, especially with the wine to counter the unusual treat.

"I told you it's good." Paul breathed in deeply, inhaling the sweet perfume she was wearing, trying to keep his attention on the food—at least while they ate.

"May you order, please?" A new waiter appeared.

"We don't need a menu." Paul looked at the girl. "Do you like lobster?"

"Love it!"

"Good! Because they make some of the finest in the world here," Paul smiled at the waiter and ordered in French: "*Homard, ecrevisse de mer.*"

"I didn't know you spoke French!" Natasha was tickled by Paul's expertise. "It sounds so . . . so romantic!"

"I looked the words up in a dictionary before we left," Paul grinned.

The meal was delicious beyond comparison. Paul and Natasha ate slowly and entangled the peaceful night air between them in soft smiles that were flashed at each other whenever their eyes met. An occasional fish jumped in the river, sending ripples racing to the shoreline that added to the quiescence of the evening. Neither of them kept track of the time, something they realized only after the waiter approached their table and tactfully informed them that curfew would be imposed on the city in a half-hour. Paul ordered another bottle of wine and two clean glasses.

"I don't want this evening to end just yet. Let's take the wine and go back to the hospital patio to drink it." Paul paid the bill as he talked, adding an extra twenty dollars to cover the glasses.

"I'd love to!" Natasha picked up the glasses and Paul carried the wine bottle, which the waiter had been kind enough to open and recork for them.

Paul parked the jeep next to the stone wall surrounding the dark patio of the hospital. Natasha giggled as they snuck over to one of the far corners and pulled up two wicker chairs near the wall closest to the sea. Paul pulled out the cork with his teeth and poured the glasses half full. He allowed a little of the wine to drop down on the sand below the stone wall.

"A little libation for whoever allowed this evening to happen!"

The soldier and the nurse locked fingers and stood looking out over the water that was streaked with slivers of romantic moonlight. Words were not necessary. Paul pulled up a chair and signaled for Natasha to sit on his lap. She slipped out of her shoes and curled up in his arms. Natasha lay against his breast listening to each single beat of his heart.

The morning light was creeping across the water, bringing early-rising seagulls crying as they flew skimming the water for their breakfasts.

The cries woke Paul. Natasha had taken a seat on the stone wall watching him.

"Have I slept long?" Paul was embarrassed.

"No . . . not long at all."

"Well, I'd better get you back to Sue's room."

Natasha watched him and nodded.

They walked very slowly along the sandy cement walkway holding hands loosely. Natasha carried her shoes in her free hand and Paul carried the empty wine glasses. The room appeared too fast for both of them. It signaled an ending of the evening.

"I enjoyed tonight very much. . ." Paul turned toward her.

"So did I. . . ."

They kissed lightly. Natasha dropped her shoes in the sand and wrapped her arms around his neck, changing the tempo of the kiss to passion.

She pushed the unlocked door open and they entered the dark room together. The enchantment of the evening was still with them as they undressed each other.

Chapter 6

Lieutenant Bourne picked up his gray B-4 bag off the ground where he had thrown it from the helicopter and walked toward the white Special Forces Group Headquarters building. He automatically absorbed every noteworthy detail surrounding him along the walkway: locations of bunkers, trenchs, clumps of thick vegetation, and avenues that led between the buildings to the outer perimeter. He stored the data in his mind for possible further use in case the compound came under attack.

"Hey, Paul!" The call rang out from behind a screened tin-roofed hooch window. "Wait a minute!

Paul dropped his handbag down on the hot sidewalk and waited for the caller to appear. A second lieutenant burst from behind the plywood building.

"Jay!" Paul took a step forward with his hand extended. "You leg son of a bitch!"

Jay grabbed Paul's hand and shook it violently. "*Whoa!* Not a leg any more!" He pointed to the new cloth wings sewn above the left pocket of his jungle fatigues. "You are observing one bad-assed paratrooper!"

"I'll be damned! So you did make it to jump school after Officer's Candidate School, after all," Paul grinned. "So what are you doing here in Nha Trang?"

"I was shipped to an infantry unit up in Quang Tri when I first arrived in-country. All kinds of shit broke loose. Hell, it's a long story that should be told over cold beers." Jay looked at his watch. "I'll tell you what. Let's meet at the Officer's Club for supper. I still have a few hours of in-processing to do, and then I'll be free." Jay's face expressed the joy at finding his closest friend from OCS stationed with him in Vietnam. They had spent many hard days together getting through the officer cadet program.

"Sounds good to me, Jay. I have to report in at Group Headquarters myself." Paul picked up his B-4 bag and adjusted the cloth handles in the palm of his hand. "See you later."

The entrance to the Special Forces Group Headquarters was exceptionally well-manicured by an aged Vietnamese Nung. There were a pair of captured North Vietnamese heavy machine guns that had been painted black and mounted in the cement next to the main entrance. A quote from the famous revolutionary Ranger, Major Rogers, had been expertly painted on a scroll sign and nailed on the wall next to the entrance doors. Paul caught only part of one sentence as he stepped inside the air-conditioned building: "Keep your tomahawk sharp and your powder dry."

"Can I help you with something, Lieutenant?" a sergeant major addressed Paul from behind the duty officer's desk.

"I came to see the group adjutant." Paul glanced down the dimly lit hallway and saw the hand-lettered sign that identified the adjutant's office.

"The third door on your left." The sergeant major continued looking at the green binder he held in his hands.

"Thanks, Sergeant Major." Paul shook his head. Once an enlisted man reached the top grade of sergeant major, they rarely addressed a second lieutenant as sir. It was sort of their way of showing superiority to the officer corps.

Paul slowed down as he neared the adjutant's office. He paused to read the information bulletin board before meeting the officer who was in charge of personnel assignments.

An unmarked door at the end of the hallway opened and the Special Forces group commander stepped out in the hall.

"Lieutenant Bourne!"

"Hello, sir," Paul shook hands with the colonel.

"It's good to see that you've healed well." The colonel took ahold of Paul's shoulder and guided him toward the adjutant's closed door. "I want to personally insure that you get well taken care of by my people."

The major sitting behind the cluttered desk stood up casually when the white-haired colonel burst into his office. "Can I help you, sir?"

"Yes, Bill. I want you to take good care of this young lieutenant for me. He's going to be the new executive officer for the My An detachment in the delta." The colonel couldn't hold back the grin when he looked over at Paul.

"That's great, sir! I thought you had forgotten." Paul's worries over ending up as a rear-area desk jockey vanished. "Thanks a lot, sir."

"Save the thanks. You might end up hating me before this is all over with. Building a new A-Camp is a lot of very hard work." A frown flashed across the tanned leathery face on the older man. He was thinking about an irritating conversation he had had the day before with the C-Team commander in charge of the Special Forces activities in the delta region. "Lieutenant Bourne, I'd like for you to do me a personal favor when you're down there. Stop by my office before you leave."

Paul listened to the group adjutant and when he left the administrative office took the stack of processing papers with him to be turned in to the records clerk down the hall. After Paul dropped off the processing papers he knocked on the colonel's private door. He was called into the well-decorated room by the colonel's private enlisted secretary. A huge Persian rug covered the handlaid teakwood floor, and two red-leather wing-back chairs dominated the setting across from the colonel's desk. The group commander joined Paul in the leather chairs and crossed his legs preparing to talk personally.

"Paul." The opening first name alerted the lieutenant to a session that was going to be confidential. "I have some problems accepting the detachment commander that the C-Team commander selected to head up the My An operation. I normally don't ask subordinates to check up on their superiors, and normally I don't personally select an executive officer for an A detachment, but in this case, I'm doing both." The colonel was careful not to use the word spy. "I need an inside eye down there. Lieutenant Colonel Bakersun turned down my offer to use Captain Blake to build My An. Blake has built *five* special forces camps as an engineer team leader operating out of the First Group on Okinawa. He's the very best man I know of for that job, and he's available right now. Bakersun was adamant in his choice of Captain Hetten, who is currently serving as his personnel officer in Can To. Hetten's been with Special Forces for only six months; he extended in-county from a supply officer's post in Long Bhien. The man reeks of a glory grabber who is out to line his chest with a couple rows of ribbons before heading home." The colonel glanced over at Paul. "That's the main reason why I want you there. You have some combat experience, and the rest of the team just might need some hardened leadership before this is all over and done with." The colonel removed a cigar from an ivory-inlaid box on the coffee table in front of them. "I want you to keep this conversation very confidential, but if Hetten can't handle that team, I want to know!" The colonel placed his visual attention on lighting the cigar. "You'll leave for Can To in the morning."

"Yes, sir." Paul stood and saluted.

"And Paul . . ." the voice softened, "take care of yourself."

"Thanks, sir."

"Oh, one more thing. I had a Sergeant Braverman assigned to your team. You can trust him. We served together in Korea during the war in the 3d Ranger Company."

Paul exited the colonel's office and returned to the in-processing station, which took only a few minutes to change over his records from the Duc Co Special Forces camp to My An. He drew his Bachelor Officer's Quarters assignment and walked over to the row of sleeping quarters. The sun had just begun to set, and he paused on the cement sidewalk to assimilate the beauty. There were many incidents during the war that he knew he would forget, but the Vietnamese sunsets with their mystical colors were incidents that remained with a person forever.

The building was dark, but enough light to see still came in through the open windows. Paul looked along the row of steel cots for one that wasn't being used and saw a green dufflebag on a bed near the rear exit. He walked over and read the name of the owner: Lieutenant J. B. Loveless. Paul dropped his B-4 bag on the cot across from Jay's. When you had your choice, it was wise to sleep near an exit in case there was a rocket attack during the night. Paul undressed and wrapped a towel around his waist. The officer's latrine and showers were located in a separate building down the street.

He could hear a shower running as he approached the brightly lit shower room. Paul slapped the screen door with the palm of his hand to remove the night bugs before opening the door.

"Jay?"

Paul picked up a red cigarette-butt can off the floor and filled it full of cold water from the row of sinks lining the wall. Paul was about to throw the bucket of water on the man in the shower, but stopped at the last second when he saw the occupant of the shower was an older man. He felt like a fool and quickly placed the red can on the seat outside the shower-room door and unwrapped the towel from his waist.

It was the first time in months that Paul had taken a really hot shower. The luxury of visiting an established headquarters was always highlighted by the showers and the real commodes. Paul took his time drying himself, then walked the short distance back to his quarters naked in the dark. He removed his leather shoulder holster from his B-4 bag and slid his 9mm Smith & Wesson pistol into the molded pocket. He changed into a clean set of tiger fatigues and brushed the dust from his boots. The rules for the base camp were posted on the back of each BOQ door, and the first one stated that it was against regulations to carry a concealed weapon in the clubs. But Paul had decided when he had first returned to Vietnam that he wasn't going to die because of stupidity.

The night air was cool with the mountain breeze coming from the northwest, out of the highlands. The floodlights surrounding the large base camp gave off enough peripheral light for him to find his way to the

Nha Trang Officer's Club. The Special Forces club was famous for its good food and star entertainment nightly. Most of the big-name movie stars from Hollywood would give free shows to the Green Beret troops when they made their USO tours. The best feature about the club was the high-stakes poker games that seemed to go on continuously day and night. There were a lot of rumors going around about big winners at the tables, but the top-dollar man was a supply officer who was supposed to have won over a million dollars playing poker in the club over a three-year spread.

Paul stopped to glance in the dining room for Jay but didn't see him at any of the tables, so he went up the stairs to the bar. Jay wasn't there either. Paul ordered a double shot of bourbon and carried it with him over to the card room. Floating cigar smoke in the long room was a permanent fixture. The chairs circling the three felt-top tables were all filled with players. Paul ordered another bourbon from the bargirl and took a seat on one of the high-backed rattan chairs used for observers. The poker game to his immediate left was an unlimited pot, with over fifty thousand dollars in chips showing in front of the seven players. To his right the action was faster, but for smaller stakes, with very few of the dark-blue hundred-dollar chips showing on the green felt. Fifty-dollar red and ten-dollar white chips were neatly stacked in front of each player. Paul watched five hands being played to pace the intensity of the betting. He waved for the club attendant to come over to him and told the small man that he would like to play at the next open seat on the second table. The officer's club took a ten-dollar chip from every winning poker hand dealt. The Vietnamese monitor stationed at each of the tables insured that the winner of each hand dropped a ten-dollar chip in the wooden box attached to the table. There were very few complaints over the revenue-collecting system, because it was only the winner of each hand who had to pay the club tax, and each hand of poker averaged between fifty and a hundred dollars, minimum. Paul converted five hundred dollars into chips at the cashier's window. The table attendant was waiting for Paul when he returned, and beckoned for him to fill an empty seat. There weren't any introductions when Paul sat down. Poker playing at the club wasn't a friendly camp game but a money-making enterprise. Most of the talking was saved for around the bar.

"I hope that you have better luck with the damn seat than I had," growled a voice from behind Paul's chair. "I dropped three grand in less than two hours."

Paul didn't answer the loser. He stacked his small pile of chips in front of his seat and looked up at the man dealing the cards.

"We're playing dealer's choice with a fifty-dollar limit on each bet with three raises. Fifty dollars opens a hand." The dealer spoke in a monotone trying to act nonchalant. "You can draw money from anywhere. We don't play like the high-stakes table. Of course, we ain't going to wait here while you run all over the compound trying to raise a bet."

Paul nodded his head. The first hand lasted only a couple of minutes with Paul losing a hundred dollars.

"Hi, Paul. I figured I'd find you up here." Jay pulled a chair up behind Paul's. "Mind if I sit here?"

"Sure, no problem." Paul glanced around at the rest of the players. "Any of you mind?"

"Naw—as long as your friend only looks at *your* cards." The dealer smirked. Paul didn't answer the wisecrack.

"The name of the game is hi-lo. Straight flush can be used either way." The dealer flipped the first round of cards, cracking each one as he pulled it off the top of the deck.

"I haven't played this game before. How about passing me this hand, so that I can see how it's played." Paul didn't like learning a new game, especially at the stakes being bet.

"Sorry, buddy. Play every hand or give up your seat. House rules." The dealer grinned with a cigar flipping up and down in his fat mouth.

"The game is simple, Paul." Jay leaned over Paul's shoulder so he wouldn't have to speak loudly. "You play with seven cards, like in stud, except you can also go for the lowest hand using five cards. In this case, ace, two, three, four, and five of any suit would be low, or could also be used as a high hand. According to the dealer's rules the perfect hand would be a straight flush, ace low card."

All seven cards had been dealt. Each player picked up one white chip and one red chip from the stacks in front of their seats and held them under the table, ready to declare which way they were going, high or low. If they opened their palm on the table and it contained both chips, that meant they were going both ways.

Paul declared with a red chip, meaning he wanted to go high, and lost the hand. The next person dealing also wanted to play hi-lo, and Paul anted his fifty dollars. He lost again. Hi-lo was a game where the betting was always heavy, because most of the time there were two people betting for the pot. It was very rare that a player would drop out before all seven cards had been dealt.

"Let's try that game again." The player to Paul's left had just won the pot and the deal went to him.

Paul looked at the first two cards dealt to him, the ace of clubs and the four of clubs. Paul met the fifty-dollar openers and raised fifty. He was bumped fifty by the man dealing the cards. Everyone around the table stayed in the game.

"Jay, do you have any money?" Paul had a few hundred dollars left back with his gear in the BOQ, but didn't want to take the time to go back and get it.

"Sure—I'll get it changed into chips." Jay left and went over to the barred cashier's window.

"Let's get some refill on the booze while we're waiting for the lieutenants," a major who was sitting directly across from Paul spoke with a confident grin on his face.

Jay returned and placed twenty red chips in front of Paul. He bent over and whispered into his friend's ear, "This is my R & R money, so don't lose all of it."

Paul nodded.

The next card face-up for Paul was the two of clubs. Paul had been dealt four cards and all of them played directly into a straight flush. He felt Jay's hand on his shoulder. The fifth cards were dealt around the table and the major received the six of diamonds, while the player to Paul's right got the six of clubs. The dealer paused and leaned forward against the table. He held Paul's card out in front of him. "Looks like this stops your flush!"

"Deal." Paul didn't waste time looking over at the major.

"Wait!" The major was glaring at Paul." Before you get your next card, I want to make a side bet with you. I'll bet you one thousand dollars that you don't draw a straight flush!" The major was getting scared over the high stakes already in the pot and was trying to bait Paul to see if he had confidence in his hand.

Paul didn't hesitate at all. "You're on, sir—a grand."

The next card to Paul was the five of clubs. He allowed a fake frown cross his face. Lieutenant Bourne glanced at the arrogant major, who had been watching his expression very closely.

"You think that helped?" The major smiled using only half of his mouth.

Bourne's sixth card was the six of diamonds.

The major led the betting with all seven of the players staying in the game. Paul's seventh card was the queen of hearts. He clenched his teeth and pushed the card away from the rest that were lined up in front of him.

"What's wrong, Lieutenant? No more clubs in the deck for you?" The major's voice echoed laughter. "You'd better drop out and save yourself a couple hundred dollars."

Paul released his-sucker catching grin at the major. "Shut up and bet . . . sir."

"Shit—you're bluffing!" The major was confident he held a better hand than the lieutenant.

"Bet." Paul looked down at the bottom of the whiskey glass he brought up to his lips.

The last round of betting drew half the men from the bar who had been watching the match between the braggadocio major and Paul. The pot contained almost six thousand dollars—plus the thousand-dollar side bet between Paul and the major.

The major declared both ways. Paul also had declared both ways with the remaining players split.

"Well, Lieutenant. Read them and weep." The major flipped his hole cards over. He had a damn good hand. A six-high straight, and a two-through-six for the low hand.

Paul casually turned over his cards and sorted through them until he had his ace-low flush arranged in numerical order.

"I guess you lose, Major. I've got an ace-through-five straight flush for high win, and an ace-through-five for low win." Paul used both of his arms to pull the chips over to his side of the table. "I'll take the thousand either in chips or MPC."

"I'll be a son of a bitch." The dealer picked up Paul's cards from the green-felt cloth. "I've played a lot of poker, but this is the first time that I've seen a pinwheel in hi-lo!"

"You're a lucky bastard, Lieutenant." The major was trying to overcome the beating he had taken at the card table, both in ego and money. "You don't play poker worth a shit!"

Paul raised his eyebrows. "Who won?"

Jay helped Paul carry the chips in his beret to the cashier's cage where they converted them back into ten-dollar-denomination military payment certificates. Paul counted off two hundred of the bills and handed them to Jay.

"I only loaned you a thousand."

"Interest rates are high in Vietnam." Paul divided the remaining stack of bills into separate piles and wrapped rubber bands around them.

Paul paused as they passed the poker table where he had given up his seat. "If you come down to the dining room later, Major, I'll buy you dinner."

"Fuck you, Lieutenant!" The major kept his eyes glued on his cards.

Paul ordered a special cut T-bone steak along with Jay. They both had brought drinks with them from the bar upstairs.

"Man! That was poker at its best!" Jay shook his head. "I was really about to lose it all when you drew that five of clubs!" Jay slapped the tabletop with his open palm. "Say, don't they get the ass when someone wins and then leaves right away?"

"Not here." Paul took a long draw from his bourbon.

"You have to understand, Jay, those games up there are cutthroat. Take that major up there. He probably spends his nights playing poker with drunks coming in from the A-Teams who come back here for a couple of nights of fun. They really don't care if they win or lose as long as they're having fun. The major and his rear-area-support buddies are like vultures. They wait until the men are too drunk to think right, and then they rip them off at the poker tables. You'll never see one of them in the club before ten at night."

"I guess some of those guys don't have much of a chance to spend any money at their A sites, do they?" Jay leaned back, giving the waitress room to place a huge steak in front of him.

"You're right. They have five or six months of accumulated pay and no place to spend it. They're ripe for the taking when they get here." Paul paused and looked out of the dining room at a group of drunks trying to make it out of the front doors. "Well, I've made enough money in one night to last me for years here in Vietnam. I think I'll put it in the 10% savings program."

"That sounds like a great idea. Wake me when you get up in the morning and I'll go over to finance with you." Jay concentrated on the steak in front of him.

When they had finished eating Paul spoke, "Let's have a nightcap up at the main bar."

"Sounds good to me." Jay checked his side pocket on his jungle fatigues, insuring that the bundle of money he had stored there hadn't slipped out.

"You haven't told me why you left Quang Tri." Paul led the way up the stairs.

Jay located a pair of overstuffed chairs near the stage in the large bar room and sat down before answering Paul's question. "You know, Paul, I have always admired you, and I was really very jealous of your airborne wings when we were in OCS." Jay blushed but continued, "I checked with MACSOG's liaison officer here and they've accepted me for one of their reconnaissance team leaders. I'll be based out of Command and Control North at Da Nang."

"Do you know what you're getting into, Jay?" Paul slid straight up in his chair. "That's *big*-time stuff up there."

"Yes, I realize the danger—but I'm sick and tired of busting my ass for chicken-shit outfits!" Jay averted his eyes from Paul's.

"Hey! Chicken-shit units are one thing, but CCN has a reputation as being one tough unit to stay alive in!" Paul emphasized his words. "Don't get me wrong—they're damn good doing what they do for the war effort and they have the cream of the crop when it comes to selecting people—but they have the toughest missions going in the war!"

"I realize what you're trying to say, Paul," Jay's face took on a frustrated look, "but I'm a *soldier* and I came here to fight, not hide somewhere in a damn bunker waiting for the war to end."

"Whoa! Back up a bit, Jay." Paul leaned back in his chair. "What's really bothering you?"

Jay looked over at the bar, trying to decide if he should get another drink before diving into the story he had to tell Paul. He decided against it. "I told you when I first got in-country they had sent me to a unit up in I Corps near Quang Tri. Well, I was assigned as a platoon leader to one of the brigade's infantry companies. We fought a couple good fire-fights up near the DMZ and lost a couple men. I even won a medal."

"Which one?"

"The Distinguished Service Cross."

"That's great!" Paul was sincerely happy for his friend. "Now I know a *real* hero!"

"Cut the shit! You won the DSC when you were a sergeant with the 173d, didn't you?" Jay's voice was filled with mock anger. "Believe me, the DSC I won saved my ass in the long run."

Paul relaxed in his seat as Jay continued his story.

"Remember a few months ago, when one of the big Stateside magazines published that story about the high percentage rate of minorities being killed in combat compared to whites?"

"Yes, I remember reading about that bullshit. You know, Jay, that they can make statistics say what they want them to."

"*We* know that, but the blacks in my brigade played that story to the hilt! Last week my company was cycled back to the brigade's base area at Quang Tri for a week of perimeter guard duty. I went over to the artillery battalion headquarters to coordinate with their fire-direction officer for nightly protective fires. I took our forward observer with me, and we stayed at the battalion headquarters for supper. After we had eaten, we went back to the tactical operations center to finish coordinating artillery fire, and it was around nine o'clock when a soldier ran into the bunker and told the duty sergeant that there was a large group of black soldiers raising hell in the Artillery Bowl. The artillery unit has set up an area in the center of their camp where they showed movies at night—they called the place the Artillery Bowl. Anyway, the soldier said that the situation was really getting out of hand. I told the sergeant that *I'd* go and check it out, seeing that the artillery officer was busy conducting a fire mission and I didn't have anything to do. I didn't think it would take long, so I told the duty sergeant to stay with the artillery officer."

"Weren't there any of the battalion officers around to help?"

"Yes, but the battalion commander was having a party for one of his staff officers in the officers' quarters, and at the time I didn't think they needed to be disturbed. I thought that I could handle it without any trouble. I went over to the Artillery Bowl using a path between two of the buildings. When I got there I could see between sixty and a hundred black soldiers packed together around the plywood stage. I stayed in the dark between the buildings and watched for a few minutes, trying to get the pulse of the situation. The blacks were really getting wound up. I noticed that there were a couple of white soldiers watching from a distance and they they were carrying their rifles. After listening to what the blacks were yelling, I could understand why the whites were nervous.

"Were there any black NCOs in the group?"

"You can bet your ass there were! Talk about pissing me off! You would think the NCOs would try and calm the younger soldiers down—but instead, they were the leaders!"

Paul frowned. He was interested in what Jay was saying, because he had heard rumors that there were racial problems in the regular line units and that senior officers were covering the incidents.

"Anyway, based on what the blacks were saying, stuff like 'we ain't going to fight no white man's war,' and 'we ain't going to fight against our colored brothers from the north' and shit like that! It sounded like a damn commie rally! I mean one of them even said that if you had a choice you should kill whites when you got in a firefight and shoot over the heads of the NVA!"

"Jay!" Paul was getting upset. He knew a lot of very loyal American black soldiers. "Come on! Even if the blacks were a little upset about the magazine article, they wouldn't advocate killing fellow Americans!"

"If I'm lying, I'm flying! I'm not bullshitting you!"

Jay's eyes reflected that he wasn't. "I hope that all of the blacks standing there didn't feel that way, but the speaker sure did."

"Just hearing about it turns my stomach!" Paul shook his head. "I have known a lot of damn fine black soldiers who would have shot that bastard just on the principle of the thing!"

"Yeah! Well, none of them were at Quang Tri that night." Jay swallowed half of his drink before he continued, "The uproar that they were causing drew the attention of the brigade duty officer, who was located about a hundred meters away from their assembly. I watched as a group of about five white officers approached the black group. I stepped farther back into the shadows and continued watching the show. One of the officers was the brigade commander himself. When he reached the black crowd, he pushed his way through the group up to the stage and climbed up, followed by two of his staff officers. *Man*, did the blacks start yelling then! It took the black leader five minutes to quiet them down. The brigade commander asked them what the problem was, and they all started to scream really nasty stuff at him all over again.

"The black sergeant, who was acting as the spokesman for the group, told the colonel that his people weren't going to go out in the bush and fight the white man's war against their brothers." Jay's voice was becoming emotional as he retold the story. "I noticed two white soldiers about fifty feet away from me setting up an M-60 machine gun in the dark alley between two of the troop sleeping huts, and I slipped around the back of the building to them. I asked them what in the fuck they thought they were doing, and one of them told me that if the blacks started shooting they were going to blow their racist asses away. I noticed that most of the blacks in the group were carrying their combat gear. I told the white soldiers that they would open fire only at *my* command, which seemed to make them happier. I think they were just waiting for someone to take charge of the situation."

Jay looked over at Paul and grinned.

"I had to gain control, or they would have surely opened fire at the first sign of trouble."

"I understand." Paul drained his drink.

"Two minutes hadn't passed after I left the men with the machine gun to get a better view of what was going on, when three of the blacks standing next to the stage below the colonel reached up and pulled him off the stage. The next thing I knew, the machine gun opened fire. At first they were shooting over their heads, but some of the blacks started shooting back trying to kill anything white. The end result was fourteen blacks killed and wounded, including four sergeants."

"Hmmmm . . . heavy! It's hard to believe something like that would happen in an American unit. Why haven't we heard about that incident down here?"

"Come on, Paul! What commander is going to report to anyone he's having racial problems in his unit? Shit! Whoever would do that definitely won't see stars on his collar." Jay tapped the bottom of his empty glass on the top of an endtable next to him. "Paul, you know as well as I do that Germany is really having some bad racial problems. Blacks are roving through the military casernes in packs, hunting down lone white soldiers at night and beating them half to death—and *nothing* is being done about it! The generals don't see shit!" The blacks call their nightly entertainment 'rabbit hunting.' "

"I've heard those rumors, Jay, but *shit*! I thought most of the stuff was really exaggerated." Paul was having a real tough time believing that racial crap was going on in Vietnam, especially since all the Americans were in it together. "What was the outcome at the Artillery Bowl?"

"Shit! Would you believe the two white soldiers were court-marshalled! And by the damn colonel whose ass they saved!" Jay shook his head. "I was sucked into the investigation because the white soldiers told the court that I had given them permission to fire. Like I said earlier, my DSC saved my ass, and I was transferred here to keep the peace, but actually the blacks had placed me on their death list."

"What happened to the black troublemakers?

"Are you ready for this one? The brigade commander gave into their demands and had all seventy-three of them transferred to positions in the rear, filling desk jobs and supply slots."

"What about the soldiers who were already in those jobs?" Paul couldn't believe his ears.

"They double-slotted most of them, but the Mexicans and whites got so disgusted working with them that they volunteered to fill the empty infantry positions."

"Jay—I don't want to call you a liar, but this story is really hard to believe!"

"I swear the story is true!"

"All I can think of his how all the loyal, hard-working black soldiers are really going to take it in the ear when this story gets out!"

"You can believe that it's a well-kept secret up in Quang Tri. They said that an NVA special sapper unit infiltrated the camp, but too many troops know the real version."

Paul shook his head slowly from side to side. "Let's get drunk."

The two men were well past caring when they stumbled to their billets during the early hours of the morning.

Paul held his head under the cold spray and put his hands against the tile on the shower wall in order to brace himself up. He should have known better than to get drunk the night before he had to fly. Paul heard the shower on the far side of the room start, and saw Jay standing under the cool water in the same manner.

"Hey, dipshit! Why didn't you stop me last night!" Paul yelled over the roar coming from the duo showers.

"You're a big boy now, Paul."

Both men allowed a laugh in spite of the throbbing pain in their heads.

In the drying room, Paul slipped on the clean tiger fatigues he had brought with him, and was lacing his nylon-mesh jungle boots when Jay stepped out of the shower room.

"I needed that." Jay shook his head from side to side, checking to see if the pain from his hangover was still lodged behind his eyes. "Are you going over for some breakfast before you leave?"

"I've got a flight from the cargo ramp in twenty minutes. I'll grab an egg'n' bacon sandwich. Damn, I dread a Caribou flight after drinking. Those damn planes are so small they bounce all over the damn sky!"

"Look at the bright side—at least an NVA gunner will have a tough time locking in on you." Jay shook hands with his school bunkie. "Listen, Paul, if you're ever up around Da Nang . . . " The sentence didn't need to be finished; they both knew that they would go out of their way to look each other up if they were within a hundred miles of each other and time permitted.

"Sure . . . you know I will." Paul packed his shaving gear into his B-4 bag and then zipped it shut. "Keep your powder dry, brother!"

"Yeah, you take care, too . . . brother." Jay was

touched by Paul's reference as kin.

Sergeant Braverman stood by the open guard gate next to the compound wall and watched the olive-drab Caribou airplane land. According to the back-channel message he had received from the group commander, the new My An executive officer would be aboard. Braverman turned and looked at the buck sergeant standing next to him.

"Sergeant Teeter, go pick the lieutenant up." The senior sergeant left and went over to the temporary A-Team headquarters that was a room converted from a BOQ suite. He paused in the doorway and called back to the young sergeant starting the jeep, "And don't make him wait!"

"Don't make *who* wait?" Captain Hetten stepped over to the doorway and peered out.

"Your executive officer, sir. His flight has just landed over on the main runway."

Sergeant Braverman had served fourteen years of his career with different Special Forces outfits and Ranger teams. He had joined the newest Special Forces organization before President Kennedy gave them the green beret as their special symbol of excellence. Braverman didn't like Captain Hetten. The man seemed far too self-centered to suit him, and didn't seem to really care about the welfare of the rest of the eleven-man team assigned under him. Braverman had seen a lot of young officers in his years, and he knew that he would have to pay special attention to Hetten if any of them were going to come home alive.

"Well, I hope he's as good an officer as I have been told he was. You know, I had already picked a lieutenant for the job. It was really embarrassing having to tell Rodney that he had been aced out by someone who hasn't been in the Delta before." Captain Hetten had a habit of whining when he talked, and the sound of his voice had a grating effect on Braverman's nerves.

"I've heard that this lieutenant is one tough hombre." Braverman was baiting Hetten. "They say he's kicked a lot of ass up in II Corps and has earned the Silver Star."

At the mention of the high valor award Hetten's eyes flashed jealously. "If the new detachment operational area is going to be as hot as the intelligence reports have projected, maybe you can police yourself up an award, Sergeant." Hetten slipped back into the shadows of the office. His voice filtered out. "Send the lieutenant to see me before you get him settled in his room."

"Yes, sir." Braverman hadn't missed Hetten's jealousy concerning the lieutenant's Silver Star. Sergeant Braverman lost respect for the captain each time the man opened his mouth. A good commander would have checked each of his men's personnel records before he even meet them, especially in a Special Forces outfit, where there weren't that many people. Hetten had been the personnel officer before he had gotten this assignment, which meant that he had had access to all of the records. If he would have made just a cursory review, he would have seen Braverman wasn't interested in winning a Silver Star.

Sergeant Braverman had won the nation's highest valor award while serving in Korea with the Rangers: the Medal of Honor.

Lieutenant Bourne exited the aircraft walking down the lowered rear ramp. The muggy damp heat of the Delta reached him instantly as he left the area cooled from the fan action of the plane's engines. Paul followed the other passengers to the tin-roofed operations building that doubled as a passenger waiting room.

Sergeant Teeter saw the lieutenant crossing the runway on the perforated steel planking and drove his jeep around to the front of the small terminal.

"Lieutenant Bourne! Over here."

Paul stepped over the packages and boxes lining the walkway surrounding the building and joined the sergeant. The humidity was so high in the Delta city that Paul's fatigue jacket was already saturated with sweat.

"You're with the My An detachment, right?" Paul stuck his head under the jeep top.

"Yes, sir. I'm Sergeant Teeter, junior radio man for the team. Welcome to Detachment A-444." Teeter smiled and waited for Paul to load his personal gear in the back and slide onto the sun-heated front seat.

"How long have you been in-country?" Paul placed his CAR-15 across his lap.

"Been here three weeks, sir. I graduated from the Special Forces commo course two months ago and took a thirty-day leave." Teeter pulled the jeep out into the Vietnamese traffic on the main road that went through the heart of Can To city.

"What did you think of the school at Fort Bragg?" Paul watched the side of the road as Teeter maneuvered around a herd of water buffalo.

"Pretty good. I graduated at the top of my class. I guess that's why they allowed me to join this team."

Paul detected the pride the sergeant felt over becoming a Green Beret active team member on a new detachment.

"You're sort of young to be with the Berets." Paul figured he was around eighteen or nineteen.

"Just turned twenty, sir." Teeter had a natural curve at the corner of his mouth that made him look as if he was always grinning. "My brother has been in Special Forces for over ten years. He was the one who turned me on to the Berets."

The jeep slowed down and turned in at the C Detachment Headquarters and stopped in front of the two-story BOQ.

"Our team office is set up in room seven. The captain wants to see you right away." Teeter shifted gears. "See you later, Lieutenant. Maybe at supper."

"Sure. Thanks for the ride." Paul turned with his hands full of his gear and saw Sergeant Braverman approaching him.

"I'm Master Sergeant Braverman, Lieutenant. The team operations sergeant." Braverman paused. "The captain wants to see you."

"Good. Show me to my room so that I can unload this gear, and we'll go see him." Paul adjusted his grip on his B-4 bag.

"Sorry, sir. The captain said he wanted to see you as soon as you arrived."

Paul looked closely at the sergeant, trying to detect whether or not the sergeant was playing games with him. "His name's Captain Hetten, right?"

"Correct, Lieutenant!" Hetten stepped out from behind the office door.

Lieutenant Bourne reached out to shake hands.

"Maybe you should try coming to attention and reporting to me, first. We're soldiers, aren't we?"

Paul didn't argue, even thought he was standing with the sergeant under the porch of the building and a salute wasn't required. Paul brought his heels together and saluted the captain. "Lieutenant Bourne reporting, sir."

"Better. Lieutenant."

Braverman had seen enough, and had already turned to leave the two officers when Hetten halted him.

"Sergeant, have the rest of the team assemble here

tonight. Now that we have all finally arrived, we can have our first team meeting."

"Yes, sir. Around 1900 hours?"

"No, make that 1830 hours."

Braverman left the two officers.

Captain Hetten slipped behind his desk and took a seat in a well-worn gray office chair. He was trying to establish a power position with the new lieutenant and felt more secure with the desk separating them. "Well, Lieutenant, I hear that you're quite the hero up in II Corps," he said, sarcasm lacing the captain's words, "That Corps has produced a lot of valor awards lately. I read the different Corps' statistics last week for awards. Someone might even think that a lot of those awards issued up there were phony ones, considering the huge difference between, say, II Corps and IV Corps."

"I don't know how many awards they gave out last year, sir, but I do know there's a lot of heavy fighting in the camps along the border to Cambodia. We've taken a lot of casualties." Paul kept his voice intentionally neutral as he tried figuring out the captain's reason for bringing up the topic.

"Bullshit!" Hetten's face was filled with hate-produced contours. "Here! Right here is where the toughest action is!" He stood and swept his hand across a map hanging on the wall behind his chair. "The Delta is the new action spot, and my camp is going to be in the very middle!"

Hetten's overreaction amused Paul. If the asshole wanted to believe his camp is the most dangerous one in Vietnam, then fine. It should make him more cautious and help save some lives when they patrolled. At least he wouldn't be overconfident.

"If you say so, sir."

"If I say so? Damn it, Lieutenant, you sit on your ass up in II Corps and then you come down here acting like you know what in the hell is going on! This is the Delta and you don't know shit! Fighting down here is different! We use airboats—we have rice paddies that are miles across—and we have water everywhere!"

Paul watched the captain's face and thought to himself that the man was crazy.

Hetten detached himself from direct conversation with Paul and went off on a tangent about warfare in the Delta region of South Vietnam. Paul wanted to ask Hetten how much action he had been in, but wisely decided against it and settled back in his chair and watched the captain go through his verbal tirade. Hetten was wearing a starched camouflaged tiger-suit with silver insignia on the collar. Hetten wore his blond hair cut very short in the crewcut style of the late fifties. Paul thought if Hetten would just keep his mouth shut, he would look like a nineteenth-century Prussian officer.

"Are you German, sir?" The words slipped out before Paul realized that he had interrupted Hetten.

"Am I *what*!" Hetten looked amazed.

"German, sir. Are you German?" Paul switched to a compliment. "I noticed the way you were standing there that you have an exceptional military bearing and I wondered of you were of Prussian extraction."

Hetten smiled for the first time since meeting Paul. "Why, yes! I am. My family came from East Germany after the Second World War. In fact, my father was an officer in the regular forces." The smile stayed on Hetten's face. "You are very observant, Lieutenant. Maybe I've judged you too quickly. By the way, my family has had officers going back two hundred years serving in wars across the world."

Paul returned Hetten's smile, but his thoughts were on Hetten's foolish vanity—a fault that always caused death to soldiers on the battlefield.

"Why don't you go and get cleaned up, Lieutenant Bourne. Room number four has been reserved for you down the hall." Hetten turned back to his battle map and began studying the details of the contour lines. "Supper is at 1730 hours. You may join my table."

"Thanks, sir." Paul saluted and left the office.

Sergeant Braverman was sitting in a chair on the veranda attached to one side of the combined clubhouse. He watched Lieutenant Bourne leave the team office shaking his head slowly from side to side and enter the room reserved for him. Braverman crossed his legs on the railing and smiled. Maybe the lieutenant would work out.

The space in the tiny office was cramped as the eleven team members and the five-man KD engineer team took seats and positions along the walls of the room. It was ten minutes past the time that the meeting had been called for, and Captain Hetten still hadn't shown up. The muggy heat seemed to hang in the room, causing the heavy masculine body odor from the assembled men and the tobacco smoke to stifle the smells of Vietnamese cooking that usually came from the nearby kitchens.

Paul watched as each of the team members tried unobtrusively to check each other out with small talk. It was imperative that weak team members be identified quickly, especially when a new team was being formed. Paul looked at his watch: it was seven-thirty, and Hetten still hadn't shown up for the meeting that he had called. Sergeant Braverman left a group of NCOs and wandered over to where Paul was standing.

"I think he's over at the club talking to a couple of his buddies," Braverman nodded in the direction of the building. "Maybe you should go over and fetch him."

Paul nodded and left the smoke-filled office. The night air was warm, but felt good compared to the cramped meeting-room's nervous human smells. Hetten's whining voice reached him from inside the bar located on the other side of the large open courtyard that dominated the camp. Paul entered the consolidated clubhouse and immediately saw Hetten talking at a table to an anemic-looking lieutenant.

"Sir," Paul stepped between the chairs occupied by the two officers, "the men are waiting for you over at the team office."

"Sit down, Lieutenant." Hetten turned his attention back to his friend and continued telling a war story.

Paul waited ten minutes and then spoke. "Sir, the men have been waiting for you."

"Damn it! Hasn't anyone ever taught you not to interrupt your superiors?" Hetten glared at his executive officer and then shifted his eyes back to the other lieutenant at the table. "Rodney, this is the lieutenant who beat you out of the XO's job."

Paul decided to give the skinny lieutenant a chance even though he had a negative impression of the man. "Nice meeting you, Rodney. I hope we can get together sometime for a beer, once things settle down a bit."

"Don't hand me any of that friendly bullshit, Bourne! You screwed me out of My An!" Hate filled the lieutenant's face, making the man's appearance shift from one extreme to the other. "Fuck you!"

Paul reacted instantly to the threat coming from his peer. "I don't know what your problem is, fella, but if you ever talk to me like that again I'm going to *tear* your fucking face off and shove it up your ass . . . hear?"

Rodney averted his eyes, knowing he had just encountered someone who wasn't going to take any of his cowardice-based intrepidity, even when his mentor was sitting at the same table.

"Stop!" Hetten jumped to his feet. "I'm not going to allow cheap threats like that to be made in front of me!" Hetten's face turned a dark red with the realization that his neophyte's ego had been hurt. "Now *you* apologize to Rodney!"

"Sir, I have nothing to apologize to Lieutenant Rodney for." Paul turned to face Hetten and spoke calmly. "Your troops are still waiting for you." Paul took a step toward the western-style swinging doors.

"Lieutenant! Get your ass back here and apologize!"

Paul turned and waited until the other lieutenant looked at him from staring at the floor. "Lieutenant Rodney . . . I apologize for the tone of my voice when I spoke to you; if it scared you, I also apologize for that—but what I said . . . I meant it."

Paul left the bar without looking back at his commander. He had gained most of his composure by the time he entered the office. All of the room's occupants stood awaiting the team leader.

"Take your seats." Paul walked directly to the front of the room and faced the assembled sergeants. "I'm Lieutenant Bourne. I have been assigned as the executive officer for this A-Team. Recently, I have been working out of Duc Co." Paul looked at the faces in the room as he spoke, "I was going through your files in Nha Trang and, quite frankly, I'm very impressed with the talent I saw."

Paul had used the standard opening lines for a new member to an A detachment. It always paid to compliment the men you were going to trust your life to. Also, most Special Forces men worked very hard to gain their berets, and were proud of the fact that they had been hand-picked to serve on a new detachment.

Paul continued, "The captain is tied up right now and will join us as soon as he can break away. I thought that I would use this time to tell you a little bit about myself and what I expect from team members that I have to share time with." A light chuckle filled the room at that comment. It sounded as if they were all going to go to prison instead of combat. "Let's start this meeting with each of you introducing yourselves and telling us where you're coming from."

Each of the experienced sergeants took their time telling the rest of the men what schools they had attended and where they had served during their assignments in Special Forces. Anything prior to wearing the Green Beret was incidental and skipped over. The last man to speak was Sergeant Yater, an impressive-looking black soldier. The man's list of schools seemed to go on forever, and included attendance at all five of the Special Forces combat specialties. Yater had come from a detachment that in itself was very famous: Sigma Project, a highly dangerous reconnaissance unit. The sergeant let everyone in the room know that he wasn't at all happy at being taken from the project and assigned to a regular A detachment. Yater was the epitome of a Special Forces soldier, both in bearing and expertise. Paul was very impressed with the sergeant. Here was a black soldier anyone would be proud to serve under. Black professionals like Yater had their work cut out for them in the future.

The door to the office snapped open and slammed hard against the wall. The rifle-shot sound echoed in the room.

"Set . . . your . . . fucking . . . ass . . . down . . . *Lieutenant!*" Hetten strutted to the front of the room and stopped next to the wall maps. "When I say wait for me, Lieutenant . . . that is exactly what I mean! *Wait!*" The captain glared from face to face as if to scare all of the men in the room with his awesome presence. It was a couple of minutes before he spoke again. "A lesson can be learned from this . . . a good lesson!" He placed his hands on his hips and spread his feet apart in an arrogant stance. "I command this team! I alone! That is your first lesson . . . Lieutenant Bourne commands nothing . . . *nothing!* He does exactly what he is told . . . that's something he has to work on."

Sergeant Braverman turned his head away in disgust. An officer should never embarrass his fellow officers in front of enlisted men, regardless how senior the sergeants are.

"Sir, the lieutenant was organizing the meeting waiting for you." Braverman spoke slowly so that he wouldn't lose control of his voice. All of the NCOs present noticed that their senior NCO had sided with the lieutenant.

"Bullshit!" Hetten's eyes lost their focus. "I have been standing outside the door for the past half hour! He's trying to take over my command!"

One at a time the team members looked down at the floor between their feet. Hetten had just lost all respect from them. They would still obey his orders but only because the law placed the captain above them.

The captain rambled on for over an hour without saying anything important. The men received little additional information about building the proposed A detachment along the Sap Rau canal. Paul glanced at his watch: it was close to midnight, and he felt the weariness from the night before and the early-morning airplane ride.

The screen door opened with a squeak and a young-looking major called the room to attention for the colonel who entered, followed by members of his staff.

"Captain Hetten. We heard you talking as we passed and I'd like to say a few words to your team. If I may?" Lieutenant Colonel Bakersun shook hands with the captain and turned his attention to the assembled team. "I haven't had the opportunity of meeting most of you yet, but I'd like to welcome all of you to the Delta."

The colonel talked for a few more minutes and then turned the meeting over to his operations officer, who covered some very important aspects of fighting in the Delta. Paul, along with most of the men, quickly became interested in the officer's briefing. The men stayed absorbed in the detailed report on the area that they were going into. The operations officer talked for over two hours, mostly because of the encouraging questions he was getting from his audience.

"Well, that sort of puts it all in a nutshell for you . . ." The major paused, ". . . tomorrow we'll have some copies of our proposed operations order sent over for you all to review."

Captain Hetten took up a position in the center of the room. "Hold it, men! Thank you for stopping in this evening, Colonel. We enjoyed your words of wisdom. I have a few more points that I'd like to cover with my men, if you'll excuse us."

The colonel and his staff left the small office. Paul could see that the operations officer snapped a quick glance at Hetten, but the captain failed to see it. Hetten continued talking until three o'clock in the morning.

Paul stepped out onto the veranda and felt the cool morning air blowing in from across the rice fields. A slight smell of water buffalo added to the fragrance.

Braverman placed his hand on Paul's shoulder in the dark. "Don't let him get to you. We're going to have to stick together if we're going to make it through this one." He nodded his head in the dark toward the room where Hetten still stood in front of the map.

"You're right," Paul smiled. "See you in the morning, Sergeant."

Paul slipped his boots off and stretched out on the

unmade cot in the dark room. The moonlight filtered in through the open window. Paul's thoughts slipped back to Duc Co and Captain Pellam. He smiled and fell asleep. It looked like he was batting a thousand.

Chapter 7

The thick muddy water seeped out of Paul's jungle boots through the built-in air vents as he stood on the low dike that overlooked the canal junction. The combat walk from the Vietnamese District Headquarters compound had turned out to be a Sunday stroll compared to what Captain Hetten had told the team to expect. The Special Forces-led Hoa-Hoa Companies, combined with the fighting force of the two local Regional Forces Companies, had patrolled the banks of the main canal leading to the location that had been selected from an aerial photographs for the new A-Camp site. Three elite Mike Force Companies composed of Cambodian Mercenaries had air-assaulted 10,000 meters west of the proposed camp site and planned on linking up with the Special Forces team within two days. A total of nine combat companies had taken part in the infiltration operation, with the total losses during the operation being three men killed by booby traps that had been placed along the trails. The allied forces had not encountered a single Viet Cong during the operation.

Lieutenant Bourne and Sergeant Yater had walked the canal with the lead platoon of the First Company, taking turns patrolling with the point element and sharing the danger. Paul was the first American to reach the proposed building site.

"At least it's a good day, Sergeant." Paul squatted Vietnamese fashion on the muddy side of the dike. The sky carried billowing clouds without any sign of rain.

"Yes, sir," Sergeant Yater joined the lieutenant, "these are the kinds of combat operations that I like—no dead."

"Three from the locals." Paul lit his first cigarette of the day. He felt the menthol burn his lips with the touch of the filter.

"I thought that I heard that coming over the radio early this morning, but I wasn't sure." Yater removed the ammunition clip from his CAR-15 submachine gun and checked the receiver for mud.

"Hetten should be arriving here soon. Let's get the First Company into their defensive positions before he arrives." Paul stood to survey the surrounding low ground for anything that could be used for cover. He placed his hand above his eyebrows to block the bright glare from the sun. "The captain wants First Company placed about six hundred meters from the center of the new camp site so that he can use the two companies with him for the camp's inner security." Paul pointed. "That treeline over there looks like a good position. With those rice paddies on each side, the machine guns will have a good field of fire."

"I don't see anything better. I can't believe how open everything is around here. I mean, three banana trees are considered a lot of cover!" Yater stood up next to Paul for a better view of the terrain.

The mudbank between the two soldiers released a low-frequency *wonk* sound and mud splattered on Paul's leg. Yater rolled forward, pushing the safety off his weapon with his thumb. He sighted in on a slight movement that caught his eye in a clump of wild vegetation next to the canal, directly in front of them fifty meters away. Yater's CAR-15 erupted fire in a crescendo of death. Two main-force Viet Cong wearing the traditional battle dress of the Delta fell from behind a mature banana tree.

The Hoa-Hoa Company reacted immediately without being told what to do. The banana grove was surrounded on three sides within minutes of the first shot. The only avenue of escape for any Viet Cong survivors was the canal. A special team broke off from the company and searched the surrounded banana grove, finding only the two dead Viet Cong.

"They must have been canal watchers." Paul turned his selector switch back on safety and rested his weapon on his ammo pouches that surrounded his waist. "That was damn good shooting, Yater!"

"I developed those reflexes playing basketball," Yater grinned at his lieutenant. "We need one more VC to even the score."

"Right," Paul nodded his head down the canal to their rear. "Looks as if the captain has arrived."

Sergeant Yater changed magazines in his weapon, then looked back over his shoulder and saw the first element of Captain Hetten's task force moving cautiously along the canal toward them.

We'd better get our company set up quickly. You take them over to the treeline; I'll handle the captain when he arrives and join you later." Paul adjusted his BAR belt, distributing the weight better on his hips and shoulders. He pointed with the barrel of his weapon.

"Gotcha." Yater waved for the company to get ready to move. "I'll come back with a squad before dark to pick you up."

"Thanks, Sergeant."

Paul made room on the narrow dike for the soldiers to pass and waited for Hetten.

"Lieutenant Bourne!" Captain Hetten appeared on the trail flanked by Sergeant Dryman and Sergeant Braverman. The Vietnamese commander and Sergeant Loau, the Vietnamese operations sergeant, were slightly behind Hetten's command group. Paul frowned. The A-Team medic, Sergeant Dryman, should have been with a more forward element, where he could have helped if contact had been made with the enemy. "We heard shouting!" Hetten's voice was filled with excitement. "Any contact made?"

"Sergeant Yater killed two Viet Cong canal watchers over by that grove of wild banana trees." Paul used his weapon to point.

"Let's go over there and search the area." Hetten pushed against Paul, forcing him to step back into the rice patty that bordered the dike.

"The Hoa-Hoa Company has already cleared the area, sir," Paul could feel the cool water filling up his boots.

"Maybe so, but the Vietnamese don't know how to do a really thorough job."

Paul looked at the two Vietnamese standing behind Hetten. The Vietnamese commander spoke poor English and had missed the insult, but Sergeant Loau spoke fluent English. Paul apologized for his commander with his eyes. Loau nodded slightly, his acceptance.

Hetten lead his company toward the wild banana grove, followed closely by Sergeant Dryman, who was becoming his shadow. Paul followed reluctantly, a few meters behind the combat patrol. The company swept through the small growth of thick plants and then stopped for a short break along the dike before returning back through the undergrowth. Captain Hetten walked over to the dead VC bodies and removed the ponchos the Hoa-Hoa soldiers had placed over them to keep the flies off.

"Why in the hell did they waste good ponchos on this vermin?" Hetten used a tone of voice that he felt sounded seasoned with combat experience.

"Hoa-Hoa respect the dead—even Viet Cong," Braverman spoke.

"Bullshit! Communists are vermin and shouldn't be treated like humans!" Hetten placed his muddy boot on the face of the nearest body.

"I wouldn't do that, Captain," Sergeant Loau frowned. "The dead are to be treated with honor."

The Vietnamese commander was speaking rapidly to Sergeant Loau and pointing at Hetten with a waving finger.

"My commander says to leave the dead alone. He is very angry."

Hetten smirked and removed his foot from the dead man's face. A hunk of mud broke loose from the sole of his boot and fell into the dead man's eye socket. Paul bent over and removed the dirt before replacing the poncho over the bodies.

Captain Hetten jerked and struggled to get his weapon off his shoulder. Paul turned quickly to see what the captain had seen to make him react so erratically. A trap door next to the canal twenty meters down the dike began to open slowly. The Viet Cong spider pit was located between the command group and the returning element of the company that had swept through the banana grove. Hetten pointed his CAR-15 toward the trap door and began to squeeze the trigger just as Paul grabbed the barrel. Bullets screamed through the air above the heads of the Vietnamese troops in the banana grove. Paul could feel the heat from the barrel in his hand as he yanked the machine gun from Hetten.

"Damn it, sir! You'll hit our own men!"

"It's a VC! A Viet Cong!" Hetten was screaming and struggling with Paul, trying to take his weapon back.

The sound of the CAR-15 firing caused the occupant of the spider hole to exit rapidly and throw both his hands high in the air.

"He is surrendering," Loau spoke.

"Don't trust him! He could be armed!" Hetten had recovered his weapon from Paul and pointed it at the lone figure. He pulled the trigger but nothing happened. He had forgotten to replace the empty magazine.

"He's not carrying a weapon." Braverman touched Loau's arm, "Tell him to stand still."

Loau gave the command in a loud voice, and the Vietnamese communist raised his arms even higher in the air.

"I'm not going to risk any of my men's lives! *Kill him!*" Hetten yelled at Sergeant Loau.

"*No!*" Paul stepped out from the group. "He's a prisoner of war!"

"Christ, sir, look—he's just a kid!" Braverman pointed at the youth.

"He still could have a grenade under his clothes!" Hetten was obsessed with killing him.

"Sergeant Loau, tell the boy to remove all of his clothes and turn around in a circle." Paul was bordering on an insubordination charge, and knew that he had to do something quickly or the boy would be killed.

Loau spoke rapidly to the youth, who hesitated over the command and then slowly started removing his clothing. He removed the black Viet Cong hat and pajama-style pants and shirt, and stood naked, shaking with fear in front of the group of armed men.

"Damn it, sir." Paul was angry over having to humiliate the child. "The boy's almost dying from fear! Do you want to start killing kids?"

Paul turned, with his face showing the contempt he felt for Hetten, and spoke to Loau, "Go get the boy and let him get dressed."

Sergeant Loau smiled at Paul and ran over to the small boy and spoke softly in Vietnamese.

By the time Sergeant Loau returned with the child, Hetten had gained control of himself. The boy ran straight over to Paul and wrapped his arms around the soldier's waist. The young boy tried talking between the sobs that wracked his thin body.

"The child is thanking you for his life," Loau's voice was near-breaking as he explained what the child was saying. "The VC forced him to bring them food from the village while they were occupying this outpost."

Paul looked down at the boy who was still holding onto his waist and noticed that he had light reddish brown hair. He reached down, lifted the child's chin, and looked into the tear-filled dark blue eyes.

"His father was a Frenchman," Loau's voice softened. "The VC used his half-French mother as a whore until she took her own life. The boy has been used as a slave ever since. I am ashamed to say this, but sometimes my people are very cruel to half-breeds, especially those children whose fathers were French soldiers that were defeated by the Viet Minh. It is a double shame."

Sergeant Braverman laid his hand on the small set of trembling shoulders. "Christ—my oldest son isn't much bigger than he is," Braverman smiled down at the child. "Loau, ask him his name."

"Tuc Tre." Loau patted the boy's wet cheek.

"Tell him his name is now changed to . . . Bobby." Braverman looked over at Paul, who nodded his approval. "He has to have an American name if he's going to live with us."

The boy's face lit up when Sergeant Loau translated Braverman's words.

"Get the kid something to eat and bring him with us," Lieutenant Bourne spoke to Braverman, realizing that the seasoned sergeant had taken a shine to the small boy.

"Yes, do that. He should be of some use to us. We can send him back to the C-Team for interrogation and get credit for a POW at the same time." Hetten had regained some of his composure and had completely forgotten his totally unprofessional actions over the last few minutes. "Actually, Lieutenant, if you would have tried to kill the child, I would have stopped you. I was testing to see if you would commit an atrocity under combat conditions. I'm glad that you've passed the test." Hetten spoke loud enough for all of those assembled near him to hear.

"Really, sir? A test?" Paul felt his stomach roll. "How about giving me a break on the testing in the future?" Paul beckoned with his head at Braverman. "Let's get the base area defense set up for the night."

Paul and Braverman spent the rest of the daylight hours inspecting the defensive perimeter and recommending changes to some of the crew-served weapons. The active day was beginning to show in Paul's posture as he sat down next to one of the radios lined up in the shallow depression that had been selected as the command center. He slipped his pack off his shoulders and unhooked the buckle on his BAR belt.

"How do they look?" Hetten spoke with a new-found friendliness.

"Good, sir. We have a company set up in each quadrant surrounding this canal junction, and two companies forming an inner perimeter and reserve force." Paul opened a can of C-rations with the P-38 opener he carried on a chain around his neck. He stirred the cold beans and franks with one of the white plastic spoons that came with the boxed combat rations while he briefed his commander. "We should be in a reasonably good fighting posture in case we get hit tonight." Paul crunched up two of the canned crackers into the beans.

"Tonight will be our most vulnerable for attack," Hetten patted the stock of his submachine gun. Paul agreed with the captain's reasoning for the first time since they had met back at the C-Team. The first night in a new location was always a disadvantage to the patrolling force.

The sun hiding behind the horizon left a faint glow in the sky waiting for the predicted full moon to appear. Paul was glad that the C-Team operations officer had held off on the insertion of the new A detachment until the moon was full. It was much easier to defend new territory when you could see the enemy. Total darkness would have been to the VC's advantage for the first week while the Special Forces detachment was building fighting bunkers and digging in. Sergeant Braverman had learned from the boy that the VC had a main-force battalion stationed less than three thousand meters from them down the canal. It was just a matter of whether or not they wanted to fight tonight. Paul placed his half-eaten can of beans and franks between his feet and called Sergeant Yater on the nearby radio, informing him that he would be staying at the command post for the night and that the sergeant wouldn't have to send a squad back for him.

The defensive position was quiet, with very little movement among the troops as they settled in for the long night. Paul looked around the area for a place where he could stretch out for a couple hours' rest before early morning arrived and he had to check the guards. His body was wracked with short stabs of pain coming from his overworked muscles. Paul located Braverman lying next to a low paddy dike and decided to occupy an open spot twenty meters away. The moon broke through the light cloud cover and revealed hundreds of soldiers lying in small groups around the perimeter anywhere there were spots of thick vegetation or dips in the flat terrain that would provide some cover against grazing fire.

"Lieutenant! One last thing before you take off for your rounds," Hetten was stretched out on a poncho with a camouflaged poncho liner pulled over him. "Would you insure that the prisoner is tied up for the night?"

"I don't think Sergeant Braverman would take too kindly to that idea, sir," Paul pointed to where the sergeant was resting with his neck leaning against his rucksack. Cuddled up close to his side was the boy, sound asleep. "Sergeant Braverman has seven kids of his own and I don't think this one can pull the wool over his eyes."

"I don't think we should allow him the chance to escape or, worse yet, throw a hand grenade in the commander post!" Hetten was determined to have his way.

"Sir, Sergeant Braverman is awake. He's just resting against his pack. I'm sure the boy can't move an inch without him knowing about it." Paul stood and walked to the place he had selected for the night, carrying his pack in one hand and his CAR-15 in the other. Paul could see Braverman's open eyes glisten in the moonlight as he passed his position. Tonight was probably the first time since the boy's mother had died where he slept securely. Tuc Tre—Bobby—moved closer to Braverman in his sleep. There had been an immediate bond formed between the boy and the crusty old sergeant, and like it or not, Paul knew that Braverman had adopted himself another son.

Paul eased his head against the rucksack frame and

stretched his legs out on the ground. The relaxation felt as good as a hot bath to his muscles. He let his mind drift over the day's events and closed with a personal thought to God for letting him save one small life in the miserable war being fought. Paul smiled. He was glad he hadn't said that out loud. Special Forces soldiers weren't supposed to feel that way. There was an image to maintain.

The bright moon drifted through the night sky to its early morning position. Paul read the dial on his watch: 0212 hours. He felt rested after the light combat sleep. He was slightly angry at himself for taking the luxury of sleep during the first night. He was sure that the VC would try attacking the outpost before the men had a chance to dig in and fortify their positions. Paul stood up and stretched the stiffness out of his muscles. He could see small groups of sleeping men lining the dikes with one man in each group sitting up, wrapped in ponchos to keep the heavy night dew off.

Paul looked down when he passed Braverman's position and noticed Bobby sleeping alone under a wet poncho. Sergeant Braverman approached Paul from the direction of the perimeter.

"Looks good so far out there," Braverman slipped down to the damp ground and took a seat on the folded-over edge of the boy's cover. Paul joined the sergeant. "The guards realize how vulnerable we are tonight. I don't think we have to worry about them falling asleep."

"I saw Sergeant Loau walking the perimeter earlier," Paul whispered.

A loud snore carried across the damp ground from where the command post was set up. Hetten was in a deep exhausted sleep.

"I'm really impressed with Loau." Braverman sat looking out at the perimeter. The tough sergeant was unconsciously brushing the youth's hair with his fingers, a reflex that was comforting to the sleeping boy and the man alike. "Look over there . . ." Braverman pointed to a green tracer round spiraling high in the night sky. The round burned out at its zenith.

".51 caliber. Wake up the ol 'man." Paul and Braverman both grabbed their weapons and rushed to alert the base camp. The watching guards had also observed the North Vietnamese round and were quietly waking the sleeping soldiers around them. Two minutes later the whole camp was alert and in fighting positions waiting for the attack. Not one word had been spoken. The lone tracer was joined in the sky by hundreds of others. At first only green tracers danced in the sky, then they were joined by the red American brand. The Mike Force companies were locked in battle.

"Lieutenant, turn up the radio that's on the Mike Force frequency!"

Paul obeyed the captain and turned up the portable speaker attached to the radio so they all could hear the messages coming from the Mike Force commander.

"Are we also under attack?" Hetten was having difficulty orienting himself after taking the luxury of sleeping so deeply.

"Not yet. It looks like the Mike Force is locking horns with something big!" Paul turned down the volume on the speaker and picked up the attached handset to monitor the radio better.

"Damn! They just punched through my First Platoon!"

Another voice came over the radio.

"Turn your A-6 over here!"

"Shit, where are you?"

A calmer voice cut in on the near-panicked voices. "This is Skull Six . . . Four and Five . . . Hold your positions . . . I'm popping smoke and star clusters for

Spooky to orient me . . . mark your perimeters. . . ."

"Roger."

"Roger, Six . . . they've just backed off a bit . . . popping smoke. . . . Four out."

A static-filled voice broke into the conversation taking place on the ground, "This is Spooky 44 . . . I see you . . . red smoke?"

"Roger that Spooky 44 . . . Smoke is red. . . ."

"Everything west of those star clusters is fair game?"

"Roger . . . west of the star clusters is fair game . . . I spell W-E-S-T . . . over."

Paul saw the solid red stream burst from the dark patch in the moonlit sky. It resembled a moving water hose that sprayed death instead of liquid. The Gatling guns mounted in the C-130 aircraft spit forth hundreds of thousands of pieces of steel a minute that covered areas as wide as a football field in seconds. The battle aircraft flew the skies nightly over the Delta track waiting for calls of assistance from ground-based units. The Mike Force's call for help had reached the plane just as it had been passing by overhead. The timing couldn't have been better.

"Man, you're blowing their shit away!" The unknown voice filled the speaker on the radio.

Another voice joined in, "You see that, Skull Six? Spooky caught that VC company in the open rice fields. . . . Nobody is moving out there!"

"Roger, Skull Five. . . . Regroup your men and withdraw to my position while Spooky can still protect us."

"Roger that transmission. . . ."

"Skull Four . . . Skull Six. . . . Pull back and link up with me also. . . ."

"Roger, Six!" The operator's adrenalin was still flowing in huge amounts through his body, causing his voice to stay high in excitement.

Captain Hetten tore at the radio handset and pushed the talk switch. "*Skull Six! This is Rimmed Tire Six . . . Over!*"

"Rimmed Tire Six . . . this is Skull Six. . . . Get the fuck off my command net and come up on the alternate!"

Hetton dropped the handset as if it had burned him. "That ungrateful son of a bitch! I was only trying to offer our help!"

"Sir, the Mike Force commander is fighting for his ass. He'll call us if he wants our help."

"Whose side are you on?" Hetten slid closer to the radio.

Paul ignored his captain's question. "We had better get our shit together in case the attack on the Mike Force was a diversion."

Hetten looked wide-eyed around the area. "Take the spare radio with you and I'll stay here and monitor the Mike Force command net . . . in case they call for help." Hetten placed his ear against the external speaker.

"Tire Six . . . Skull Six . . . over . . ."

Captain Hetten fumbled for the handset. "Skull Six . . . *This is Tire Six . . . OVER!*"

"This is Skull Six . . . Spooky can't stay up there much longer. He has to refuel, and it'll be at least forty minutes before another one can get here from Ton Son Nhut Air Base . . . Do you have any heavy mortars with you?"

"Yes . . . but they're still on the barges—"

"On the fucking *what*!" The Mike Force commander's voice rose for the first time that day. "You mean you haven't set up your defensive protective fires yet? You have to be one of the dumbest fuckers in the Infantry. . . ." The contemptuous words didn't lose their force filtering through the headset.

"Don't talk to me like that! What's your rank?"

"I'm a Captain . . . you asshole!" The voice sounded threatening, even with the owner's face not present. "Now listen to me! You have thirty minutes to get those mortars set up and laid on my defensive grids! Now move your sorry ass!"

Captain Hetten stumbled to his feet and yelled for Sergeant Braverman but failed to receive an answer from the darkness. He saw Sergeant Dryman and McGrath and ordered them to get the two 4.2-inch mortars off the barge and set up near the canal bank. McGrath tore the canvas off the boxes trying to control the anger he felt. Hetten had sent both of the team's small-arms men out on patrol with the companies, even after they had told him they had to set up the heavy mortars. Loau and a squad of Vietnamese joined the American NCOs in their frantic effort to uncrate the weapons and ammunition. It took them thirty-five minutes to break out the tubes and three dozen rounds of high explosive ammunition. The Vietnamese soldiers continued breaking out ammo while McGrath ran over to Hetten's position.

"Is it still quiet out there?" McGrath was breathing hard from the effort of setting up the weapons.

"They're still digging in, but they think the VC are getting ready to hit them soon . . . are the mortars set up?"

"Yes, sir," McGrath ran his hand down the stock of his weapon in anticipation of the upcoming resumption of the fight.

"Skull Six this is Tire Six . . . We have the mortars ready and locked on your grids . . . OVER."

There was a long pause.

"Skull Six . . . good . . . We're almost ready . . . I'll tell you when to fire. I want rounds dropped along both of our flanks . . . understand?" The voice coming over the radio was a very soft whisper.

"Roger . . ." Hetten whispered back.

Lieutenant Bourne and Braverman finished their inspection of the perimeter and moved back to their vantage point, from where they could control the defense of the camp, regardless from which direction the VC chose to attack. Bobby had been awakened during Hetten's yelling session and was lying on the ground shaking under the poncho. Sergeant Braverman sat down next to the boy and patted him on the head. The shaking stopped.

"I want to send him back to the C-Team tomorrow." Braverman wasn't asking; he had taken it upon himself to care for the boy's welfare. "He can stay with Sergeant Willroy, the senior medic."

"I agree with you. The first aircraft coming in tomorrow will take the boy out." Paul felt Braverman's concern and agreed that a combat area was not the place for a child.

The Mike Force unit had reorganized its position and was waiting for the attack to renew. The Spooky gunship had left to refuel. The commander of the elite fighting unit had moved his wounded men and medics to the center of the circular fighting perimeter. He didn't have to tell his men that if the thin line of soldiers was breached, the wounded would be butchered by the Viet Cong. The Mike Force battalion had suffered eighty-six casualties during the initial assault.

"Skull Six . . . I see movement to my front. . . ." The voice was barely audible in the speaker Hetten had pressed to his ear.

"Four . . . Five . . . get ready . . . Tire Six . . . fire at my command."

Ten minutes passed in silence. Hetten heard the handset click as a keyed tone emitted over the air waves. Soft breathing could be heard. Five more minutes passed with the speaker keyed.

"Tire Six . . . *Fire!*"

Hetten screamed across the open ground to the mortar crew and the *plop-whooossssh* sound of the rounds sliding down the tube and then igniting established a rhythmic pattern of sound. Six rounds were sailing through the air before the echo of the first round's explosion reached Hetten's command group.

"Tire Six . . . right on target . . . continue firing . . ." A sense of control of the situation was in the man's voice. ". . . Four and Five . . . open fire!"

The night sky was again lit with dancing tracers, only this time there were far fewer green ones.

"*Skull Six . . . Five . . . They're all around us! We're fighting Hand-to-hand*!" A pistol firing was transferrd over the radio. "*Shit, one just tried grabbing my handset!*"

The fighting continued for ten minutes and then tapered off into sporadic rifle shots. Spooky's replacement arrived on target and began harassing the remainder of the Viet Cong force, who were trying to escape the deadly fire by hiding in the thick undergrowth along the canal. The sky suddenly filled with blinking lights as the med-evac helicopters arrived to haul out the wounded and dead Mike Force soldiers.

Daylight shot out over the flat horizon, and the strikers started lighting small cooking fires around the base camp. The glow coming from the fires out at the outposts looked eerie through the early-morning ground mist. The wind began blowing gently from the west. Paul could smell overripe fish and a faint odor of burnt gunpowder. The battle smell of gunpowder sent a shiver of excitement along Paul's spine.

"Lieutenant Bourne!" Hetten's high-pitched voice broke the tranquility of the camp. He was standing next to the canal bank. Heavy ground fog was clinging to the tops of his jungle boots. "Bourne! Come here!"

Paul walked around the discarded ammunition cases and cardboard packing from the mortar rounds.

"Yes, sir," Paul's tone of voice reflected his lack of desire to talk to Hetten so early in the morning.

"Why didn't you set up the mortars last night?" Hetten urinated into the canal as he spoke.

Paul gathered his thoughts before he spoke. "I was with the lead company, sir; you and the weapons sergeants were with the main body of troops—"

"*Damn it Bourne!*" Hetten swung around, trying to replace his penis in his pants before he was through urinating. He only succeeded in forming a large wet spot around his fly. "Because you forgot to do your job, the Mike Force battalion damn near got overrun!"

Paul looked calmly at the stoop-shouldered captain standing with his hands on his hips glaring at him, and answered, "You're right, sir. I should have insured that the mortars had been set up and the base perimeter established." Paul paused. "I've been around long enough to know that you're too busy to handle the small details."

"Don't you get smart-mouthed with me, Lieutenant!" Hetten was trying to pass the responsibility for establishing the camp's defense to Paul; they both knew that the Mike Force commander was going to come into the base area and look for the one responsible for the mortars. "Lieutenant Bourne, I want to be prepared when the Mike Force commander gets here, to explain to him why you failed and screwed up the mortar support." Hetten was using his best defensive weapon—making his subordinates take the blame for his shortcomings—to insure that he was never wrong in the eyes of his superiors.

"Is that all you wanted me for, Captain?" Paul pulled a folded drive-on rag from his back pocket and wiped the light coating of night dew from his weapon. "I'm having Sergeant Braverman send the boy we found yesterday back to the C-Team on the first chopper going out. I'm *sure* the intelligence people back there will want to talk to him." Paul rolled his eyes thinking about a half-dozen men standing around the frail child.

"That's the first good idea you've had lately, Lieutenant! Use the radio to call for a chopper and tell them that we have a captured Viet Cong canal watcher at this location."

Paul made the call on the radio and then joined Sergeant Braverman, who was squatting near a small cooking fire, opening a can of C-ration eggs and ham for the boy's breakfast.

"I called in for an aircraft to send him back on," Paul nodded down at the child. "It should be here within the hour. Hetten wants to send the boy back as a POW."

Braverman frowned.

"When the chopper lands, tell the pilot to inform the people that will be waiting at the C-Team that the VC jumped from the chopper and that the only cargo they have is the boy for Sergeant Willroy." Paul smiled and joined Braverman for breakfast.

"I'll write a note and pin it to Bobby for Willroy." Braverman displayed one of his rare grins and looked up in the sky. "There should be a lot of visitors flying in here as soon as they've eaten their breakfasts and received their morning briefings. The Mike Force fight will be the main attraction."

Braverman's statement was fact.

"I'm taking one of the companies out on a sweep to our south. The KD Team is supposed to get their D-4 dozer airlifted in here today; also expect the shuttle to start hauling in gravel by Chinooks this afternoon." Paul glanced over to where Hetten was sitting on the ground concentrating on a 1:500,000 scale map. "Hetten reamed my ass over the 4.2-inch mortars. How about getting with the weapons people and finding out what happened."

"I already know the answer." Braverman's expression became almost sinister. "The captain told Sergeant DeTunor not to set up the mortars last night and to go out on the perimeter with Third Company last night. DeTunor came to me bitching about it, because he thought it was stupid to leave the mortars on the barge all night. Hetten called him a coward and told him that he was chicken to go out with the company—needless to say, DeTunor is pissed!"

Paul shook his head from side to side. "He's going to get us killed."

"You're wrong there, Lieutenant. I have children to raise back in the States and nobody is going to get me killed." Braverman's voice reflected his determination. Bobby smiled at the Sergeant, not understanding a single word spoken but responding to the comforting hand resting on his shoulder.

A column of soldiers dressed in faded striker jungle fatigues drew Paul's attention from Hetten. The remaining members of the Mike Force battalion would be arriving at the base camp soon.

"I'm going back to talk to Hetten and clear today's operation with him. I want to get moving before the sun gets too hot." Paul picked up his ammo belt, rucksack, and weapon. He patted Bobby on his head and then pulled his own short-brimmed jungle hat down low over his eyes.

"Thanks for helping me out with the boy, sir," Braverman stood. "I'm going to have Sergeant Loau brief the boy on what's going on so that he won't be scared when they put him on the chopper."

"*Da nada.*" Paul checked the safety pins in his hand grenades while he sauntered over to where Hetten was camped.

"We're going to have company, sir," Paul announced as he pointed toward the long single column of Mike Force strikers weaving through the thick undergrowth bordering the canal leading to the new base camp.

"Good! I need to clear the air with their commander before the C-Team arrives this morning," Hetten said, folding his map. "I don't want a bad impression formed over My An right off the bat!"

"I plan on taking a company and sweeping the area to our south this morning. I'd like to clear the area out at least four thousand meters before dark." Paul was not asking for permission.

"All right, I was going to have you do that anyway." Hetten stood and bent over to adjust his trousers in his boot top.

The Mike Force started entering the loose perimeter of the A-Camp just as Hetten finished adjusting his uniform. A tall captain broke off from the column and walked over to where Hetten waited under the cover of a makeshift poncho tent.

"Hi, I'm Captain Hetten, the My An commander." He stepped forward holding out his hand.

The Mike Force commander ignored the greeting. "You're the S-1 at Can To, aren't you?"

"Not anymore." Hetten lowered his unshaken hand to his side.

"Too bad. . . ." The captain turned and faced Paul, extending his hand.

"I'm Lieutenant Bourne, sir. The new executive officer here at My An." Paul shook hands with the weary-eyed leader.

"I'm glad to meet you, Lieutenant." The captain turned to his side and introduced his two lieutenants to Paul, ignoring Hetten in the process. "We'd like to set up our operations base here today and let our men get some rest before they're extracted tomorrow."

"No problem! Glad to help!" Hetten interjected. "By the way, did Colonel Bakersun tell you he was coming out here today?"

"Yeah, he'll be arriving soon." The Mike Force captain gave directions to set up their base camp over by the banana grove.

"I have to leave," Paul made a general statement to all gathered around the tent and to no one in particular. "It was nice meeting you all." He nodded to the lieutenants, and left to join Sergeant Loau, who had been waiting for him off to the side.

Hetten waited until Paul was out of hearing range and then spoke to the Mike Force leader. "I chewed his ass good for not having those mortars ready last night! He should have known better, but you know what kind of officer OCS produces!"

The other captain smiled and looked at Hettern under the brim of his sweat-soaked hat. "I'm an OCS grad." He nodded for his lieutenants to follow him. "Hetten, you're an asshole!"

Captain Hetten stood under his poncho tent shaking with uncontrollable rage as he watched his peer stalk away.

Sergeant Braverman kept himself busy on the far side of the established base area bringing in helicopters laden with supplies and equipment for the new A-Camp. Since the ground would not support any kind of fixed-wing aircraft, all the supplies had to be brought in by choppers or LOLEX dropped from low flying C-130 cargo aircraft. The bundles were wrapped in waterproof containers and dropped in the wide canal.

The special, engineering KD Team was working hard hooking the blade to the small D-4 bulldozer and setting up the two large five-hundred-gallon-capacity water purification tanks that looked like small black rubber swimming pools. One of the large tanks would hold muddy water pumped into it directly from the canal, and the other would have the settled clear water from the first tank pumped into it and then purified with strong chemicals, to kill the bacteria before being used as drinking water for the soldiers. The complete process to insure safe drinking water took two days, and then the cycle was started all over again after the clean water had been emptied into five-gallon water cans and the dirty tank scrubbed clean. The troops were showing signs of dehydration, and it was becoming imperative that they had good water soon, or they would go to the canal for water—and it was a sure thing a lot of them would contract amoebic dysentery or cholera.

Braverman joined Sergeant Yater over by the water tanks and helped him connect the interlocking hoses.

"I'm going to speed up the process so we can have safe water for tonight. It won't be crystal clear, but it'll be drinkable for the men." Yater was sweating profusely from working hard under the relentless Delta sun.

"Fine, just throw in a few extra gallons of chemicals! I had amoebic dysentery once, and I don't need another round of that kind of suffering ever again!"

"Sergeant Dryman is the bug expert on this team." Yater paused in his work and stood straight to work a kink out of his back muscles. "He will keep us healthy. Where's the lieutenant going?" Yater pointed.

"He's taking a company out on patrol to our south." Braverman lifted a heavy section of rubber pipe. "That company is going to be plenty thirsty when they return tonight."

"That's one of the ironies of the Delta-region—water, water, everywhere, and not a drop to drink!"

"Hey! I've heard that line somewhere else . . ." Yater

chuckled and wiped the sweat from his brow.

Braverman swirled the water in the tank with his hand. "This stuff *feels* like muck!"

Sergeant Braverman left the working engineer and went over to see Captain Hetten about the evenings patrol that needed to be sent out from the camp site. It took over two hours to convince Hetten that it would be safer if the majority of the men were spread out and not all bunched up together in the small camp. Hetten had finally agreed to Braverman's recommendations, leaving the sergeant almost exhausted from the effort and from the lack of sleep the night before. Braverman left the command post and found himself a shady spot under some banana trees, where he could catch a couple of hours of sleep before the night patrols started.

A loud voice coming from somewhere outside of his head woke Braverman from his deep sleep, bringing him back into the hot world of the late afternoon Delta sun. He had been dreaming of his wife and children and had woken in a good mood. He noticed that the sun was setting as he oriented himself, and saw Lieutenant Bourne standing near one of the large black rubber water containers with sweat saturating his complete uniform. Sergeant Yater and three other team members were running across the camp site toward the lieutenant, who was screaming at Hetten—who was standing naked inside the clean water tank.

"I can't believe you're *taking a fucking bath* . . . A *bath!* In our *drinking water!*" Paul hit the side of the container with the barrel of his CAR-15. ". . . *in our drinking water!*"

Sergeant Yater reached Paul just as he flicked the safety off his weapon and pointed it at the side of the water tank. Captain Hetten stood waist-deep in the clear water holding a bar of soap in his hand.

"Easy . . . easy, Lieutenant . . . calm down . . ." Yater tightened his grip around the lieutenant and felt Paul's muscles form into knots. Braverman rushed over and helped Yater keep Paul from doing what they all knew would be very stupid.

Paul regained some of his composure and turned to speak to Braverman. "Ever since I received Dryman's call this morning about water being available when we returned, I kept my men from drinking canal water!"

Hetten rubbed some soap on his arm, but stopped when he saw all the glaring looks he was receiving from the team members. "What call did you receive!"

Braverman answered for Paul. "There's a cholera epidemic in the village upstream, and the water here is probably contaminated." Paul was shaking from controlled anger in the sergeant's hands. Braverman squeezed harder. "I told Sergeant Dryman to call the lieutenant and make sure he stopped his strikers from drinking local water that wasn't treated, and to tell him that we would have safe water waiting for him when he returned to camp."

"I've got a hundred and twenty-five men *damn near dead* from thirst and he's *washing his ass in our drinking water!*" Paul tried to break away from the two NCOs who were holding him back from the edge of the tank.

"Sir, I'll take care of the lieutenant—while you're getting dressed." Braverman could see the film of soap around the edge of the water tank. "It wasn't a very smart thing to do, sir, taking a bath in the drinking water."

"Well! I'm not washing in a damn cholera-infested canal, Sergeant!" Hetten regained his courage watching the sergeants pulling Bourne away from the water tanks back toward the camp perimeter. "Tell the lieutenant, when he gains control of his emotions, that I want him to take an airboat and attend the district commander's meeting tonight." Hetten stepped over the wall of the tank and lifted a green towel from a crate nearby to dry off with.

"I don't think it's a good idea sending him up the canal this late at night . . . and alone," Braverman frowned.

"Send him! Damn it, doesn't anyone obey orders anymore!"

Sergeant Braverman instructed Loau to pick two good men to go with the lieutenant and had the airboat engine warmed up. There wasn't more than twenty minutes of light left for the canal trip to the village. One boat moving fast might have a slim chance of making it without being blown out of the water by VC canal watchers.

Braverman found Paul resting against a banana tree and eating slowly from an open can of C-ration peaches. "The ol' man wants you to attend the district chief's meeting tonight. Stay the night and return in the morning with the work barges." Braverman added the last part, knowing the lieutenant would travel back during the night just to piss the captain off.

"Thanks, Top . . . but first I have to scrounge up some water for my men."

"I'll handle that for you. Just get your ass moving for the village before you lose all the daylight dicking around."

"See you in the morning." Paul picked up his gear and ran toward the boat docks.

Sergeant Braverman stood by the canal next to Yater and watched the airboat skimming over the water. "I can't believe that dumb son of a bitch took a bath in our drinking water! It's really unbelievable!"

Yater remained silent and shook his head slowly.

Chapter 8

"All right, men, get your sick bodies over here for chow!" Braverman was the assigned American cook for the day. "You'll love these Texas-style beans and canned Spam."

"One thing unique about your cooking, Braverman, is the amount of hot sauce you use." McGrath, the team communications sergeant, moved over toward a comfortable-looking sandbag, carrying a tin plate stacked with food. "Hey, has the lieutenant returned from district headquarters yet?"

Sergeant Braverman straightened his back and looked over at the temporary boat dock. The green fiberglass assault boats were all there. "He's here somewhere. Why do you want the XO?"

"The captain told me last night when I was on radio watch to tell the lieutenant that he's detailed for tonight's ambush patrol. He had better get his ass in gear. The patrol is due to leave camp in an hour," McGrath blurted out the words between mouthfuls of beans.

Braverman looked down at a half-opened can of Spam. "The lieutenant was on patrol yesterday and up at district all last night and most of today; hell, he hasn't slept in the past forty-eight hours."

"Who hasn't slept?" Lieutenant Bourne looked over

Braverman's shoulder into the pan of frying Spam slices.

"The ol' man wants to see you ASAP." McGrath kept looking down at his plate and stirred the food with his fork.

"I'm going to get some chow first. I haven't eaten since this morning. We stayed up at district and helped the Vietnamese doctor with the cholera patients. By the way, I brought back some fresh French bread," Paul grinned. "It's in the airboat."

"Great!" McGrath slid his half-full plate over on a nearby table and left to get the bread.

Paul gobbled his food down and rushed over to the captain's command bunker. He saw Sergeant Dryman running to meet him, but continued jogging in the direction of the command post. Paul had developed a dislike for the team's senior medic, based on the man's close relationship with Hetten.

Dryman caught up to Paul just as he reached the entrance to the well-fortified bunker. "Sir, we're on patrol together tonight. Has the captain talked to you yet?"

"No, I haven't talked to him since I left for the district headquarters yesterday. By the way, the doctor up in the village sure could use your help."

"We have problems inside the camp that need attending to first, Lieutenant. Besides, the captain doesn't want me working with the villagers until we get the area pacified. We don't want to cure any Viet Cong, do we, sir?"

"Having the team medic help the villagers is the best way that I know of to pacify an area." Paul continued walking. "Why don't you go and check our patrol, and make damn sure they've put on their camouflage make-up."

"Yes, sir." Dryman looked sheepishly out of the

corner of his eye at the lieutenant.

Bourne entered the captain's bunker through the packed-mud entranceway. The bunker was the first defensive position made in the camp and served as the radio room and secure area until other bunkers could be assembled.

"Lieutenant Bourne! I'm over here!" Captain Hetten was washing his face from a basin of clean water that had been placed near the medical stretcher in case of emergencies dealing with wounded or injured soldiers. Paul frowned but kept quiet. It was becoming obvious the captain would never learn.

"You wanted to see me, sir?"

"Yes; you're taking the ambush patrol out tonight. I'm giving you forty Hoa-Hoa commandos—they're the best fighters in camp."

"Sir, I don't want to sound like a crybaby, but I was on patrol yesterday and up all night at district headquarters and helping out with the sick in the village all day. I haven't slept in three days . . . not a damn minute," Paul's voice was strained.

"If you don't want to sound like a crybaby, don't—and do what you're told. The other team members and I have been working hard, too!"

"Sir, I thought you said that the officers were going to rotate going out on patrol. I have been out every day since we left Can To, and you haven't left this base camp." Paul's eyes were red and hurt from lack of sleep. He blinked.

Hetten wore a smug grin. Paul immediately regretted having tried reasoning with the senior officer.

"Lieutenant, you seem to have forgotten that I run this camp . . . *me*! And *you* don't tell *me* a *damn* thing! I would go out on patrol and place my ass underneath a banana tree all day if I wasn't needed to stay back here and *work* building this camp!" Hetten was fidgeting with the towel he held in his hands. "Besides, I have a lot more personal responsibility than you do."

Paul raised his eyebrows in anticipation of what the captain was trying to say.

"I can't afford to get myself killed. I have a wife and a small son to take care of back in the States." Hetten shifted his attention to the maps lining the bunker wall. "I'm not a coward, you understand! But I have responsibilities!"

"What you're saying is that because I'm a bachelor . . . I can afford to get killed in combat and you can't?" Paul's temper began rising. "I can't believe what came out of your mouth!"

"Lieutenant! You have *five* minutes to have your ambush patrol in the field or I'll have a chopper brought in to haul you back to the C-Team—under arrest for insubordination!" Hetten threw his towel on the mud-packed ground. "I won't forget this, either. . . . If you mention a word of what was said between us—to anyone—your efficiency report will reflect your attitude to your superior officer!"

"Sir, I haven't refused to go on patrol. . . . In fact, I rather enjoy the challenge of leading men in combat . . . but I take the responsibility very seriously, and don't feel that I am giving them my best when I'm so damn tired I can't see straight."

"Get the hell out of here, Lieutenant, or I'll relieve you on the spot!"

Paul went over to his lean-to and slipped on his combat gear. He checked his CAR-15 submachine gun and locked a round in the chamber. Sergeant Dryman was with the commandos when Paul arrived at the clearing where they had assembled.

"Are we about ready to leave, Dryman?"

"Yes, sir, they have been checked. Each man is carrying three hundred rounds of ammo and four hand grenades."

"How much ammo do the BAR men have?"

"Five hundred rounds per weapon."

"And the grenadiers with the M-79s?"

"Forty-five high-explosive rounds. Sir, you don't have to sweat anything; I've got them all squared away." A proud smile etched itself on Dryman's face.

"Is this your first time out?"

"No, sir, I've seen plenty of action up in III Corps before coming here."

"It's getting dark. We had better start moving. The ambush site is fifteen hundred meters from camp. Pass the word: no smoking, talking, or any kind of noise when we leave camp. I don't want this ambush patrol getting ambushed."

"Yes, sir!" The thought of being ambushed hadn't occurred to the medic.

Paul stepped to the side of the trail and inspected each commando as he passed his position. He wasn't too worried about the patrol since the men were from the Hoa-Hoa sect that lived in the villages surrounding Can To city. Each of the soldiers was carrying his bayonet and had secured every item he was carrying so that there was no sound from any gear as the column slipped into the long shadows along the canal.

Sergeant Loau stepped from the ranks and stood next to Paul, watching the remainder of the men file past.

"Glad to have you along on this patrol, Trung-si Loau," Paul whispered.

"You have quickly gained a reputation already among the Hoa-Hoa warriors as a man of honor." Loau was referring to the incident with Hetten and the dead trail watchers. "Did you notice how the commandos were acting as they left the camp?" Loau cast an approving glance at the young lieutenant. "You also have a reputation for finding a fight. The men are ready!"

"Thanks, Trung-si Loau." Paul pointed down the canal. "I want a pointman out checking for booby traps, seventy meters to our front. Tell him to follow the canal to the first junction and then turn left and follow the smaller canal for eight hundred meters until it intersects a stream. The ambush will be set up in that area." Paul thought to himself that out of all of the trouble he was having with Hetten, he was lucky enough to have some good people with him. The pointman was the best tracker in camp and could detect a booby trap from fifteen feet away in the dark! Paul glanced back over his right shoulder and located Private Ro-Den, his radioman, and nodded for him to get ready to move. Ro-Den placed himself a foot or two behind the lieutenant and stayed there while Paul walked next to the column trying to get up front. Ro-Den had just turned fourteen years old and was small for his age. Boys started patrolling with the Hoa-Hoa companies before they reached full manhood, so that they could prove their courage.

The patrol moved slowly along the canal bank lined with thick patches of undergrowth. Paul believed in moving a patrol slowly, insuring that he controlled the moving fighting element instead of it turning into a mob. Hetten disagreed, and moved a company as fast as the troops could walk, disregarding the threat from booby traps and ambushes.

"Rimmed Tire Five . . . this is Tire Six . . . over. . . ."

Private Ro-Den handed the handset to Paul.

"Tire Five . . . over," Paul whispered between his teeth.

"Tire Six . . . Where in the hell have you been?" Hetten's voice sounded even more high-pitched than normal coming over the radio. "I've been trying to reach you for the past five minutes! Have you reached your ambush site yet?"

Paul's skin shivered. Hetten had broadcast over half the Delta what the patrol's mission was. "No . . . we're at the first checkpoint. We've just finished scouting the area to the left on my map."

"Tire Six . . . You've been gone for over an hour! How damn long does it take you to move fifteen hundred meters? Get your ass in gear, Lieutenant!" Hetten released the push-to-talk switch on the handset he was holding and scanned the map on the bunker wall. He placed his finger on a circled location and pushed the transmitter switch. "I want you to cross the rice paddy to your left and get your ass over to your designated location!"

"Tire Five . . . I would rather continue along the route you agreed on back in the TOC—crossing rice paddies is something you just don't do in the Delta unless you have a force securing the far treeline. . . ."

"Damn it! Do as I say— and you had better not try faking your location with me! Be at the ambush site by 2130 hours or I'll have your ass!"

Paul looked back over his shoulder for Sergeant Loau. A hand touched Paul's arm in the dark shadows provided by the thick vegetation bordering the canal. Loau leaned over and whispered next to Paul's ear. "I heard. He is a crazy man!"

Paul whispered back, "You're right, but the son of a bitch will court-marshal me if I don't obey. What do you think our odds are crossing the rice paddy?"

"The idea is so stupid that it just might work." Loau pointed over the moonlit standing water in the paddies. "We should go further down the treeline before we cut across the open field. That way, we won't expose the men too long—and if the VC are waiting for us in the streambed, we have a small chance of making it back to the canal for cover."

Paul whispered so low that only Loau could hear, "Good plan."

The moon broke out from behind a cloud cover just as the patrol left the protection of the canal bank and started crossing the open paddy. Paul ground his teeth and thought about the old tale of bad luck coming in sets of three.

Paul turned in his low crouch position and signaled for Sergeant Loau to join him from farther back in the column.

"Trung-si, tell the men to stop and sit down, making as small a target as they can. They'll blend with the clumps of rice straw and mud, and when the moon is covered again by clouds we'll move to the streambed." Paul turned slightly to face the stream. "You and I will crawl forward with the pointman and selected fighting positions for the patrol."

Loau tapped Paul's shoulder in consent.

"Sir, what do you want me to do?" Dryman was panting from the effort of crawling in the mud.

"Stay with the men and help get them in line parallel to the stream. When I signal you, have them crawl forward. Two clicks on the cricket will be the all-clear sign; once click will mean trouble." Paul repeated the basic signals for Dryman to make sure the medic remembered them.

Loau started crawling forward the instant a cloud-bank covered the moon. He was followed closely by Paul. Crawling across the mud was a lot easier than it was on dry land. The wet earth spread a coat of slime over the front of Paul's uniform that stunk of human feces the Vietnamese used as fertilizer for the rice crops. Paul remembered the trick Braverman had taught him, and had unbuckled his BAR belt and then had rebuckled the ammunition belt behind his back so that his shoulder straps held the gear in place out of the mud. He slid his Randall fighting knife around his waist belt until it was centered along the small of his back, then he took his CAR-15 by its barrel and laid the weapon across his shoulder within easy reach if he needed it in a hurry. Paul pumped his legs and followed Loau's lead through the mud to the edge of the streambed. Paul and Loau were stopped by the point-man crawling toward them with the speed of a fright-ened salamander. The man's legs were flopping back and forth like a pair of tails. He was moving so fast that when he reached Paul and Loau he was almost hydro-planing, and his momentum pushed him against the lieutenant.

Mud streaked the man's face when he spoke. "Beaucoup VC! *Trung-uy* . . . Beaucoup VC!"

Paul raised his head slowly above the thick rice stubble that bordered the streambed depression—and felt his bowels lock and his breath catch in his throat. The moonlight glimmered off so many rifle barrels that the field on the far side of the stream looked like a parade ground. He recovered from his initial shock and analyzed the situation within seconds. There were three Viet Cong about sixty meters from the stream to his direct front, followed by three long lines of at least two hundred main-force soldiers wearing camouflaged uniforms. Paul glanced at Loau, who had also been analyzing the enemy formation, looking for any weak spots.

"Get the men into the streambed . . . quick!" Paul slapped Loau's shoulder, "and don't fire until I give the command!"

Paul reached his hand back without looking and felt the radio handset against his palm." Tire Six . . . Five . . . over . . ."

Pause.

"Tire Six . . . come in, Five."

"Five . . . We're going to be in deep shit shortly . . . Have the mortars laid on by defensive grids and stand by . . . out."

"Tire Five! What did you say?"

Paul handed the handset back to Ro-Den and pushed the selector switch on his CAR-15 to full automatic. He aimed slightly to the left of the rapidly approaching VC pointmen, who were less than twenty meters from him on the far side of the narrow stream. Paul felt a hand touch his boot and then move rapidly up his shoulder. He quickly responded to the shoulder tap and saw Loau pointing with the barrel of his carbine to the far right flank. Another column of Viet Cong was moving along the canal close to the treeline. Paul's heart rhythm turned into one continuous beat. Fear flashed forcing him to release his bladder. The warm fluid felt good against his cold stomach. Almost instantly, Paul gained control of his fear and disregarded it as a solution. All of the military training he had acquired came to the forefront of his thinking. He glanced back behind him and saw his commandos almost at the edge of the streambed.

The enemy pointmen had reached their side of the stream and had stopped to scan the narrow ditch. All three of them were looking to their left when Paul pulled the trigger on his submachine gun. The moon framed the Viet Cong, lighting up their streamside stage as they performed a macabre dance with the help of the bullets striking their bodies.

"Charge!" Paul's voice carried above the roar of the gunfire. The only chance the small patrol had was to reach the protection the streambed could give before the VC gained control of the only defensible piece of terrain within a mile.

"Hai-yeh! Hoa-Hoa! . . . Hai-yeh! Hoa-Hoa!" The commandos screamed their thousand-year-old war cry, sending shivers down Paul's spine. A battalion of Scottish pipers couldn't have had a better effect against the unwary Viet Cong soldiers. They had been too lax, and were about to pay for their folly.

The commandos climbed up the far side of the stream bank and gained excellent protection for their firing positions. One of the Hoa-Hoa commandos stood up on the far bank and fired his BAR from the hip, screaming the tribal war cry like a chant.

"Fix bayonets!" Paul gave the command followed by Loau, who repeated it in Vietnamese.

The chatter from the Browning Automatic Rifles, carbines, and M-79 grenade launchers produced a weird musical background for the chanting Hoa-Hoa. The first rank of VC were decimated before they could even unshoulder their weapons. The second rank wavered and then charged the stream.

"Fight, Hoa-Hoa! Do not dishonor your ancestors!" Paul's voice rose above the sounds of battle for a fraction of a second and then was lost. Loau repeated what Paul had said, and the Hoa-Hoa war cry became deafening.

Lieutenant Bourne reached down in his ammo pouch for a new magazine and felt mud jamming his weapon receiver when he tried inserting it. He dropped the useless weapon onto the rice stubble and reached for his handgun and Randall knife. Paul stood to meet the first VC coming over the edge of the stream bank. He aimed and shot the soldier in the face, using his right leg to kick him backward. The second and third Viet Cong soldiers came at Paul together, with their needle-shaped bayonets pointed at his chest. Paul crouched down under the second VC's bayonet, lifting the rifle with his shoulder and ramming his Randall into the enemy's exposed throat, shooting the third enemy in the stomach at the same time. Paul whirled around and checked the surrounding area for more soldiers and saw Sergeant Loau holding the barrel of an AK-47 assault rifle and trying to kick the owner of the weapon in the groin at the same time. Paul side-stepped and pushed his Randall into the back of the VC's neck. He twisted the handle of the sharp blade and pulled the red steel out of the dead man's flesh.

"Thanks, Lieutenant," Loau gasped for breath, and yanked the AK-47 from the VC's quivering hands. The sergeant pushed the enemy soldier over on his back and tore the full ammo pouches from the VC's chest packs.

"Did your carbine jam?"

"No, sir, out of ammo. . . ." Loau choked as he tried breathing and talking at the same time.

A trumpet could be heard above the din of battle. The remainder of the Viet Cong soldiers began withdrawing immediately. Paul aimed his pistol at one of the enemy soldiers who looked like a leader and squeezed the hair trigger. The soldier dropped down on his knees, holding his chest. Paul shot again, and the man pitched forward with his face smacking the mud.

"They're pulling back. . . ." Lieutenant Bourne sat back in the water and mud, exhausted from the hand-to-hand fighting.

"They will return." Loau waved his arm at one of his squad leaders, beckoning for him to come over to where he was located.

The adrenalin continued coursing through Paul's veins, causing his body to begin shaking when the natural chemical couldn't find an exit through active muscles.

"Loau . . . we need to get an ammo count and I need to get an idea how many casualties we got . . ."

A hand touched Paul's shoulder, bringing an involuntary jerk from the still-nervous lieutenant. Ro-Den handed Paul his CAR-15. Paul felt along the side of the weapon and could see in the bright moonlight that the submachine gun had been disassembled and cleaned. The boy had cleaned the weapon during the fight!

"Thanks, Ro-Den! You are very brave!"

"No, you brave men. Ro-Den no fear VC . . . Trung-uy will protect Ro-Den!"

Paul smiled at the young warrior. He sure did have a lot of faith.

"Give me the radio, Ro-Den," The boy handed the handset to Paul. "Tire Six . . . Five . . . over."

"Tire Six! What in the hell is going on out there!"

"We were hit prior to reaching the stream junction," Paul whispered into the handset. "Five minutes later and we would have been caught in the open rice paddies!"

"What kind of unit did you run into? A squad?" Hetten's sarcasm lost all of its effect as it traveled the airwaves from the command bunker to the patrol.

"Squad! My ass, sir!" Paul looked up over the edge of the stream bank and saw only dead VC in the moonlit rice paddy. "I need some mortar fire placed to my east and along the far side of the canal to our northwest . . ." Paul whispered the request.

"Tire Six . . . how many casualties do you have?"

"Wait. . . ."

Lieutenant Bourne turned on his side looking down the line of soldiers for Sergeant Loau and located him crawling along the mud bank toward him.

"Loau! *Lai-day!*" Paul waved for the sergeant to join him. "How many casualties do we have?"

"Twelve wounded . . . no dead, but the problem is ammunition. We are out of BAR ammo and M-79 grenades."

Paul nodded and pushed the handset switch. "Tire Six . . . Five . . . over."

"Six . . ."

"Five . . . twelve wounded and no dead."

"That's all! You were shooting like you really had a fight going on out there!" Hetten's voice cut through all of Paul's mental defenses.

"We did have a fight! We were lucky to have reached the stream before the VC did. They took a lot of casualties . . . We need a resupply of BAR ammo and grenades for the M-79. . . . What's the status on the mortars? I haven't heard any explosions. . . ."

There was a long pause before Hetten answered.

"I've thought about it, and I don't think they will attack you again tonight. It was probably just a chance encounter with a small scouting party. Let's wait and see—maybe we can get this fight to develop into something worthwhile."

Paul choked on the emotion that was welling up from his stomach. "If you're going to do that, then let me withdraw from this position to better ground. Hell, I'm facing at least two companies!"

"I said that I want the fight to develop!" Hetten's words were sharp. "If they attack again, I'll come out and relieve you, but there won't be any 4.2 rounds wasted tonight!"

"You stupid son of a bitch!" Paul's voice rose above a whisper, and he immediately regretted it. "If they attack again, we've had it."

"Lieutenant! I'm getting really tired of your smart-ass mouth!" Hetten yelled into the handset.

"Out. . . ." Paul handed the handset back to Ro-Den. He looked at Loau and couldn't control the hate filling his voice. "Loau, we must stay here. Tell the men to crawl forward and get as many of the dead Viet Cong weapons and ammunition as they can. We're going to have to fight the next round with their stuff." Anger tightened Paul's vocal cords making him sound hoarse.

"The captain will not fire 4.2s?"

"No! He's the biggest shithead in Special Forces! If I ever get out of this alive, I'm going to report his ass!"

Paul's anger-filled speech was interrupted with the heavy thudding sound coming from a Chinese-built .51-caliber heavy machine gun. The green tracers from the weapon smacked against the muddy stream bank removing huge clods of grass. Paul's courage waned. Only battalion-sized units in the Delta carried heavy machine guns with them on patrol.

Sergeant Braverman stood on the camp's berm watching the green tracers dance in the sky. He looked at Captain Hetten who was standing nearby with a pair of binoculars hanging around his neck.

"Sir, squads don't have .51s in the Viet Cong units."

"It could be a squad coming to harass the camp."

"Sir, I think Bourne's patrol is in trouble and needs some help. I'll take the reserve companies and reinforce him."

"And then who will defend the camp if that's only a diversionary tactic out there?"

"Sir, if there's a battalion out there, and I so happen to think there is, our people need help and quick! We can cover their withdrawal with the 4.2s or reinforce them . . . either way. . . ."

Braverman's voice concealed the rapidly developing hatred he felt for the team commander. It wasn't difficult to mentally change positions with the lieutenant and be in a fire-fight without support.

"We'll wait and let the fight develop for awhile." Hetten lifted his binoculars to his eyes.

Sergeant Braverman turned and jumped down from the berm. He rushed over to the closest 4.2 pit and told Sergeant McGrath what was happening and what Hetten had decided.

Braverman added, "The lieutenant needs our help. Let your conscience be your guide, but remember one thing—you might be the next man out there under fire." Braverman left the pit.

Sergeant McGrath paused for only a second and then lifted a mortar round off the ready rack, removed the pin, and dropped the high-explosive round down the prelaid tube. He made small adjustments in the weapon deflection to disperse the rounds over a large area around the lieutenant's defensive position.

Braverman arrived at the alert company's position just as the first faint crump from the 4.2 round reached him. He smiled. The captain would probably relieve him and McGrath, but the lieutenant's life would not be on either of their consciences.

Braverman spoke in broken Vietnamese. "The ambush patrol is in a big fight. They need ammunition and help. I will not order you to come with me, but I am going to help them. Anyone who wishes to follow me is welcome."

The guards at the main gate unlocked the chain for the team sergeant. Braverman did not look back as he walked down the narrow path out of the base camp. He stopped when he reached the treeline and checked his M-16. When he looked up, he saw that the whole company, plus the gate guards, had followed him.

"Sergeant Loau, do you have any hand grenades?"

"Five."

"Good. You crawl to the right, and when you get within range of that machine gun, throw. I'll go around to the left side." Paul handed his CAR-15 and his BAR belt to Ro-Den. He held an M-26 grenade in each hand and had Ro-Den pull the pins. If they jumped him, he planned on taking a few more VC with him. Paul started to crawl, at an oblique angle, to the starting point of the green tracers. Bourne's platoon couldn't lift their heads above the stream bank to return fire, which allowed for VC sappers to start crawling forward. Paul could hear a pair of flank guards talking to each other as he neared the machine gun. The Viet Cong commander was smart in posting the guards, but they should have remained quiet. Paul raised his torso up from the ground just enough to locate the barrel of the weapon spitting out the deadly metal. He rolled over, using the movement to give himself additional momentum, and heaved the first grenade at the weapon's position, followed closely by the second grenade, which was aimed at the flank guards. The two locations were encompassed with orange flashes. The machine gun stopped firing. Paul pivoted around on his belly and slid through the mud faster than the fish he had watched in the shallow inlets feeding into the large canals. He slid over the edge of the stream bank seconds ahead of a stream of tracer rounds and smashed into Sergeant Loau.

"You made it back OK?" Paul wiped the mud off his face with the back of his hand.

"I didn't even have a chance to leave the stream. The machine gun had me pinned down."

"Check the men and see if we have enough ammunition to withstand another attack."

"I've already done that, sir. We're in real good shape, considering that the most of the men who can still fight are using AK-47s and SKS rifles." Loau spoke rapidly as if he sensed an impending attack. "Our A-6 machine gun was jammed during the whole fight, but we've got it working now—the head-spacing and timing was off. I had the crew give the BAR men some of their ammo."

"Great! Have the machine gun placed in that clump of brush to our rear—over there by that bomb crater."

"To our rear, sir?" Loau thought the lieutenant had cracked under the pressure.

"Yes, we can cover either flank from there at the same time. The next fight will be at close range, and if they mass at either of our flanks, they'll just plow right along the stream through our ranks, never facing more than a couple men at a time." Paul felt an urgency to hurry, even though he couldn't see any enemy troops.

"Good idea, sir," Loau spoke over his shoulder as he ran bent-over down the stream.

"Ro-Den, have you seen Sergeant Dryman?" Paul laid his head back against the wet bank, trying to rest a little before the next major assault.

"Him go."

"Go where? Help hurt men?"

"No, him go," Ro-Den pointed toward the A-Camp.

A bugle broke through the early morning mist and Lieutenant Bourne didn't have time to pursue the topic any further. Paul narrowed his eyes as he strained to locate a target. The A-6 machine gun started firing in short bursts and then broke out in a solid stream of fire. Paul became angry, knowing that it wouldn't take the VC long to locate the machine gun and destroy it with the kind of identification the crew was making by firing continuously. Screams sounded above the clattering of the gun. The enemy had tried attacking the small ambush patrol from the rear and had run into the A-6 machine gun.

A large group of VC, who had been low crawling, sprang to their feet near the edge of the stream and charged. Paul's platoon opened fire sporadically, trying to save ammunition. Off to Paul's left, a tremendous volume of fire erupted. The camp had sent a relief force and the enemy was caught in a crossfire. Paul heard the renewed Hoa-Hoa war cry as the company formed a skirmish line and assaulted the VC positions.

"Lieutenant Bourne!" Braverman's voice reached Paul as sweet music to his ears.

"Over here!" Paul stood up in the knee-deep stream. "It sure is good to see you! What in the hell changed Hetten's mind about sending a relief force?"

"Nothing." Braverman changed the subject. "Sir, there're dead Cong lying all over the place! Damn, this reminds me of Korea, when the Chinese would make one of their human-wave assaults."

Loau interrupted, "We have eighteen wounded men."

"How many dead?"

"None yet, but a couple of the men are hurt bad and probably won't make it."

"That's great, Lieutenant! No dead and you really kicked ass! You're lucky!" Braverman was giving one of his rare displays of emotion.

"Not luck . . . it's Easter Eve, isn't it?" Paul looked over at the senior sergeant from the corner of his eye.

"I'll call for a med-evac." Braverman took the handset.

Paul removed the small plastic bag containing his cigarettes and matches from the inside of his hat. He pulled one of the menthols out and straightened the white paper with his muddy fingers. He held his bush hat up in front of his face as he lit the cigarette. He inhaled the first drag of white smoke deep into his lungs and held it there.

"Sergeant Braverman, have you seen Dryman?" Paul released the smoke with his words.

"Yes, we picked him up about a thousand meters from here. He said that you sent him back after help." Braverman reached for the radio. "Something wrong?"

"No . . . just getting my thoughts together."

Braverman looked closely at the lieutenant. He sensed that there was something bothering him.

Morning arrived, along with a thick mist sweeping the ground in front of a mild wind coming from the east. The med-evac ships appeared on the horizon with the first light. Paul helped with the wounded, and then joined Braverman and Loau when the helicopters departed for the nearest hospital.

"Would you get the men ready to sweep the area, Sergeant Loau?" Paul pushed his hat back on his head and wiped his brow with the back of his hand. It was already hot and it wasn't even noon.

The Vietnamese sergeant formed the relief company into a skirmish line. Morale was high as they swept the battlefield, searching bodies for intelligence information and the field for weapons. The men returned from the sweep an hour later. Sergeant Loau half-ran to where Paul and Braverman were sitting in the shade.

"Sir! There are a hundred and six bodies out there!" Loau could barely contain his excitement, "and there's a hundred and ten weapons—including two .51-caliber machine guns and four rocket launchers!"

"We sure whipped them this time!" Paul's mind reeled over the report. The VC never left their dead behind and only did so if there weren't enough remaining men to carry them off the battlefield. It was a great victory for Paul's small ambush patrol.

"Have you talked to Hetten lately?" Paul spoke to Braverman.

"No, sir. He tried to reach me last night but I didn't answer him," Braverman spoke without any real concern over what the captain might do. "Hetten will probably try and have my ass, but I have a few aces in the hole to play if I really have to." He knew that he had done the right thing by reinforcing the lieutenant's patrol—and he would face a court-marshal if need be to clear himself.

Paul wrinkled his nose and then spoke, "I hate to do this, but tell Ro-Den to put a bullet through the radio and we'll tell Hetten it got hit during the fight." Paul turned and hesitated. He saw the look on Ro-Den's face and changed his mind. "Wait! On second thought, I haven't done a damn thing wrong! Screw him!"

Sergeant Braverman smiled as he turned to muster the troops and head back for the camp site. One of the things he liked most about the lieutenant was that the man could be relied upon for telling the truth. He told it the way it was and took praise or an ass-chewing, whatever he deserved.

Sergeant Dryman caught up to Lieutenant Bourne as they were walking in single file along the narrow dike. "Sir, do you need . . ."

"Shut up, Dryman. I don't want to talk to you just yet. You know damn well I didn't send you back for help." Paul cut the sergeant's words in mid-sentence and started walking faster. He had already decided that he wasn't going to push the issue with the sergeant, nor was he going to report the man for cowardice. Paul believed every man was entitled to one mistake under fire, but only one.

Captain Hetten was standing next to the makeshift gate leading into the rapidly formulating A-Camp when the night patrol returned. Sergeant Loau was with the point element, and he stopped next to Hetten and briefed him on how many dead enemy were still out on the battlefield and on the weapons captured. Hetten's eyes were on the men filing through the gate. Each Hoa-Hoa carried at least two enemy weapons along with a lot of main-force VC combat gear. Paul and Sergeant Braverman brought up the rear guard. Hetten was estatic with joy when the two Special Forces soldiers reached his position at the gate.

It had worked. Paul had read during one of his college history classes about a Roman general who had angered one of the emperors during a major battle by going against the leader's poorly directed plans. The general had won the battle but had been in great danger for his life. In order to calm the enraged emperor, the general ordered all of his soldiers to carry the captured loot to the emperor's camp ahead of him. The ruse had worked then as it was working now, almost two thousand years later.

"Lieutenant Bourne! You've done a great job!" Hetten's eyes were counting the loot and his mind was reeling with the glory he would received from the C-Team leader for all the captured enemy arms.

"No swear, sir. You made the right decisions last night. They could have been waiting for you in ambush outside the main gate," Paul's words dripped with a sarcasm that Hetten missed. Paul's anger burned like a hot coal in his stomach. "It was really smart of you to send Sergeant Braverman out with a small force to test the enemy's strength." A voice deep inside Paul screamed for him to kill the captain.

"Yes, I was very worried about a counterambush force. They pulled that off last year at Lai Duc, if you remember," Hetten stammered.

"Check, sir. If you don't mind, I'd like to get some chow and a little sleep," Paul talked as he watched the exhausted commandos drop their gear and wrap up in their sleeping blankets. He kept his eyes off Hetten, knowing that he would kill the captain if he looked directly at the man.

"Go ahead—I want to inspect some of these weapons for unit markings." Captain Hetten half-stumbled, rushing toward the growing stack of communist weapons.

Paul forced himself to walk over to the commo shack and dig out a can of beans. He nearly fell asleep eating the cold food. Paul set the half-empty can on one of the nearby folding tables and started walking toward his fighting bunker, on the perimeter, that also served as his sleeping quarters. He glanced over to where the pile of enemy weapons had been stacked in the center of camp and saw Hetten and Dryman talking, each of them holding an AK-47 Russian assault rifle. Paul thought to himself that they made a compatible pair. He dismissed the danger of the two of them conspiring under the hot sun. He only wanted to sleep.

The bunk felt good as he sat on it and loosened the laces of his boots. He was covered with layers of drying mud from his hair down to his boots but he didn't care. He'd wash when he woke up. Paul dropped back against the folded poncho liner he used for a pillow just as Hetten stuck his head through the bunker entrance.

"Lieutenant Bourne. I wanted to say something to you out there, but it would be better said in private."

Paul kept his eyes closed and waited for the captain's apology.

"Paul . . . You fought a good fight last night. You brought back a lot of good weapons, which always makes a good impression on the brass. It *proves* that you were in a big fight. . . ."

Paul remained lying down with his eyes closed. He could feel the slight burning sensation under his eyelids that was caused from lack of sleep.

"I'm going to recommend you for the Silver Star," Hetten reached over and touched Paul's arm. "I would like for you to sign this document for me before you go to sleep. There'll be a lot of choppers coming in soon, and I want it processed as soon as possible."

Lieutenant Bourne tried figuring out why Hetten wanted him to sign his own award, and in his half-dazed state he was having trouble. Paul opened his eyes and raised himself up on one elbow. He reached for the papers and read.

"I know that I was back here, but I did expose myself on the berm when I was directing the 4.2 fire. . . . There were VC snipers out there. . . ."

Paul's eyes narrowed. "Those were ricochets, probably five hundred feet over your head. . . ." he said. Paul slowly realized what Hetten was doing and the full impact worked its way through his exhausted mind.

"Get the fuck out of here before I blow your fucking brains out!" Paul reached over for his pistol.

Hetten stumbled backward toward the door holding his phony recommendation for the Silver Star in his right hand. "Lieutenant, the right hand washes the left!"

Paul pointed his pistol at the captain and cocked back the hammer. "Get out. . . ." Paul couldn't control his urge to kill the man and fired a round into the roof of the bunker, inches above Hetten's head.

The sound of the echoing explosion filled the confined space in the bunker. Hetten fell backward out the doorway and shuffled on his hands and knees away from the dark opening.

A voice filtered back into where Paul was stretched out. "Bourne! I'm going to ruin you!" Hetten's voice had taken on an insane quality that had been brought on by fear.

Lieutenant Bourne didn't care. He just wanted to sleep.

Chapter 9

The light from the afternoon sun covered Paul's feet on the cot inside the machine gun bunker. Sergeant McGrath stepped into the narrow entrance, changing the light pattern filtering through the doorway. Lieutenant Bourne rolled over and pointed his Smith & Wesson at McGrath's left eye.

"Hold it, Lieutenant!" McGrath leaned back against the steel frame. "Christ, you're jumpy!"

"You should have knocked," murmured Paul in a sleep-filled voice. "What time do you have?"

"It's almost 1700 hours, sir."

"Hell, I must have been really tired—I slept ten hours! Damn, I feel rotten." Paul stretched and leaned forward on the cot. "Is the Australian shower set up?"

"Yes, sir. We thought you'd want to get the mud off when you got up. I put two five-gallon cans of water on top of the bunker. They're been up there since early morning, so you should have a warm shower."

"Thanks, McGrath . . . 'preciate that."

The mud had dried and caked on his hands, cracking and flaking when he made a fist. Paul reached down to finish unlacing his boots. "Is the ol' man at the Tactical Operations Center?"

"Naw, he left yesterday—in fact, right after you got back. What in the hell did you say to him?" McGrath shrugged his shoulders and raised his eyebrows. "He came over to the commo bunker right after he had talked to you and told me to call a chopper to come and get him."

"I just couldn't take the man's bullshit last night."

"We all could hear what you were saying to him," McGrath lowered his head. "Hell, both of you were yelling. I guess that's why Sergeant Braverman told him that he had some personnel administration matters that he needed to take care of and rode back with him. At least you've got someone there who's on your side."

"Braverman's a good man . . ." Paul stood and wrapped a camouflage-colored towel around himself, "but I think the ol' son of a bitch has my ass in the palm of his hand." A grin flickered across his face. "I was going to kill him last night. You know what he can do with that back at the C-Team. His good buddy, Major Reth, will believe anything Hetten tells him."

"I wouldn't sweat that too much, Lieutenant. There's not a man in this camp who wouldn't side with you, except for maybe Dryman . . . but I've heard talk . . ."

"What kind of talk?"

"Just NCO talk . . . . doesn't concern you, sir."

Paul stepped out into the hot sunshine and stretched again before walking along the narrow path constructed from empty 4.2 mortar-round crates to where the outdoor shower had been built next to the canal. He poured one of the five-gallon cans of water into the canvas bag and stood directly under the shower head before rotating it, releasing a fine spray of warm water. As the liquid covered his body, he could feel the tension in his muscles mix with the soothing, sun-enriched molecules and drain off into the ground. Paul poured the second can of water into the bag just as he heard a helicopter in the distance. He hurried to finish the single pleasure that My An furnished.

The helicopter landed on the newly constructed helipad outside the camp and Captain Hetten jumped off, followed by Sergeant Braverman. The crew chief threw two boxes from the chopper as the pilot dipped the machine's nose and pushed the left rudder, forcing the helicopter to cant sideways over the canal. Braverman picked up the two cases of frozen meat by the steel bands.

Paul strapped on his leather NVA pistol belt and adjusted the canvas French holster on his hip. He started toward the helipad and met Hetten halfway to the TOC.

"Lieutenant Bourne, meet me in the operations center in ten minutes." Hetten didn't even slow his pace as he passed his XO.

"Yes, sir," answered Paul as he turned to help Braverman with the heavy cases.

"What did you get?" McGrath yelled across the clearing from his bunker doorway.

"A case of T-bone steaks and fifty pounds of frozen french fries!" Braverman smiled

"Whahooo!" McGrath yelled above the roar of the D-4 dozer operating on the berm behind him. "Throw a steak over here and I'll eat it raw!"

Braverman waved the commo sergeant off. "Tonight, McGrath . . . tonight!"

Braverman and Paul went over to the outdoor kitchen and put the cases of food under the lean-to cooking shelter in the shade.

"Well, what's he been up to?"

Braverman took a seat on a stack of rice bags. "His case is real shaky, sir. He tried pressing charges against you, but I had a talk with the team sergeant major and he sat in on the conference with the commander." Braverman stepped on a centipede crawling next to the food cases with a twisting motion of his boot. "You owe the sergeant major one. He told the commander about your excellent war record."

"I knew Hetten would try to cut my throat," Paul's words filtered through his clenched teeth. "I think I'd better make a trip to headquarters myself."

"I'd let things cool for awhile, if I were you. You've a damn good reputation with those who count up there." Braverman threw a cover over the meat case. "Anyway, if he tries to smoke you, he'd get burnt—and he knows it. Just be careful when you deal with Hetten in the future. He's going to really try and catch you cold, without any recourse. The son of a bitch is vindictive as Satan himself!"

"I'll agree with that comment, Top." Paul stood and stretched from the strain his muscles had taken squatting. "I'd better not keep him waiting."

Hetten was playing with a black grease pencil on his battle map when Paul entered the Tactical Operations Center.

"Pull up a seat and sit down," Hetten gave the order with a tinge of fear left in his voice from the earlier encounter with his lieutenant. He continued looking at the map as he spoke. "Major Reth has given me a new area to work. Do you realize with these additional thirty square clicks added to what I already have as an operational area, I'll have the largest combat AO in Vietnam!"

"I really thought the AO was already too big for our camp, sir." Paul wanted to reach over and slap the captain's face so bad that his hand actually hurt in anticipation. He knew damn well that Major Reth hadn't given the extra area to Hetten. The team headquarters operations officer had probably been begged until he relented and gave the ground to Hetten, just to have some peace.

"Lieutenant, about what happened last night . . ." Hetten started scribbling lines on the battle map as he talked, ". . . if you're worried. I didn't mention the incident up at the headquarters. I realize that you were under considerable strain and battle fatigue and didn't really know or mean what you were saying to me. . . . So . . . we'll forget about that incident in the bunker. . . ." Hetten waved for Paul to join him by the map. "Come here. See this area? I bet there's a VC battalion hiding around this lake to our south."

"I doubt that, sir," Paul tapped the map with his finger. "Too much marsh, low shrubs, and a high water table so they couldn't dig in against artillery or bombs. Also, there's not a village close enough for them to get food from."

"Well, I told Major Reth that I was going to patrol through that area," Hetten kept his eyes averted from Paul's. "Have three companies ready to leave a dusk. You can hold the camp using the reconnaissance platoon, can't you?" Hetten shrugged his shoulders. "I mean, the berm is almost finished and the fighting bunkers done."

Paul forced a grin, "Sure, sir. Anyone can hold this camp with sixty men. By the way, did anything else happen up at the headquarters?"

"Oh, nothing much, except . . . we're getting another lieutenant on the team. Seeing that we're the hottest A-camp in the Delta, they let me have him to take over part of the load patrolling. He should be arriving tomorrow sometime."

"Good! We can use another officer to rotate combat patrols," Paul's voice revealed a genuine relief. "What's he called?"

"First Lieutenant Vainbane. He's coming from the III Corps Mike Force. He outranks you, but that shouldn't be a problem."

Paul ignored the obvious slight. "Did you turn in my after-action report for last night?"

"Thanks for reminding me. I took it with me to headquarters. The commander wanted to see it right away and I thought that you would rather have the extra time sleeping, so I filled it in for you."

"That was considerate of you, sir. Who signed the report?"

"I hope you don't mind. I signed your name for you." Hetten quickly looked back at his map. "Don't you have something to do, Lieutenant?"

"Yes, sir."

"One more thing. If you want to stay in the army, I expect you to show a little more loyalty. General Pick is going to come here tomorrow to present some impact awards, and I expect you to act like my executive officer and not some damn kind of maverick!"

"Impact awards?" Paul was puzzled. "For what action?"

"That's not your concern, Lieutenant. Go and alert the companies for tonight's patrol."

"Yes, sir."

"Oh . . . have the camp cleaned up and the men that are staying back here with you in clean fatigues. I should be returning right after dawn, so we'll have a chance to clean up before the general's arrival."

"See you at supper, sir."

"I almost forgot. Tell Sergeant Braverman not to open those cases of steaks and fries tonight. We can wait until I get back from patrol tomorrow."

"Sir, you know as well as I do that the men haven't had steak since we left the launch site to build this camp. There's at least fifty steaks in the box, sir, and the men are really looking forward to a good meal tonight."

"Damn it! Why do you *always* question what I say?"

Hetten's face contorted with hate. "Now go and tell Sergeant Dryman that he's going on patrol with me tonight!"

Paul left the Tactical Operations Center feeling a deep frustration welling up inside of him. He was the executive officer on the team and should have the right to speak his opinion to his boss. The pressure Paul placed on his foot caused the PSP flooring to squeak as he left the entrance to the TOC.

Sergeant Braverman was standing outside the bunker, waiting for the lieutenant.

"Hey, sir. We can keep the steaks until tomorrow. No problem."

Paul realized that Braverman had been standing outside the TOC just in case there had been a reoccurrence of the evening before. "Damn! He acts like the men would eat all of the food on him. The bastard has steak three times a week when he goes up to the headquarters to brief the commander and his buddies!" Paul had released his anger and changed the subject. "Let's get the word out about tonight's patrol."

Captain Hetten watched the First Company pass through the main gate from his overview position on the ten-foot-high berm the KD Team engineers were building around the entire camp site. He was going to travel with the Second Company and use the Third Company as a rear guard. Sergeant Dryman was standing on the slope of the berm with his CAR-15 slung Saigon-style over his shoulder.

Lieutenant Bourne and Sergeant Braverman walked up to the dyad, stopping near the gate. Braverman broke the silence.

"Good luck on patrol, sir."

"Uhhh . . . yes . . . thank you, Sergeant." Hetten

checked his magnetic compass as he stood next to the rows of barbed wire that covered the outward slope of the berm. "But you don't need luck when you know what you're doing." The comment was directed at Paul, who was having a difficult time controlling his urge to laugh as he watched Hetten tap the side of his compass because the needle was acting erratic.

"Yu de bes', Suh!" Paul mocked his subservient position. He was almost beyond caring what the captain thought of him.

Captain Hetten turned and slid down the side of the berm without answering his lieutenant's sarcastic remark. He edged into the ranks of the Second Company followed closely by the senior team medic.

"Keel dem Congs, Suh!" Paul raised his voice slightly so Hetten could hear. He saw the captain's shoulders hunch when the words reached his ears.

"Sir, you should back off a bit on him," Braverman was smiling.

"Why? We both know that Lieutenant Vainbane is coming out here to take over my job as the executive officer of My An." Paul's voice was calm. "Do you know him?"

"We've crossed paths a couple of times up in III Corps Mike Force. That's where he's coming from on loan." Braverman's voice took on a hardened tone. "Do you know that Hetten asked for him by name? He's a bastard first class who's after all the medals he can get and at *any* price. I feel sorry for you with two of those kinds of assholes in camp at the same time!" Braverman glanced over at Paul. "I hate to say this to you, Lieutenant, but I think you should get your ass out of this camp. Hetten is bringing him here as an officer witness against you."

"I hear what you're saying, Top. The only problem is, I'm the only person who can keep Hetten halfway honest. I couldn't leave here and place the other team members at his mercy." Paul was watching the beautiful Vietnamese sunset as he spoke.

Braverman nodded his head in agreement with what the lieutenant had said. He didn't like it, but he agreed with the rationale.

"I've got to check the guards. With only sixty men in camp tonight, we'll have to stay up till morning."

Lieutenant Bourne walked slowly over to the communications bunker thinking about the day's events and trying to mull over what Hetten's next move would be. Paul could smell the fresh scent of brewing coffee ten feet away from the bunker. McGrath seemed to always have a fresh pot of the eye-opener brewing, even if the supply of coffee grounds was low. Paul entered the bunker and blinked as his eyes adjusted to the glowing red lightbulbs. He chuckled under his breath as he remembered when Hetten had drawn a battle plan on the map inside the bunker using a *red* grease pencil. It had been a rather elaborate plan, with detailed thrusts and counterattacks that covered fifteen square miles of Delta rice paddies. Hetten had left the bunker to eat chow and McGrath had changed the lightbulbs from the normal white to the red ones, so that during the night you wouldn't lose your night vision coming into the bunker and then leaving again to check the guards. When Hetten returned after eating supper, the red bulbs had made the battle map look as if it had been erased. Hetten had raised all kinds of hell with McGrath before the sergeant could explain that the red grease pencil and the red light cancelled each other out.

"What's so funny?" McGrath looked up from his code book.

"I was just thinking about the *red* battle plan." Paul was still chuckling under his breath.

McGrath broke out in a loud laugh, "Yeah, he sure did jump all over my ass!"

"How about letting me bum a cup of coffee?"

"Sure, help yourself to the pot."

"Mac, do you know where Braverman put my model 70 rifle with the starlight scope mounted on it?"

"Awww, shit! Sorry, Lieutenant. I was supposed to give it back to you, but forgot. It's over there behind the table." McGrath pointed with the lead pencil he was holding.

Paul picked up the leather case that held the Winchester model 70 bolt-action rifle. He unzipped the butt end of the case and slid the walnut stock out from the sheepskin lining.

"You sure do like that rifle," McGrath said, adjusting the zero beat on his radio.

"It took me four hours to put that starlight scope on and zero it." Paul rubbed his hands along the smooth finish on the weapon. "Would you believe the rounds for this rifle cost three dollars each!"

McGrath kept his attention on the waving frequency needle and answered, "Matched ammo?"

"Yep, shipped special from the States." Paul slid open the oiled bolt and pressed down on the ammunition spring with his thumb, turning the barrel toward his eye so that he could look down the grooves at his thumbnail shining in the glow from the lightbulb. "I think I'll go sit up on the water tower for a couple of hours. If Charlie was watching the camp when Hetten left, he'll be back to check us out tonight and maybe harass us a little."

Paul took his time finishing the thick-brewed coffee and then picked up his rifle by its leather sling and slipped a Pancho Villa style bandoleer over his chest. "I should be back around 0300. Save me a cup of coffee."

"Will do, sir," McGrath looked up from his radio

panel and watched Lieutenant Bourne slip out of the bunker behind the cloth flap covering the entrance. A thin vapor of cigarette smoke followed him out into the darkness. Paul stopped just outside the doorway and butted his cigarette against one of the steel engineer stakes that held up the sandbags surrounding the bunker.

Paul waited for his eyes to adjust to the moonlight that broke through the thick cloud cover in brief glimpses. He looked down at the light meter he held in his hand, and judged that he should be able to detect a moving ant at four hundred meters with that much light for the scope. Paul walked over to the water tower and climbed the wooden ladder that was secured against the twenty-five-foot structure. He found a comfortable-looking spot next to the black rubber tank and removed the bandoleer from his chest, laying it next to his left leg.

The water-covered rice paddies reflected the soft moonglow for hundreds of meters surrounding the camp. Paul took up a good sitting position and flicked on the starlight scope. A dim green light filled the inside of the device. Paul removed the protective cover from the front of the scope and raised the rifle to his shoulder, placing the soft rubber eyepiece up against his cheek. Everything looked light green as he slowly scanned the terrain. The scope changed the shadows and night into a detailed iridescent daylight. Ten minutes passed before Paul lowered the heavy weapon across his lap. He stretched his arms and flexed his shoulders. The biggest drawback of the special weapon was its weight. He looked around the inside of the camp from his vantage point. Everything remained quiet; even the guards moved like noiseless specters in the light ground fog coming off the canal. Paul replaced the rifle butt against his shoulder and adjusted the eye pad until he was comfortable. He aimed for the treeline that ran parallel to the camp's north berm. The rifle moved slowly in his hands from left to right, scanning the edge of the underbrush three hundred meters away. He stopped and zeroed in on a slight movement in the rice stubble bordering the trees. He locked himself into a stable firing position and waited. The cross hairs covered the area where he thought he had seen movement.

Five minutes passed. Paul's arms were beginning to cramp from the statuelike position he was holding. The movement could have been an animal hunting along the treeline for food. He was about to change positions when, slowly, a head and then a pair of shoulders appeared. Paul waited until the man emerged from the brush and took up a crouching position. He was wearing the full battle-dress uniform of a main-force Viet Cong. Paul's right thumb crept along the smooth surface of his weapon stock and pushed against the steel safety lever. His right index finger squeezed softly against the cold trigger. He held his breath, and very gently began the final squeeze. Paul closed his left eye.

The sound of the explosion from his rifle echoed over the placid rice paddies. Paul switched the rifle to his left shoulder, ejecting the spent cartridge in the same movement. The flash had disrupted the pattern in the starlight scope. Paul's left eye waited for the foggy image to clear again. He could hear the camp below him start to stir as the men moved to their battle positions.

Paul saw the dead VC lying half in the shallow water. He waited.

Suddenly, out of the foliage appeared two more VC crawling toward their dead comrade. Paul blinked his eyes and thought how foolish he had been not thinking about putting a flash suppressor on his rifle. He moved the crosshairs in the scope to the VC who was farthest away from the dead man and fired.

Paul was having a turkey shoot. He fired seventeen times during the next twenty minutes, killing fourteen VC. The enemy soldiers in the dark assumed the camp guards were firing wildly into the night, failing to realize that the starlight scope revealed them despite their cloak of darkness.

Paul smiled and whispered, "Keep coming . . . please . . . keep coming!"

There were no more targets. A hand gently touched Paul on the shoulder and he lowered his rifle.

"What in the hell are you shooting at?" A tinge of fear was in McGrath's voice.

"I think I've zapped seventeen gooks!"

"What!?" McGrath scooted closer to the lieutenant to see if the man had lost his senses. Their eyes locked and the moonlight revealed to the sergeant that his lieutenant was only very excited, not crazy.

"No joshing!" Paul's voice wavered from the pent-up excitement that he had controlled during the firing. "They must have been a recon patrol sent out to check on us. They were moving along that treeline north of camp."

"Sir, the general is going to really flip!" McGrath remembered the message he had received over the radio in morse code while Paul was shooting. "I just broke the message from headquarters alerting us that General Pick will be arriving here at My An right after first light." McGrath shook his head. "What's weird, though, is that Captain Hetten must have known about the general's early arrival, because the message stated that he was arriving on schedule. I had to ask for the coded time."

"Let's get down from the tower." Paul stood and stretched. "It should be light in a couple of hours. You had better get back to the radios. I'm going to put on a clean uniform for the brass! Gotta play the game!" Paul slapped McGrath on the shoulder.

"So do I," McGrath answered, and took the lead on the ladder. The radio was broadcasting when McGrath reentered the bunker.

"Tire Four . . . Tire Six . . . over . . ."

McGrath picked up the handset. "Tire Four . . . over . . ."

"Tire Six . . . we heard shooting . . . what's going on?"

"Tire Five has intercepted a VC patrol north of camp. He thinks he hit quite a few of them firing from the water tower with his Winchester . . . over."

"How many?"

"We don't know yet . . . It's still dark and we haven't had a chance to sweep the area, but he thinks he hit seventeen . . . over"

"Did you say seventeen?"

"Roger . . . seventeen . . . over." McGrath grinned as he visualized what Hetten's face looked like. "Our visitor will arrive at ZY00 hours . . . over." McGrath coded the time.

"Roger . . . We'll be back in camp by then . . . out."

"Tire Six. . . . Tire Five . . . send me your present location . . . over."

"Forget it; by the time I code it and send it to you, we'll be near the camp . . . out."

Dawn broke quickly over the flatlands of the Delta in a soft light. Water buffalo were calling to each other across the diked paddies as Paul stepped out of the entrance of his bunker dressed in his best uniform, the one with all of the patches sewn on it. McGrath and the rest of the A-Team who had remained inside the base camp had also changed into clean uniforms and shined boots for the general's arrival.

Paul waved for McGrath to join him. "Mac, take thirty men and check out those bodies. See if they were carrying anything that the intelligence detachment can use. You might as well bring back to camp as much gear as you can and bury the bodies before the heat gets to them. I don't want to have to patrol that area and smell decomposing corpses."

"I wish you would have let me known before I changed clothes, sir," McGrath grumbled under his breath.

"Sorry, I thought about it when I was dressing," Paul smiled. He knew McGrath didn't like being around senior officers and would enjoy being away from the radios for a couple of hours.

Paul and McGrath heard the main radio crackle, and then a loud voice through the static coming from a helicopter.

"Tire Six . . . Black Dragon Six . . . over"

"Black Dragon Six . . . Tire Five . . . over."

"Dragon Six . . . We'll be landing in one-five . . . over."

"Tire Five . . . roger."

"Dragon Six . . . out."

Lieutenant Bourne stepped out of the bunker and looked into the morning sky trying to detect the first sign of the aircraft. Sergeant McGrath was leading the sweep patrol toward the main gate when the guards pulled open the steel-meshed frame and allowed Hetten's First Company to begin passing through into the camp. McGrath's small patrol stepped aside and dropped down into squatting positions as they waited for the long line of commandos to pass through the narrow opening. Paul went over to the north berm and climbed to the top of the wedge-shaped earthen barrier. He held his hand up over his brow to shield them from the reflected light off the water in the paddies and saw a column of commandos moving toward the camp from the northern treeline. He could just make out the VC bodies strung below bamboo poles as if they were dead tigers instead of men.

The helicopter appeared on the horizon at the exact same time that Hetten strode through the main gate.

"I'll guide in the chopper!" Hetten screamed over the sound of the engine.

Sergeant Dryman took up a squatting position next to the berm and waited for his captain.

Paul could see that both Hetten and Dryman were covered from head to toe with a thick rice-paddy mud that hadn't completely dried. The normally immaculately clean uniform Hetten wore was torn, and mud covered half of his face. The commandos entering through the main gate had mud on the front of their uniforms but the backs were clean. The troops wore angry expressions on their faces, daring anyone to laugh or say anything to them.

Paul spoke to Dryman, "I thought you were going to the area south of here?" His mind was rapidly beginning to piece together what was going on around him. "How in the hell did you all get so damn muddy?"

"We crawled for about a hundred meters." Dryman's face tried to take on the airs of a combat veteran, but failed as soon as Paul stared at him.

"Crawled?" questioned Paul. "With three companies of some of the best fighting men in the Delta . . . you crawled!"

"The commandos didn't patrol well, so Captain Hetten had them practice low-crawling . . ."

"Bullshit!" A slow smile spread across Paul's face as he pieced together the charade. Hetten knew that Paul would have followed the camp policy for senior visitors and have all of the men in the base area in clean uniforms. Hetten and Dryman would be the only two

Americans to greet the general in battle-worn fatigues. The slick bastard! Hetten had probably been waiting just outside the camp all night.

"It should be a Hollywood production this morning in the operations center—right, Dryman?" Paul threw his head back and laughed, "You phony bastards!"

Dryman's only answer was the smirk spread over his face.

Paul cupped his hands around his mouth and called across the camp to Sergeant McGrath. "Forget the patrol! Captain Hetten is bringing in the dead VC!"

The general's chopper landed in the center of a circle of dried mud. Captain Hetten was standing outside the sphere of the rotor blades at rigid attention. The captain's CAR-15 was slung under his right arm in a combat-ready position.

General Pick stepped out of the chopper door followed by his aide-de-camp. A lieutenant emerged alone from the left side of the idling helicopter and made a wide circle around the helipad.

"Captain Hetten, Commander . . . Team A-477 . . . reports, sir!"

"At ease, Captain," General Pick's voice complemented the black combat camouflaged stars on his collar. "It looks as if I caught you coming off a patrol. We could see some commandos carrying bodies this way. Did you have a fight that I don't know about?"

"Yes, sir. A small fire-fight. My patrol caught a recon unit observing my camp over by that treeline." Hetten turned and pointed.

"Any intelligence information on them that my people can use?" the general asked as Hetten escorted him through the open gate into the camp.

"We haven't had time to search them thoroughly, sir, but so far it looks as if they were traveling sterile."

Lieutenant Bourne had the American A-Team lined

up near the main gate. He could hear the whole conversation between Hetten and the commanding general. Disbelief covered his face for an instant just before the general's party reached him. Paul couldn't believe that Hetten was actually taking credit for those kills. He was lying to a general officer.

"Sir, this is my team," Hetten stated the words as if he owned the men, "and Lieutenant Bourne here is my executive officer. He normally stays inside the camp and runs things for me while I patrol."

Paul felt like puking as he watched Hetten move down the line, introducing each man to the general. When they reached the end of the formation, Hetten looked back over his shoulder and spoke to Paul, "Lieutenant, give the men a break. Sergeant Dryman and myself will brief the general in the TOC on our most recent operations."

"Just a minute, Captain, before you dismiss your men," the General held his hand out toward his aide.

Paul called the troops to attention and moved to stand next to his captain.

"Lieutenant, please fall back in with the troops," the general smiled, and Paul obeyed.

"Officers, Americans, and commandos, I'm proud to be out here today and a bit surprised also . . ." the general started his speech, "I came here to award the Silver Star to a very gallant officer, who engaged a vastly superior enemy force and with only forty Hoa-Hoa commandos . . . he defeated them!"

Paul grinned. He wasn't expecting to win a Silver Star, actually he was glad just to be alive after what had happened out there.

The general continued, ". . . but upon my arrival here at My An, I find that he followed one outstanding feat with another! Back to back! I am very impressed with this kind of leadership and guts!"

Paul glanced over at Braverman, who had been watching the lieutenant with a spark of pride in his eyes.

General Pick cleared his voice. "As soon as I return to my headquarters, I am going to have my G-1 upgrade this Silver Star into a Distinguished Service Cross!" The general turned and looked at the A-Team and saw Sergeant Braverman, but this time he recognized him. "I see another old war horse is amongst us." He faced Hetten again before speaking. "If you keep this up, young man, you'll end up with a Medal of Honor like Sergeant Braverman."

All eyes flashed to where Braverman was standing at attention. No one on the team knew that Braverman was a Medal of Honor holder, and the sergeant blushed over all the attention he was receiving.

"You men must be proud to have an officer of Captain Hetten's caliber for your leader!" The general pinned the Silver Star on Hetten's muddy jacket pocket.

"Thank you, sir," Hetten saluted.

"You deserve it, Captain!"

"Sir, if you would follow me to the operations center, we'll begin our briefing."

"Please, lead the way." General Pick smiled, but something was bothering him as he walked with the captain. He couldn't quite place what was wrong.

Paul started to follow the general and Hetten toward the bunker.

When the party was out of hearing, Braverman spoke, "He's gone too far!"

Paul stopped following the general's party and changed directions. He went over to the commo bunker and poured himself a cup of coffee, then went back outside the bunker and slid down into a Vietnamese squat next to the sun-warmed sandbags. A large wasp flew by carrying a dead spider and circled a few feet over Paul's head. Paul focused his gaze on the flying insect.

"Sir! that has to be one of the guttiest fucking liars in the Army!" McGrath roared out the words.

"Mmmmmm . . ." Paul watched his wasp gain altitude.

"Sergeant Braverman is madder than hell!"

Paul didn't hear the communications sergeant. He was totally absorbed watching the black two-inch-long insect struggling with its load.

Chapter 10

The curled edge of the steel canteen cup burned his lip as Paul took a sip of hot coffee. The wasp that he had been watching was only a speck in the light blue sky. What Captain Hetten had done in front of the whole team occupied his mind. A soldier just didn't lie to a general officer, under *any* circumstances. Paul had started to regain his feet and go over to the operations center when the new lieutenant stepped around the corner of the communications bunker.

"Hello, I'm Lieutenant Vainbane," his hand was held out. "Heard a lot of good things about you."

Paul accepted the handshake. "Heard about you, too, Vainbane."

"I hope it was half as good as the stuff they're spreading about you all over group headquarters in Nha Trang," Vainbane tried complimenting his rival. "By the way, what in the hell is going on here at My An? Everyone looks as if their best friend just got zapped."

"It's rather obvious, My An is not a happy camp." Paul's eyes were expressing as much information as the words he was speaking. "What's your first name?"

"Hell, it's a loser; most people call me Bane."

"Fine! Well, Bane, Camp My An is having a few internal leadership problems." Paul glanced over to where a half-dozen of the team members were talking under the kitchen lean-to. "Why don't you get some chow? I've got some work to do over at the TOC."

"I'm not really hungry. If you don't mind, I'll just tag along with you."

"Whatever flips your skirt."

Vainbane followed Paul across the open parade grounds in the center of the small camp and around the water tower to the Tactical Operations Center where Hetten was briefing the general and his party. The two lieutenants arrived just as General Pick and Captain Hetten stepped from the sandbag entrance of the bunker.

General Pick was speaking to Hetten. "Captain, you're doing a damn fine job securing this new area."

"Thanks, sir! We try hard!"

"Well, keep up whatever you're doing!" The general angled toward the helipad as he walked. He looked up and saw the two lieutenants watching him from a few meters away and smiled at Vainbane, "Captain Hetten has just informed me that you're some kind of real fighter from III Corps." The general pulled the visor of his field cap down to protect his eyes from the bright sunlight.

"I try to do my best, sir." Vainbane's tone of voice implied he was a professional who was very humble when his talents were being discussed. Just the opposite of what he truly felt.

"Stand at ease, Lieutenant," the general waved his hand at Paul and continued speaking to Vainbane. "Captain Hetten tells me that you've been recommended for the Medal of Honor, but I haven't seen any of the paperwork yet."

"That's true, sir. I was caught in an ambush and had to fight my way out after all of my men were killed. I ended up killing seven NVA with my K-Bar knife,"

Vainbane kept a partial grin on his face as he briefed the general.

"Very good, Lieutenant," General Pick turned slightly to address Paul. "It must be difficult for a young man like you to have to stay in camp all of the time while your commander sees all the action." The general was looking deep into Paul's eyes as he spoke, and added, "You have a very smooth-running operation here."

Paul slowly glanced over to where Captain Hetten was standing, shadowed by Dryden, and then he looked over at Vainbane. The long pause before answering the general was becoming awkward for the captain. Paul mustered up a wide smile without changing the expression his eyes radiated and spoke, "Yes, sir, I'm really fortunate to have officers of the caliber Captain Hetten and Lieutenant Vainbane represent to teach me the facts of life about surviving in the U.S. Army." He added, "They're the kinds of leaders you need to have just once to learn how things are really done."

The general was observing the body language emitting from Paul as he spoke. The two men's eyes touched gazes with neither man withdrawing. General Pick had known a lot of fighting men in his thirty-five-year career that spanned three wars. The young lieutenant's eyes told him that here was a man who had seen too much killing and too much of the darker side of mankind. He knew that he was looking at a battle-scarred warrior. The general broke the stare with a smile spreading over his face. It was as if they had reached an understanding.

Captain Hetten shattered the moment between the two warriors. "Sir, your chopper is ready. Do you want to leave now, or do you want to tour the camp before you go?"

"No, I have to leave very soon. Thanks for the offer of the tour but I have to be back at my headquarters before noon."

The general had developed a sixth sense during his career that told him there was something about My An that wasn't jelling as it should. He studied Hetten and saw that the man's face failed to match his torn jungle fatigues. The lines weren't there to show evidence of long combat patrols and the strain of leadership under extreme combat. He thought that if Bourne and Hetten would change uniforms, then things would be right. The sound of the helicopter cranking up broke the general's thought pattern.

General Pick turned and spoke sharply to his aide, "Let's go!"

The chopper roared and then changed pitch to a cracking sound as the pilot changed the angle of the rotor blades. General Pick leaned out of the rising aircraft and flipped Paul a slow salute. He liked the lieutenant's style. The aircraft shot forward as the general leaned over to his aide and shouted above the helicopter's noise, "Take a note! Lieutenant Bourne . . . Camp A-477 . . . I want to keep an eye on him!"

Captain Hetten whirled around to face Paul the instant the General's helicopter was out of sight. "*Damn you, Bourne!*"

Paul sauntered casually over to where Hetten stood shaking with uncontrolled anger. "Yes, sir?"

"*Damn you ! Who . . . Who in the hell do you think you are!* Don't you realize that you made the general angry! He can make or break anyone in Vietnam! Probably the whole damn army!"

"Angry, sir?" Paul remained extremely calm on the outside. "Why should he be angry? I didn't tell him anything . . . now that I've thought about it, I should have. I mean, lying to a general? . . . shame on you,

Captain!"

"*God damn you, Lieutenant!*" Hetten was gearing up to his tantrum level. "*Get your ass to the TOC! We're going to have a chat!*"

Lieutenant Vainbane had left in shock as soon as Hetten started into his tirade against Paul. He had never witnessed anything like what was going on before in his military career. Vainbane took up a position near Sergeant Braverman under the mess tent lean-to.

"Hi, Sergeant." Vainbane's voice reflected the nervousness he was feeling watching the captain lay into Bourne. The level of the attack was almost sick. "Does that go on all of the time?"

Braverman kept his eyes on Hetten. "Most of the time when there aren't any outsiders in camp. You're having your first real look at your new leader."

"Why does he do that?"

Braverman half-closed his eyes and looked at the young lieutenant, who in ten years would probably be a replica of Hetten. The sergeant held the lieutenant's attention for a few seconds before he spoke. "Lieutenant Bourne can outfight, outcommand, and outlead the captain—and Hetten damn well knows it!" Braverman held out his hand and turned his palm from side to side. "It's rather basic—Hetten is jealous of Bourne to the point of being neurotic."

Captain Hetten strutted out of the command bunker and joined Sergeant Braverman and Vainbane. "Well, Lieutenant Bourne is finished!" Hetten's voice was marbled with the hate he felt for the junior officer. "I'm going to the C-Team this afternoon. Sergeant Braverman, have a chopper here around 1600 hours to take me. I should return from my meeting with the district chief before 1400 hours. When I get back from the village, I want that damn lieutenant waiting for me at the helipad!" Hetten looked at the new lieutenant.

"Vainbane! You're the new detachment executive officer now!"

Lieutenant Vainbane looked at the captain and tried to smile, but he was wondering if being Hetten's XO was an honor or one of those positions from which you just couldn't win.

Braverman tried remaining nonchalant when he spoke to Hetten but his voice broke halfway through his sentence. "You're coming down awfully hard on the lieutenant, aren't you, sir?"

"Heavy? That damn lieutenant hasn't been loyal to me! I should have his ass shot!"

"Loyalty is something that has to be earned. I've been around long enough and been through enough wars to know that blind loyalty can get a lot of people killed." Braverman wasn't backing off. "The men on this team really think highly of Lieutenant Bourne, and if he leaves it would create a real morale problem."

"All of you people are mine, damn it! I'm your leader and you will do whatever I say has to be done!" Hetten had transferred his hatred to the senior sergeant, "and I don't give a damn if you do have the Medal of Honor!" There was a pause and Hetten added, "It was probably a phony award just to appease the Mexicans. . . ."

Hetten's words cut through Braverman like laser beams of hot light. He was half Mexican and very proud of his south-Texas upbringing in a poor but loving family.

Braverman had been pushed too far. "Sir, I've been in the army twenty-four years, and I have never even seen an officer with morals and a code of ethics as low as yours. I've put up with your self-centered horseshit for the past two months, and I did that only because I am a professional soldier and had faith in whoever allowed you to be appointed as an officer." Braverman pointed his finger at the awestruck captain. "But listen to *me*, if you hurt that lieutenant in any way . . . I . . . me . . . Braverman . . . the Mexican . . . am going to get your ass!"

Captain Hetten was shocked and couldn't respond to Braverman's outburst. Lieutenant Vainbane looked as if he wanted to crawl underneath a sandbag and hide.

"Mu . . . ma . . . mutiny!" The words stuck in Hetten's throat as he tried forcing them out. "Sergeant! You've gone too far! This is mutiny!" Hetten was acting like a trapped animal. "Lieutenant Vainbane! Have three gunboats ready to go to district headquarters in ten minutes!" Hetten refused to look at the sergeant. "I'll see you when I get back!"

Vainbane ran toward the boat dock, being only too happy to leave the scene.

Sergeant McGrath met Braverman next to the berm.

"Well, Mac, I guess we're going to have to go ahead and do it . . . and do it quick!"

"I told you we should have greased that bastard a long time ago!" McGrath pulled a rice weed from between his teeth. "Is he about to do the lieutenant a job?"

"Yes . . . but Hetten has added me to the list." Braverman looked down at the ground. "If only he would show just one good point!"

"Should I get Sergeant Loau?" McGrath asked.

"Yeah, and bring the AK-47s. Hetten is leaving for district headquarters in a few minutes. We can meet him on the canal."

"You really want to go through with this?" McGrath was getting a flash of cold feet.

"No . . . not really, but if we don't kill that bastard,

or at least wound him bad enough to be evacuated, he's going to end up getting us all killed trying to get himself a chest full of medals!"

"Should I have Loau instruct the boat guards?" McGrath turned to leave.

"That's a good idea," Braverman was watching Vainbane ready the boats.

Sergeant McGrath's pace increased once he regained some of his confidence in the task; after all, he had killed a lot of VC who were only soldiers like himself trying to do their jobs . . . but Hetten, he deserved death.

Lieutenant Bourne sat in the chair with his feet crossed on a nearby field table. He tapped the edge of the olive-drab table with the end of a grease pencil. A crease appeared on his forehead as he slipped into deep thought. Paul hated Hetten. The sound of the forty-horsepower Mercury outboards met his ears. Paul got up, went over to the door, and looked out. Lieutenant Vainbane was standing on the short dock untying the ropes that held the three eighteen-foot gunboats to the wooden structure.

"You leaving, sir?" Paul yelled above the sound of the revving engines.

Hetten turned around on the dock and screamed back, "To district! When I get back, you be ready to leave with me to the C-team!"

Paul shrugged his shoulders. So what, he thought. He left the operations bunker and went over toward the mess tent, passing the communications bunker on the way. He could hear the radio call sign for the My An Camp being broadcast by someone who wanted to talk to the new site.

"Rimmed Tire . . . Rimmed Tire . . . Rimmed

Tire . . . Crowfoot . . . over."

Paul paused outside the bunker and waited for the caller to repeat the long call over again. He entered the bunker and looked for McGrath or Sergeant Teeter. The bunker was empty. Paul picked up the handset and answered the call, which turned out to be a radio check. He paused before leaving the bunker and looked around in the storage area for McGrath, but couldn't find him. The communications sergeant never left the bunker without someone else monitoring the radios for him. Paul stepped back in the doorway until he had a view of the latrine located next to the berm. McGrath wasn't inside. Paul left the bunker and ran over to where Braverman usually stayed during the day when he wasn't occupied with camp duties and found him gone. Ro-Den was sitting with the Vietnamese medic against the shady wall of the small dispensary.

"Ro-Den! Have you seen Sergeant McGrath or Sergeant Braverman?"

"Him go *Trung-uy*! Braverman, McGrath, and Loau . . . him go . . . take Viet Cong AK-47 to target shoot . . . him go . . ." Ro-Den pointed down the canal.

Paul knew.

He ran out the main gate and onto the narrow trail that bordered the canal leading to the district headquarters. He knew he had to stop them. Hetten was a first-class son of a bitch, but he was still a commanding officer. Paul ran harder. His lungs hurt. He reached down with his right hand and held his French canvas holster against his side. The awkward movement threw him off balance, but he continued running as fast as he could, dodging through the overhanging branches.

Ten minutes of hard running brought him to a gradual curve in the manmade canal. He heard voices filtering through the dark green growth and slowed down. Hetten's boat was drifting in the middle of the wide ditch.

"Damn it, driver! Get this thing running!" Hetten was standing in the front of the boat.

"One minute, *Dai-uy*!" The Vietnamese driver pulled on the start cord.

Lieutenant Bourne crouched and slipped past the drifting gunboat in the underbrush. The team sergeants couldn't have had time to travel much farther up the canal. A sharp bend in the muddy water appeared off to Paul's right. He stopped creeping and lay down against the cool, mud path. This was an excellent spot for an ambush. The boats would have to slow down in order to negotiate the curve. Paul's eyes scanned the canal banks. A brief flicker of reflected light caught his eye. Paul heard the boat motor roar to life as the operator gunned the throttle. He knew that he wouldn't have time to reach the group of sergeants. The lead boat was already passing the bend in the canal. Hetten's fiberglass craft was beginning to reach the danger point of the curve. Paul noticed that the rear boat was intentionally falling back in the distance and hugging the canal bank. Paul knew that he would have to act.

He stood up and yelled, *"Ambush!"*

Hetten's boat reached the bend at the same instant. The driver jumped overboard and three AK-47s opened fire from the underbrush bordering the canal. The rounds shattered the fiberglass hull, throwing pieces of the green plastic across the water. Hetten fell backward into the thick muddy water. Paul couldn't tell from where he was if Hetten had been hit or if he had jumped.

Seconds passed.

Hetten's head appeared through the brown water. He still had his camouflage hat on his head.

The last boat slowly moved through the kill zone

without receiving any fire. Hetten's head bobbed in the boat's wake.

"Over here, Captain!"

Hetten turned in mid-canal and dog-paddled over to Paul's position on the slanted canal bank.

"Shoot, Bourne! Give me cover!" Hetten swallowed water as he struggled to talk and swim at the same time.

Paul sat on the canal bank in full view of the ambushers and watched Hetten drag himself up out of the water and scurry over to where he was sitting.

"Get down, Lieutenant! You dumb ass!" Hetten sprayed water from his mouth as he yelled to his lieutenant.

"You haven't figured it out yet, have you, Captain?" Paul's voice remained on one level. "You can stand up."

The three sergeants stepped into view on the trail, carrying their captured AK-47s balanced in the palms of their hands. Braverman wore a determined expression. It was cold and mean. Hetten looked up at the sergeant and then lowered his eyes to the weapons the three NCOs carried. He knew then what had happened.

"You're the ones!" his voice dropped in amazement, ". . . you tried to kill me?" Hetten turned on the muddy canal bank, slipping back into the water up to his waist, and faced Paul. *"You're their leader!"*

"Shut the fuck up, Captain!" Braverman whispered through his teeth and glanced over at Paul. "Sir, I don't want you mixed up in this . . . Would you leave?"

"No . . . it's over, Sergeant. . . ." Paul stood firmly between the sergeants and Hetten. "Put the weapons away."

"Can't do that, Lieutenant. You know that . . ." Braverman placed the still-warm barrel against Hetten's wet temple, causing the captain to flinch.

"Braverman, don't kill him." Paul gently pushed the

weapon aside and stepped over to place his body between the two of them. "There are other ways of handling Hetten. General Pick seems like a fair man and I'm sure he'll understand why . . . why you would be pushed into doing this . . ."

The three combat sergeants stared at Lieutenant Bourne for a long time. The pause gave Hetten courage.

"You are all under arrest!" Hetten stood up, and water dripped from his clothes to the packed mud causing a large puddle to form around his feet. He stuttered, "I promise you will all receive a fair trial for this attempted murder of your commanding officer."

Paul looked at the captain with undisguised disgust. "Damn it, Captain! Set your ass down and shut up for once! Unless you would rather die?" Paul shook his head. The dumb ass didn't realize that he was within a hair's breath of death. Bourne reached into his shirt pocket and pulled out a squashed package of cigarettes. He offered them to the sergeants and then lit himself a menthol. Paul squatted and the men followed suit. An idea had occurred to Paul, and he nodded for Hetten to sit down where he was.

"Hetten, just sit there and stay quiet until I finish talking." Paul frowned to insure the captain realized that he was very serious. Smoke left the lieutenant's mouth and drifted against the captain's face. "We're at a Mexican stand-off. If you press charges against these men, a court-marshal will surely bring out your phony Distinguished Service Cross—and that will be the end of your career," Paul spat out the words. "I don't think General Pick will take kindly to being made a fool out of by you." Paul could see that Hetten was interested in making a deal and he looked over at the three sergeants. "And if you kill him, regardless how much he deserves to die, sometime, somewhere . . . the word will get out about the murder," Paul could see he was beginning to get through to them, ". . . so, Captain Hetten, will you agree to what I'm going to propose?—we will keep quiet about the phony Distinguished Service Cross and, by the way, the Silver Star, and allow the medals to go through channels without trying to stop them. Your part of the bargain will be to forget about this ambush and allow for the team members to transfer out of your command without any black marks following them."

Hetten saw his opening and grinned, "I'll go along with you, Bourne, but under one condition: the sergeants are free . . . but I want you!"

Paul smiled.

"The lieutenant goes free, too!" Braverman raised his AK-47.

"I'll forget the ambush, Bourne, but don't forget—I write your efficiency report." Hetten knew Bourne wouldn't commit murder, and that he wouldn't allow the sergeants to either.

Sergeant Braverman pushed off the safety selector switch on the communist weapon. Paul put his hand on the barrel and gently pushed it down. The lives of his men meant a lot to Paul, much more than his own career in the military.

"It's a deal." Paul felt sick to his stomach. He motioned for the sergeants to head back to camp.

Paul waited until the two officers were alone on the canal bank and then spoke to the captain. "Hetten, do you really want the DSC that bad?"

Hetten didn't look at the lieutenant. "I have a career to look out for, Lieutenant. You have never been a part of the peacetime army—I have." Hetten's face showed no signs of guilt. "If your numbers haven't been punched in war, you can hang up seeing stars on your shoulders . . . even eagles."

What about respect from your men? Does that mean anything to you? Paul thought. He was beginning to get so frustrated in his attempt to reason with Hetten that he felt like crying. "What about your own pride? Service to your Nation? . . . Don't you think the survival of the Nation is more important than one single man's career?"

Hetten's head turned from looking out over the water and his eyes locked on Paul's. The captain's face reflected no remorse, only hate for the lieutenant. "Sure, Lieutenant . . . if it's not mine."

Chapter 11

Captain Hetten and Lieutenant Bourne hurried toward the jeep parked near the C-Team helipad. Paul slipped onto the rear seat as the driver started moving the vehicle away from the dust cloud created by the landing helicopter.

"The colonel wants to see you ASAP." The driver seemed very uptight and uncomfortable talking to the two officers. The sergeant slowed the vehicle down to negotiate around a screen of barbed wire, and then he floored the gas pedal for a couple hundred feet, braking to a jerky halt when they reached the main compound gate. The guard waved them through without getting up from his seat in the shade from a low building.

Lieutenant Colonel Bakersun was standing in the hallway when Hetten and Bourne entered the headquarters building.

"Lieutenant Bourne, wait in the S-1's office until I call for you." Bakersun's voice was sharp. He turned to face the captain. "Did you bring the sworn statements with you?"

"Yes, sir." Hetten was smiling.

Lieutenant Bourne went through the open office area to the narrow hallway that led to a dead-end door marked with the adjutant's name in black lettering. He wondered as he walked what Hetten and the colonel were having a private meeting about, and what he had meant when he mentioned getting signed statements.

"The colonel told me to wait in your office, sir."

Major Cragmore raised his eyes over the top of the paper he was reading from and held out his hand. "Hello, Bourne. It's been a long time."

"I haven't seen you since you were promoted to major. Congratulations!"

"Thanks!" Major Cragmore motioned to Paul with his head. "Let's go in the back, I've got a good bottle of bourbon stashed away."

Paul noticed that all of the clerks had stopped typing when he had entered the major's office and were listening to what was being said between the two officers. Paul closed the door to the major's private quarters, which were attached to the building, and dropped into the soft lounge chair. The major fixed two stiff drinks with ice cubes and handed Paul one of them.

"Sir, do you know what the colonel wants to talk to me about?"

"You don't know yet?" Cragmore didn't try to conceal his surprise. "Hell! Every clerk in the compound knows why you were brought back here!"

"Knows what?"

"Well . . . I had better let the colonel tell you, seeing that Captain Hetten hasn't mentioned anything." Cragmore looked quickly down at the floor. "I still have to work here . . ." He looked back up at Paul's questioning eyes. "What in the hell did you do to piss Hetten off so damn bad?"

"You should know what kind of officer he is. . . . He was the S-1 here before you," Paul reined in the frustration he was beginning to feel and spoke slower. He was on Hetten's old stomping grounds, and he had to be careful what he said—and to who he said it.

"Captain Hetten and I aren't exactly friends." Cragmore threw his head back against the chair. He stared at the young lieutenant and wondered if Hetten had been telling the truth when he had briefed the colonel.

Paul changed the subject. "Sir, what do you know about Lieutenant Vainbane?"

"Vainbane!" Cragmore grinned, "he's out of the same mold as Hetten. Hell, when Vainbane reported in here, he was carrying his own paperwork for a Medal of Honor recommendation—for *himself*!" Cragmore sat up in his chair. "It really cracked me up. He said that his old team leader might lose the documents, so he personally hand carried them here. I'll say one thing—if he did what those papers said he did, then he's one hell of a super soldier!" Cragmore smiled a knowing grin. "The only problem is, he is the only American who's written a statement. All the rest are Vietnamese strikers."

"What you're saying, in effect, is that he's recommended himself for the Big One?" Paul shook his head in disbelief. "How in the hell can the guy even try to pull that off?"

"His commanding officer signed off on it." Cragmore swallowed his laughter with a sip from his bourbon. "So I'm forced to process the paperwork."

"Are you sure his commander signed the document?" Paul spoke softly. A month ago, he wouldn't have believed that something like that could happen; today, he wasn't sure.

"Maybe we had better check and see if the colonel is ready to see you." Cragmore stood and motioned for Paul to remain sitting, "You wait here." He wiped the back of his mouth with his hand and left the room.

Paul leaned back in the soft chair and enjoyed the

luxury. He wondered if he should just give in and agree with whatever Hetten had said or if he should try and explain what had been going on at My An. He knew that a second lieutenant didn't have a chance standing up against a captain, especially a commander. Paul frowned. It seemed as if nobody cared if they *won* a fight with the enemy; the awards afterward seemed to be the name of the game in Vietnam. Paul became angry over the thought. Someone had to stand up to the Hettens in Special Forces units.

Major Cragmore entered the room wearing a coat of white around his jaws where his teeth were locked together. He was controlling a great deal of anger. "Paul, the colonel wants to see you now. Just be very careful what you say."

"Thanks for the drink and the conversation." Paul adjusted his pants legs at the tops of his jungle boots.

The clerks stopped typing when he walked through the outer office, and then almost simultaneously began banging away at the typewriter keys as Paul approached the colonel's office door. Paul realized that something was very wrong and knocked cautiously on the closed door.

"Come in!"

Paul glanced back over his shoulder and saw that all of the clerks were watching him as they typed. Major Cragmore was leaning against his door frame watching with a tight smile on his face. He looked more sad than content.

Paul faced the grizzled senior colonel. "Lieutenant Bourne reporting as ordered, sir."

"Shut your damn mouth, Lieutenant!" The colonel's voice penetrated through the thin walls of the office back out into the clerk area. "You're the sorriest example of a lieutenant that I have ever ran across in my thirty years in the army! You are one fucking *sorry* officer!" Colonel Bakersun's face was red with rage. "I can't believe that a Special Forces officer would do what Sergeant Dryman stated in his affadavit!" Bakersun stood and slammed the paper in his hand down onto his wooden desk. "And you're a damn officer!"

Hetten sat in a high-backed chair on the far side of the large room. A sick smile was pasted on his face. He was enjoying every minute of the colonel's conversation and every second of his rage that was directed at the lieutenant.

Paul frowned. "Sir, what are you talking about?"

The colonel lowered his voice and struggled for control of his surging emotions. "Sergeant Dryman's sworn statement concerning your conduct during the Easter Eve fire-fight at My An." Bakersun wiped the sweat off his forehead with the back of his fatigue jacket sleeve. "How in the hell could you just run off and leave him to fight alone during the Easter Eve attack against My An? How? *How!* And you're supposed to be a damn leader! A commissioned officer!" The glare in the colonel's eyes changed from pleading for an answer to steel. "You are a damn coward!"

The colonel's words cut into Paul deeper than any whip. "Sir! I am *not* a coward!" He looked over at Hetten and saw the look of triumph written on the captain's face.

"*I say you're a damn coward!*" The door shook from the colonel's fist smashing down on the desk. "There's a plane leaving this camp for Nha Trang in an hour. You have your worthless ass on it or I'll have you fucking shot! This unit has *never* had an officer even suspected of cowardice in combat, and I'm not going to mark that record with the likes of you! The only thing that's saving your ass, Lieutenant, is the memory of the good Special Forces men who've died—and Captain Hetten, who begged me not to use you as an example and give his camp a bad name! Consider yourself very lucky!"

"Sir—"

"Don't you sir me! Take that beret off your head and get the hell out of my office!" The colonel waved his hand at the lieutenant in disgust. "And don't let the door hit your ass on the way out!"

Lieutenant Bourne caught a swift glance at Hetten when he saluted and turned to leave. Captain Hetten looked like a contented Cheshire cat.

Paul kept his eyes on the exit as he walked the long gauntlet of wide-eyed clerks.

Hetten had won.

Lieutenant Bourne pushed both of the swinging doors open with his palms and left the C-Team headquarters building without looking back over his shoulder.

Major Cragmore, along with all of his clerks, watched the lieutenant walk down the narrow dirt road toward the officer's quarters. The colonel's voice had carried through most of the building during the conversation with Bourne, leaving nothing to the imagination of the clerks. Major Cragmore slowly shook his head from side to side with the realization that the lieutenant had been dismissed from his A-Team for cowardice. The word would be spread, via the grapevine, to all of the operational detachments before the end of the week. The lieutenant's reputation would be destroyed. The major stood and walked across the office floor holding Bourne's green personnel data card close against his chest. He stopped and scanned the information listed on the personnel form until he reached the section containing the man's awards and decorations.

Captain Hetten stopped in front of the major's open

door; he was smiling viciously, still enjoying the aftereffects of his victory over Bourne. Hetten felt very secure.

"Hi, sir!" Hetten leaned up against the door frame. "How's the new job coming along?"

Cragmore raised his eyes from Bourne's personnel record and folded the document without moving his head. "I want you to take a look at this, Hetten." He handed the green file to the captain. "I hope you're happy, branding a Distinguished Service Cross winner a coward!"

Hetten couldn't hide the surprise expressed on his face. "He won a DSC?"

"If you would have taken the time to have checked your peoples' files when you were the administrative officer for this detachment, you would have seen that you were given a lot of first-rate soldiers for your A-Camp . . . A blue-ribbon team!" Cragmore yanked Bourne's personnel card out of Hetten's hand. "You fucking disgust me! Get out of my office!"

Hetten slid sideways away from the angry major and looked back over his shoulder wearing a sly grin that covered half of his face. "You didn't have that whimpering *coward* under your command, Major!"

"Get out!" Cragmore kicked his office door shut, barely missing Hetten's hand on the door frame.

Cragmore waited in his dark office until his temper had cooled off before he went out into the central office and called his clerks over to him. He motioned for them to form a circle around him.

"Men . . . I can't force you to keep quiet about what has gone on here today . . . but before any of you take part in spreading anything about Lieutenant Bourne around the headquarters . . . I want you to review his personnel file . . ." The major slowly looked into each of the eyes watching him as he continued. "He's one of the most decorated soldiers in Special Forces; a DSC . . . two Silver Stars . . . two Purple Hearts for wounds in combat. . . . I'd say before any more damage is done to the lieutenant by spreading half-assed rumors, that we had better wait and see what really is true and what isn't. . . . I want all of you to remember, especially those of you who worked for Captain Hetten when he ran this shop, that we have only heard one side of the story so far . . ."

The major stopped talking when he saw his clerks nodding their heads in approval and murmuring to each other about Hetten.

Paul went to his room in the visiting officer's quarters where he had hastily dropped off his B-4 bag that contained all of his private possessions; his mind still reeled from the shock he had received back in the colonel's office. Paul dropped down on the steel springs of the bunk bed and leaned back against his B-4 bag. He couldn't begin to accept the fact that the C-Team commander had openly accused him of the worst crime a Special Forces soldier could commit—cowardice in the face of the enemy. He had really underestimated the extent to which Hetten and Dryman were willing to go to. Sergeant Dryman's shame over what he had done during the Easter Eve fight must have been so great that his mind was rationalizing all of the blame for his acts onto the lieutenant. And Paul couldn't defend himself, because he had pledged to remain quiet to protect the team sergeants who had participated in the ambush and attempted murder of Hetten. Paul smiled to himself, knowing that he was trapped in a well-laid snare by Hetten and Dryman; he gave the son of a bitch credit for being able to trap him.

Paul pulled his old, well-worn Ranger cap from the

bottom of his bag and slapped the faded fabric against his leg a couple of times in order to re-shape it. He removed his green beret and rolled it carefully before tucking it into one of his spare boots and rezipping his B-4 bag. A surge of black despair surged through him, forcing him to collapse on the cot. The cold barrel of his CAR-15 pushed against his cheek. He spent a couple of seconds thinking about Hetten. Should he kill him before leaving the C-Team? Paul knew that he would probably end up saving a lot of people's lives if he did end the miserable bastard's life. Paul frowned, knowing it would be so damn easy to do. He envisioned tearing Hetten's throat out using his own teeth. Paul could taste the salty blood and swallowed. A smile crossed the lieutenant's face. He knew that killing Hetten would not prove anything and would probably end up making Hetten look right. Paul decided that he would let his own record stand up for him. He would wait, and when the time was right, he would make Hetten pay dearly for what he had done to him.

Major Cragmore ran down the main road through the center of camp to the helicopter that Paul was about to load up onto for his trip to Nha Trang.

"Bourne!"

Paul didn't turn to face the caller, but kept walking.

Bourne!" Cragmore reached the aircraft just as Paul started to strap himself into the seat. Cragmore placed his hand on Paul's arm, trying to draw his attention. "I'll get with Sergeant Braverman and clear this misunderstanding up! Lieutenant Bourne . . . don't take any stock in the colonel's charge!" The major couldn't force himself to use the word coward.

The helicopter crew-chief motioned for Cragmore to stand clear as the turbine engine gained RPMs for takeoff.

Paul turned his head to face the major. Tears streamed down his cheeks unchecked. Major Cragmore's mouth opened, but there were no words passing his lips. The red clay dust that covered everything in the C-Team headquarters had coated the lieutenant's face, and the tears of anger had mixed with the red dust. The effect was scary. It looked as if Lieutenant Bourne were crying blood.

Chapter 12

Lieutenant Vainbane stood on the wooden boat-dock and smiled as he drew in a lungful of dew-laden early morning air. He was now the unchallenged executive officer at My An Special Forces camp, and he planned on showing Captain Hetten what a loyal second-in-command could do. Lieutenant Bourne had been too close to the enlisted men and Hoa-Hoa commandos for the good of the camp's mission as far as Vainbane was concerned; after all, how could you lead men in combat if they were your friends?

Vainbane's thoughts were interrupted when the swirling ground fog parted and Sergeant McGrath, followed closely by Lieutenant Bourne's old radio operator, Ro-Den, appeared from behind the tall berm.

"Did you inspect the patrol yet?" Vainbane's tone of voice was patronizing and almost insulting. Next to Sergeant Braverman, McGrath was the most loyal to Lieutenant Bourne.

"As best as I could. . . ." McGrath looked both ways, up and down the canal. The fog was thick, allowing for only a few feet of visibility. He could barely make out the dark green vegetation marking the far bank of the canal twenty-five meters away. "We should wait until this fog burns off before we leave camp and walk into an ambush."

"What!? And waste three hours?" Vainbane frowned at the young sergeant.

"Lieutenant Bourne never had any problems finding the Viet Cong . . . during the day . . . or for that matter at night . . . but he always *picked* the time to meet them. . . ."

"Fuck Bourne!" Vainbane hissed the words. "I'm the XO of My An now, and if you're half-smart, Sergeant . . . you'll stop referring to Bourne."

Sergeant McGrath looked back over his shoulder and located Sergeant Loau squatting next to the berm near a line of battle-ready commandos. McGrath nodded his head and Loau motioned for the column to follow him.

"Do you want to cross the canal now?" McGrath kept his eyes averted. He was never very good at hiding his emotions, especially the contempt he felt for Vainbane and Hetten.

"Yes. By the time we get to the other side and organized, it'll be full daylight, and the fog should be pretty well gone by then." Vainbane stepped over to the nearest olive-drab fiberglass boat and untied it from its mooring. "I'll go over in the first boat."

McGrath spoke before he thought. "That's a brave thing to do. . . ."

Vainbane turned and glared at the sergeant. "Listen, goddamn you! I haven't been thrown out of an A-Camp for cowardice!" Vainbane pointed his finger at the sergeant's chest and continued, ". . . but your buddy-buddy lieutenant has!"

"That remains to be *proven* . . . sir."

Vainbane stepped into the boat without answering and motioned for the first boatload of commandos to join him. The ride across the canal only took a few seconds and was almost a time-consuming hassle—except for the comfort of knowing the canal was a natural barrier that protected the camp from a ground attack along that perimeter.

Sergeant McGrath rode in the last boat over to the day patrol's location. He was visibly relieved. The heavy ground fog could easily have hidden a large enemy force, and once the Americans were separated, half on each side of the canal, it would have been very easy for the enemy to kill the trapped commandos on the far bank.

Vainbane's attitude had changed, and he was almost friendly toward McGrath when he spoke. "Sergeant, you travel with Sergeant Loau behind the point squad. I'll be traveling between the platoons so that I can control both of them."

McGrath nodded and beckoned for Loau to join him. He enjoyed controlling the lead element of a patrol more than being with the command element. Action was normally at the point. McGrath nodded at Loau and racked a round into the chamber of his CAR-15 submachine gun. The rest of the patrol followed suit. The ritual marked the beginning of a combat patrol, where talking was forbidden along with smoking and the making of unnecessary noise. Lieutenant Bourne had taught him that small trick, and it worked very effectively with the troops. It signaled the beginning of a war patrol.

Captain Hetten stood up from his squatting position next to the bunker. He had been squatting next to the fighting bunker and eavesdropping on the conversation between Vainbane and McGrath. He was pleased with his new executive officer. The heavy fog had chilled the captain and he shivered, thinking that a hot cup of coffee would hit the spot.

The two-platoon patrol moved slowly during the early morning hours along the canal checking for booby traps. By eleven o'clock the sun had burned off most of the fog, leaving only small pockets along the borders of the treelines that marked the rice paddies. The south side of the canal was much different than the north side where the A-Camp had been built. To the north the rice paddies were huge, over a thousand meters across; while due to the swamps and streams that meandered through the southern marshes, the rice paddies to the south were much smaller.

The patrol reached a major canal junction almost exactly at noon. McGrath felt that it would be a good time for a break so that the men could eat and rest awhile before they tackled the longer, southern leg of their patrol. He whispered in Loau's ear for the men to take up a defense position tucked into the ninety-degree corner of the canals, and then he walked back down the patrol to meet with Vainbane.

"I think we should break here for lunch before heading south," McGrath whispered close to Vainbane's ear, and guided the lieutenant to the edge of the trees by placing his hand on his shoulder. Both men squatted down and looked out over the abandoned rice paddy. The owners of the field must have been killed, or perhaps the VC-controlled area prevented them from working the small field. The canal intersection formed a cross lined on both sides by a thick border of vegetation composed of thick layers of trees and jungle plants. The treelines could hide anything in them, but they were, at the most, only fifty meters wide, and always concealed a wide path bordering the water. McGrath looked across the narrow strip of paddy and frowned when he saw another treeline less than a hundred meters away. The map had shown a stream wandering through the paddies, but he hadn't figured that it joined the canal this close to the junction. The unsecured treeline so close to their location made McGrath nervous. "We had better send a squad along the canal and check out that treeline before we make ourselves too comfortable." McGrath pointed.

"Fuck it!" Vainbane was hungry and tired. "We haven't even seen a footprint . . . not even a single old booby trap. . . . There aren't any VC around here."

"That or . . . or they haven't put out any booby traps because *they* use these trails regularly at night." McGrath kept his eyes on the opposing treeline. He couldn't take his mind off it. The darkness behind the bright green sunlit trees seemed sinister. He thought about what Lieutenant Bourne would do in the same situation.

"Listen . . . we're safe here . . . they would be dumb shits to try and attack us across that open paddy . . . *if* they were over there. . . ."

McGrath nodded in agreement. The two light machine guns they had with them could decimate even a battalion trying to cross the open ground between them. There were only clumps of wild rice growing in the untilled soil. And an inch of muddy rain water covered the plate-flat field, which would also act as a deterrent to anyone who thought of attacking the sixty-three-man patrol. McGrath positioned the two machine guns facing the open ground before he joined Sergeant Loau and Vainbane for a C-ration lunch.

Private Ro-Den sat near Lieutentant Vainbane, cleaning the outside of the PRC-25 radio he carried for the lieutenant. Ro-Den had liked Lieutenant Bourne much better than the new lieutenant, but the teenager was loyal to his job as a radio operator, and whoever was in command could totally depend on him. Ro-Den removed an oily rag from the side pocket of his rucksack and wiped down the sides of the radio while he waited for the command party to finish eating.

Vainbane smashed the empty C-ration can with his heel and turned to where Ro-Den sat waiting.

"Ro-Den! Bring the radio here."

The boy was handing the lieutenant the handset before the officer finished talking to him.

"Rimmed Tire Six. . . . . Rimmed Tire Five . . . over."

The answer came almost instantly, "Tire Six . . . over."

"This is Tire Five . . . we've reached our first objective and will be traveling due south from here. . . . We haven't even seen a footprint so far . . . this area is clean . . . over." The radio faded out and hissed with a soft background static. Vainbane looked at Ro-Den and spoke, "The battery is going in this thing . . . change it as soon as I've finished."

"Tire Six. . . . you're doing a good job, Five . . . continue your patrol and try and make it back to this location before dark. I want you in camp tonight . . . over."

"Tire Five . . . . that should be no problem. . . ."

The transmission faded out and then came back in weakly, Vainbane continued talking, ". . . we've rested up and should be able to travel fast throughout the afternoon—"

Vainbane stopped talking. The words stuck in his mouth. He had been sitting with his back up against a small tree and looking out across the small rice paddy, his eyes scanning the strip of dark green foliage a hundred meters from where he was. Three black-clad Viet Cong, one holding the barrel of a .51-caliber machine gun, stood with their backs to Vainbane. One of the VC dropped down on one knee, reached up for the barrel, and began sliding it into the other portion of the heavy weapon.

"Jesus! . . . Holy shit! . . ." Vainbane spoke over the radio that he held in his hand. McGrath turned and looked to where the lieutenant was pointing with his free hand. The sergeant saw the enemy at the same time Loau did. Both of them grabbed their gear and ran to where the commandos were waiting. Loau went to command the First Platoon and McGrath ran bent-over to the Second Platoon, which held the canal junction position.

"What's going on?" Hetten's voice brought the lieutenant out of his shock. So far, only ten seconds had passed from the time he had spotted the enemy.

"Fucking VC! . . . . they're setting up a .51 . . . less than a hundred meters from us . . ."

"I want it! Bring me back that damn weapon and I'll give you a Silver Star!" Hetten screamed into the handset.

"Yes, Sir!" Vainbane threw the handset at Ro-Den and grabbed his weapon, ignoring his backpack. He paused only long enough to scream an order to Ro-Den, "Change that damn battery before you catch up!"

Ro-Den looked puzzled at the lieutenant, but obeyed. He untied the canvas straps on his rucksack and removed the spare battery.

Lieutenant Vainbane broke through the brush and stepped out into the rice paddy. The shallow water covered the tops of his jungle boots. He paused only long enough to scream back over his shoulder, *"Follow me! . . . . . Attack!"*

McGrath couldn't believe his eyes. He watched the lieutenant slip and fall down on one knee and then get up again. He squatted and emptied a magazine from his CAR-15 at the three VC, who immediately abandoned the .51-caliber machine gun. McGrath could see the black barrel and the front wheels of the prized weapon.

Vainbane paused again and screamed back over his shoulder, *"God damn you . . . . Charge!"*

Neither Loau nor McGrath were cowards. They obeyed. A compact line of commandos broke away from the treeline that protected them and ran as fast as they could toward the waiting trees that would protect them again. McGrath kept his eyes locked on the security of the closing trees.

Ro-Den had been left alone in the trees bordering the canal with his radio. He hurried to snap the bottom half of his radio with the fresh battery in it to the top half and join the lieutenant. He was mad because he had been left behind. His position was with the commander. In his haste, Ro-Den dropped the battery case in the dirt. He cussed, pulled the new battery back out of the container, and started cleaning the particles of dirt off the electrical connectors. He swore again, knowing that he would not be able to catch up to the lieutenant until after he had reached the .51-caliber machine gun. The lieutenant would be very mad at him, but he had to make sure the radio worked when he got there, so he began cleaning the dirty parts.

Sergeant McGrath ran in front of his attacking commandos, trying to catch up to Lieutenant Vainbane who was almost to the machine gun the VC had abandoned. Vainbane entered the shade of the treeline fifty meters ahead of McGrath.

The commandos were at the halfway point between the treelines and started slowing down. Two of them sensed the danger and dropped down in the mud.

The three concealed .51-caliber machine guns opened fire simultaneously on the order of their commander.

McGrath didn't even hear the first rounds fired. One of the enemy gunners had been tracking his approach in his sights, and the first rounds from his heavy weapon hit McGrath in the face. The sergeant's body crumpled to the ground without a head. Loau survived just long enough to realize that they had fallen into a trap. He told himself that he knew better as the steel-cased bullets smashed through the soft mud and tore his body apart.

Ro-Den had flattened against the ground at the first crack of weapon fire. He looked up from the ground and watched the massacre. Bodies bounced in the water from the powerful thumb-sized bullets tearing into them. After ten seconds there were only a handful of commandos left alive. One of them stumbled to his feet, screamed the Hoa-Hoa war cry, and charged directly into the green machine-gun tracers merging in front of him. His body danced from the two streams of projectiles hitting him from different angles before it dropped torn to the muddy water.

Lieutenant Vainbane turned away from the prized weapon at his feet and looked back at the destruction of his patrol taking place in the untilled rice paddy behind him. It was too early for shock and fear to set in. He looked surprised. A sound coming from his rear forced him to turn, and he saw the three Viet Cong, who had earlier ran, coming back. What Vainbane saw that registered first in his mind was the smiles on their faces, and then the full impact hit him.

Ro-Den watched the muddy water in the rice paddy turn red and then pink. Sixty-one bodies lay scattered in the water.

Lieutenant Vainbane stumbled out of the treeline and started running back toward the safety of the canal. He dropped his submachine gun in the water and swung his arms trying to gain speed. Ro-Den watched as three Viet Cong ran behind the American, laughing as they closed the gap between them and the lieutenant. A group of black-clad VC stepped out from the treeline and watched the chase. Twenty-five meters before Vainbane reached the trees, the first VC caught up to him and jumped on his shoulders, bringing him down face-first in the muddy water.

The lack of fire from the side of the paddy where Ro-Den lay in hiding reassured the Viet Cong that they had killed all of the patrol, and they stepped from their hiding places to watch their comrades capture the American. The Viet Cong who had knocked Lieutenant Vainbane down pulled the lieutenant up on his knees and forced him to stay in that position. The VC held up one arm in victory and screamed a war cry.

Vainbane looked up at his five-foot, five-inch captor in shocked disbelief.

A party of VC wearing black uniforms with tan pith helmets left the treeline and waded through the water to where Vainbane was, followed by a dozen VC who began policing the battlefield for weapons and souvenirs. One of the VC removed a French pistol from a holster at his side and placed the barrel up against Vainbane's head. He smiled, exposing a set of perfectly white teeth.

Vainbane began crying.

The Viet Cong leader laughed and replaced his pistol. He pointed to the treeline where Ro-Den lay hidden and gave a rapid set of orders. Ro-Den could make out most of the words and realized that the area he was in would soon be swarming with Viet Cong searching for any survivors.

Ro-Den dragged his pack and the PRC-25 radio down to the edge of the canal. He shoved the radio into the muddy water and watched it sink, followed by his pack filled with cans of C-rations. Voices came from the treeline in whispers as the VC cautiously entered the shady cover. Ro-Den slipped naked into the water and let the strong tidal current pull him toward the A-Camp. The boy flattened out on the water and started doing a slow breast-stroke, using his legs and arms as rudders to keep him under the overhanging shrubs and brush. He ducked underwater to miss large branches and very thick clumps of brush that might harbor snakes. Ro-Den's teenage mind thought only of survival, and did not dwell on the massacre he had witnessed.

Captain Hetten held the handset tightly in his fist and yelled into the mouthpiece, ". . . *Damn it! Answer me! . . . . What's going on out there!*"

BOOK TWO

Chapter 13

Ro-Den breaststroked in the dark brown water, holding his head above the surface. The canal was subjected to the strong tidal currents found in the waterways of the southern Delta region of Vietnam. Ro-Den realized his good fortune in finding the current flowing back toward the American A-Camp.

The muffled sound of an A-47 disrupted the stillness occasionally when a Viet Cong soldier performed a coup de grace on one of the wounded Special Forces commandos lying in the open rice paddy a mile upstream from where Ro-Den swam. The boy winced each time he heard the sound. He had been a commando since he was ten years old and had worked hard to become a radio operator for the Americans. Ro-Den though about the radio he had sunk in the canal and felt like crying. What would he tell the American captain when he returned to the A-Camp without his radio? Shame made the boy duck his face under the water. He swam a half-dozen strokes feeling the cool liquid wash the tears from his cheeks, and felt better. A Hoa-Hoa warrior did not cry, not even a fourteen-year-old one.

The distance along the canal from where the patrol had been ambushed to the A-Camp was about ten miles, maybe a little less. Ro-Den remembered Lieutenant Bourne telling Sergeant Loau that from the canal intersection where the A-Camp was built, to the main intersection where Lieutenant Vainbane's patrol had just been massacred, all sixty-one men, was twelve thousand meters. Ro-Den felt like crying again when he thought about Sergeant Loau lying dead in the muddy rice field. Lieutenant Bourne had always warned the other Americans about that junction in the canal system surrounding the A-Camp. Lieutenant Vainbane and Captain Hetten had never really believed the young American, and now one of them had paid for that mistake. Ro-Den nodded his head as he swam. They would listen to Lieutenant Bourne now.

The boy's eyes constantly scanned the near bank of the canal as he swam downstream. He let the strong current push him along, but he stroked occasionally to maintain his position

Ro-Den saw the snake's head appear from the thick grass at the same time the reticulated python saw the boy. Five feet of the snake was already in the canal when Ro-Den collided with the reptile. The boy could feel the cold skin of the snake rub against his legs and then across his bare stomach. Ro-Den kicked out at the ten-foot python and cursed the snake under his breath. The wedge-shaped head of the snake jerked from side to side as it thrashed its coils, trying to disengage and get away from the human. The instant the boy and the snake had seen each other they had both known that there was no threat to either of them. The boy was too big to eat and the python was almost a protected species in the Delta of South Vietnam. The villagers allowed the snakes to live in the fields and eat rodents. Only when the pythons reached a length where they threatened small children were they killed. A ten-foot snake was no threat to the boy.

Ro-Den smelled the camp before he saw the smoke

coming from the cookhouse. He left the safety of the underbrush near the far bank and eased himself out into the center of the canal, so that he could be seen by the camp guards and not be mistaken as a Viet Cong spy. The boy floated on top of the water and guided himself over to the boat docks that had been built by the Americans. A party of guards was standing around Captain Hetten on the dock when Ro-Den grabbed one of the loose pilings and pulled himself from the water with the grace of an otter. The boy had been raised swimming in the canals, and the float downstream had been easier for him than walking the same distance.

Captain Hetten glared at the naked boy, not knowing what to ask him. Ro-Den flicked the hair out of his eyes and sent a volley of water pellets against Hetten's pressed fatigue jacket. The boy watched as the water drops spread out in the dry cloth and thought about witnessing spots spreading out on fatigue jackets, but instead of water, they were blood spots.

Hetten ground his teeth and spoke. "What in the fuck is going on?"

Ro-Den understood more English than he spoke, but the question didn't make any sense to him and he shrugged his shoulders.

"Damn it, boy! Answer me! . . ." Hetten grabbed the young commando by his shoulders and shook him.

Ro-Den twisted free from the man and looked at one of the guards, who was his uncle. The older commando removed his M-16 from his shoulder and stood ready. If the American tried hurting the boy, he would kill him.

Ro-Den spoke to his uncle in Vietnamese, telling him of the massacre upstream. The older commando groaned and turned to inform the rest of the camp about the deaths of their friends and relatives. A patrol had to be assembled immediately to go get the bodies.

Hetten watched as the camp became a fury of activity, not understanding what was going on. He turned back to the boy, who still stood on the dock, and tried smiling before he spoke. "Ugghh . . . boy . . . what happened? Where is Lieutenant?"

Ro-Den understood the question. "All dead . . ."

"What!" Hetten gasped and felt fear at the same time.

"All zapped . . . VC kill . . . ambush."

Lieutenant Bourne opened his eyes slowly and then let them ease shut again. He felt the soft comforting vibration of the jet engines coming through the seat cushions and allowed his mind to drift back into a restful state of wandering thoughts.

Paul had enjoyed the five days of R & R in Australia a great deal more than he wanted to admit. The events that had taken place at My An Special Forces Camp and the C-Team at Can To had drained him of just about all his emotional reserves. Captain Hetten had plotted well with his followers, and had won the first round—on the surface. He still couldn't believe that he had been relieved as executive officer of the team for cowardice in the face of the enemy. The thoughts running through his mind about the incident forced Paul to open his eyes. He pushed the shade back on the window and looked down at the water thousands of feet below. Anger flashed through his mind, and thoughts of violent revenge filled every fiber in his body. Paul had no way of knowing that, at exactly the same moment he was looking down at the ocean below him, Sergeant McGrath was dying along with two platoons of Hoa-Hoa commandos. Paul felt a sudden chill traverse his spine, and he reached up to screw shut the air-conditioner vent above his head.

The whitecapped South China Sea gave way to a dark green landscape to the west of the aircraft. The coast of South Vietnam drew closer to the banking aircraft. Paul looked over the back of his seat at the row of faces staring out the window. It didn't take much imagination to guess what most of the returning soldiers were thinking about. Paul's mind was occupied with the same thoughts: Would he return from this landing in Vietnam alive, or in a cold steel coffin?

Paul reached over and yanked the window shade shut. He forced himself to think about happier thoughts and the good times he just had in Australia. A friend he had made, who was serving with the Australian SAS unit in Vietnam, had given him the address of his family at Kingscote on the island of Kangaroo, located in the Indian Ocean south of Adelaide, South Australia. Paul had taken a great risk leaving the R & R port of Sydney and flying to the island. His R & R pass had been only good for the large capital city, and travel around Australia without permission was forbidden. But he had taken the risk and had enjoyed the freedom from the military tremendously, especially after leaving My An.

Paul thought of his Australian friend's female cousin. He had told Paul that she was cute, but when Paul had seen her sitting in the dust-covered Land Rover, he had nearly embarrassed himself by busting the steel buttons on his Levis. She was a red-blonde with a smile that forced you to smile back at her. The loose bush jacket she had worn was solely to keep the sun off her well-tanned shoulders. She had had on a tight black swimsuit under the long jacket.

The three days and nights they had spent together on the very private beaches of the island were etched forever in Paul's mind. People dreamed of just one night in their lifetimes like the ones he spent swimming and making slow love on the beach. The second day, Paul had asked her to take him out to the small islands and do some scuba diving with him. She had laughed, and told him that first they would go on a little boat cruise. They had boarded a fifty-foot oceangoing craft that belonged to a friend of hers and headed out to the small rock outcroppings that surrounded the larger island. The boat captain kept his craft well away from the sharp rocks hidden under the breakers, but they had gotten in close enough for Paul to learn why she had laughed when he had said he wanted to go scuba diving off the small islands. Seals covered most of the rocks and cruising off the sanctuaries were white sharks hunting in large numbers. She had told Paul that Kangaroo Island was famous for the record-breaking white sharks taken off the coast. Scuba diving around the island when the seals were there in large numbers was the best way to commit suicide in Australia.

The jet hit a small pocket of turbulence and brought Paul out of his personal thoughts. He felt the solid erection pressing against his pants and adjusted the light blanket on his lap to hide it. He thought that maybe he should have made love to his Australian girl just one more time before he had left, but grinned; they had made love five times during the last four hours he was on the island. He was sore.

The wheel wells on the aircraft opened, and the loud hum from the motors that lowered the landing gear alerted Paul that they were about to land in Saigon. He sat up in his seat and adjusted the seatback for landing. A sigh slipped out of Paul's mouth. The war would be very real again, very soon. He knew the colonel who commanded the Special Forces group in Nha Trang, but he had already decided that he was going to leave Special Forces and get back in a regular line unit.

Captain Hetten had cured him of serving on an A-Team again. The only way he would ever go back to an A-Team site was if he were the commander and could control the team. He had had his fill of glory-grabbers for a lifetime.

The smell of burnt jet fuel filled Paul's senses the second he stepped from the aircraft. A wall of heat and dust hit him in the face shortly thereafter; welcome to Saigon, the thought flashed across his mind. Paul gave a cock-sided grin and jauntily hopped down the steps to the waiting tarmac.

Chapter 14

The helicopter Paul was riding in was the daily courier flight between Saigon and Nha Trang. The flight was a fairly long one, lasting two hours. The chopper landed on the private pad behind the main Special Forces complex. Paul could see a clerk waiting to exchange courier pouches with the chopper's crew chief. Paul threw his B-4 bag out the door onto the PSP matting and jumped off the low-hovering helicopter without giving the pilot the customary thank-you wave. He walked around the building and headed directly across the large asphalt quadrangle toward the BOQ office.

A group of senior officers stepped out of the officer's club entrance located at the far corner of the large parade grounds just as Paul reached the sidewalk. Paul continued walking, without trying to identify any of the officers. He heard his name called and paused a second to look back over his shoulder. Paul wasn't in the mood to talk to any of the acquaintances that he had met in Special Forces.

"Get over here, Lieutenant!" The voice of a lieutenant colonel boomed over the open pavement.

Paul watched the senior officer jog toward him from the waiting group.

The officer stopped a few feet from Paul and grined,

"Didn't you hear him calling you?"

Lieutenant Bourne saw one of the officers wave for Paul to join him.

"That's the group commander, boy . . . get your ass moving!" The lieutenant colonel's voice was good-natured, but it irritated Paul nonetheless.

Paul gave the senior officer a glaring look and dropped his B-4 bag down on the sidewalk before he took off at an easy lope to join the commander where he waited. Later in the evening, the lieutenant colonel would tell one of his friends how he thought the young lieutenant was going to kill him with a look of pure hate emitting from the young man's eyes. He hadn't been far from the truth.

"Lieutenant Bourne, reporting, sir." Paul's eyes didn't focus on the colonel when he brought his salute straight down to his side, and he remained standing at attention. Paul wanted to get this uncomfortable meeting over with as quickly as possible and be on his way. He was getting really tired of senior officers yelling at him.

"Paul, what in the hell are you doing with that Ranger cap on your head?" The colonel held out his hand to shake hands with Paul, and when the lieutenant failed to respond he reached up and patted Paul's shoulder. "Why aren't you wearing your beret?"

Paul forced his eyes to focus. "Haven't you talked to Lieutenant Colonel Bakersun yet?" Paul had been expecting an ass-chewing or worse from the colonel. He figured that the C-Team commander would have talked to the group commander by now, especially since Paul had taken an R & R that had totaled seven days; five in Australia and two days travel.

"Hell, no . . . I've been up in I Corps for the past week inspecting our A-Camps along the Laotian border. . . . Why? Is there something Bakersun has to tell me about you?"

"Sir . . . you had better check your mail from Can To. . . . I think Bakersun has a message for you about me. . . ." Paul intentionally failed to address the colonel by his rank.

The group commander sensed something was going on that he didn't like. If there was one thing that really got under his skin, it was petty politics. He had warned all of his senior commanders that he wouldn't tolerate that kind of peacetime bullshit—especially when there was a war going on. "I don't know what in the hell is going on, Paul! But I have a feeling that something is really going to piss me off!"

That was the second time the group commander addressed Paul by his first name. The officers who had been standing quietly waiting for the senior officer to address the young lieutenant all realized that there was a special bond between the crusty old colonel and the lieutenant. The colonel rarely addressed one of his senior staff by their Christian names.

The group commander grabbed ahold of one of the brass handles on the headquarters door and flung it open. He called back over his shoulder as he stalked toward his adjutant's office, "Paul! wait for me in my S-1's office. . . ." The tone of the colonel's voice changed as he addressed his adjutant. "Major! Get me my dispatches from Can To!"

"Yes, sir!" The major rushed toward the message center.

Paul dropped emotionally exhausted onto the nearest chair the adjutant had lined up along his wall and waited for what he knew would be a very bad scene. He became absorbed in the details of a U.S. Army print hanging on the wall that depicted an Indian War scene. Paul liked the painting of the proud warriors riding their painted pinto ponies and carrying their wooden pole hoops.

The roar that came from the colonel's office filled the entire first floor of the building, ". . . and you get that dumb son of a bitch on the scrambler!"

The colonel's door flew open and the adjutant exited, heading down the hallway toward the operations center. The colonel followed close behind taking long strides and holding a yellow sheet of crumpled paper in his hand. "Paul! Get over here!"

Paul felt sorry for the adjutant, who was catching all kinds of hell for something that he had no part of, except he was the closest one to the colonel.

"Yes, sir." Paul followed the raging colonel into the cement bunker attached to the wooden office structure.

The older officer looked directly at Paul before he spoke. "Paul . . . what this letter states . . ." he waved the wrinkled paper in the air, ". . . is it true in any way . . . even slightly?"

Paul felt the day's accumulated anguish rolling in his stomach. "No . . . no, it's not."

The colonel stood up straight from the desk he had been leaning against. "Then take that hat off! You'll wear your beret until I tell you to stop!" His face was beet red when he turned and looked out of the small gunport-sized window. "I have never—never—in my career, seen a dumber group of sons of bitches assembled all together in one damn place than at Can To!" The colonel looked over at Paul. "You don't have to wait here. I'm going to talk to Bakersun on the scrambler. Why don't you go get something to eat and clean up. . . . Wait for me over at the officer's club." The colonel turned and vented his anger on the desktop with his fist. "Christ! I can't believe what he implied! And he took action without notifying me first!"

Lieutenant Bourne saluted and eased out of the colonel's sight. Paul knew that he couldn't push too hard, but he had the feeling that maybe things would work out. Hetten couldn't say anything if the group commander investigated the charges. Paul was almost out of the building when he sensed someone approaching him from behind. He turned quickly and nearly bumped into the lieutenant colonel who had jogged over to him earlier outside in the quadrangle.

"Lieutenant Bourne? I'm Lieutenant Colonel Clewell. I'm the commander up at Command and Control North. We launch out of Da Nang." He spoke of his organization with a lot of pride.

Paul recognized him and tried grinning. "I have a friend in your command—Lieutenant Jay Loveless." He sensed that the senior officer was very professional and re-evaluated him from their first encounter.

"Loveless is proving out to be one of my best team leaders." The colonel continued talking, but watched Paul's expression closely, "Would you like to join us?"

Paul didn't hesitate a second. "Yes, sir."

"Good! I'll see you up in Da Nang. I'll take care of getting the assignment approved with the colonel."

The conversation was brief, but carried in it a great many unspoken words of trust and professionalism as the two officers parted.

Paul waited at the officer's club for the colonel until eleven-thirty. He avoided having any conversations at the bar and even stayed away from the poker tables. He had found himself a very quiet corner and slowly became loose from the bourbon he was consuming. He finally stood, checked his watch again, and then decided to wander over to the headquarters building. The duty officer informed Paul that the colonel had been called to MACV headquarters for a conference with the commanding general. Paul took the written message that had been left for him at the desk and went to his room. He propped a couple of blue-striped pillows, without cases, up against the wall and lay down on his bunk. He opened the letter.

Lieutenant Bourne:
I am sorry, but I have been called to Saigon tonight and cannot personally talk with you. I spoke with LTC Bakersun and told him that I wanted *proof* of any action or charge. He has thirty days to produce or he will have to withdraw all charges and take action against Hetten. LTC Clewell saw me shortly after you had left my office. He wants you up at Da Nang. There aren't many officers who are better than him. The two of you should get along fine. Take all the time that you need to get yourself together and then report to his headquarters. Paul, have no fear for your future. I promise you that I will sort out this mess and get a pound of flesh!
Regards! GPH

Lieutenant Bourne folded the note and slid it into his jacket pocket. He zipped up his B-4 bag and left the building, walking in the dark toward the flight operations office on the attached airfield. A cargo flight was leaving for Da Nang in ten minutes. The duty officer gave Paul the tail number and pointed to where the aircraft was located on the line. Paul ran past the parked airplanes and hopped on the lowered rear ramp.

It was nearly four in the morning when Paul arrived at the front gate leading into the Command and Control North Headquarters. He could see the U.S. Marine guards standing in the distance on top of Marble Mountain. They looked like miniature men as they stood and stretched in the early morning light. The gate guard stopped Paul and asked for identification. Paul told him that he had just been assigned to CCN and asked for Lieutenant Colonel Clewell. The guard told Paul that the colonel was still at Nha Trang on business. Paul waited while the gate guard called the duty officer. Twenty minutes passed before a jeep came down the road bearing a young captain. Paul stood as the officer entered the guard shack.

"You say that you've been assigned to us?" The captain looked suspiciously at Paul. "I'm the personnel officer for the unit, and I haven't received any messages on your assignment . . . What's your name?"

"Lieutenant Paul Bourne, sir," Paul slung his CAR-15 across his shoulder by its canvas strap. "The decision to have me assigned here was made last night between Lieutenant Colonel Clewell and the group commander." Paul handed the captain the colonel's note, but he had folded it so that only the portion referring to his assignment could be read. "If you can show me a place to stay and point me in the direction of the mess hall, I could get fed and settled in before your commander returns."

The captain looked Paul up and down as he tried deciding what to do with him. The CCN compound was top secret, and entry was strictly controlled. "Hell, I guess it'll be all right as long as I stay with you." The captain led Paul to the jeep. "Throw your stuff in the back and get in." He held out his hand, "Welcome to SOG, Lieutenant."

"Thanks, sir, but what does SOG mean? I thought this was Command and Control North."

"Studies and Observation Group. The name changes all the time. I think they're calling us Studies and Observation Augmentation now. . . . Whatever, but we always refer to ourselves as SOG."

"Do you know where Lieutenant Loveless is living?"

"Sure, but he's out on a mission right now. Jay lives in the recon compound—he should be back today or late tomorrow. . . . It all depends on what they find or what finds them . . ." The captain left the comment open-ended.

"Can you show me where he's billeted. We're good friends."

"Sure, Jay's the team leader for RT Cobra. They're located over near the sea. Where do you know Jay from?"

"We went through OCS together." Paul heard the soft sound of waves breaking somewhere ahead of them and then caught a good whiff of salt water. "How close are we to the sea?"

"Hell! We own a mile of beach-front property!" The captain jerked the wheel and made a sharp turn next to a row of buildings. "Let me show you our little set-up." The jeep slowed down, but spun its way over a sand dune and stopped ten meters from the nearest hooch. The waves were breaking at six feet and rushing over the packed sand to touch the first rows of barbed wire on the perimeter.

"Man, is that beautiful!" Paul could feel his body automatically relaxing as the sound of the waves played a familiar rhythmic lullaby to his ears. It was perfect. He knew that he would enjoy this part of his assignment very much.

"They originally had planned on building the camp a mile from here on the far side of the highway. Someone used their heads and switched to the location here. It's a lot easier to defend with the sea to our backs, and at night there's a cool breeze that comes off the water." The captain eased in the clutch and slowly rolled back down the sand dune. "I like it here, myself. We have a lot of good times down on the beach. We've made agreements with the American units to our north and south, so that the beach is open during the day for a five-mile stretch. The units on the ends have run barbed wire out to sea that blocks off anyone from entering except from the water. So in effect we have a five-mile-long private beach to run on or just enjoy. The only unit to our south is the Marine outpost up there on Marble Mountain," the captain pointed.

"Can I get a hooch by the sea?" Paul held his breath. He had to live as close to the water as he could. "I'm from around Malibu, and I guess salt water has gotten into my blood."

The captain thought for a few moments before answering. "I really don't know what the ol' man has in store for you, but seeing that you're a lieutenant . . . about the only thing open for you is with the recon company as a team leader." The jeep stopped. "Hell, I might get my ass chewed, but for now I'll put you in Nappa's old hooch. I hope you're not superstitious—he was killed last week on a mission, along with his whole team."

The captain drove the jeep between the hooches and slowed down when he reached a spot of loose sand. Across a narrow stretch of windblown sand and separated slightly from the other buildings stood a small plywood hooch that was perched on a mound. The jeep found traction and angled up the side of the long dune and stopped next to the hooch Paul had been looking at. Paul held his breath. The sea rolled ashore seventy-five meters away, with only a few bunkers and barbed wire separating the hooch from the water. The small hooch had been placed between two of the perimeter bunkers, allowing for an unhindered view of the water if you looked straight ahead from the top of the dune over the wire.

"This is perfect!" Paul felt happy for the first time in

months. "Thanks a lot, Captain!"

"Don't thank me yet! The colonel still has to approve the assignment and the recon company commander has to hack off . . . but I do have a *little* influence around here." He smiled. "Put your gear inside and we'll run over to the mess hall and eat."

A hand-painted picture of a bright green snake winding its way through a clump of bamboo was painted above the door with the words *RT Viper* stenciled beneath the drawing.

"Lieutenant Nappa was the RT leader for Viper. If you're lucky enough to get a team, you'll have the hooch."

"I'll get a recon team. . . ." Paul's words were a statement. He couldn't bear to see anyone else living in the hooch so close to the sea. The floor was made out of three sheets of plywood built up on four-by-four stilts off the sand. Plywood composed the sides and tin sheets covered the roof. It was very simply constructed and was painted white to reflect the hot sun during the day.

Paul followed the captain over to the mess hall and ordered after the senior officer. They had a feast of T-bone steak with two eggs on top.

"You have a damn good set up here, sir," Paul looked around the barn-sized room and counted ten standard-size air-conditioning units mounted in the walls.

"We're fortunate to have the best mess sergeant in Vietnam assigned to our unit. He built this place starting from a field mess tent with a sand floor!" The S-1 forked a huge piece of well-done steak into his mouth. "The place should start filling up pretty soon with people from the recon teams. As soon as we finish eating, I'll show you the headquarters and get your in-processing started."

Paul was very curious as to what the special top-secret SOG teams actually did. He had heard his share of the barroom rumors.

"What do you people do here?"

The captain smiled. "Our operations people will brief you after your clearances have been verified. It'll probably be sometime this afternoon if there aren't any glitches." He laid his fork down against the side of his plate and looked across the table at Paul. "You'll find out that we have the best equipment in the world and we live very well . . . in garrison . . ." The captain emphasized the last two words.

They finished breakfast just as the first of the SOG team members appeared in the mess hall wearing their short-brimmed black hats.

"Only recon team members are allowed to wear the black hats with the skulls on the front." A slight hint of jealousy escaped from the captain in the tone of his voice.

The drive from the mess hall to the headquarters building was a half-mile along the road bordering the perimeter fence. Paul observed two large training areas built along the south side of the camp. One was a large, walk-through range, and the other looked like a Hollywood screen set with a conglomerate of junk piles pushed to one side of the field.

"What is that training area used for?" Paul pointed to the Hollywood-style buildings that had only fronts, with no sides or rears.

"That's a special mission training site," the captain cut his answer short and changed the subject. "Looks like the ol' man is back."

Lieutenant Bourne saw the colonel walking up the private sidewalk from what was probably the colonel's hooch to the side entrance of the main office building.

"He'll probably want to see you the first thing this morning," the S-1 said, parking the jeep in a marked slot. "Have a seat in my office while I talk to him."

The headquarters building was only partially air-conditioned, but the high ceilings helped cool the office space. Paul smiled as he looked around at the well-furnished rooms. CCN must have some darn good scroungers assigned to the unit.

"He'll see you now." The captain had caught Paul daydreaming. "And don't forget to report to him."

Paul looked down and checked his uniform before entering the colonel's office. "Lieutenant Bourne reporting, sir."

The lieutenant colonel remained sitting and returned Paul's salute. He smiled and spoke, "Looks like you're eager to get to work. Have a seat," he pointed to a nearby chair. "My adjutant, Captain White, tells me that you'd like to command RT Viper . . . is that true?"

"Yes, sir," Paul felt his heart racing. "I think that I can do a good job for you in that capacity."

The colonel threw his head back and laughed. Paul was amused at first, but became concerned when the laughter continued for almost a minute.

"Lieutenant . . . please . . . excuse me . . ." Clewell wiped his eyes, "I'm not laughing at you . . . but you really are a humble young man. Your being assigned here wasn't by chance; in fact, I worked very hard to get you from all the other SOG operations and the Greek Teams that wanted you. You are a very famous young man within SOG circles! The mission that you conducted for Mister LeBlonde has become a rather classic mission that any recon man in the program would give his left nut to have under his belt! Maybe you thought that I was acting through kindness back in Nha Trang . . . I wasn't. . . . it was more from selfishness. . . ." Clewell leaned back in his swivel chair and laced his fingers behind his head.

"Thanks for the compliment, sir, but I had a lot of

very talented help on that mission . . ."

"Sure . . . I know," the colonel grinned. "I'm going to assign you to the recon company. Captain Atkins is the commander and will make the decision on what team you'll be assigned to, but Captain White has informed me of your love for the sea and I'll see what I can do. . . ."

"Thanks, sir!"

"Oh . . . you might have a problem here for awhile . . . I wish I didn't have to say this . . ."

Paul felt his stomach knot as he waited for the colonel to mention Hetten and My An.

"There's a lot of pride in this unit. We have a number of men who think they are the world's answer to the recon man . . . some of them come damn close . . . but you might find some professional jealousy. Most of the men here are looking for that one mission that will make them a legend among their peers." The commander looked over the top rim of his glasses at Paul. "You've already accomplished that . . . or so the legend goes. . . ." The colonel turned and looked out of his plexiglas window. "Did you really kill Colonel Jean Paul LaTruseau?"

"Who, sir?" Paul had been debriefed that the mission was still listed as top secret with a need to know. "I'm sorry, sir; I don't know who you're talking about."

Clewell spun around and faced Paul from his chair. His eyes flashed for an instant and then he smiled. "You'll do all right here, all right!" He sipped from the cup of lukewarm black coffee on his desk and continued, "We had been hunting for LaTruseau for over a year on a *dedicated* special mission criterion. SOG had lost a lot of good men tracking him down and we'd lost complete teams that were inserted in areas where we heard he might be. We heard through our CIA contacts that Colonel LaTruseau was eliminated—just about the time you returned from a special mission and had used our site to launch out of. A real coincidence!"

Paul shrugged his shoulders. "He sounds like a real smart commie. I don't think I'm that good to have aced him out in the jungle, especially on his home turf."

Clewell took the hint and dropped the subject. "Have my S-1 show you around the camp, but first I want you to hit the operations people over in the TOC."

Paul stood to leave and paused. "Thanks, sir, for helping me get here."

The commander smiled and nodded his head.

Captain White had been waiting for Paul to leave the colonel's office and he escorted him through the gate guards at the top-secret TOC that was surrounded by a ten-foot-high cyclone fence with three strands of barbed wire lining the top and rolls of concertina stretched out along the bottom. Paul noticed twelve cement blocks strategically placed on the inside wire, back from the fence. The cement blocks were designed to hold three claymore mines facing at different angles and protected from each other by a steel triangle, so that they could be detonated individually or together. The four corners of the building each had a cement fighting bunker. The whole reinforced cement structure reminded Paul of an old-time French foreign legion outpost located in the Algerian desert.

The steel door opened on the recessed side of the building and a tall thin major stepped out into the bright sunlight, blinking his eyes.

"You have quite a fortress here, sir," Paul said, continuing to scan the fighting positions.

"A lot of thought went into building this open vault. We don't have to constantly keep the top-secret papers locked up, and we can run the place like a regular office inside, once a person has the proper clearances to enter." The major spoke as if he was confident in his operation. "By the way, I'm Major Galviston. I run this operation."

"Lieutenant Bourne, sir."

"Your reputation has preceded you, Lieutenant. LeBlonde is a *personal* friend of mine . . ." Galviston looked at Paul with a knowing twinkle in his eye. "C'm'on, I'll brief you off the operational map; it'll give you the big picture that is in operation right now."

Paul followed Galviston through the maze of offices that contained plans and equipment. The area they entered looked like the main floor of the New York Stock Exchange, with men runnning from map to map and posting hundreds of pieces of current data.

"Your people look like they have their hands full, sir." Paul tried focusing his eyes on the huge map that covered most of the back wall.

"We all take our jobs here very seriously. One minor mistake can cost a whole team their lives." The major stopped in front of the huge map that Paul had been looking at. The map was on a scale of 1:50,000 and encompassed the land mass of five countries. Paul was impressed when the major picked up a small control box and pushed one of the buttons. The lights along the back portion of the room dimmed and the lights behind the map brightened, depicting the locations of the recon teams that were presently inserted on the ground, along with hundreds of other items of information including airports, roads, supply depots, NVA headquarters, and large enemy concentrations. The map was a constantly changing work of military art.

"Take a seat over there." The major pointed with the control box he held in his hand to a row of high-backed chairs.

"Do we work the whole area, sir?"

"No, but we have a need to know what is going on along the whole land mass so we can do our job."

Galviston took his time briefing Paul on the unit's mission and periodically he pushed a different button to highlight different areas and topics as he talked about them. Paul was very impressed with the professionalism the CCN personnel displayed in their jobs.

"Any questions?" Galviston turned off the map lights and faced Paul.

"None . . . I'm rather dazzled . . ."

"You're supposed to be, Lieutenant," Galviston chuckled under his breath. "One of our people was a Hollywood light director before working for us; this map was his pet project."

"Thanks for the briefing, sir." Paul had taken up enough of the major's time.

"Part of the job. Captain White is waiting to take you over to the logistics shop and draw some equipment."

Paul met the captain at the main entrance and they walked together, cutting across the compound through the loose sand to the huge warehouses that lined one side of the compound. Paul didn't draw a weapon because he had brought his CAR-15 with him from My An. The S-4 officer took his time, and reflected a great deal of pride in showing the new lieutenant his operation. One thing that Paul was beginning to notice was that there wasn't any overt jealousy between those who supported and those who conducted operations; each man was judged on how well he did his particular job. The warehouses were stuffed full of all kinds of special gear, food, and clothes.

Captain Atkins was waiting outside the supply building, parked on the shady side, when Paul exited carrying an armload of equipment.

"Hop in, I'll drive you back to the recon company," Atkins nodded.

Paul took a front seat and thanked Captain White for his help. The jeep ride back to the area was quiet.

Captain Atkins acted as if he were deep in thought. They passed the orderly room and drove back behind the row of team hooches. The captain stopped his jeep in front of the RT Viper hooch.

"It's yours," he grinned.

Paul hopped out of the jeep and felt the heat coming down from the sun almost instantly. "Thanks, Captain! You won't regret making this decision!"

"Get your gear squared away and wander over to my office when you get a chance and we'll talk." He eased out on the clutch. "And don't hurry! Enjoy your first couple of days in camp!"

Paul pushed open the door to his new home and dropped his gear down on the wooden floor in one big pile. He noticed immediately that a portion of the wall facing the beach was covered with a modified blanket so that it could slide back and forth on a thick bamboo rod. Paul reached up and pushed the makeshift curtain aside and caught his breath. A five-foot-long by four-foot window made out of plexiglas was built into the wall, making a beautiful bay window overlooking the South China Sea.

Paul dropped back down on the bare bunk and drank in the beauty of the powerful waves. Damn, he felt happy! He wanted to strip naked and run down to the beach and dive into the sea. He watched the wave action for over an hour and then stretched out on the hard bed and looked up into the open rafters. His eyes locked onto a pair of familiar shapes.

"Surfboards!" Paul jumped up from the bed, not trusting what his eyes alone were telling him. He wanted to touch them to make sure. He removed a bright yellow board from between the rafters just as a knock echoed through his hooch.

"Come in!"

The door swung open and a young American stood

in the bright light wearing a pair of cut-off jungle fatigues.

"Hello, sir, I'm Sergeant Cooper from RT Cobra." The sergeant paused in the doorway.

"Come on in." Paul rubbed his hand along the surfboard, checking to see how well it had been waxed.

"Lieutenant Nappa and I were pretty good friends." Cooper watched Paul admire the board as he spoke. "We used to surf a lot together when we were back in base camp."

"This your board?"

"No, Lieutenant Nappa had those boards shipped in from California. He was from Florida and was a surfing nut. The Air Force makes a lot of supply trips to Oakland, so Nappa paid one of the pilots four hundred dollars to bring these back for us." Cooper paused. "Nappa said that if anything ever happened to him that he wanted these boards left here for anyone to use."

Paul turned the board that he was holding over and checked for dings. "They've been really well cared for." Paul handed the board to Cooper. "You going surfing right now?"

"Yes, sir; there's still a few good hours of daylight left. Do you surf, sir?"

"I thought that you'd never ask!" Paul pulled his clothes off as he spoke. "I'll meet you down there in ten seconds!"

Sergeant Cooper was paddling out through the soupy white water as Paul reached the beach through the gate, carrying the other surfboard under his arm. Within five powerful strokes Paul had broken through the breakers and was pulling behind Cooper.

"This is really living!" Paul's voice startled the sergeant.

"Christ, sir! That was quick!" Cooper sat up on his

board. "Before you try your luck, Lieutenant . . . you ought to know that this area is full of sea snakes. They normally leave you alone, but watch out for them."

"Thanks." Paul saw a swell starting a hundred meters out from him and started paddling hard. The wave caught him perfectly and he stood up on the board. He shot through the water-created tunnel and hot-dogged his way to the beach. Paul heard clapping and for the first time noticed a small group of men sitting back in the sand dunes who had been watching him come in.

The man nearest to him spoke, "You're pretty good with that thing, Lieutenant!"

"Thanks." Paul turned and joined Cooper, who was still waiting out past the breakers for a respectable wave.

Paul was in one of his elements.

Chapter 15

"Paul! Paul!" The loud pounding on the plywood door woke Paul from his deep sleep. *"Damn it! Paul! Open up!"*

Lieutenant Bourne sat upright on his cot and swung his legs over the edge. He looked at the luminous dial on his army-issue watch and frowned over the early hour.

"Come on in, the door's unlocked," Paul stretched and stood up. He could feel the fine grains of sand between his toes.

The door flew open and Lieutenant Loveless strode into the small hooch wearing a set of worn camouflaged tiger fatigues. Jay flicked on the overhead light and grabbed Paul in a firm bearhug.

"How in the hell did you land an assignment here?" Jay dropped Paul back down on the floor and stood back.

"Get your ass away from me, you queer bastard!" Paul laughed. "Can't you see I'm fucking naked!"

"I know a lot of women who've wished that I was a little queer! Especially after they've had one of my super fucks!" Jay laughed with his friend, releasing some of the tension that had built up inside him during the long, six-day patrol. Jay slapped the side of his leg. "Damn your skinny ass! It's good seeing you, Paul!"

"Well . . . I figured that I had better get assigned up

here to watch after you . . . I remember how piss poor you did during night patrols during OCS," Paul slipped Jay a sly look, "and I did promise your parents that I would look after you in Vietnam." Paul pulled a pair of black peasant pants on over his hips and tied the drawstring around his waist. "How's your Dad doing?"

"He's fine. Mom's worried shitless about me being over here and Dad still has his job in Orlando." Jay slipped down in a chair that had been made out of empty ammo boxes and sandbags and crossed his legs in front of him. "Do you still have your Randall?"

Paul reached up to a wooden peg that was holding his web gear and pulled the seven-inch blackened blade from its oiled brown-leather sheath. "It's just like new." He handed the blade handle first to Jay, who ran his thumb slowly down the extremely sharp cutting edge.

"Have you used it on any gooks?" Jay didn't expect an affirmative answer and held his thumb out for Paul to see the thin red line the sharp blade had cut. "Just like the Gurkas of India! Once a knife has been drawn from its sheath, it must bring blood before it is replaced."

"Dipshit! You know how sharp a Randall knife is!"

Jay frowned at Paul. "You haven't answered my question. Have you used the knife on any VC?"

"That's a long story that should be told over a lot of booze." Paul's voice dropped and his voice thickened. "The answer to your question is yes."

Jay sensed that his buddy desired to change the subject of their conversation and reached back on his own pistol belt and pulled his Randall from its sheath. He held the two knives side by side. Both knives were identical, except for the names engraved on the combat-blackened blades near the hilts. *Officer's Candidate Class 2–66* was engraved under each of the names.

"I really appreciate your parents buying me that

knife as a graduation present." Paul took his knife from Jay and placed it back in its sheath.

"Hell, it wasn't that big of a deal. The Randall Company is right next door to my parent's house—Gary Randall is a friend of the family!" Jay stropped his blade against the edge of his boot.

Paul knew better. It was a big deal getting a Randall fighting knife. Since the Vietnam War had started, there had been a big demand for the custom-made knifes and the normal waiting time for one of the blades was well over a year.

"So, anyway . . . where in the hell have you been?" Paul sat back down on his bunk.

"Fightin' the fuckin' war . . . Bro!" Jay looked up at the ceiling and folded his hands behind his head. "Man, we had a great mission! My people are cra-ee-zzzy! My team sergeant has got to be el nut-o! We accomplished what we had set out to do, plus we killed a passel of NVA . . ." Jay's eyes took on a very tired look but he continued talking. ". . . My sergeant . . . Christ, did he pull off a good one! Right before we were due to be extracted, we heard a convoy of trucks passing by close to our extraction site. Sergeant Nimon took a claymore mine from his rucksack and attached two sets of detonating wires together. He looped the long wire like a cowboy's lariat in his left hand and held the Claymore in his right hand while he took up a position behind a large tree waiting for the last truck to pass his location next to the narrow road. He threw the mine over the tailgate and waited for the wire to play out of his hand before he pushed the detonator. It blew thirty NVA soldiers all to hell!" Jay rolled his eyes. "Love it!"

"Seems like you're getting to see a lot of action." Paul smiled as he recalled patrolling with Jay in the Georgia swamps. Jay had been afraid of almost everything during that training phase, and now he was the team leader of a damn fine recon team. "You're getting to be a big boy!"

Jay shot out of his chair and tackled Paul around his waist, pushing him back down on the bed.

"Get your weak ass off me! Shit!" Paul twisted, trying to break Jay's grip. Paul maneuvered Jay until he could slip him into a full-nelson and then he felt his friend's body go limp.

"You all right, buddy?" Paul rolled Jay over on his back.

"Sure . . . I just didn't realize just how damn tired I am. . . . We haven't slept in five days . . . been on amphetamines. . . ." Jay's eyes closed. Paul reached down, grabbed Jay's feet, and flipped them up on his bed. Jay was lost in a deep sleep before Paul left the hooch for breakfast.

All of the mess hall lights were turned off except for the row directly in front of the serving line. Paul was the first one to enter the building for breakfast and found himself a quiet spot next to the corner wall.

"Have you seen Lieutenant Loveless, sir?"

Paul looked up from his eggs and bacon. "He's sleeping in my hooch."

"I'm Sergeant Nimon. Would you tell him we have a debriefing at 1700 hours in the TOC?"

Paul quickly checked the sergeant out. The man wasn't much over five feet tall and couldn't have weighed over a hundred and ten pounds. "Sure . . . Sergeant . . . Will do." Paul turned his attention back to his breakfast. He didn't want to try and push a relationship with any of the other recon team members. He figured that they would either accept him or reject him, but it would be based on what he did in the future, not his past.

Paul was interrupted for the second time.

"Mind if I join you?" Captain Atkins placed his tray on the table across from where Paul was sitting.

"Have a seat, sir," Paul nodded for the captain to sit down. A young sergeant wearing a name tag that said "Cooper" was standing behind the captain.

"This is Sergeant Cooper from RT Cobra."

"We've already met, sir," Paul shook the offered hand. "We surfed together yesterday."

"Oh, shit! Not another one of those fucking surfing freaks!" The captain grinned as he joked, "Damn, why can't you be normal and get drunk like the rest of us!"

"I do that, too. . . ." Paul continued eating his food that was already getting cold.

The recon commander wasted no time and got down to the reason he chose to sit with Paul.

"Sergeant Cooper would like to transfer to your recon team." He paused. "RT Viper lost its senior NCO along with Lieutenant Nappa. What I'd like to do is consolidate the Americans on Viper and Cobra to make one effective operational team. Cooper is the only survivor from his RT." Captain Atkins cut his omelet with his fork. "Cooper is one of our experienced men."

Paul glanced over at Cooper—who was concentrating on his food—and then looked over at the captain. "Sure . . . it's all right with me. Cooper can't be all bad if he knows how to surf." Paul had added the last comment to needle the captain.

"Then it's settled . . . Cooper will report to Viper as of today." Atkins took a long drink from his lukewarm coffee and checked his watch for the time. "Darn! I've got to run . . . Oh . . ." he looked directly into Paul's eyes, ". . . I hate to alert you for a mission so soon, but we're short on operational teams."

Paul's expression turned to a fake bewildered expression. "Isn't that what we're all here for?"

Atkins reached across the table and slapped Paul's shoulder. "You're lucky I like you. . . . You could piss a working man off!"

Paul wondered if Atkins knew about Hetten.

Atkins stood to leave the table. Most of his food remained untouched. He reached down to his plate as he spoke and picked up a half-slice of toast to take with him. "The operations people have a preliminary briefing ready for RT Viper."

Sergeant Cooper waited until Captain Atkins was out of hearing range before he addressed Paul. "Damn! That was embarrassing, sir! I didn't think Captain Atkins would approach you in front of me like that."

"Don't worry about it. I was very impressed with you when we met yesterday." Paul finished the last bite from his plate. "We should be able to form a darn good team."

"I heard about your mission," Cooper eased the sentence out cautiously.

"You know, this is the third time that someone has alluded to a mission that I am supposed to have conducted. . . . Just what are you talking about?" A faint smile flickered at the corners of Paul's mouth.

"We don't loan out facilities to anyone except CIA people, and when they bring a special crew in here it's usually really big stuff." Cooper looked sheepishly at Paul and continued, "Hell! CIA missions are always hot and everybody wants to be selected for them. So anyway, LeBlonde told our operations officer what you did and the word spread quickly through the recon teams. . . . Don't worry . . . we bullshit to each other but nothing passes through the gates!" Cooper frowned. "We lost a lot of good men trying to kill that French bastard! I think we had the right to know when that son of a bitch was zapped!"

"The mission was top secret," Paul spoke softly.

"*All* of our missions are top secret, sir." Cooper's voice reflected the hurt he felt over not being trusted.

"I apologize, Cooper, but I was told not to talk to anyone about the mission." Paul sensed that he should back off a little.

"No sweat, sir; most of the recon men have a lot of respect for you because of that mission." Cooper's face flushed pink. "That's why I asked the captain to get transferred to your team."

Paul slapped Cooper gently against the side of his head. "Let's go over to the TOC and get briefed."

Major Galviston and Captain Atkins joined the team members from RT Viper in the briefing room. Paul looked over at the two officers carrying steaming cups of coffee. Galviston was wearing a solid gold ten *bot* chain around his neck with a disk hanging from it with the word WAR cut out from the circle of gold in the same style the hippies used for their peace medals that the soldiers referred to as chicken feet.

"Are you ready to go to war, Lieutenant?" Galviston sat down in a chair that had been placed in front of the large map. He tapped his foot with the wooden pointer he held in his free hand.

"Guess so, sir," Paul didn't know exactly how to respond to the major.

"You seem to have good taste in NCOs," Galviston acknowledged Cooper's presence in the room.

"I hear you have a mission site selected for us, sir."

"Yep, and it's a good one." The major turned on his seat and tapped the map with his pointer. "Somewhere in this area we have a very big problem developing . . ." He paused as he checked the location of his pointer on the map. ". . . I think both of you have heard the rumors circulating around I Corps that concerns American soldiers who have changed sides and are fighting with the North Vietnamese against American forces."

"I've heard bits and pieces, but nothing that is really believeable," Cooper answered the major.

"Well, you can relax, Cooper—it's true." Galviston sipped from the coffee mug. "Last month a Marine patrol in this area . . ." Galviston located the small arrow on the map and pointed to it, ". . . spotted what they thought was a caucasian wearing a red bandanna around his head. He was patrolling with a squad of NVA. The Marine patrol thought that he was a prisoner and attempted to rescue him. They were very surprised when the caucasian flipped an AK-47 from behind his back, opened fire on them, and then led the NVA squad in an attack. The Marines regained their composure and returned fire. Two Marines swear that they killed the white man, but a search of the area revealed no body."

Paul interrupted, "You want us to go looking for him?"

"Hold it, Lieutenant! Let me finish . . ." Galviston gave Paul a sharp look, teaching him his first lesson in dealing with the senior officer: that you didn't interrupt him. "We have a confirmed sighting and a B-2 level information packet that confirms there are at least two more caucasians and a black who are acting as patrol leaders for an NVA regiment," Galviston tapped his pointer against the map, "probably working out of this area."

"I'll be a son of a bitch," Cooper hissed the words out between his clenched teeth.

"Let's not be too quick judging them. They could still be prisoners made to *look* as if they are fighting against their own people." Galviston raised his eyebrows. "After all, blanks in the AK-47s, forcing them to lead down dangerous paths . . . all of that *looks* like they're leading a patrol, but in actuality they're still prisoners . . ." Galviston took his time bringing his coffee cup up to his lips, ". . . but . . . if they are working for the NVA . . . well, your mission is to go in there and find them, give them the choice of staying or coming back to American control . . . if they stay . . . eliminate them. We can't have Americans fighting with the commies. Hell, we already have a group led by an American movie star touring Hanoi! Morale is getting low among the line troops and we have to nip this one in the bud!"

"What if we can't get close enough to offer them a choice to come with us?" Cooper's voice didn't sound as if he relished the mission at all.

"Kill them," Galviston's voice held a matter-of-fact tone. "But given a choice, we'd like to talk to them."

"When do we leave?"

"Late tomorrow. We have to move fast. The Marines are upset over this whole thing and they're afraid that the NVA regiment will move south out of the area and we'll lose them."

"I wouldn't mind taking on this mission for myself." Captain Atkins spoke with a tinge of jealousy, but failed to reveal that he had already asked for the mission only to be turned down in favor of the Bourne-Cooper team.

Atkins stood up. "Lieutenant Bourne, follow me and I'll show you the mission-alert system we use here at CCN. The first step was the briefing that you've just received; during the second phase you choose what types of special equipment and personnel you think are necessary to fulfill your mission requirements."

The captain stopped in front of a door marked RT Viper, the removeable sign placed in a slot on the door. Atkins led the way into the room. "In here is some special equipment we feel you can use. You, as the team leader, have the option of adding or subtracting whatever you want to, but I think that you'll find our logistics people quite effective in their selections."

"What do you mean by special personnel, sir?"

"An example: You have to destroy a gas pipeline. We would find you an expert in pipelines and try to get him to volunteer for the mission."

Galviston entered the small room, which was dominated by a table and five chairs with a narrow display table placed up against the far wall. A detailed map covered the wall nearest the work table. The major removed the white sheet that covered the table against the wall, revealing a display of special equipment.

"Here are your URC-10s." He handed one of the pocket-sized radio transmitter-receivers to Paul. "Have you ever used one of these before?"

"No, sir."

"They are preset on two broadcasting and receiving channels. One for communication with the FAC aircraft, which will be constantly flying near you during your mission." Galviston caught Paul's immediate concern. "Don't worry. They don't stay over your position but within the range of the radio. The other channel is set on the Air Force's emergency frequency that is constantly monitored by every ground station and aircraft in flight. We want you to use the emergency freq only if the forward air control aircraft gets shot down."

Paul ran his hand over the case of the small radio. "This is good stuff."

"Here's your primary radio," Galviston placed his hand on a PRC-77 secure voice radio set. "It comes in three pieces so that you can divide the load among your team members."

"I've used those before, sir." Paul picked up one of the

silenced .22-caliber pistols. "I've used one of these, too."

"I've heard." Galviston stepped over to a closed box and flipped open the lid. "Here's one of your special pieces of equipment for this mission." The major removed a beautiful Weatherby .300 with attached scope.

"Man! Is that nice!" Cooper took the weapon from the major. "This has to have cost a bundle!"

"Five thousand dollars, to be exact. We bought this weapon in case you have to make a difficult long shot and we had it modified . . . we don't . . . ahh . . . like I said . . . we would really like to talk to them . . . but . . ."

The two team members checked their equipment as Major Galviston watched. Paul was familiar with most of the stuff but noticed that the packaging and re-taping of the items was unique. The LRRP rations had all been opened and re-sealed with a strip of special green tape that didn't make any noise when it was pulled free.

"Have you ever ridden a STABO rig?" Galviston sat down in one of the chairs at the work table.

"No, sir," Paul had heard of the special extraction rig and had seen it used during a Gabriel demonstration at Fort Bragg, North Carolina. "I'm familiar with the harness and think I can handle it. The supply officer gave me a STABO rig with my issue, and Sergeant Cooper helped me set it up on my web gear."

Galviston looked over at Cooper. "Make sure the Lieutenant's gear is squared away tomorrow morning when you go into isolation." The major turned back to face Paul. "I hate having to put you on a mission so soon, but this is an important one and all of our teams have already been committed to other areas."

"No sweat, sir; between Cooper and I, we can make it."

"All right, then!" Galviston slapped Paul on his back. "Tomorrow we'll get you out to your launch site at Quang Tri."

The day was still young when RT Viper was released from the TOC, leaving them most of the afternoon free. Paul went back to his beach hooch and found that Jay had left. The sound of the surf carried on the soft wind, sending a message to Paul. He pulled off his sweat-stained clothes and slipped into a pair of cut-offs. He ran over the sun-heated sand down to the sea, not stopping until he had reached the cool, wet sand lining the shore. Waves that had been formed by a distant typhoon were smashing their ten-foot walls of water on the packed sand beach. The roar combined with the salt spray filled all of Paul's senses. He turned left at the gate and started running at a fast pace along the beachfront. The effect of the huge waves caused Paul to begin daydreaming as he ran down the open beach. Mythology carried Paul two miles. The wind tears in his eyes blurred his vision, causing him to slow his pace. He saw a twenty-foot-high sand dune to his left and turned, increasing his speed to the top of the hill. Paul stopped abruptly at the peak and placed his hands on his hips as he looked out over the rolling sea. The wind picked up drops of seaspray from the waves and threw them against Paul's bare chest. He now became an Indian warrior and dropped down into a cross-legged squat. Thoughts of war filled his mind and then slipped back to Malibu and the Countyline surfing beaches located in southern California. Minutes passed.

Out of the corner of his eye, Paul saw a figure running along the beach. He watched the quarter-inch-high runner grow larger, and at a half-mile Paul could see that the man was running naked, carrying his shorts rolled up in his right hand like a baton.

Jay saw Paul sitting on the top of the sand dune and changed course to join him.

"You always run around bare-ass?" Paul came out of the trance.

"Try it sometime . . . talk about feeling free!" Jay slipped his dry running shorts over his wet hips and then sat down next to Paul. "Because of the war, this is probably one of the most private beaches in the world."

"Look at that!" Paul pointed at the monster white-caps smashing into each other far out at sea. "I could live here forever."

"How did your in-processing go?" Jay's words broke the mood.

"I'm on a mission alert for tomorrow." Paul wiped the salt spray off his face. "Oh, before I forget, you have a debrief set for five o'clock in the operations center."

"Shit! I forgot all about it!" Jay stood. "I can't believe that they put you on a mission so damn soon!"

A giant wave rushed across the sand and touched the base of the dry sand dune.

"Well . . . I've got to get my ass back there and get ready." Jay jumped down from the top of the sand hill and turned back to face Paul, who remained sitting crosslegged. "Do you want me to hold your mail for you?"

"What do you mean?"

"Well, normally, the S-1 handles all of the mail, but when someone goes on a mission, usually a friend picks up his mail and holds it just in case something happens . . ." Jay turned his head away from Paul and looked out over the waves. "If the S-1 has the letters, he has to send them unopened to the next of kin. If a friend is holding the letters, nothing embarrassing gets forwarded back home to wives and mothers."

"I gotcha . . . no letters from girlfriends being sent

to wives," Paul laughed. "You guys think of everything! Sure, Jay, get my mail—but you'll be bored to death reading it if I get zapped."

"Let's hope that I don't have to go through being bored!" Jay started running hard down the beach. He paused long enough to yell back over his shoulder. "Coming . . . Pussy?"

Paul grinned before answering his friend, "Later. . . ."

Lieutenant Bourne pushed the padlock shut on the door of his hooch and slid the brass key under the wooden steps between a crack in the boards. He looked down at the hiding place, and wondered if he would be able to return and remove the key from its hiding place or if someone would have to bust the lock. He shrugged and flipped his rucksack over his shoulder. The pack was light, containing only the barest of essential items he would need during the mission. Paul had cleaned his CAR-15 thoroughly the night before, and had even removed each round of ammunition from his magazines and cleaned them singly with a cloth. He might die during the mission, but it wouldn't be because he hadn't taken the necessary precautions and insured that his equipment operated perfectly.

"Wait up, sir!"

Paul stopped and waited for Sergeant Cooper to catch up to where he was standing between the hooches in the hot sand.

"You look like you're ready for some war, Sergeant."

"Bet your ass I am!" Cooper adjusted the shoulder strap on his CAR-15 and commented, "Don't worry, sir, we'll carry you through this mission."

Paul smiled. He understood that Cooper was nervous and was talking to control his trepidation. "I hope someone *else* is looking out for me . . . Rookie Sergeant . . . someone who carries a bit more of a wallop!"

Cooper glanced at the lieutenant out of the corner of his eye with a rookie-my-ass look. The sergeant smiled and added, "We should be meeting the Montagnards who are assigned to RT Viper at the isolation building. The whole team is new . . . maybe that's going to be a good-luck sign."

"I would have liked to have run a few practice missions before we tackled a big one," Paul talked as they forced their way over the soft sand. "It makes me nervous not having had the chance to have worked together."

"I feel the same way, lieutenant, but the major said all of the Montagnards speak English and have worked on other teams before."

The gate guard at the isolation building recognized Cooper and allowed them to pass through and join the three Montagnard warriors who had been waiting for them inside. The senior Montagnard was inspecting the two junior team members' gear that had been laid out carefully on the stripped cots.

Paul was impressed, and nodded his approval to the senior warrior as he helped Cooper inspect the special gear. Major Galviston joined the two Americans, entering the room through the rear exit.

"I see you're not wasting any of your time," the major smiled without showing his teeth.

"We don't have any time to waste, sir." Cooper didn't look up from the radio he was checking for batteries.

"Good! Your mission insertion has been moved forward ten hours. The weather is starting to close in around the plateau and we're going to have to move fast to sneak your team in before the clouds settle into the valley."

"When do you want us ready to leave, sir?"

"Can you have your team ready to leave for the launch site in, say . . . an hour?"

"Yes . . . all we have to do is break down the special gear and pack up." Paul joined Cooper and helped him divide the heavy radio amongst the team. The Weatherby would be a problem since the Montagnards were too small to carry the big rifle.

"I'll take the rifle, sir, seeing I'm a school-trained sniper." Cooper handed his CAR-15 to the major. "Will you make sure this gets back to my hooch?"

"Sure." Galviston took the submachine gun. "There's a van waiting out in back when you're ready to load up."

Cooper removed all of the 5.56 ammo from his web gear and slipped the .300 rounds in the empty pouches. He took his silenced .22-caliber pistol and slid it into one of the empty pockets on his rucksack.

"Just in case!" Cooper spoke to no one in particular. He tied the strings on his rucksack and looked up. The other members of his team were standing in the doorway waiting for him to finish.

"Let's go!" Paul led the small recon team out to the van. The driver was standing next to the open rear door and slammed it shut behind the last man. All of the windows in the stepvan had been painted over with black paint, giving the tight quarters an even more cramped feeling. Paul had a flash of claustrophobia mixed with fear rush through him. The ride over to the private helipad took only a few minutes, but it seemed like hours to Paul. The van was still rocking from the sudden stop when the rear door flew open, letting in the bright sunlight. Paul jumped out and felt a cool sea breeze brush his wet face. He hadn't realized that he was sweating profusely. The helicopters were parked fifty feet away from the van with their blades beginning a slow rotation, their high-pitched whines rising in intensity as the turbine engines gained RPMs. The team loaded up in one of the choppers, leaving the partner empty to act as an escort. The helicopters became airborne with the click from the last seat belt and headed out over the South China Sea, making a low sweep across the open water and a wide arc as the flight banked toward Quang Tri to the north.

The last hour had passed so quickly for Paul that he hadn't had time to think about what he was doing or where he was going. Fear, his old enemy, began creeping up along his spine into his consciousness against the helicopter's rapid descent. The Quang Tri launch site was spread out below them. Four Cobra gunships were nestled in a grassy defilade, warming up their engines. Two Huey gunships squatted on a PSP pad waiting to load the team. SOG units used only a special group of pilots for insertions so that secrecy could be maintained.

A pair of camouflage-clad launch site officers ran toward the landing choppers from the opposite side of the field. Paul met the leader on his way toward the waiting passenger choppers.

"We're ready to insert your team now. . . . Do any of you have to use the john?" The officer yelled above the roar of the turbine engines surrounding them.

Paul glanced back at his team that followed closely behind them in single file. All of them had heard the officer yelling and shook their heads in the negative.

"*Good!*" Board your slicks and good luck!"

Paul ran bent-over to the pair of waiting slicks and waved Cooper and two of the Montagnards into one of the aircraft. The old Montagnard and Paul slid backward onto the floor of the first chopper. All of the team members sat in the open doorways with their feet hanging outside the choppers. Paul took the headset from the nylon net that served as a seatback and placed it over his ears.

"You ready, Lieutenant?" The pilot was looking back over his armored seat at Paul, who nodded and gave the aviator the thumbs-up sign. The six helicopters lifted off the pad rapidly, one after the other. The roar from their engines was deafening to those who stood watching the departure. Two of the Cobra gunships shot out ahead of the formation, with one of the Cobras bringing up the rear and dropping down to treetop level. The aircraft armada headed west, away from the American base camp.

The flight from the safe launch site to the thick jungles bordering the network of mountain rivers and streams was uneventful. Forty minutes out from Quang Tri the slicks started circling, waiting for the Air Force A1E flight to finish prepping the area. The lead Cobras made a quick pass over the open landing zone with their mini-guns blazing, followed closely by the slicks carrying Paul's team. The slicks had barely touched the dark green jungle mat before they gave a burst of speed and followed the A1Es back to the coast.

Paul ran hard for the cover of a thicket of small trees. The roar of aircraft engines rapidly faded, followed by the muffled echoes coming from a fake LZ that was being prepped ten miles south.

Total, absolute silence. Paul thought for a second that he had gone deaf as he watched the dust settle from the bombs that had exploded in the clearing only seconds before. He saw the old Montagnard lying in the thick grass twenty feet away. Paul rolled over and located the remainder of his team slipping through the bamboo toward his location. He pulled his compass out of its canvas case attached to his web-gear harness and shot an azimuth. Paul pointed in the direction he wanted the team to travel. The old Montagnard tapped one of the men on his shoulder and tilted his head in the direction Paul had pointed. The pointman slipped ahead of the team and quickly disappeared, followed by the team. Everyone knew that the faster they left the insertion area, the better chance they had of completing their mission. The NVA would be arriving very soon in large numbers, like sharks drawn to the smell of blood in the ocean.

The small team moved silently through the meshed jungle growth for an hour before Paul signaled for a halt so that he could take an accurate bearing on their position and judge how far they had to travel before reaching their first objective. He checked his map and judged that they were less than three thousand meters away from the main river. The team was making good time. Paul placed his mouth next to Cooper's ear and whispered, "We'll stop at the river."

Cooper nodded in agreement and took over from the pointman. He set an even pace through the thick jungle, using a pig run to travel on through thick bamboo growths.

The team had traveled most of the day with very few rest breaks. Paul could feel the sweat rolling down his back forming a wet band around the top of his pants. His muscles felt good from the smooth steady pace. Paul took a deep breath and held the sweet jungle air deep in the bottom of his lungs for a second and then released the air with a soft hiss. The man moving through the jungle in front of Paul came to a halt, dropping down to one knee. Paul slipped past him and joined Cooper, who was still traveling as the team's pointman. The riverbank was at Cooper's feet. Paul had never seen vegetation growing so thick next to a mountain river. The monsoon rains up in the highlands had brought the lazy jungle river to near flood level with a slow current. A deer trail ran parallel to the water about six feet from the river bank.

Paul checked his map sheet and found a bluff represented by close-together contour lines about two hundred meters north of their present position. Cooper looked over Paul's shoulder to where he was pointing on the map and smiled. The sergeant took the lead again and headed for the high ground. The team slowed its pace, using extreme caution as the men moved up the wide deer path. All of them knew that natural jungle trails would be watched, especially those running next to natural obstacles. Paul was hoping that the deer trail would be too new for the NVA to have found. The two hundred meters Paul had estimated to the bluffs turned out to be closer to five hundred, but he was still happy with his map reading, considering the dense jungle they had just negotiated.

The bluff rose seventy-five feet above the water. It was a perfect place from which to observe the flowing river, and was an excellent location for an enemy outpost. The team adjusted their weapons and crept up the gradual rear slope to the clifftop. The Montagnards moved over the crest in a fan-shaped formation and checked every nook and cranny in the immediate area. Bourne and Cooper found good fighting positions that afforded quick escapes on top of the crag. All of the five positions had a clear view of the river for a half-mile in each direction. The Montagnards returned to where Paul and Cooper waited, satisfied that the area was clear of NVA and cobra snakes. More than one recon patrol had made the fatal error of not checking the area around them for snakes and had lost team members because of it.

Paul signaled for the men to eat while he and Cooper confirmed their position on his battle map. In the event that a large enemy force located them, it was imperative for Paul to know exactly where they were so he could call in air strikes accurately. The bluffs helped them confirm their location to within ten meters. All five of the recon men were within twenty meters of each other, yet no one spoke, since sound carried very far in the jungle. Paul took a few minutes to study the terrain and contours around him before opening a packet of rehydrated fish and rice. With the first bite of the food he realized that he was starving and wolfed down the whole packet in minutes.

A cool breeze coming off the water ruffled the loose lock of hair hanging in Paul's eyes that had slipped free from under his camouflaged jungle hat. Paul brushed the hair back with his hand and looked up through the trees at the black monsoon clouds racing through the sky above them. Bourne tapped Cooper and pointed up. The sergeant shook his head and slid over to the Montagnard nearest to him just as a huge drop of water smacked against the dry ground causing a miniature explosion of dust to erupt. The team closed into a circle, and within ten minutes it was as if night had arrived as the rain clouds darkened the sky. The men took up prone positions in a small circle with their legs forming wide V's, each of their feet touching the man's lying next to him. The team would remain in the circle defense the rest of the night and would warn each other with foot pressure.

The center of the storm hit the small team like an ocean wave. Paul pulled the brim of his hat down closer to his nose. The bill on his hat deflected the rain into small waterfalls. Within minutes everything the men carried that hadn't been wrapped in waterproof bags was saturated. The rain lasted three hours, stopping as quickly as it had started. The heavy downpour had created some good for the recon team by wiping out their trail through the jungle. Nothing could now follow their tracks from the LZ to the cliff.

The night slipped by and brought only a warm

sunshine and no unwanted visitors. Paul had tried staying awake without having to take any of the amphetamine tablets he carried. Drugs were not a part of his makeup. But the early-morning hours had caught him dozing off and he'd swallowed one of the small white pills. A troop of small monkeys began a racket as they moved through the trees along the far bank of the river. The animals were headed downstream in the direction of the hidden recon team, pausing occasionally to fight over choice morsels of food.

Paul crawled forward from his hidden position to a more open area along the edge of the cliff to get a better view of the river. Two of the dominant male monkeys were stationed on flat rocks that bordered the river edge, watching for predators while the troop took turns coming down to the water to drink. Paul's eyes slowly scanned the opposite treeline looking for any signs of NVA soldiers. The monkey sentinels would have alerted the whole area if any people were nearby, so Paul stopped his search when he neared them and looked for a river crossing site. He planned on giving the fast-flowing water time to lower a few feet and then cross over during the night.

Cooper touched Paul's elbow and slid against the lieutenant so that he could whisper in his ear, "We have ten minutes before our first broadcast to the FAC aircraft."

Paul nodded and scooted back from the edge of the cliff. Cooper had already assembled the secure voice radio from each of their packs. Paul looked at the face of his watch and realized that he had less than a minute before he had to broadcast. He waited and then keyed the handset.

"Thor . . . situation green . . . line alpha . . . five . . . line bravo . . . Nighthawk . . . out."

Lieutenant Bourne had informed the FAC pilot who was flying somewhere within their radio range that the team had made the insertion without detection and that there weren't any members sick or injured. He had also told him that he was continuing his mission.

The radio receiver crackled, "Thor . . . roger . . . Foxfire 22 . . . out."

The message had been acknowledged. Paul quickly dissassembled the radio and handed back each part to the man who had been carrying it. The senior sentinel monkey screamed a warning and followed his troop up into the safety of the trees. Paul slid back to his former position on the cliff edge. The monkeys flashed against the dark green leaves and headed farther downstream, away from what had scared them.

Paul waited.

The brush parted directly across from where the recon team was hiding and two NVA soldiers stepped out onto the river rocks lining the far bank. Paul instinctively pushed his chest down against the dirt and granite when one of the NVA looked up at the top of the cliff. The heavier of the two spoke rapidly in a deep Vietnamese and then the scouts disappeared back into the jungle. Paul could hear muffled voices coming from the bamboo thicket where the men had vanished. The brush again parted and three naked NVA jumped into a shallow hole next to the riverbank. A half-hour passed as the enemy soldiers frolicked and splashed in the five feet of river water.

Paul arched his neck when he heard voices calling out to the washing NVA from the bamboo thicket on the far bank. The three soldiers laughed and called out to the hidden men. Five minutes later two more naked NVA stepped out of the jungle and joined their comrades in the swimming hole, followed by three caucasians.

Paul's muscles tightened against the stone as he felt Cooper's foot tap against his boot. There was movement in the underbrush a hundred meters upstream, followed by a tall black man stepping out from the thick jungle growth onto a small flat rock snuggled up against the green overhang close to the bank. The black man was dressed in NVA battle gear and he carried an AK-47 assault rifle with a folding stock. The black took up a squatting position on the dry rock and looked slowly up and down the far bank of the river. The ends of the dark green bandanna he wore around his head flipped against the back of his neck. Paul tapped Cooper and pointed at the black guard. He felt Cooper's shoulder grow tense when the sergeant saw the rifle clenched in the black's hands. Cooper slid open the breech of his sniper rifle and insured that he had chambered a round.

Paul slid up close to Cooper's ear. "Get the range but don't fire until I tell you to . . ."

Cooper nodded and waited.

"Hey, you big motherfuckers! I'll beat you over to the other side!"

The loud words spoken in English startled Paul, followed by an instant erasure of all doubt as to the caucasians being either French or Russians. They were Americans.

The smallest of the three white Americans made a shallow racing dive from the rocks bordering the NVA swimming hole. He glided just under the surface of the clear water, then started swimming for the riverbank at the bottom of the cliff on which the American-led recon team was hiding. Paul glanced over at Cooper, who half-closed his eyes and squeezed his rifle.

"*We ain't going to chase your punk ass!*" One of the bigger men yelled over the water after his friend. "*I hope a damn garfish bites your cock off!*" The two white men laughed as they visualized their partner cockless.

The small swimmer reached the rocky shoreline and turned his head to call back over his shoulder to his friends, "*Hey, watch out for me! I'm going to take a shit over here in the brush!*" The small man climbed over the rocks and disappeared in the thick bamboo.

Paul saw his opportunity and exploded into action. He whispered quickly to Cooper, "Give me time to grab that bastard and then kill as many NVA as you can . . . starting with the traitors. . . ."

Cooper nodded his head and slipped into a good prone firing position. He placed the crosshairs of his scope on the second jacket button the black was wearing and waited. Sweat was dripping off the black's chin and running down his chest.

Paul motioned for the old Montagnard to join him, and the pair of hunters slipped over the rocks and down the hill. Paul held his silenced .22-caliber pistol in his right hand and a set of interlocking plastic handcuffs in his left. The duo moved quietly but rapidly through the patchy jungle. Paul wanted to take the American alive, but he knew he would have to kill him if he started swimming back to the NVA-held side of the river. Paul paused when he reached the base of the cliff. He listened and heard a low grunt coming from a small stand of bamboo ten meters away. Paul crouched and slid through the green vegetation as silently as a hunting tiger, with the old man following close behind him. A single medium-sized wild banana tree separated Paul from the American. Paul paused and listened for the forced breathing of his prey. One rapid move around the tree revealed the small American squatting down with his back toward Paul. Feces were halfway out of the man's rectum.

"*What in the hell are you doing over there . . . playing with yourself?*"

The voice startled Paul.

"Shut the fuck up and let me take a shit in peace!"

Paul covered the remaining meters in seconds under the cover of the man's voice. The pistol butt caught the unsuspecting traitor on the side of his head, knocking him unconscious. Paul swept up the limp form and threw it over his shoulder. He was very surprised at how light the body was.

The old Montagnard led the way around the backside of the cliff and stopped to cover Paul as he handcuffed the prisoner's hands and feet. Paul unrolled a piece of green cloth tape from around his pistol belt and grabbed the man by his wet hair, turning the face toward him.

Paul paused in his work. The man couldn't be older than eighteen. Bourne pressed the sticky tape over the closed mouth.

The old commando reached Cooper's hiding place just as Paul finished securing his prisoner. The Montagnard grabbed Paul's rucksack and signaled for the other tribesmen to join him.

Cooper nodded and sighted his rifle. The sound of the explosion echoed over the water. He switched his sights from the black man, who fell face-first into the river, to the white man who stood waist deep in the river looking over at the far riverbank, and fired again. Blood spread out in the brackish water. The NVA started scrambling up the riverbank toward their weapons. Cooper locked the crosshairs on the back of the head of the last white traitor and squeezed the trigger. He watched the man slip on the wet rocks and spin around. Cooper could see the fear on the white enemy's face change when the bullet entered his skull just below his nose.

Cooper reached out without looking and wrapped his fingers around his rucksack straps. He found the trail and ran at top speed until he reached the rear guard of his recon patrol. Automatic fire cut through the leaves above their heads. The NVA were firing wildly into the jungle. Cooper sighted Paul running ahead of him carrying the naked traitor over his shoulder. Paul dropped down on one knee and waited for his men to pass by; he counted each of them and signaled Cooper to stop.

"Use your URC-10 and call for an extraction. We'll have to STABO out of here through the trees . . . Tell them that we have a prisoner and will be needing a McGuire rig."

"Right, sir!"

"Have the pick-up in the small clearing a hundred meters downstream . . ."

Paul flipped the man back over his shoulder. A slight movement from the body told Paul that the man was regaining consciousness. The team moved rapidly through the jungle. Time was very important. The NVA would be calling for help and would cross over the river in full force within the hour. Paul was sweating heavily when they reached the extraction site. He flipped the body off his shoulder and let it land on the ground hard. All five of his team were present. Paul pointed out fighting positions to each man and then looked down at his prisoner. The man's eyes were wide open and centered on Paul's face.

"You had better be hoping that our choppers get here before your friends do . . . one way you'll end up living . . . the other way your ass is going to be dead. . . ." Paul waved the business end of his CAR-15 at the wide-eyed man.

The jungle sounds began again around the hidden recon team. Cooper whispered to Paul who was lying next to him under a thick jungle plant, "I told them to bring a McGuire rig for the prisoner . . . they sounded really surprised . . ."

The helicopters could be heard coming from a long way off. Paul began preparing the prisoner for the extraction. Cooper removed three syringes of morphine from his first-aid kit and handed them over to Paul. The young prisoner's eyes enlarged when he saw the needles.

"Feel damn lucky that this is all that's going into your fucking body . . . you damn traitor!" Cooper watched Paul shove the first needle deep into the man's buttocks. "Lieutenant, why don't you put the other two shots in his nuts!"

The prisoner started thrashing around on the dead bamboo leaves. Cooper placed his knee on the soldier's chest and grinned. A muffled scream came from behind the tape.

"Let him be, Cooper!" Paul nudged his team mate.

"Just trying to make him sweat a bit, sir!" Cooper frowned.

The first of the choppers appeared and hovered over the small clearing. Three rapelling ropes with sandbags attached to weight them down were dropped out of the open side doors. The fourth rope had a horse-collar-shaped device attached to it. The two Americans carried the semiconscious man to the harness and strapped him into the seat. Two of the Montagnards hooked their STABO "D" rings to the ends of the dangling ropes. Paul yelled for Cooper to ride with the prisoner. Cooper hooked up and grabbed the McGuire rig at the same time, wrapping both of his legs around the prisoner. Lieutenant Bourne would never forgive Cooper if the prisoner managed to jump from his seat when they were airborne.

The second helicopter appeared shortly after the first one had pulled away from the opening in the jungle floor. Cobra gunships opened fire near the riverbanks, covering Paul and the old Montagnard as they rushed to hook up.

Paul looked up at the crew chief and gave a thumbs-up sign for them to take off. The old Montagnard grabbed Paul's left strap on his web gear and held his CAR-15 under his left arm. The old commando motioned with his head for Paul to do the same thing. The helicopter dropped its nose in the screen pattern of green tracers. The Montagnard pointed his weapon and opened fire at the spot of the jungle from where the tracers emerged. The last chopper turned and dashed for safety with Paul and his team mate firing down at the enemy.

Chapter 16

The two helicopters carrying Bourne's recon team continued climbing toward the protective cover of the thick clouds rolling over the jungle. The Cobra gunships continued making passes over the extraction site, returning fire to the enemy gunners. The jungle below Paul changed from individual trees into a solid dark green carpet as he hung suspended on the nylon rope. He relaxed his body in the STABO harness once they had gained enough altitude to leave the arching tracers below them. The wind blowing against Paul's sweat-soaked fatigues withdrew his body heat, causing his muscles to shake.

Lieutenant Bourne looked over to his right and saw the helicopter carrying Cooper and the prisoner. Sergeant Cooper had the naked man held in a tight bearhug, trying to keep the hundred-knot wind from killing him. Paul looked up at the bottom of the helicopter and saw one of the door gunners leaning out over the skids. The only device holding the man to the aircraft was a thin nylon safety strap. The gunner was pointing down toward the jungle. Paul followed the door gunner's arm with his eyes and saw where he was pointing. A Marine fire-support base stood carved out of the foliage, less than a mile away. Paul let go of his CAR-15, allowing it to hang from its sling, and gave the door gunner the thumbs-up sign. The pilot was planning on landing in the clearing near the old base to let the recon team scramble inside for the long ride home. The helicopters approached the unmanned fire-support base with extreme caution, since the NVA were fond of scrounging around abandoned American bases for C-rations and equipment that had been left behind by American soldiers.

A Cobra gunship appeared from the west, flying at treetop level as Paul's helicopter hovered above the base area, descending slowly to the ground with its dangling human cargo. Paul watched the ground as it rose up toward the toes of his boots. He instinctively stretched his toes toward the safe brown earth, and felt the pressure ease up in his harness when his legs absorbed his weight. It felt good to touch the dry clay. Paul and the old Montagnard stumbled into the open side doors of the idling helicopter on blood-denied legs. The harnesses from the STABO rigs had cut off the circulation of blood to their lower extremities. Paul felt his cheek touch against the cool metal deck of the chopper as the door gunner nearest to him grabbed his pistol belt and pulled him into the vibrating machine. Paul and the Montagnard remained lying on the steel floor, neither of them having the energy to pull themselves up into the nylon mesh seats. They were safe.

The four Cobra gunships left the slicks over Quang Tri and headed for their home base at Camp Eagle. The slicks banked and aimed toward the South China Sea's coastline in the distance. The lead chopper turned south at the waterline and angled for the CCN base camp located at the base of Marble Mountain. Paul's body relaxed in increments as he recognized familiar landmarks. Large groups of Vietnamese fishermen covered the calm sea in their round bull boats. All of the bobbing craft remained within sight of the shoreline and maintained a respectable distance from the cruising naval gunboats. The tail of the helicopter dipped as Paul's aircraft slowed its speed for a landing. Paul looked out the door and saw the black van parked near the fifty-foot-long "H" marker. Lieutenant Colonel Clewell and Major Galviston were both standing near the open van doors, looking up at the approaching craft. Paul forced himself to pick up his rucksack and ignore his sore muscles when the skids touched the PSP pad. Galviston grabbed him by his arm and helped Paul into the van.

"Damn it, Lieutenant! You did it again!" Galviston and the colonel were both smiling. "We were expecting your team to stay on the ground at least a week . . . I'll be damned! One day out and you're back in camp . . . mission accomplished! Great job!"

Paul tried grinning. "I have a good team."

"Let's get in the van!" Clewell patted Paul's shoulder as they all entered the dark chamber inside the vehicle. Cooper and the rest of the team joined them, carrying the naked prisoner. The doors closed and the van shot across the helipad. The black vehicle came to a rocking halt in front of the isolation area.

"Get our friend inside. . . ." Galviston helped Cooper carry the half-conscious man through the open door. "Paul, use the intercom and get a medic over here . . . pronto!"

"Christ! He's a kid!" Clewell picked up a poncho

liner off one of the bunks and wrapped it around the shaking body. "Cut those handcuffs off his wrists . . ."

Cooper obeyed and used his knife to cut the man's hands free. He pulled the tape slowly off the soldier's mouth and watched as the man inhaled a deep breath of air and partially opened his eyes. He still suffered from the effects of the morphine shots and the cold air from flying underneath the chopper.

"He'll need some rest, but he should be able to talk in the morning." Paul dropped back down in a nearby chair.

"He's shaking like a leaf." Clewell placed his open palm on the prisoner's chest and felt his heart rate and breathing both at the same time. "Damn! I hope he's not going to die on us!"

"He may be suffering from exposure. Our ride back was pretty cold." Cooper stood behind the colonel.

"Pull that blanket off and start rubbing him down." The Special Forces medic edged his way in between Cooper and the colonel. "He's suffering from extreme heat loss and will slip into terminal shock if we don't hurry!"

"Shit! If that son of a bitch dies on us . . ." Cooper grabbed one of the man's legs and started rubbing vigorously.

"Let's put him under a hot shower." Paul walked around to the far side of the bed.

"Good idea!" The medic picked up the light body in his arms and carried him into the open shower room. The warm water spraying against his shaking body woke the prisoner. He looked around at the staring faces and gained control of himself. The expression of surprise surrounding his eyes changed to fear. He knew what he had done and realized that he would have to face a lot of trouble.

"How are you feeling, boy?" Clewell's voice was fatherly and allowed the prisoner to relax slightly on the tile floor of the shower.

"I didn't do anything wrong!" The young soldier tried standing up on the slippery floor.

"Lieutenant Bourne, see if you can find him some clothes," the colonel kept his voice soft.

"They forced me to help them!" Fear crackled through the youth's voice. "After they captured us, the NVA said that they would torture us if we didn't help them . . . really!" His eyes traveled from face to face, looking for someone who believed what he was saying. "They tortured Jim . . . he died! . . . I just want to live!"

"Relax, son . . . We'll find you some clothes and get some hot chow in your stomach and then we'll talk some more . . . just rest for awhile . . . OK?" Clewell stepped back and allowed the medic to hand the shaking youth a towel to dry off with before leaving the shower. Paul appeared in the doorway carrying a new set of camouflaged jungle fatigues.

"The S-4 had these sent over. I guess they saw us carrying the prisoner in." Paul handed the uniform to the medic.

"Bourne, come over here a second." Clewell stepped over to one of the beds at the far end of the room and put his foot up on the steel frame. "Every time you get near that kid he starts shaking harder. . . . Why don't you release your team and come back over to the command center in the morning for your debrief. I'd like to talk to this kid alone so that he'll calm down." Clewell nodded over to the man and asked, "Why is he naked?"

"He was swimming in the Sapone River with two of his buddies. A third was playing guard carrying an AK-47 . . ."

"What happened to them?"

"I killed them." Cooper had joined the officers. "I didn't have much of a choice . . . either kill them or they would have joined the NVA against us. . . . I mean, the black was carrying an AK-47 and he was guarding the swimming group. The man could have escaped at anytime . . . if he had wanted to."

"Don't start feeling guilty. You followed orders—and remember, the Marines reported that they were fired on *first* by the Americans . . . that doesn't sound like POWs waiting for a chance to escape!"

Lieutenant Bourne hung his web gear and weapons on the wall pegs in his hooch. He went over to the window and pushed back the curtain, allowing the bright sunlight to burst into the small room. Paul opened the ammunition box under his bed that he used for a storage container and removed the partially full bottle of Jim Beam, then laid his head back against the chair and took a long pull straight from the bottle. The whiskey burned his throat as it traveled down to his empty stomach, ending its trip in a fireball. Paul poured a plastic cup half full and propped his feet against the wall that faced the sea.

The plastic cup slipped out of his hand down to the floor.

The gentle sound of waves breaking against the beach woke Paul. The sea wind was starting to pick up with the early-evening tide change. Paul stood and stretched. He looked at his watch and noticed that it was nearing eight o'clock at night. He had slept through the whole afternoon in his chair. Paul stripped down to his shorts and grabbed a towel. The shower building was located between two of the team hooches across the small clearing of sand that separated him from the rest of the recon company buildings. The sun-heated water tanks located on the roof of the building provided a warm cleansing shower that removed the sweat, dirt, and camouflage paint from his body.

"Hey, sir!" The voice came from the other side of the wooden shower wall. "You going to the movies tonight?"

Paul called back, "What's on?"

"It's a western. . . . The commandos are sure to shoot up the place!"

"Just a minute . . ." Paul pulled his towel off the wall and stepped out onto the wooden pallet that was used to stand on while drying off. "Where are you?"

Cooper and Loveless appeared through the shower entrance. Paul wrapped his towel around his waist; he didn't want to put his dirty shorts back on now that he felt clean.

Loveless spoke, "Hey, instead of going to the movie, let's get a couple of bottles and go down to the beach and get a little drunk tonight."

"Sounds good to me!" Cooper grinned.

"You all go to the club and get the booze and meet me back here at my hooch at eight-thirty. . . . that'll give me enough time to get something to eat." Paul left his friends and went through the loose sand over to his small hooch. He hung his towel up in the rafters to dry and threw his dirty clothes in his laundry bag. He picked up his well-worn cut-offs from the floor next to his bed and stepped back when a small brown scorpion flipped its tail in the air. Paul slapped the insect with his shorts, flipping it against the wall. The arachnid spun around the floor trying to locate its tormentor. Bourne picked up one of his boots and ended the insect warrior's concern forever. A shiver went up his spine as he thought of what could have happened if the scorpion had been inside his shorts when he slipped them on. He shivered again and searched his hooch for any more buddies of his dead opponent. Paul made a mental note to go over to the S-4 shop and get some insect spray to saturate the floor around his walls. He shook his shorts again before slipping them on over his hips. Another shiver vibrated at the base of his neck as he anticipated a sting.

Paul removed his weapon-cleaning kit from the shelf above his bed, sat in his handmade chair, and placed his CAR-15 across his lap. It took him twenty minutes to give the submachine gun a quick cleaning. He rushed through his work because he really wanted to get down to the beach and get very, very drunk.

Lieutenant Bourne placed his BAR belt around his waist and slipped the sling on his CAR-15 over his right shoulder. He hung his weapon upside-down over his bare back. Light spilled through the screen on the back door of the mess hall, sending long shadows out over the sand.

"Anybody here?"

"In the back!"

"Can I make a couple of sandwiches?" Paul called to the unseen cook.

"Sure, if you don't mind helping yourself." The mess sergeant wiped his hands on his apron. "I'm baking for tomorrow."

"Thanks." Paul pushed back the cloth that covered the tray of leftovers from the evening meal and prepared himself two huge sandwiches.

"You really pulled off a great mission, Lieutenant," the sergeant yelled above the drone coming from the mixer.

"Thanks!" Paul shook his head and waved his thanks with a hand full of super Dagwood. A grin spread over Paul's face as he thought about how fast news traveled through the Special Forces units. He had no doubt that someone in the other SOG camps already knew about the mission he had just completed. Word traveled through the Special Forces grapevine via secure voice radios. Thoughts about My An flashed through his mind and how badly his reputation had to be suffering over that tour served under Captain Hetten.

Paul pushed the last bite of sandwich into his mouth as he reached the back gate of the camp that led to the beach. The guard on duty was a commando Paul had shown earlier how to surf.

"Hi!" Paul waved to the man as he approached the sentry outpost bunker.

"Chow, Lieutenant! You swim now?"

"No . . . party on beach . . . get wasted!"

The commando laughed. "VC come and get you for sure!" He waved a disciplining finger at Paul.

Paul returned the laugh and patted his CAR-15 with an exaggerated motion. "Shoot them up . . . big time!"

The guard unchained the sea gate and allowed Paul to pass through the narrow opening designed for human passage, next to the wider gate locked with chains and only opened for the passage of trucks or an occasional battle tank. The waves broke against the beach violently from the seven footer just off shore. Paul walked along the high-water line with his eyes wandering around the sand dunes, looking for any interesting objects that the sea might have washed ashore.

"What in the fuck are you carrying on your shoulder?" Jay stood up from behind the low sand dune that had concealed him from view.

"My fuckin' gun, dipshit!" Paul changed course and joined Jay and Cooper, who had obviously started partying early.

"Man, you don't need heat down here. . . . Shit, we're safe this close to the base camp." Jay started to laugh and turned over toward Cooper.

"Jay?" Paul spoke softly to his friend.

"Yeah. . . ."

"Did the war end today?" Paul's tone was cutting. "This is one fella who isn't going to die in this fuckin' country through stupidity. It only takes a few seconds to put my gear on and a little energy to carry it down her. . . . Personally, I prefer to have a weapon close-by . . . especially at night . . ." Paul grinned to ease the tension, ". . . if you don't fuckin' mind!"

"Here, Lieutenant . . . have a drink." Cooper poured a plastic cup halfway full of bourbon. Paul took the offered drink and plopped down on the loose sand that was still warm from the sun. He placed his canvas BAR belt on the sand and laid his CAR-15 on top of it.

"What in the fuck is that?" Jay stood and pointed at an object lying thirty feet away on the edge of the bubbling surf. A wave had washed the creature ashore and it was desperately trying to return to the protection of the sea. Paul and Cooper stood and followed Jay's pointing arm.

"Damn! That's a sea snake!" Paul jogged toward the two-foot-long reptile, followed by his drinking partners. He stopped a respectable distance from the snake and watched the deadly creature continue its effort to reach the water, ignoring the humans.

"Do those things bite?" Jay took a step closer to the creature but was stopped in mid-stride by Paul's outstretched arm.

"The tiger snake of Australia and the sea snake are probably the deadliest mothers crawling." Paul released his hold on Jay's arm.

"No shit?" Jay looked over to where Paul's CAR-15 was laying. "Let me use your sub and I'll blow that little mutha away!"

"No . . . shooting will alarm the camp." Paul led the way back to where their whiskey bottles stood in the sand. "Let it live . . . maybe it'll bite a VC for us."

"Hell, Lieutenant, there's going to be more shooting going on in camp tonight than a full-scale war!"

"What are you talking about, Cooper?"

"They're showing a western movie, and every time the Indians attack the cowboys our commandos open up on the movie screen with their weapons. I mean, they blow the shit out of the bed sheets we use for a movie screen!"

"The colonel allows them to do that?"

"Well, we've tried stopping the western flicks, but the morale dropped so low we brought them back. The ol' man changed the site where we showed the films. He placed the sheet screen toward the rifle range at the base of Marble Mountain. Now the commandos get target practice and it only costs us eight or ten cotton sheets!"

"I guess that's one way to train troops." Paul reached over and filled his glass again with quality bourbon.

"Shit, Lieutenant, you've gotten me all nervous. I think I'll go back and get my stuff." Cooper started walking toward the sea gate.

"Just a second, Coop! I'll go with you!" Jay trotted after the sergeant.

Paul pushed his cup of bourbon down in the loose sand and threw his cut-offs next to the cup. He watched the waves coming in and timed his entry into the sea with an eight-foot-high wall of water. The waves were spaced about one hundred meters apart, with smaller waves filling the open water between them. The beach was unique in front of the Special Forces camp. The depth of the water between the waves was less than five feet, which created a tremendous undertow that went back out to the edge of the sandbar, and then the water depth increased rapidly. The beach was excellent for body surfing at this time of day, letting Paul catch a dozen good waves before his friends returned. Paul rode a large ten-foot wave to shore and quickly ran up the beach before the returning water could tug him back out to sea. He stood on the hard-packed sand and shook his torso and head, followed in turn by each leg individually to remove as much excess water as he could before returning to his booze. He turned on the sand and faced the wind coming from the open sea to let the swift breeze partially dry him. Paul visualized that the westerly wind had originated on the California coast and had traveled the great distance over the ocean swells to him. He shook his head, allowing the wind to dry his hair.

"Hey, Neptune! Are you going to join us?" Jay's voice floated brokenly above the wind and wave sound. Paul trotted back to his gear.

"The water felt really good." Paul slipped on his shorts as he talked.

"You ain't going to get my ass in that water! Not after seeing that fuckin' snake!" Cooper poured himself a liberal drink.

Paul noticed that Jay and Cooper had brought all of their fighting gear, including hand grenades.

A great burst of gunfire erupted from the camp.

"The commandos are shooting up the movie screen." Cooper half-turned in the direction the gunfire was coming from and leaned on his elbow.

Paul's hand moved to his CAR-15.

"Shit, Lieutenant . . . don't be so damn jumpy! This happens all of the time!" Cooper sipped from his glass.

Paul looked at the dial of his watch: 2330 hours, almost midnight. He pulled his web-gear harness over his shoulders and fastened his pistol belt just as a loud explosion rippled the night air.

"Do commandos throw satchel charges, too?" Paul racked a round into the chamber of his weapon.

Jay and Cooper scrambled for their gear. "Hell, no! *We're under attack!*"

"Slow down . . ." Paul slid on his belly to the top edge of the large sand dune that separated them from the camp. Two of the American sleeping hooches near the main headquarters building were in flames. Men were running around the camp half-dressed, trying to form up into small fighting units. The trio watched the developing battle from the safety of their beachfront seats.

"Looks as if they caught the guards sleeping . . ." Jay whispered even though the gunfire covered any sounds they were making.

"Over next to the mess hall," Cooper pointed to a group of about fifty commandos wearing red armbands. "They don't look like any of ours."

"Shit! They're not! VC! . . . They must have snuck into camp dressed like commandos!"

The group of elite VC sappers moved under the camp floodlights, methodically throwing satchel charges into the buildings and shooting any stray commandos they found.

Paul spotted a gathering of Americans at the far end of the camp near the sleeping quarters for the headquarters personnel. The VC had picked a good night to hit them, with most of the fighting recon teams inserted in the jungle on missions. A large group of commandos were reinforcing the TOC guards, who had successfully kept the VC from penetrating the security fence around the cement building. The camp was rapidly mobilizing against the enemy, taking the surprise out of the attack. The sappers were hard pressed, and began to withdraw toward the sea gate and the open beach.

"Shit! They're coming this way!" Cooper chambered a round in his CAR-15.

Paul glanced down the beach. To the north, American installations stretched for miles. The enemy would have to run a machine gun gauntlet, and they'd still end up in downtown Da Nang. Paul looked out to sea. The waves were too high for boats to reach the sapper force, and they would drown trying to swim out past the breakers.

"Cooper . . . what's to the south of Marble Mountain?"

"A village of Vietnamese fishermen, nothing else. Marble Mountain is our southernmost installation." Cooper looked up to the top of the mountain. "Hell! They've wiped out the Marine outpost!"

Smoke and flames were coming from the small base on top of the mountain.

The Americans and commandos at the far end of the camp had organized and had formed a solid fighting line that was pushing the sappers back to the sea. Paul started crawling for the sea gate.

"Come on! We'll catch them in a crossfire!"

The guard at the sea gate was lying behind a small sand dune ready to defend his position with his life against the large VC force. Paul called out to him, and without any hesitation the small man joined the lieutenant's team.

"How many grenades do you all have?" Paul counted four on the commando's web gear.

"I've got four," Jay answered Paul.

"I've got two high explosive and two white phosphorus." Cooper slid next to Paul.

"All right . . . here's my plan. The commando and I will take up positions south of the gate. When the sappers start to bunch up as they reach the sea gate, I want everybody to throw two of their grenades . . . Cooper, throw both of your white phosphorus . . . throw the remainder of your grenades when you have targets." Paul smiled. "They're going to be fighting like hell to break through the sea gate, so use your CAR-15s sparingly or we'll run out of ammo."

Paul got up on one knee to see what was going on in the camp and saw that the first of the VC had reached the last of the hooches that separated them from the sea gate.

"We'd better get our asses in gear!" Paul tapped the commando on his shoulder and pointed to where he wanted him to go.

"Good luck, Paul." Jay nodded and then left with Cooper to a slight rise that gave them a commanding view of the sea gate.

Paul helped his commando push a pile of sand up in front of him, more to hide him from view than for protection, and then made a shallow depression for himself a few meters away where he could see the gate. Paul removed five magazines from his BAR belt, placing them on top of each other near his left hand.

Lieutenant Bourne and his small team waited.

The first of the sappers reached the sea gate and shot the lock off with hardly a pause. Paul had hoped that the lock would have slowed the enemy force down enough to have made them bunch up along the gate. They were obviously very good soldiers. Paul pulled the pin on his first grenade. Five more VC joined the first one and helped him push the gate open through the piled sand. Fifteen more sappers cleared the protection of the hooches and ran toward the open gate. The command party of the sapper force joined the team that had opened the barrier.

Paul leaned back and threw his first grenade. It bounced off the steel rail of the main gate and hit one of the sappers on the side of his face, falling down in the sand at his feet. Paul watched the man stare at the live grenade, and then saw the fear cover the enemy face when he recognized in the half-light what had hit him. Orange flame and black smoke engulfed the soldier and his nearest comrades. Paul threw his second grenade and it meshed with the convoy of explosions from the rest of the grenades thrown by his team. Cooper's white-phosphorus grenades lit up the beach front as they spread their white blossoms of death in a large fan of burning death fragments.

The small American team opened up on the enemy force with their small arms, cutting the massed VC apart. The surprise attack from outside the camp had caught the sappers unprepared and their commander off-guard for the first time that evening. The VC leader had expected only a single gate guard, not a fighting unit. He was trapped, and knew that he must gain momentum and break through the unknown force opposing him or his unit would be destroyed.

The sapper leader jumped up from his hidden position and screamed a curse at the Americans. The twenty-three remaining enemy soldiers followed their commander directly toward Lieutenant Bourne's position. Jay immediately saw the danger and threw his last hand grenade into the middle of the sapper charge. The bomb failed to explode.

Paul threw his remaining grenades at the charging mass of determined enemy, killing eight of them. Cooper stood up from the dry sand in a crouching position, firing his CAR-15 from the hip, trying to draw the main charge away from Paul's position. The sergeant succeeded in gaining the attention of four bayonet-carrying NVA. Cooper spun around on the sand and fell backward with his head making a smacking sound when it hit the loose-packed beach.

The enemy commander was almost on top of Paul, who was busy changing magazines, when the commando gate-guard jumped on the snapper's back and pushed his K-Bar knife through the man's throat. Paul dropped his weapon and pulled his Randall from its sheath, reaching out at the same time to grab the round-style bayonet being thrust at his naked chest. Paul flipped the sapper through the air by rolling backward and used his feet to push the short man up and over him, following through the movement so that he would end up on the enemy soldier's chest with his knees digging in the sand. Paul thrust the extremely sharp knife deep into the open-mouthed man's neck muscles, twisting the blood-covered blade as he removed it so that a channel would be opened for the sapper's blood to flow out.

Sand burnt against Paul's cheeks from the bullets clipping the ground inches in front of him. He rolled over to his left and the copper-coated slugs that were meant for him smacked into the dead sapper commander's body. Paul dove for the sapper lying on the sand less than ten feet from him and shoved his knife under the man's ribs. Paul instantaneously rolled off the soldier's back and stood in a crouch waiting for another attack.

The beach was littered with dead sappers.

Rifle fire echoed along the sand dunes from the base camp as the commandos found and eliminated small pockets of fanatical sappers.

"Jay! Cooper! . . . are you guys all right?"

"I'm fine . . . but Cooper's hit!"

The gate guard walked over to Paul. "VC . . . all dead . . ."

Paul wiped the sweat rolling down his forehead with the back of his blood-covered hand, creating a Crow Indian's war mask on his face: half red and half suntanned brown.

"Jay! Where are you?"

"Over here!"

Lieutenant Bourne helped Jay stop the blood flowing from Cooper's wounds. Paul used the commando's jacket for a temporary bandage to stem the flow of life force that was leaving his team mate.

Cooper opened his eyes. "Am I hit bad . . . Lieutenant?"

"Not too bad . . . You've got a round through your leg and a couple of creases . . . you'll live . . . but all that whiskey you've drank tonight is leaking out."

Cooper smiled. "You might not know this but you're good luck, Lieutenant . . . A man can't die working for you. . . ."

Cooper passed out.

Paul grinned and raised his eyes from the sergeant, and saw five Americans walking carefully through the sea gate.

"Over here! We need a medic!"

The five men ran over to Paul's location.

"Cooper's hit and needs help!" Paul's voice rose as he talked.

"We got him, Lieutenant! . . . The colonel's coming behind us . . ."

Lieutenant Bourne stood as Lieutenant Colonel Clewell and a small group of Americans, mixed with commandos, spread out over the beach searching for any stray or still-living sappers.

"That one over there acted like their leader," Paul pointed.

"I might have known it would be you!" Clewell walked up to Paul. "What in the hell brought you out here on the beach at this hour of the night?"

"Getting drunk with Loveless and Cooper . . . sir."

"You brought your weapons to the beach with you?"

"Don't you think it was a good idea, sir?"

Clewell wrapped his arm around Paul's neck. "I think it was a *damn* good idea, Lieutenant!"

Paul felt his face turning red and stepped back from the colonel.

"How did they get in camp, sir?"

"We don't know yet . . . but we figure they bribed the main-gate guards this afternoon and walked right in dressed like our commandos. Shit! They even had the balls to watch the movie with our troops! Talk about *big* fucking balls!"

"Yeah . . . but they all got their asses greased in the process . . ." Paul half-grinned at the colonel. "How many people have we lost, sir?"

"Don't know yet . . . they threw satchel charges into the senior NCO and officer hooches . . . killed five."

"I'm going over to see Cooper in the dispensary and then to my hooch . . . unless you need me for something else, sir."

"No . . . Bourne, you saved my camp from a total disaster . . . I appreciate that." Clewell's voice dropped.

"Damn, sir! It's all in being at the wrong place at the right time. . . . we had to fight or die."

"Well . . . I'm damn glad that I got you out of Nha Trang. . . . The group commander is going to hear about this one in detail!" The colonel's look gave away that he knew what had gone on at My An and the charges that were pressed against Paul.

"Jay! Get our bottle and meet me at the doc's!" Paul walked fast over the sand toward the center of the camp.

Jay picked up his empty magazines and the almost-empty bottle of bourbon. As he walked through the sea gate he saw an American grenade half-buried in the loose sand. He reached down before he thought and picked up the explosive, noticing that the safety handle was missing.

It was alive!

Jay nearly dropped the grenade in the sand before he caught himself. It was a dud, probably the one he had thrown earlier that had failed to explode. He unscrewed the fuze and noticed a yellow piece of paper shoved down into the fuze well. Jay unrolled the note and read the message in neatly printed block letters:

STOP KILLING EACH OTHER! PEACE BROTHER!

Chapter 17

General Pick sat with his legs crossed and his feet hanging over the corner of his desk. A picture of his wife and children dominated the opposite corner of the well-polished wooden desktop. He concentrated as he looked out the window of his Pentagon East Headquarters, causing deep furrows to appear on his forehead. The general rolled an unlit cigar between the fingers of his left hand and read the sheet of paper that he held in his right hand for the tenth time.

The senior general looked over at the door to his office when his aide de camp entered carrying the personnel folder he had asked for earlier in the morning.

"The records people kept a copy of his last officer efficiency report, sir." The young aide laid the folder in front of the general and waited while he lit his cigar.

"Sometimes it just doesn't figure up . . ." General Pick spoke between jets of inhaled cigar smoke. He dropped his feet to the floor and scooted his chair up to the desk. Telltale signs of anger appeared on the general's face when he read the highlighted parts of the efficiency report that Captain Hetten had submitted on Lieutenant Bourne. "Damn! His last commander wrote him up as a coward, and this message here . . ." the general waved the paper he still held in his right hand, ". . . states that the commander at the Command and Control North site wants to present a Distinguished Service Cross and a Silver Star to the same man!"

The aide joined the general, shaking his head in the same manner.

"There's more! . . . Bourne will be receiving the DSC with a first oak-leaf cluster! This is the boy's *second* award," General Pick stood and slapped the top of his desk with his open palm. "Someone is trying to bullshit me!"

The aide nodded his head in full agreement, but did not speak.

"Send a message to Clewell . . . Tell him that I'll fly in to his camp tomorrow and present the awards myself at his ceremony . . . also set up a private meeting between me and Lieutenant Bourne . . . but don't make it too obvious!" The general slid the folder back to the waiting aide and resumed his former thinking position with his legs crossed on his desk—but this time he was taking long puffs from his cigar.

Lieutenant Bourne woke early, just as daylight was breaking over the water on the sea, and left the CCN compound for the hospital in one of the recon company's black jeeps. It was the first day that they were going to allow visitors in to see Sergeant Cooper. Mist hung low over the rice paddies that bordered the narrow two-lane asphalt road that had been repaved by the Navy Seabees. Paul drove the five miles to the hospital holding the gas pedal down against the floorboard of the jeep. He was deep in thought that covered his first two weeks assigned to CCN. He was tired of killing and seeing his friends killed and maimed for life. Paul stopped the jeep at the main bridge on the outskirts of the city and waited for the military policeman on duty to wave him across. There were two American soldiers sitting on small stacks of green plastic sandbags on top of a huge fighting bunker, smoking pipes. Paul could smell the sweet acid odor of hashish. It was six o'clock in the morning and those two soldiers were well on their way to getting stoned. Paul's mind filled with disgust over the guards' conduct and the acceptance of the military policeman to the situation. Paul wondered what in the hell the American army was coming to! Racial and drug problems were totally out of control, with most commanders ignoring the situation—and if they did try to stop it, they would end up getting fragged by their own troops. The noncommissioned officers saw nothing and did nothing.

Paul yelled over to the pair of guards when his jeep passed the bunker, "Suck on those pipes, you worthless cocksuckers!"

One of the guards tried standing up to see who had insulted him, but fell down sideways against his buddy.

The gate guard at the hospital waved Paul through with a bored arm movement. Bourne parked his jeep in the first empty slot he could find next to the "F" wing of the single-story building and entered through the nurses' private entrance. He saw Cooper occupying the bed nearest to the on-duty nurse station.

"Hey, Leg! How you doing?" Paul approached Cooper's bed.

The sergeant opened his eyes and smiled. "Hi, Lieutenant! Hell . . . I'll be out of here in a week. The doctor said that my wounds were clean. I just lost a lot of blood . . . no broken bones."

The nurse sitting at the desk turned around to see who Cooper was talking to and growled, "Lieutenant! How did you get in here?"

"Why I walked in through the door, my lovely dove," Paul pointed to the screened nurses' entrance.

"Don't give me that kind of crap, young man! I'm a Lieutenant Colonel and expect to be treated like one!"

"Excuse me! . . . Ma'ammmm!"

"Don't get on her bad side or Christ, she'll give me another one of those shots with her horse needle!" Cooper laughed.

"Hey! Did you hear that General Pick is coming out to CCN today? He's going to present some awards to our guys for the attack on our base camp." Paul patted Cooper's bed and continued talking, "You're going to get a Silver Star for our mission with the prisoner and a *second* Silver Star for the home-camp fight . . . How about that shit! You're a fucking hero!" Paul watched as Cooper's face lit up.

"Really? Man . . . is Dad going to be proud!" Cooper said. His face quickly turned red.

Paul quickly covered his friend's embarrassment and added, "And a Purple Heart, too, for those little scratches you've got!"

Cooper nodded his head and made an exaggerated grimace as if he were still in great pain. "Scratches, my ass!"

"Well . . . have the nurse put a clean bib on you, because the general will probably come here to pin your medals on himself . . ." Paul took a seat on his teammate's bed. "Thanks for what you did for me during the fire-fight . . . those gooks would have greased my ass!"

"Cut the bullshit, Lieutenant! Hell . . . I didn't even see you! I jumped up because a crab ran into my shorts!"

Paul smiled. Cooper smiled.

"I have to shag my ass back to camp. The general is due in at 0830 hours. Do you need anything?"

"No . . . maybe a couple of good fuck books. . . ." Cooper rested his head back on his pillow.

"He doesn't need any of those kinds of books . . ." The old nurse had been listening to their conversation, ". . . we have a library in the hospital that's full of wholesome literature!"

Cooper started laughing so hard over the woman's exaggerated expression that he ended up moaning from the pain the movement gave him.

"Gotta go, Coop." Paul stood to leave and looked over at the nurse. "Bye . . . Sweetie!"

"You get out of here!" The old girl left the protection of her duty station and headed for Paul waving a metal clipboard.

"See you later," Paul waved at the nurse and ran out of the back door.

The nurse went over to Cooper's bed and tucked in the sheets around him. She watched Paul leave the ward with a small smile on her face. "Who is that lieutenant? He's a cute little thing, isn't he?"

Sergeant Cooper rolled his eyes in confusion over the woman's change of heart toward Paul.

The large steel-plank helipad at the CCN headquarters held the American troops and the commando contingent comfortably along the northern side of the large square. The men stood relaxed in formation with their CAR-15s slung over their right shoulders, waiting for the general's arrival by helicopter. The adjutant ran over to Lieutenant Bourne before he could park the jeep in front of the headquarters and spoke with a tinge of panic in his voice. "Bourne! Where in the hell have you been? The general is due to arrive any minute now!"

"I was visiting Cooper at the hospital," Paul took his

CAR-15 from the passenger seat and adjusted his pistol belt.

"Oh . . . well, let's get our asses in gear. . . . Your position is over there behind the colonel . . . hustle it!"

Lieutenant Bourne had been notified earlier that he would be receiving an award. The other medal winners were already waiting in line behind the colonel.

Lieutenant Colonel Clewell nodded and spoke to Paul in a low voice. "Where have you been?"

"Went over to see Cooper, sir." Paul assumed a parade-rest position at the end of the line. He could hear the faint drone of a helicopter coming from his front, but the view was blocked by the steep cliffs of Marble Mountain.

The colonel turned and faced his troops. "Bring your units to attention!"

Paul waited for the colonel to face about and then came to the military position of attention with the rest of the awardees. A helicopter appeared and dropped down to a hover a hundred feet in front of them. There were four white stars painted on a red background attached to the sliding door of the chopper. Paul thought that it wasn't a very good idea to advertise the cargo the aircraft was carrying, but, then again, a little show of guts added to the general's leadership image.

General Pick stepped from the chopper and adjusted his uniform before reaching out to shake hands with his escort officer. The general and his aide walked over to where Clewell stood at attention and returned the colonel's salute. The CCN adjutant took up a position to the right side of the general, carrying a dark-blue felt pillow with a number of valor awards pinned on the cloth. Paul caught the blue, red, and narrow white stripes of a Distinguished Service Cross. Music began playing over the camp's speaker system, sending a shiver along Paul's spine that ended up as a pleasant tingling sensation at the base of his neck.

General Pick approached the microphone just as the music stopped playing. "Men of Command and Control North . . . it is always a pleasure when I come here to visit your ranks. . . . You are a collection of the finest fighting men under my command! . . . Today I would like to show you the appreciation of a grateful Nation and that of a very proud Commander-in-Chief . . . for the blood and personal sacrifices you have given for this unit's mission and your fellow soldiers. . . ."

The general's address took an additional five minutes. Paul's mind wandered from the general's speech to My An and the disgrace he had suffered under Captain Hetten. Paul readjusted his vision when the CCN commander turned and called the units back to attention. General Pick and the colonel started walking in Paul's direction with the adjutant following slightly to their rear, carrying the blue pillow in both of his hands.

General Pick stopped directly in front on Paul and smiled before he spoke, "Lieutenant Bourne . . . It's a pleasure seeing you again. . . . My An? Wasn't it?"

"Yes, sir." Paul was amazed that the general actually remembered who he was and where they had met before.

The adjutant held the pillow forward and the general unhooked the Distinguished Service Cross with a bronze oak leaf attached in the center of the ribbon.

A voice came over the loudspeaker as the general pinned the medal of Paul's fatigue pocket.

"The Distinguished Service Cross . . . first oak-leaf cluster . . . is awarded to Lieutenant Paul Bourne for extraordinary valor . . ."

Paul's mind reeled while the award was being pinned on him. After the short ceremony he couldn't remember any of the small details. The general worked his way along the line of recipients, handing out well-earned medals to the Special Forces soldiers.

". . . Lieutenant J. B. Loveless . . . The Silver Star is awarded for gallantry in action during . . ." The voice droned on over the public-address system.

The command party returned to the center of the massed troops. Lieutenant Colonel Clewell saluted the general and spoke, "Sir, that concludes the ceremony."

General Pick glanced down at his wristwatch. "I have a few minutes to spare, Colonel. Would you mind showing me your operation center?"

Clewell was caught by surprise. The general's aide de camp had informed him the day before that the General would stay only for the brief ceremony and then leave for corps headquarters.

"Sir, I don't have any jeeps standing by, but if you will follow me, we can walk over to the TOC."

"That's fine with me, Colonel. I could use a little exercise after riding up here in that helicopter." General Pick placed his hand on Clewell's shoulder and looked over at his aide de camp, nodding his head toward Lieutenant Bourne.

The aide understood the general's request and nodded back in the affirmative while he walked over to where Paul was standing. "Lieutenant, please come with us."

Paul followed the aide until they were out of hearing range of the staff officers. "What's going on, sir?"

"General Pick wants to talk to you in private. Is there a place nearby where you can meet with him?"

"Me? He wants to talk with me?"

"Yes."

"Well, there're some private briefing rooms over in the operations center." Paul could see that the general and Clewell were headed in that direction.

"Good, lead the way."

Paul and the aide arrived at the entrance to the operations center seconds behind the general and passed through the checkpoint without being stopped by the gate guard.

"The rooms are to our left," Paul pointed down the hall.

"You wait inside for the general." The aide pointed into the first empty room and left Paul standing alone.

Paul pulled out a chair from the table and sat down. Something must be going on at a very high level for the general to personally want to talk to him. He looked down at the medal that was still pinned to his jacket pocket and rubbed the beautifully sculpted bronze eagle between his fingers as he thought about what the medal represented: cloth and bronze for killing flesh and blood.

The door opened.

Paul jumped to attention as General Pick entered the small room alone, carrying two cups of hot coffee.

"Take a seat, Lieutenant." He handed one of the steaming cups to Paul. "I hope you drink it black."

Paul nodded, shocked that the general was serving him coffee. General Pick removed a cigar from a black leather case and lit it before speaking. "Lieutenant Bourne . . . I'm a little bit confused about a few things and I want you to be very candid with me." The general's four stars flashed as he took a seat across from where Paul stood. He nodded for the lieutenant to take a seat and continued talking. "What in the hell went on between you and Captain Hetten at My An?"

Paul looked down into his coffee cup. There was a long pause as he thought about what he should say and what he should hold back from the general. "Sir . . . I really can't tell you anything . . . I gave my word."

The general blew a solid stream of blue smoke across

the room. The jet of burnt tobacco hit the map on the far wall and rolled out over the printed terrain like a dense fog. General Pick frowned before speaking. "I respect your sense of loyalty, Lieutenant, but I must know what's going on at My An. We have a very big operation kicking off in the Delta region and I'm afraid your old camp is going to be the hub of the whole operation. . . . That's a lot of responsibility for whoever commands that camp . . ."

Paul looked up at the general and read genuine concern in the old warrior's eyes. He knew that if he remained quiet, a lot of innocent men would die because of Hetten, who would almost surely use the operation to make a name for himself at the expense of his men. Paul made his decision after thinking about what would happen to Sergeant Braverman and the rest of the team he had left there under Captain Hetten's command.

"Sir . . . Hell . . . I. . . ." Paul stopped. He shouldn't have sworn in front of the general.

"Go on." General Pick puffed on his cigar and waited. "I've been known to curse a few times myself." A faint smile broke at the corners of the man's wrinkled mouth that broke the tension.

"I hope that you realize, sir, it's taking a lot for me to break my word, but a lot is at stake here . . . A lot of good men's lives."

The general nodded. "I appreciate your trust, and I give you my word that what you tell me will be kept between the two of us." General Pick held out his hand. "Let's shake on it."

Paul took a deep breath and began; twice during the following hour and a half the door to the room opened and both time the general waved his aide away. Paul covered all of the incidents that he could recall from My An, including the fake Silver Star Hetten had set up for himself. The general's eyebrows rose for a second when Paul told him about the attempted assassination of Hetten by the camp NCOs. The room became extremely quiet when Paul had finished talking as the two soldiers looked at each other over the tabletop.

The general broke the uncomfortable silence. He spoke very softly. "Lieutenant . . . I sensed that there was something very wrong in that camp when I visited there. My concern now is how many other isolated Special Forces camps and advisory detachments have the same problem?"

Paul shrugged his shoulders. "It's no big deal, sir . . . I mean, my case. I did what had to be done. Anyway . . . I'm not a career soldier, sir. When this war is over, I'm heading back to California . . ."

"That's the damn problem!" The anger in the general's voice alarmed Paul before he realized that the frustration wasn't directed at him. "There are a lot of men like you, Lieutenant, especially in the lower ranks, who have been the victims of overzealous career officers who are trying to establish themselves as military heroes at the expense of good leadership. We have a hell of a lot of good officers out there, but it seems as if the bad ones always make the headlines." The general paused. "Paul . . . I'm sorry! I promise that I'll clear this mess up for you . . . at least the bad efficiency report." The general smiled. "Hell, I wonder how the Department of the Army is going to react to this. You're one of the most decorated soldiers to come out of the Vietnam War so far and Hetten has accused you of . . . and in writing!" The general skipped over the insulting word.

Paul's mind reeled when he thought over what the general had said. He had never added up his awards for service in Vietnam but he did have a collection: two

Distinguished Service Crosses, two Silver Stars, three Bronze Stars, and a couple of Purple Hearts. When he wore a dress uniform, he would have quite a chestfull of ribbons.

"I've just been trying to stay alive, General."

General Pick stood and adjusted his black leather pistol belt and holster. "I really believe that, boy—but you're also a damn good leader."

Lieutenant Colonel Clewell was sitting on the top of a desk when the pair left the small team briefing room. The aide had been studying a large wall map that had all of the recon team locations plotted.

"I enjoyed the visit, Colonel. Thanks for your excellent hospitality."

Clewell nodded. "Sir, we have a jeep waiting to take you back to your chopper."

"Thank you." General Pick turned slightly to face Paul. "Thanks for the conversation, Paul." The general winked and joined his aide de camp.

Lieutenant Bourne remained behind at the operations center while Clewell escorted the general to the helipad.

"Well . . . let's call him Paulie now!" an area-studies officer kidded Paul from behind his desk.

Paul gave a shy smile and tried hiding the red blush covering his face by turning toward the map. "Get off my ass, sir."

"Don't get mad . . . Paulie." The officers working in the control room all laughed good-naturedly over the teasing of the popular lieutenant.

Paul left the building to find a quiet place to think about what had occurred between him and the general. Jay was waiting for him outside the building.

"Hey, Paul! Check this out!" He held up his Silver Star for Paul to see. "I am getting to be a full-fledged fuckin' hero!"

Paul laughed, "A full-fledged fuckin' rookie is more like it!"

The pair of lieutenants walked next to each other down the hot sidewalk to the low headquarters building. A group of men from the recon company and some clerks from the headquarters unit were standing just inside of the entranceway, where the mess sergeant had placed a cake decorated with copies of the medals that had been awarded during the ceremony. Cans of cold beer and bottles of top-shelf booze were stacked on a nearby table. There wouldn't be much work done during the rest of the day, while the camp partied.

"Lieutenants! Get your sorry asses over here!" One of the recon men was well on his way to a hangover.

Jay saw the team adjutant and beckoned for him to join them. "Where did the general go from here?"

"Over to the hospital to present some awards to our wounded."

Jay raised his eyebrows. "I bet Coop will shit when those four stars shine in his face!"

The conversation was interrupted by a loud voice calling Lieutenant Bourne. "Bourne! A DSC! Big-time stuff!"

"Thanks." Paul kept the tone of his voice humble.

Captain Atkins from the recon company joined the growing group of men surrounding Jay and Paul and spoke after the men had quieted down after laughing over Cooper meeting the general.

"Congratulations, Lieutenant Bourne; a DSC is hard to come by here in CCN."

"I heard that there aren't many of them given out," Jay answered for Paul.

"Three since I've been here—and that's been over two years." Captain Atkins grinned and looked down at the cup of Seven-Up Paul held in his hand. "You're not drinking today?"

"No . . . drying out," Paul smiled.

"Really? Maybe you want to go on an easy mission this afternoon. Seeing that the rest of the recon company is already well on their way to getting drunk."

"Awww . . . shit, Captain! Can't you give him a break!?" Jay cut in.

"Sorry . . . we just received an emergency resupply call from our Hickory relay site and need to send someone who's cleared to handle top-secret documents. I need someone just to ride up there this afternoon and return back here with the same chopper tonight."

"Shit, sir, I'll do it." Jay sensed his friend's need for a break. "Let Paul relax."

"You've already been slated for a mission alert in the morning, Loveless. You can't go."

"I'll do it, sir. Does it count as a mission?" Paul looked at his watch.

"Sure does. Be at the helipad by 1400 hours for take-off. Travel light: weapon, survival gear, and water. You'll be unloading the chopper and will need to be able to move around."

Paul slapped Jay's arm and spoke with a joking tone in his voice. "You'll be in isolation this afternoon when I return, so I won't have a chance to say good-bye. Take care of your rookie ass, ya hear!"

"Sure, Paul—just don't hurt your back unloading C-rations!"

Paul went over to the mess hall and ate before he picked up his combat gear. He took only those items absolutely necessary for survival in case the helicopter went down and he would have to evade the enemy. The supply people had just finished loading the cargo helicopter when he reached the pad. Paul looked at the black face on his military watch and read the time: 1320 hours. He was early.

"You the pilot?" Paul approached the middle-aged

man who was wearing a dark brownish-green flight suit.

"Yeah, Lieutenant, I'm the pilot." The captain's voice was rude.

Paul ignored the verbal bad manners.

"If you're ready to get out of here, let's go." Paul looked at the crates of ammunition and stacks of C-rations that filled most of the passenger space in the aircraft.

"Your request stated a 1400 hours departure time." The captain was being sarcastic. "One of the problems with you fucking recon people is that you don't know what in the hell you want."

Paul easily detected the jealousy in the captain's voice and again ignored the insult.

"I was just thinking that the earlier we get this over with, the earlier we can get back to doing better things . . . Captain."

The senior officer puckered up his lips and thought for a few seconds before waving for his crew to board the chopper. "I have a promotion party to go to tonight . . . let's go!" The pilot pulled his flight helmet on over his sweat-stained hair and waved at Paul with one of his gloved hands. "Find yourself a place back there with the cargo."

Paul took the seat that had been left open for him and strapped himself in with the dirty white-nylon safety belt. The helicopter engine labored under the heavy load and the skids under the belly of the aircraft scraped along the steel PSP, leaving a line of sparks.

The pilot kept the nose of the chopper down and cleared the camp barbed wire with only inches to spare. He banked the laboring aircraft over the water and changed his course to follow the coastline north. It took ten minutes of gradual climb to attain a safe altitude of 3,500 feet. Paul looked out the open door, enjoying the view of Vietnamese farmers working their rice paddies behind their water buffalo. Vietnam would be a beautiful country to live in if the war would stop. The helicopter banked and headed west when they had reached Highway Nine, located just above Quang Tri. The aircraft followed the highway inland until they reached the Marine camp at a place called the Rockpile. Hickory was another twenty minutes west of the base.

Paul placed his hands over the earpieces on his headset to hear a faint message that was being cut out by the pilot's bitching over the intercom at his crew chief.

"Mayday. . . ." The radio crackled and faded out for a second before coming in loud and clear. "*Mayday . . . Mayday . . . We've been hit! Going to crash! . . . Mayday . . . vicinity . . . Grid 247858 . . . Mayday . . . Mayday . . . Mayday. . .* " The broadcast began to fade out again.

Lieutenant Bourne flicked the push-to-talk switch. "Where's that location?"

The helicopter copilot plotted the coordinates on the flight map attached to his left leg and then looked up at his pilot. "That plots out about ten miles over the border into North Vietnam."

"Let's go get them!" Paul spoke to the pilot over the intercom system.

"This is a fucking slick, Lieutenant! Not a gunship! I'm not going to cross that fucking border."

"Gunships can't carry people. . . . We're close to where they're crashing . . . let's go!"

A loud transmission broke into the conversation.

"*Mayday . . . Mayday! . . . this is Devil Dancer 37 . . . May—*" The radio broadcast was cut off.

"Turn this fucking aircraft, Captain!" Paul couldn't listen to the fear-filled voice over the radio and not help.

"We can't! We're carrying too much already!"

"I can solve that problem right now!" Paul started pushing the heavy crates overboard.

The voice coming over the intercom hurt Paul's ears. *"Stop doing that, Lieutenant!"*

Paul used both of his legs to finish pushing the last stack of supplies out the open door. "Now we have room to pick up that pilot! Go get him!"

"No!"

Paul didn't hesitate and placed the cool barrel of his CAR-15 under the back edge of the pilot's helmet. The man stiffened when he felt the cold steel against his neck.

"You won't shoot! We'll crash!"

"I *will* blow your fucking head off! And then, if your copilot is as fucking dumb as you are . . . we'll *all* die!"

The helicopter started a slow bank to the north. Paul checked his weapon over quickly and felt around his waist for the gear that he figured he would need once they reached the crash site. He was traveling light, but he had enough gear and ammo to suppress anyone on the ground long enough to get the crashed pilot into the chopper.

"*Door gunners! Get ready!*" Paul released his seat belt and slid on his rear over to a position on the floor behind the pilot. "Can you see the crash site yet?" A large black cloud rose out of the jungle in answer to Paul's question.

"*There's a parachute!*" The helicopter's copilot pointed with a gloved finger to the right at a lone parachute landing in the trees.

"What kind of aircraft went down?" Paul spoke to the copilot, who had taken over flying the aircraft.

"I think it was an Air Force Phantom jet . . . an F-4 . . ." The copilot looked back over his shoulder at Paul.

"There're two people in a Phantom. . . ."

"Can you land this thing in that rice paddy bordering those trees where the parachute is?"

"Sure. . . ." The copilot's voice was filled with fear but he kept the chopper under control. The pilot had removed his pistol from its shoulder holster and was searching the nearby jungle for enemy soldiers. Beads of sweat dripped down from his forehead.

"Good! Drop me off over there. . . ." Paul slid over to the edge of the doorway. "When I locate the pilot and his crewman, I'll call you on my URC-10 . . . monitor the emergency frequency . . . take off and wait for me up where it's safer. . . ." Paul leaned forward, ready to jump when the chopper went into a hover five feet above the muddy field. The helicopter started to bank away just as Paul jumped, causing him to hit his arm against one of the steel skids. Before Paul could recover on the ground, the chopper was out of sight.

Paul ran hard for the treeline. The familiar smell of the jungle and the silence after the helicopter had departed made Paul nervous. He hurried over to where the white chute hung from the trees and searched the low underbrush for the parachutist. Paul kept looking back at the open paddy for NVA soldiers, who would most assuredly be arriving soon.

A low groan followed by a short sentence reached Paul from the jungle. "Ohhh. . . . I'm hurting. . . . uhhh . . ."

Paul quickly found the man lying on the ground still attached to his parachute harness.

"Where's your partner?" Paul released the emergency links, detaching the man from his canopy.

"He went down with the plane . . . He's dead," the man groaned. "I think my legs are both broken. . . . *mmmhhhh*."

Paul leaned over and quickly checked the man

wearing the flight suit. There were no broken bones protruding through the cloth of the one-piece outfit. Paul figured that he had fractured both legs in his landing.

"Help me get you on my back . . . I have a helicopter waiting to haul us out of here!" Paul grabbed the pilot's harness and tried lifting him up without hurting him. The pilot groaned, but took ahold of Paul around his neck. The distance back to the open field was less than twenty meters and Paul covered it carrying the pilot piggyback. He lowered the man to the thick matted vegetation and yanked out his URC-10.

"Chopper . . . Chopper. . . ." Paul had forgotten the helicopter's call sign, ". . . chopper, get your ass back here!"

Paul saw the NVA squad the instant it stepped out of the jungle on the farside of the field.

"Chopper! Come in!"

No answer.

Paul held the small radio in his hand and eased back into the jungle. A radio transmission broke the silence.

"Unknown Station . . . this is flight leader Alpha Six. . . . identify yourself. . . ."

Paul pushed the rubber-covered switch, happy to hear a friendly voice. "This is Lieutenant Bourne . . . CCN . . . I have a wounded Air Force pilot. . . ." Paul looked at the man's rank that was sewn under plastic tabs on his shoulders, ". . . a lieutenant colonel . . . he crashed in a Phantom jet . . . I need a pick-up aircraft . . . what are you driving?"

"I have four A1Es with me . . . We heard a Mayday and came. . . . We can't land . . . Do you need air cover?"

"Hell, yes! This area is crawling with NVA! . . . They're crossing the rice paddy now!"

"I see them!"

Paul covered the wounded pilot's body with his own as the A1Es made a gun run against the exposed NVA soldiers. Dirt flew in all directions from the aircraft cannon rounds plowing through the mud, leaving a couple dozen NVA for fertilizer.

"I got them!" The voice coming over the URC-10 was younger than the first voice Paul had heard.

Paul pushed his talk button. "I'm going to take this pilot and head south to the river . . . try and cover me!" Paul slipped his URC-10 back into his pocket without waiting for an answer and lifted the wounded pilot onto his back. He was glad the fighter pilot wasn't overweight.

The A1Es danced and swooped around Paul, spraying the jungle with bombs and cannon fire. Paul traveled three thousand meters carrying the man until his legs gave out from under him. He fell face-first to the ground. The pilot moaned. Paul reached down without looking and removed his URC-10.

"Have you found my chopper yet?"

"Sorry . . . we saw a slick heading south on our way here . . . but he ignored our request to turn back . . ." The A1E leader's voice dropped, "Listen, buddy . . . I hate to tell you this but we're almost out of fuel. . . . Leave him there and we'll try to call in for some help . . . save yourself. . . ."

"Bullshit!" Paul's voice cracked. "I've got him this far and I'm bringing him home!"

"You're a gutsy little shit!" A deep respect filled the pilot's words. "I'm Colonel Wilson . . . look me up when you get back!"

The flight of four A1Es dipped their wings and the lead aircraft did a victory roll in honor of Lieutenant Bourne before they banked south.

Colonel Wilson raised his protective visor and wiped the tears from his eyes.

Lieutenant Bourne felt a little strength returning to his legs as the friendly sound of the A1Es turned into a low hum. Fear had a way of making adrenalin enter the bloodstream. He groaned with the pilot and crossed the wounded man's arms around his shoulders. As he stood with flashes of pain bursting through his muscles, Paul looked up and saw rain clouds racing toward him from the south. He grinned and thought that he was actually happy to see a monsoon downpour. He lowered his head and struggled the first few steps forward.

The lone helicopter landed on the CCN pad. Colonel Clewell looked out of his window. A frown crossed his face. The chopper had only left an hour ago and wasn't due back until late afternoon. Clewell raised his hand to stop the officer who was briefing him and turned to Major Galviston, who sat in the chair next to him. "Have someone go out there and find out why the resupply chopper has returned so early."

The briefing officer from the corps headquarters was half through his weekly report when a jeep slid to a halt under the colonel's window. Clewell stood up so that he could see what was going on. Captain Atkins had the helicopter pilot by the back of his neck, shoving him toward the entrance of the building. Clewell and Galviston met the recon company commander in the hallway.

"This son of a bitch left Bourne!" Atkins's face was red from the anger he was venting. "This bastard flew back here to press charges against Bourne for attempting to kill him!"

"Hold on!" Clewell eased Atkins away from the helicopter pilot and continued speaking to him. "What in the hell has happened?"

Atkins adjusted his field jacket, "Sir . . . Bourne had the pilot land his chopper in North Vietnam so that they could pick up an injured Air Force pilot who had called for help. . . ." Atkins reached over for the pilot, but was blocked by Galviston. "And that punk just took off and left them on the ground!"

"You . . . *what?*" Clewell couldn't believe what he had just heard.

"Sir . . . I don't have a gunship. . . ."

Clewell spoke to his deputy. "Galviston, get over to the TOC and crank up anything we can launch . . . Get a Brightlight Team in the air . . . Loveless is in isolation . . . use his team."

Major Galviston hadn't finished briefing Jay before the lieutenant had his team assembled and ready. Loveless didn't wait for the black van to take them to the helipad, instead he ran over to the single helicopter on the pad, followed by his team.

"Is this machine ready to go?" Jay jumped into the cargo area followed by his commandos.

"We're almost out of fuel." The copilot spoke cautiously to the armed recon men. He had warned his pilot that coming back to the CCN camp was stupid, but the senior officer had ignored his warning and had been hauled away.

"Is this the same chopper that left Bourne?" Red slivers of fire flashed from Loveless's eyes.

The copilot was careful to answer the lieutenant holding the submachine gun. "Our pilot gave the orders—"

"Get this fucking coward's craft off our helipad! If I ever see you here again . . . I'll tear your fucking heart out and feed it to Vietnamese pigs!"

The copilot didn't need to be told twice. He jumped into the cockpit and cranked the engine. He didn't wait for the pilot or for the aircraft to warm up.

Jay sat down on the hot PSP and placed his head between his legs. He thought clearly for the first time since he had heard what had happened to Bourne. He should have kept the chopper.

Lieutenant Bourne stumbled through the bamboo thickets without paying any attention to the noise that he was making. He was walking in a pain-wracked stupor, and didn't care any more if the NVA found him or if a tiger jumped out of the jungle and ate them. Pain attacked every muscle in his body, telling him to drop the load off his back. All of his survival instincts told him to cut the wounded pilot's throat—no one would ever know. Paul responded to his thoughts by squeezing the man's upper thighs harder under his arms.

The pilot released a low moan.

Paul carefully placed each boot in front of each other, taking extreme care not to slip on the mud. He knew that if he fell he would never get back up again. The sound of frogs croaking broke through the mental block that had separated him from reality. He stopped walking and allowed his knees to bend down to touch the ground. The pilot on his back slipped sideways down to the damp earth.

Lieutenant Bourne had reached the north bank of the Ben Hai River that separated the two Vietnams. Later, when Paul tried to recall how he had reached the river, he would draw only a blank.

Paul forced himself to cover the pilot with brush and then found himself a shady spot to rest. The sound of helicopters brought Paul back to reality. He could see a flight of three Huey slicks and six Cobra gunships flying north toward him. He reached down into the side pocket of his camouflaged pants and pulled out his

URC-10.

"Unknown helicopters . . . this is Thor . . . Thor . . ." Paul used his secret code name.

Jay wore the headset off his ears around his neck. The Brightlight rescue ship he was riding in was approaching the DMZ from the south. He nearly jumped off his seat when he heard his friend's voice coming weakly over the air.

"Thor! Thor! Where are you? . . . This is Bacchus. . . ."

"The north bank of the Ben Hai . . . You're flying straight at me!" Paul took a deep breath to control the pain in his body. "I'm going to turn on my strobe light . . . *Now*!"

The first bright flash from the strobe bounced against the plexiglas window on the chopper as a pin mark and started growing larger. The light came from a location a mile away to their one o'clock.

"I have you located! Hang in there!"

Paul allowed his eyes to close.

"Get your gunships shooting up anything that moves around that strobe light!" Jay yelled into his mike and readied his team for the landing.

The helicopter carrying Jay and his team hovered ten feet from the ground and started a slow descent to the tops of the high grass growing next to the riverbank. Jay hit the ground running. He grabbed Paul's flashing strobe light and turned it off. It had done its job. The chopper sat down and Jay loaded on the wounded pilot, then went back for Paul. Jay carried his friend to the waiting safety of the chopper, allowing no one else to touch him. Paul's head rested against Jay's leg as the chopper made a 180-degree low-level turn and shot back across the narrow river.

The gunships continued their assault on North Vietnam and answered the thousands of green tracers flying up at them from the jungle. The NVA had been nipping at Lieutenant Bourne's heels but had arrived minutes to late to reap the glory of their chase.

The Brightlight Team had played the modern-day role of the old wild-west cavalry, and had rescued the pair of warriors from the jaws of certain death.

Chapter 18

Captain MacReal sat alone on the wide patio outside the hospital snackbar, lost in her own thoughts. The coffee was cold as it touched her lips. She looked down at her watch and realized that she had spent forty-five minutes daydreaming.

"Natasha! Come over here and join us!" One of her coworkers waved from across the way. Natasha smiled and shook her head from side to side. She wanted to be alone for awhile and just think things out for herself. The doctor she worked for had said he would bring her the test results before he went off shift. She checked her watch again: forty-eight minutes had passed.

"You shouldn't be sitting alone out here without a dozen handsome young men vying for your attention!" The doctor turned the steel-framed chair around and sat down cowboy style. He began talking candidly to the waiting nurse. "Well, what you've suspected is correct. Let's say that the rabbit died and you'll be a mother in six months or so, give or take a week."

Natasha looked directly into the doctor's smiling eyes. "Are you sure?"

"Yes, very sure, Captain MacReal." He looked down at the table top. "If you don't want to keep the child, I can perform an abortion . . ."

"Thanks, Doc, but I've already decided to keep the baby."

"Do you know who the father is?"

The hurt flashed over her face, cutting the doctor to the quick. "I'm going to be a mother—that doesn't make me a whore."

"I'm sorry . . . that statement was uncalled for . . . I just . . ."

"I know what you mean. . . . The answer is yes . . . I know who the father is." Natasha placed her hand over the doctor's.

The path leading along the walkway bordering the hospital was lined with banana trees and flowering bushes. Captain MacReal walked along with a light bounce in her step. Now that she knew for sure, she was very happy. When she had first realized that she might be pregnant, she had felt shame and confusion. Paul Bourne had been the only man she had been to bed with since she had arrived in Vietnam, and her experiences with sex before that had been limited to one long relationship with her ex-fiancee. She was a girl from the old school, who believed in loving someone before having sex with him.

She removed a pad of writing paper from her desk drawer. Paul had the right to know, even though she wasn't going to push him into a marriage.

Lieutenant Bourne opened his eyes. He was lying on one of the infirmary beds in the ten-man hospital that the CCN medics operated for the recon team commandos. Paul felt pain coming from all of the muscles that he tried moving.

"It's best if you get up and walk around a little," the medic sitting behind the desk at the far end of the ward spoke over the case of bottles that he was labeling.

"Easy to say . . . hard to do," Paul made an emphatic effort and sat up. Black spots flashed in front of his eyes and he stopped moving for a few seconds.

"You've been lying there asleep for the past eighteen hours. Your muscles should be really sore." The medic lifted the telephone receiver on his desk and dialed. "The colonel wants me to call him as soon as you woke up. We kept you under because you were really beat when you got here."

Paul's mind began recollecting what had happened to him and then he remembered the crashed pilot. "How's the Air Force fighter jock doing?"

"We don't know. They rushed him to the main hospital in Da Nang and then evacked him to Japan yesterday." The medic spoke into the telephone. "He's awake now, sir . . . yes, sir . . . I'll have him wait here. I really don't think that he's going to be able to go very far on his own for a couple of days, though." He looked over at Paul and watched him struggle to his feet.

Lieutenant Bourne held the bed frame and placed one hand against the wall for support. "Shit! I feel like I'm a hundred years old!" The pain was still there, but with each short step his body began to return to normal. When the colonel arrived, Paul was walking slowly back and forth between the row of beds.

"Well, Lieutenant Bourne, I see that you're up and about!" Colonel Clewell was followed into the room by a smiling Major Galviston.

"Barely, sir." Paul reached out and shook the offered hand and added, "How's the pilot doing?"

"Fine . . . real good! He was evacked for some repair

work on his legs. I think there was some bone fragmentation. By the way, he sent a message back through our headquarters thanking you and your effort."

Paul shook his head from side to side. "He'd have done the same for any of us. Oh . . . by the way . . . a flight of A1Es did a real super job covering for us. If it wasn't for Colonel Wilson and his people, the NVA would have gotten us at the crash site."

"I know. He called here yesterday and couldn't praise you enough! In fact, the Air Force is recommending you for a Silver Star and a Distinguished Flying Cross!" The expression on the colonel's face changed and he introduced another topic. "One other thing, Paul—what happened between you and the helicopter pilot?"

Paul's face instantly reflected the contempt he felt. "That son of a bitch!"

"Now calm down," Clewell's voice released some of his own frustrated anger, "a lot has happened in the past twenty-four hours and I need some facts!"

Paul sensed the pressure his commander was under and became sedate. "What do you want to know, sir?"

Clewell took a deep breath and released the first question almost too fast. "Did you place a gun on the pilot's neck?"

"Yes."

"Did you threaten to kill him?"

"Yes."

Clewell flinched and Galviston broke out in a wide grin.

"Did you also threaten the copilot?"

Paul paused and then answered, "Yes."

"Why! *Damn it!*"

Paul shrugged his shoulders. To him, the answer was

very black or white. "They refused to go after the downed pilot."

Clewell slapped his own leg with his open palm and eased out his words between clenched teeth. "Damn, Paul! Why do you always get so involved?" The statement was more of a plea than accusation.

Lieutenant Bourne looked over at Galviston, who had taken a seat and was still grinning over the whole conversation. He had approved of everything Paul had done and had told the investigating officers that he personally would have shot the pilot and then talked to the copilot.

The colonel sighed and continued, "Do you know the pilot of the helicopter went directly to the commanding general of the XXIV Corps and demanded that you be punished for threatening a senior officer?"

Paul had taken enough and his nerves broke. "So! If that's the fucking bottom line . . . punish me!"

"Damn it, Bourne!" Clewell turned and left the room.

"Relax, Lieutenant. He's on your side, but the corps commander is trying to force him into giving you an Article 15," Galviston said.

"So? I get an Article 15. I would do it all the same if I had to do it again. Let me ask you a question. What would you have done if you had been in my place?"

Major Galviston smiled and left the room, leaving Paul's question unanswered.

Paul dressed, ignoring the low-key pain coming from his sore muscles, and left the infirmary. He walked stiffly toward the beach and the sound of the waves breaking against the sand. He knew that he had done what was right, and if the brass couldn't understand that, well, then fuck them.

A half-dozen of the camp's commandos were catching sea snails and Paul stopped walking and sat down to watch them. The commandos had fashioned special nets out of broom handles and heavy wire with a fine nylon net attached. The technique they used in catching the snails, which were burrowed an inch or two under the sand in the surf, was to walk through the shallow surf dragging the net in the sandy bottom. A ten-meter walk in the waist-deep surf would harvest a couple dozen snails. The commandos had five-gallon cans positioned along a hundred meters of the beach, where they would empty their catches into for a community feast later that night. One of the older commandos sat on the packed sand and acted as a judge for whoever brought in the most snails in one pass along the beach.

Paul felt an urge to join the commandos and take his mind off the events that had happened with the helicopter pilots. He stripped naked like the commandos out in the surf and picked up a spare net lying next to one of the five-gallon cans. The water felt good as he waded out to the deeper water, which the shorter commandos couldn't stand up in and still use their nets. Paul buried his net in the sand at his feet and pulled it along for twenty meters in the soupy water before raising it to see what he had caught. There were two or three hundred small snails trapped in the fine mesh that threatened to break the fibers. Paul eased the net back into the water in order to ease the pressure and walked slowly back to the shore where he emptied his catch under the approving eye of the old commando.

Two hours passed quickly as Paul enjoyed wading in the surf. Then a yell from one of the commandos nearest to where Paul was using his net drew his attention to where the man was pointing out to sea. A foot-high fin cut powerfully through the water a few meters past the drop-off where Paul was standing. The commandos near Paul struggled through the surf and ran up on the sand, followed closely by the lieutenant—who used the escape effort to drag his net on the bottom. Paul knew that the knee-deep water was too shallow for the big shark to attack. Yelling from the commandos forced Paul to take another look at the shark and saw that the fin was coming directly toward him.

The commandos pointed at the American lieutenant and laughed good-naturedly between sentences spoken in Montagnard. One of the younger boys had puffed out his chest and was strutting along the beach, and then acted like he was picking up his skirts and running. He met Paul at the edge of the water and pointed at him. Paul joined the laughter and held his leg as if the shark had ahold of him.

"If I want to find you, all I have to do is check the beach." Jay joined Paul and the circle of Montagnards who were still watching the hunting shark circle out past the reef.

"Hey, Jay! What's been going on?" Paul tried slapping the wet sand off his legs and then pointed at the nearest five-gallon can that was filled to the top with a mass of moving snails.

Jay's eyes were on his friend and were filled with concern. "Paul . . . "I've heard what happened . . ."

Paul smiled. "*What* happened?"

"Paul! Damn it, don't play games! This is really serious!"

"Jay . . . I really don't give a shit what they do. What

I did was *right*! Understand that! . . . I can sleep very well at night. . . . Can they?"

Jay's face shivered with hurt. "Hey, Paul . . . I'm on your side!"

Paul reached down, picked up a handful of loose sand, and threw it into the sea breeze. "Shit, I'm sorry for taking it out on you, Jay. . . . It's just that—"

"You don't need to say any more . . . I gotcha!" Jay changed the subject. "The reason I came out here to find you is the old man sent me." Jay slapped Paul's wet back. "I think better minds than ours have formulated a plan."

Paul slipped on his clothes over his still-wet body while Jay watched the shark cruising back and forth, waiting—as if someone would be foolish enough to go swimming out beyond the reef.

Paul walked next to his friend on the sun-baked sand halfway to the headquarters building before speaking. "Jay, I want to say thanks for Brightlighting and getting me out of there." Paul kept his eyes down on the sand. It was always hard and embarrassing to thank a fellow recon man for helping you—mostly because it embarrassed the recipient.

Jay stopped dead in his tracks and grabbed Paul, spinning him around. "Let me make one fucking thing clear! I didn't *volunteer* for any fucking thing! My team was already in isolation and was ready for insertion. We were the standby team for a Brightlight mission for *any* other team . . . You know that!"

Paul nodded in agreement.

". . . but . . . I would have volunteered . . ."

Paul placed his arm over his buddy's shoulder and they continued walking the remaining distance to the headquarters. "Thanks anyway . . . asshole!" Paul pulled Jay backward, causing him to fall down hard on his rear. "Meet your sorry ass in the colonel's office!" Paul began running hard for the building.

Jay sprang to his feet and tore out after the stiffly running figure ahead of him. Jay passed Paul ten meters before he reached the building and stopped in the shade to wait for his friend.

"No wonder your ass is always in trouble. You can't run worth a shit!"

Paul grinned. "You don't know how close to the truth you are!"

Colonel Clewell had been looking out of his window watching Loveless and Bourne racing toward the headquarters building. He smiled and thought about how they reminded him of competitive school children.

Paul met the colonel in the hallway.

"Lieutenant Bourne, wait for me in my office." Clewell kept walking toward the communications room.

Paul found himself a comfortable chair and waited quietly for the colonel to return.

The door to the office opened and Clewell entered carrying a yellow piece of paper in his hand. "It's not as good as I had hoped for, but it's good enough."

"What's that, sir?"

Clewell looked up from the message and grinned. "How long will it take you to have your team ready for insertion."

"This afternoon," Paul's lungs automatically inhaled a deep breath.

"Good, but that's too soon. Be ready for insertion tomorrow morning." Clewell turned in his chair and stared out the window over the rows of buildings that separated the headquarters from the beach. "I can't stop a lieutenant general . . ." Clewell turned back to face Paul. "The corps commander wants to make an example out of you. I sent a message to General Pick asking for him to intervene in this case, but he's back in Washington, D.C., testifying before the Congress and can't make it back here for at least five more days. I have to keep you away from the corps commander until then. What we're going to do, Paul, is insert your team in one of our cold recon areas and hide you out there until General Pick returns."

Lieutenant Bourne smiled at the colonel's plan. He couldn't get an Article 15 if he wasn't available. "Appreciate your concern, sir, but I don't think the general is going to like you pulling this off under his nose." Paul bent over and tucked his pant leg into his boot.

"That's my problem, Paul. The war is still going on . . . remember?" Clewell grinned. "You go get ready for your mission. Major Galviston is waiting for you."

Paul stood and saluted the colonel.

Jay had been waiting outside the closed door. "Well?"

"I'm on a mission alert." Paul kept walking, with Jay walking rapidly beside him.

"Damn! You just came off a mission . . . *two* missions!" Jay's voice rose. "What in the hell do they think you are? A fuckin' Superman?"

"This one is a good deal, Jay. If I'm out on a mission they can't give me an Article 15—unless they want to come out *there* and do it." Paul half-closed his eyes and left the rest unsaid.

"When are you being inserted?"

"Tomorrow morning. I'm on my way to get briefed by Major Galviston right now." Paul stopped talking and looked at the man entering the building dressed in civilian clothes, accompanied by Captain White.

"Lieutenant Bourne! Loveless! Come over here for a minute; I want you to meet somebody," Captain White waved them over.

"Yes, sir? What do we have here? A new recruit?" Paul returned the man's friendly smile as he spoke to the captain.

"John Michaels. I'm with *Newsweek* magazine."

"A reporter! How in the hell did he get in here!" Jay mocked alarm but became instantly wary of the man. Reporters had gained a very bad reputation in Vietnam among the soldiers, and most of it was justified.

"Easy, Lieutenant . . . He's been given a special clearance and has permission to do a story on recon operations. The MACV Commander himself gave the clearance!"

The reporter grinned. "I'm aware of the special security problems here at CCN and I'll respect them. I want to write a story about real recon people and take a few pictures."

"Well, you're talking to the right officer, buddy! He's Mister Recon himself!" Jay nodded at Paul and continued talking, "He's the most decorated recon man in the country!"

The reporter looked back over at Paul with a renewed respect. He had instantly caught Paul's photogenic good looks and had planned on using him for a photo session, but now a feature story started appearing in the back of the reporter's mind.

Paul laughed. "Bullshit, Mister Michaels! I'm the camp's mess-hall officer." Paul risked a glance over at Jay and started walking away from the group. "Sorry to leave you all, but I have to see Major Galviston. Nice meeting you, Mister Michaels."

Jay waited until Paul was out of sight and then

spoke. "Mess officer, my ass! He's on mission alert right now! The modest son of a bitch!"

Michaels started at Jay and sensed that there might be a little bit more than the average amount of jealousy in the man's tone of voice. "You don't like him very much, do you?"

"I hate that pompous bastard!" Jay frowned. "He's nothing but a damn show-off and tries to make us other recon people look bad!" Jay shook his head and left the reporter standing with Captain White.

"He *really* hates Bourne! I haven't seen a case of professional jealousy that bad in a long time!" Michaels looked over at the S-1 who was smiling at him.

Captain White shook his head. "Those two are like peas in a pod! You mess with one of them and the other one will get you! Come on over to my office and I'll tell you about the Brightlight operation we just had a couple of days ago that involved both of those lieutenants."

"Brightlight?"

"Yes, a Brightlight is an operation that involves a recon team that goes into a very hot area after another recon team too shot-up to help itself, or they go after the remains of what's left of a wiped-out team; either way, it's very dangerous. Sort of like going to hell carrying a Bible—you're not wanted in the first place, and when you get there . . . well . . . it gets worse."

Lieutenant Bourne received his briefing from Major Galviston and was very pleased with the intelligence package that had been assembled for him. RT Krait had originally been scheduled for the mission and most of the insertion planning was already completed. There wasn't any special equipment required, but Paul asked that silenced .22-caliber pistols be added to his list. The area that Paul's team had been given to reconnoiter was twenty grid squares large, ten more than the normal area of operations for a team. CCN hadn't sent a recon team into the area for over three years due to the inactivity in the past. The terrain was made up of patches of bamboo and a lot of elephant grass that didn't allow much cover in which large units could hide. Photographs and intelligence reports confirmed that the area was never used by the NVA. Their insertion would be different from the normal helicopter landing. The team was going to be dropped off at a Marine Corps patrol base, and then they would be infiltrated into their area on foot. Lieutenant Bourne figured that the change in tactics was made for his benefit, to use up as much time as possible. The mission directive was simple: Check the area for any past enemy activity. Sergeant Cooper had recently been released from the hospital and would be joining the team. He figured that the easy terrain would be a good way to get back into shape quickly from his wounds.

Paul skipped supper and went down to the beach. He saw the *Newsweek* reporter walking across the compound on the far side of the camp, heading toward the mess hall. Captain White was still with him and talking with his arms moving in the salty air. The pair had stopped in front of one of the camp bunkers and the captain was showing the reporter something inside. Paul figured White was telling the young newspaper man about the fight inside the camp.

Paul spotted Jay sitting on the steps of his hooch and changed course to join him.

"Hey, Jay!"

Jay looked up from his weapon. "How did your briefing go?" He ran a patch down the barrel a half-dozen times waiting for Paul to answer.

"Good. It's an easy mission. Looks like a lot of walking, though—but I can use the exercise. I hate trail-watch missions where you have to sit in hiding for days on end; at least we'll get to move around a bit." Paul pointed at Jay's weapon. "You missed a spot."

"Why in the fuck don't you go bother someone else!" Jay wiped the missed spot with an oily cloth and placed the CAR-15 down on a clean step.

"What's wrong with you?" Paul took a step backward.

"Shit! It pisses me off!" Jay looked at his friend. "They're keeping your ass out there on patrol, and I know of some teams that haven't been inserted in fucking *months*!"

"Doesn't bother me any. . . ." Paul shrugged his shoulders. "Anyway, it makes the time go by faster. . . ."

Jay tightened his lips and frowned before speaking. "You going over to the club?"

"Naw . . . I think I'll wander down to the beach for awhile." Paul shuffled his feet as if he were nervous and added, "Have you seen Coop since he got back?"

"Yeah, he just went over to his hooch from the mess hall. Are you sure you don't want to go over to the club? They're having a big poker game tonight in honor of the *Newsweek* reporter . . . they plan on really fleecing his ass good!" Jay picked up his ammunition belt from the steps and opened one of the pockets.

"Naw, thanks anyway. . . . Uhhh . . . will you pick up my mail for me while I'm out on patrol?"

"Sure . . . no problem," Jay grinned as he looked into his friend's eyes. He tried to control the very weird feeling that flashed through him.

Paul caught the change in his buddy. "Something wrong?"

"No . . . ahhh. . . ."

"Don't worry, Jay, this soldier isn't going to get his ass greased . . . not just yet!"

Paul went over to Sergeant Cooper's hooch and briefed him on their upcoming mission and the easy target area. Cooper was a little upset that he hadn't been included in the original briefing, but relaxed as Paul told him what they would be doing. It was a cakewalk and needed very little prior planning. Paul explained the real reason for the mission to his partner, which took the edge off the normal pre-mission jitters. This mission was planned so that they wouldn't find anything.

Coop told Paul that he wanted to go over to the club and get in the poker game, so Paul went back to his hooch and changed into his cut-offs, picking up his weapon and ammo belt as he exited the building.

Mister Michaels stepped out of the mess hall and spotted Paul walking in the distance down the narrow camp road. He spoke to Captain White. "Where's he going?"

"Hell, I don't know. It could be anywhere, but I'd suspect he's heading down to the beach—he damn near lives there!" White grabbed the reporter by his elbow. "Come on! There's a good poker game going on at the club!"

"Sure. . . ." Michaels kept looking at Paul as he followed the captain into the officer hooch that had a separate room set aside as an officer's lounge and card room. He thought that Paul would be an interesting character for the article he wanted to write and maybe even the main character for his war novel.

Paul found himself an isolated location on the beach and stacked his battle gear next to him on the sand. He loved sitting alone on the soft sand, thinking about California and all the good times that he had living there as a kid. Paul watched a bank of storm clouds rolling in from far out at sea. The strong wind moving the clouds pushed Paul's hair almost straight back. His thoughts slipped back to Linda. He had truly loved her, as much as a man could love anything on earth. Her words echoed in his thoughts and he felt a shiver etch itself on his neck just below his right ear lobe, as if she had touched him with her lips.

"Care if I join you?"

Paul broke away from his thoughts and saw Mister Michaels. He allowed his eyes to reveal his irritation over being disturbed. "It's a free beach, but it's a lot nicer down there, though . . ."

"I came out here to talk to you. The poker game was boring. Those guys in there might be great on the battlefield, but they're piss-poor poker players. I won over eight hundred dollars playing kiddy stakes with them."

Paul smiled to himself thinking about what his friend Jay was going through right about now, especially after the way he had bragged about fleecing the reporter.

"What do you want with me?" Paul turned his face back to the sea and watched the breakers.

"You have a reputation for being a damn good recon man. In fact, they say you're one of the best. I'd like to hear from you what it's like being out on patrol behind enemy lines." Michaels joined Paul, uninvited, and looked out to sea at the fury of the breakers when they hit the reef a hundred meters in front of them. The spray had the pair of them soaked within minutes.

"Recon is like working with the ocean: both the jungle and the ocean are neutral to everything," Paul turned a little on the sand and faced the reporter, "but if you can learn the ways of the jungle and don't fight the currents, then you can make the animals, bamboo—everything there—work for you."

Paul talked for hours in a soft voice that was repeatedly drowned out from the sounds of the waves. Michaels listened patiently, not daring to interrupt and change Paul's chain of thought. Slowly, over the hours on the beach, a friendship developed between the soldier and the newsman.

Morning came early; it always did when your team was due for insertion. Paul lingered under the showerhead, enjoying the relaxing effect coming from the water jets. He would have at least five days ahead of him that would be spent sweating and caked with grime. Paul left the shower and leisurely dried off and dressed in his battle gear. He stood in front of the mirror and applied his camouflage grease paint with the care of a professional clown who was getting ready for the opening act of a circus—except that the clown was getting ready to entertain and the warrior was preparing for a possible encounter with death.

Paul stopped by Jay's hooch on his way over to the isolation building, but found it empty. He found a piece of paper lying on a shelf in the hooch and wrote a note reminding Jay to pick up his mail and take care of his stuff while he was gone. Paul knew that he didn't need to remind Jay, but the note served to let his friend know that he had stopped by before leaving on his mission.

The flight to the Marine base was as relaxing as a helicopter flight could be in war-torn Vietnam. The normal tension was not there that they would have had if they were going in for a helicopter insertion. Walking into his assigned area of operations appealed to Paul. It gave the team a much better chance of survival and the opportunity to surprise any enemy soldiers who might be operating in the area.

The Marine patrol that had been assigned to escort the recon team out to their break-away site was a group of young but rugged professionals. The patrol leader briefed Paul on the tactic they were going to use to cover for the team's insertion and the route that they would be taking through the dense highland jungle. The platoon leader took his time to check each one of his men to insure they carried the proper amount of ammunition and combat gear. Paul was impressed over the young lieutenant's concern; most new officers had lost that leadership trait in the regular army, or had shucked that boring responsibility to their NCOs.

The Marine patrol departed from the barbed-wire enclosure using extreme stealth the minute they merged into the jungle, ready to encounter the enemy with the first step they took outside the base camp. Paul's team brought up the rear element of the small Marine platoon formation.

Darkness replaced the bright sunlight from the underside of the triple canopy jungle much earlier than it would have if they had been in open areas. The young platoon leader signaled for a break and walked over to check out the piece of terrain he had selected for a night lager site. He waved for his sergeant and whispered that he wanted the army lieutenant to join him. The sergeant returned five minutes later and informed his lieutenant that the recon team wasn't with the Marine column and that he couldn't tell the lieutenant when they had dropped off.

Lieutenant Bourne moved through the thick jungle using every trick and bit of stealth he had learned in the years prior to his joining CCN. He was followed at intervals by his team mates who also blended in with the jungle. It had been very important to break away from the Marine column without being detected by the Marine rear-guard element. The area of operation for the team was highly classified, and if the Marines knew what direction they were travelling in, it would have been very easy to tell where they were going.

Paul stopped his team for the night along the military crest of the hill that they were on. The recon team watched flickers of light coming from the Marine lager position from some of the guards sneaking cigarettes. The guards obviously didn't know how far the light from the end of a cigarette carried in the jungle blackness.

The night passed slowly, with the early-morning light filtering almost without notice through the trees. In the jungle, light changes happened with a gradual ease that almost caught you off-guard if you weren't aware of it. Paul watched the vegetation turn from black to gray and then to a variety of green shades. He kept looking at the jungle and then began to identify individual objects with his eyes, allowing his ears to rest.

Bourne slid over to Coop's position and alerted him that he was ready to move out. The old Montagnard took his turn as the pointman and led the team toward the river. Paul could smell the river before he broke through the jungle growth and saw the rocky banks and the water. The old Montagnard had already started downstream, looking for a fording site that they could use for a night crossing. Late afternoon found them at an excellent river crossing strewn with flat rocks the size of houses. Paul signaled for the team to take cover and wait for the sun to go down before crossing the open waterway, which was two hundred meters wide at the point Paul had chosen for the crossing. Cooper slid next to Paul and signaled for him to get some sleep before it got dark. Paul pulled the short brim down on his camouflaged hat and dozed.

A light tap on his shoulder brought Paul instantly awake and alert. Cooper was pointing at an object moving in the river. Paul rolled over on his stomach and touched shoulders with his team mate.

"What?" The word was an exhaled whisper.

"In the water," Cooper said, his mouth up against Paul's ear.

Paul focused his eyes on a large "V" mark that was moving swiftly downriver. The water following the mark seemed to be rolling, as if another water creature just below the surface as chasing the creature making the "V" mark. The mark changed course slightly and headed directly toward Paul, and then abruptly turned and headed for one of the dry river rocks surrounded by running water. Paul frowned and tried to figure out what kind of creature was swimming on top of the water and what sort of fish was chasing it.

The "V" touched the rock and answered Paul's

question.

Cooper's breath rushed into his lungs between clenched teeth. The smaller object, about the size of a standard football, touched the rock and climbed ashore followed by more and more of itself. Paul and Cooper watched in awe as one of the largest reticulated pythons they had ever seen, or, for that matter, had ever heard about, slid up on the house-sized rock.

Cooper released the trapped deoxygenated air from his lungs and quickly sucked new air back in. "Damn! It has to be damn near forty feet long.

"*Shhhhhh. . . .*" Paul put his hand over Cooper's open mouth.

The Montagnards shifted nervously in their hidden positions, sending rustling noises out over the water. Paul knew that if the water monster stayed on the sun-warmed rock when it got dark he could forget about crossing the river, and would lose another whole day waiting for it to get dark again. Paul slipped his rucksack off his back and pulled it around to his front so that he could see into the canvas side pockets. He removed his silenced .22-caliber pistol and checked the safety switch. The gun was loaded and ready for action. The snake moved slowly on the warm rock less than twenty-five feet from the team's concealed positions. A hard shot for a handgun between the constantly moving coils of the reptile at the only vulnerable spot: the head.

Paul took a half-hour crawling to the point on the riverbank nearest the reptile that offered a clear shot at the constantly moving coils. He took aim, using both hands to steady the long barrel of the weapon. Paul squinted to bring in the front sight on his weapon in the half-light of the late afternoon. The python's head emerged from the pile of tight coils and touched the water. Paul paused and looked downstream in the direction the snake was headed. A wild pig was a third of the way across the river and was swimming at an angle toward the hunting snake. Paul returned his attention to the python and saw that half of the snake was already in the water and that the second half was rapidly following. The thing was huge. Paul waited and watched the jungle drama developing between the unsuspecting pig and the hunting snake. He had no doubt as to who the winner was going to be. An involuntary shutter traversed Paul's spine when the snake reached the pig. The python first bit the pig and then threw its coils around the screaming animal. The whole event took less than five minutes. Darkness fell quickly and began hindering visibility. Paul signaled for his team to cross the river while the reptile was occupied downstream. He didn't have to tell his men to hurry across the waist-deep obstacle. Paul figured that there wouldn't be any more snakes in the area because of the size of the hunting python, but he hoped that the creature wasn't married to a hungry wife.

The team had bunched up on the far side of the river, each man breathing hard from the rapid crossing.

"Christ, Lieutenant! Why did you decide to cross the river now! I damn near pissed my pants!" Cooper's whisper was high and filled with fear.

"Would you rather have waited for the moon to come out and have that fucking beast ready for dessert?" Paul was angry at having his judgment questioned. "Now keep quiet!"

Cooper reflected for a second and winked at the lieutenant.

Lieutenant Bourne thought about the next day's planned activity as he lay in the total darkness of the jungle. He felt the comfort of Cooper's boot against his right foot and the old Montagnard's against his left leg. The team settled down and waited for the night to pass.

First light brought a large flock of multicolored birds to the fruit trees surrounding the hidden recon team. The brightly colored parrots and songbirds began to feed on the abundant seeds and rotten fruit. Paul and his team remained hidden under the thick layers of bamboo leaves on the jungle floor; any movement would alarm the birds and advertise their position to anyone within miles around.

A loud squawk followed by the whirring sound coming from hundreds of wings beating the humid air preceded the sound of truck engines. Paul pressed his chest and right ear to the black soil and listened to the sound of vehicles approaching and then passing less then a hundred meters away. Paul counted the trucks as they passed, stopping to look up when the number reached fifty. The team waited for an hour after the last vehicle had roared by, and then cautiously crept forward from their hiding places.

Cooper stepped through the jungle growth that had been covered with a thick layer of dust from the passing trucks. A gravel, all-weather road stood under the thick canopy of the jungle. The road was no more than a path twenty feet wide by American standards, but in the jungle it was a main thoroughfare. Coop slipped back into the cover of the jungle and peered out. It was becoming very clear why the North Vietnamese didn't want any attention brought to the area. They had built a main supply route south that supplied most of their army in the three southern corps areas.

Paul drew his team around him and removed his small map from its protective case. He showed each man the selected team-extraction site nearest them in case they made contact with the enemy and needed to get taken out in a hurry. Coop nodded in agreement with Paul's choice and pointed to the road. Paul nodded and took the lead, pushing the jungle aside. He felt naked standing on the edge of the highway, but turned and slipped along the easy-walking roadside back toward the river.

A large troop-transport truck was pulling into the jungle just as another truck left the special camouflaged site. The NVA were hurrying to get their vehicles across the open waterway before any early-morning American spotter planes could locate them. Paul knew that the river fording site would not show up on any of the maps and was extremely important information to get back to the CCN intelligence people.

Paul waved his hand for Coop and his team to follow him and slipped back into the covering jungle. He stopped after a few meters and spoke in a soft whisper. "Head north."

Cooper took the point and set a steady pace through the large, arm-thick bamboo. He found a low tunnel entrance at the edge of the stand, which allowed passage through finger-thick interlocking bamboo, that had been made by wild pigs. Cooper entered the tunnel crawling on his hands and knees. The team could have moved faster staying in the fairly open clearing, but the trail would offer more cover even at the risk of running into a boar, or, worse yet, a hunting tiger. Sergeant Cooper led the team for two hours of slow crawling and stopped only when he reached a fork when the trail turned sharply to the west. The cause of the trail to turn was a clear water stream. It was a stroke of good luck that allowed the team to rest and have a cool drink of much-needed water. They filled all of their canteens with fresh water and listened for any sign of approaching danger.

Paul tried orienting himself in the thick growth but had to settle for a compass direction. He guessed that they were still near the road, and noticed that one of the CCN area-studies officers had placed a symbol on his map that represented a landing-zone site nearby. Paul replaced his weatherproof map in his pocket and motioned for the team to move out. He took the point and followed the turning mountain stream until it intersected with the NVA road. The banks of the stream had been leveled so that trucks could ford the watercourse without any difficulty. A simple bamboo footbridge had been built for troops to cross the water about ten meters up from the truck crossing. Paul took ten minutes to visually recon the crossing site. He noticed that the jungle growth had crept back to within ten feet of the footbridge, with a slightly enlarged area leveled flat by use, both up- and downstream from the bridge. It was a good place to set up an ambush. The truck crossing site was deserted and the water in the stream was crystal clear, a sign that the site had not been used since the first convoy that had passed Paul's team in the morning. Paul assembled his team around him, touching heads with almost all of them, and briefed them on how he wanted the ambush set and conducted if an NVA force tried to cross the stream. The jungle to the north and south of the stream formed a shallow ravine as it dipped down to meet the water.

Paul stationed two of his men on the south side of the stream after they had placed their claymore mines along the foot trail. He placed himself and the remaining team members on the north side behind their claymore mines. The ambush was set along the western side of the NVA road, which would allow for Paul to withdraw westward—in a direction the NVA would not expect from an American-led unit. Paul slipped around from position to position checking each of his men to insure that they blended perfectly with the shadows and surrounding jungle. None of the men could be detected from as close as five feet away if they remained lying still. Paul returned to his selected ambush position and wiggled back into the underbrush near the road. He pulled the short elephant grass and vines together in front of his face and held the detonator to his claymore mine loosely in his right hand. He rearranged some of the loose vines so that he could command a view of the footbridge and dropped his chin down against his left hand. Paul hoped for a squad-sized unit or, better yet, a lone NVA courier. A prisoner to take back to the CCN camp would really make a success out of his assigned dead-end mission.

The team waited.

Sweat rolled off Paul's forehead and dripped from his chin to the dry earth forming a small puddle. The afternoon slipped by. Hundreds of bugs crawled and slithered within inches of his face, ignoring the living flesh. Paul blinked the sweat out of his eyes and felt the slight burning sensation from the strong salt. The bugs crawling all around him and over the exposed parts of his body didn't bother him, but certain hairy species of jungle spiders that grew large as a man's open hand would force him to shiver even in the greenhouse heat.

Paul felt the urge to urinate and slowly, without noise, rolled over on his side and unbuttoned his fatigues. He tried keeping the urine far enough away so that he wouldn't have to roll back in it.

Laughter came from down the trail. Paul's muscles tensed. The team waited. A group of thirty NVA soldiers appeared suddenly carrying their weapons flipped on their shoulders, holding onto them by the barrels. The enemy didn't suspect anything in their own backyard. It was a common mistake that had been made during every war ever fought. Paul had just finished urinating and had rolled back over onto his stomach without taking the time to button up his pants. He felt the wetness seep through his clothes. He waited, knowing that his team would not open fire until he detonated his claymore mine. Paul counted the group and decided that there were too many of them to effectively kill. The NVA removed their round boy-scout-style canteens and began filling them from the clear stream. A shout brought those enemy closest to the stream back up on their feet. Another group of NVA appeared on the ridgeline led by an officer, who started yelling down to the unit filling up next to the stream. Paul rapidly assumed that the first element was the point platoon for a very large NVA troop movement, and he slid deeper into the underbrush, hoping that they would all pass by quickly. Paul's thoughts slipped to where he had left his claymore mine. He hoped that it was camouflaged well enough to miss detection.

Minutes turned into eons as more and more NVA soldiers broke over the ridge and slipped down the hill to the stream crossing. The original group had passed over the bridge and disappeared into the jungle. The new group split and half of them stopped on the north side of the stream and dropped their packs, removing cooking pots. It looked to Paul as if they were going to take a meal break at the stream, or that the main body planned on stopping there for the night. Paul knew that he had made a big mistake setting up his ambush so early in the day. He felt his bowels tighten when a half-dozen NVA broke away from the main party and started walking directly toward his hiding place. The man in the lead was dressed in a pair of immaculate khakis, the men following him were very tall for Vietnamese. Paul pressed his chin down in the soft soil and listened to the older man talk to the group in Chinese. Paul's almost-shut eyelids popped open and then closed again almost as quickly. The group were Chinese advisors to a North Vietnamese unit! Paul squeezed the hand detonator gently in his palm—he wanted to blow the group away—but common sense stopped him from committing his team to a sure death.

One of the NVA soldiers broke away from the main group down by the stream and drifted closer and closer to Cooper's hiding place as he looked for small pieces of dry wood for his cooking fire. Paul followed the soldier's movement with his eyes and kept his head absolutely still. The enemy soldier stopped two feet short of where Coop was lying camouflaged from sight and unbuttoned his khaki pants, removing his penis and at the same time looking back over his shoulder as he made a dirty remark to his friends about how many women back in Hanoi had experienced his love-making.

A stream of dark yellow urine left the North Vietnamese's body followed by the explosion from Cooper's claymore mine. Paul instantly followed suit along with all of the team members. The commander of the NVA unit along with all of the Chinese advisors dropped instinctively to the ground, watching their soldiers die from the thousands of ball-bearing sized pellets filling the air. Confusion filled the faces of the NVA survivors as they crawled to their weapons and looked for the source from which the destruction had come. Artillery shells and even bombs from American B-52s gave a short warning before detonating. The NVA leader began yelling orders to his subordinates, gaining order from the confusion. Paul centered the front sight of his CAR-15 on the middle of the leader's forehead and pulled the trigger. The NVA commander flipped over on his side from the impacting bullet and slapped the face of the Chinese advisor lying next to him with his dead right hand. Paul used his right thumb to change his weapon's selector switch to full automatic and killed all of the Chinese advisors who remained lying on the open ground. He finished his first thirty-round magazine and started crawling backward, deeper under cover, as he changed clips. The recon team was raking the ambush site with a deadly volley of fire. The NVA were totally confused and failed to return fire. The ambush had lasted less than thirty seconds.

Paul gained his feet and started running deeper into the jungle. He could hear members of his team following him on both sides. Five minutes of hard traveling brought Paul to the base of a large tree, where he stopped long enough to assemble his team. Paul pointed to the north using his rifle barrel and started breaking through the undergrowth. The NVA soldiers had recovered from the shock of the ambush and were firing wildly into the jungle all around them, which was only allowing the American recon team to escape under cover of the noise.

The team stuck close together, with Paul leading them along a course parallel to the NVA highway. Voices filtered through the bamboo coming from a relief force of enemy soldiers, who were running down the highway to help their comrades. An idea flashed through Paul's mind. He knew that for the next few minutes the advantage was on his side because of the confusion in the enemy ranks. He jogged along looking from side to side until he found a piece of high ground near the road with a small ravine to the rear. Paul stopped and assembled his team.

"We're going to hit them one more time." Paul's eyes continued scanning the jungle while he talked. "They should be bringing their wounded back this way to the north. I want all of you to head for the landing zone marked number two after we hit them. Questions?"

Coop spoke, "You want us to hit the wounded?"

"We're not after the wounded, but for every wounded NVA soldier it takes two healthy men to carry him. We should have them at a disadvantage, and if we allow that huge mob down there to organize, we aren't going to make it out of here."

Paul spotted his men along the roadside, but this time he put them closer together. Without the claymore mines they would have to make a smaller kill zone.

They waited.

An hour had passed before they heard the voices filtering from the south of the roadway. A group of four NVA soldiers appeared, running in single file up the road. Paul let the messengers pass through the kill zone. He hoped that he had guessed right and that they would be sending their wounded north on the road. While Paul lay thinking if he had made a mistake, that the NVA wounded were being taken south, he noticed movement on the road at the very edge of his peripheral vision. A small group of walking wounded appeared. Some of them were using their weapons as walking sticks. Paul allowed them to pass through the kill zone. He wanted those who could still fight and who were able to chase his team through the jungle. The litter cases appeared on the road. Paul waited until his kill zone was filled with soldiers carrying wounded and then threw his last hand grenade. The team opened fire using grenades and small arms. NVA dead covered the surface of the road. The ambush was a total success. There were no survivors. Paul fired the last round from his fifth magazine and jumped over the embankment and ran down the ravine. He knew the gunfire would draw the main NVA force within minutes—and this time they would be ready to fight.

Sergeant Cooper stopped and dropped down on one knee at the edge of the landing zone. Paul broke out of the jungle and joined him seconds later. Air tore in and out of their lungs as they struggled to get their breath. The open field was crisscrossed with head-high tripwires attached to Chinese claymore mines designed to blow a helicopter out of the sky. Paul knew that at least a couple of mortar tubes were laid on the open field. Helicopters trying to pickup people in the clearing would be committing suicide. Paul checked the area for all of his team members. He saw two of the commandos hiding under a clump of bamboo, Cooper was next to him. The old Montagnard was missing. Paul knew that he couldn't wait for him; he had to move fast. Paul yanked his URC-10 out of his side pocket and called the unseen FAC aircraft that was supporting his team.

"FAC Foxfire . . . RT Viper . . . over."

Almost instantly there was a reply, "Foxfire . . . over."

"Viper . . . request immediate extraction . . . Site two is hot . . . We must move inland and STABO rig out . . . over."

"Roger transmission Viper . . . Select a site and I'll call in a team ASAP . . . over."

"Viper . . . over."

Lieutenant Bourne checked the trails entering the clearing and looked back at the jungle he had just left. He hated leaving a team member behind and wanted to go back to look for him. A look of pain covered his face as he made his decision: The old Montagnard had a better chance of surviving alone if he was still alive than any of the Americans did. Going back would only jeopardize all of their lives. Paul signaled his team to head west. The team moved silently through the jungle, listening to NVA soldiers firing signal shots to each other. The jungle overhead opened slightly and Paul stopped the team. He called the FAC aircraft and gave their approximate location.

Cooper held a small pen flaregun in his hands with the barrel pointed straight up through the trees. Paul nodded and Coop released the thumb firing pin. A soft *whooshing* sound filled the clearing and the tiny flare burst bright red a few meters above the treetops.

Paul pushed the talk switch. "Foxfire . . . see it?"

"No . . . fire another one . . ."

Cooper pulled another flare from the strap and screwed it into the barrel. He fired the second round. It ricocheted off a large beech but continued its upward course to explode above the trees.

"Marked!"

Paul prepared his web gear, hooking the nylon straps between his legs and snapping them together. Cooper was having trouble untaping his "D" rings, and Paul slipped over and helped him. Both of the men's hands were shaking from the tension and fear building up inside of them.

The sound of helicopters filtered down through the thick vegetation to the waiting team. Paul forced his ears to block out the comforting sound of the choppers, and listen to the jungle. He desperately wanted to hear the old Montagnard moving through the bamboo.

The helicopters circled the site, giving Paul an occasional flash of silver light reflecting off the plexiglas cockpits.

"Viper . . . Foxfire . . . over."

"This is Viper . . . You're almost over us. I'm flashing you with my mirror."

"Marked, Viper. . . . I'm bring in some fast movers to cover your extraction."

"Roger . . ." Paul wiggled the small mirror in his hand a few more times just to insure that he was marked by the FAC.

A pair of slicks hovered over Paul's position and dropped sandbag-weighted nylon climbing ropes through the light cover down to the waiting team.

Paul looked back over his left shoulder and saw the old Montagnard break out of the thick cover. Blood covered his right leg. Paul unhooked himself from the ropes and ran over to the old man. He picked up the small-framed man in his arms and ran back to the dangling ropes.

Paul looked up and saw a solid stream of green tracers enter the chopper through the front of the plexiglas. The helicopter banked away from the extraction site and crashed in a ball of fire. Pieces of the helicopter bounced off the trees above the team and fell to the ground.

Paul carried the wounded commando over to the single remaining dark-green nylon rope just as the chopper began lifting Cooper and the other commandos off the ground. The pilot saw Paul and lowered his chopper back down to within reach of Paul.

Lieutenant Bourne quickly hooked the old man onto the remaining lifeline and waved up to the chopper pilot to leave. The man was shaking his head, but realizing the danger he pulled up.

Cooper hung helplessly from the string that held him ten feet off the ground. He heard Paul yelling to him to drop his rucksack and obeyed. He reached down for his knife so that he could cut himself loose and join his team mate on the ground, but the chopper pilot gunned his machine to escape a stream of tracers and the ground below dropped away.

Coop screamed down to Paul but the wind erased his words as they left his lips.

Lieutenant Bourne took a second to watch the helicopter disappear carrying his team and then grabbed Cooper's rucksack and blended into the jungle.

He was alone.

Chapter 19

Sergeant Cooper joined hands with the team commandos and spread his legs apart to stabilize his flight and prevent his single rope from twisting around and make him spin at the end. The tears pouring out of the combat-hardened sergeant's eyes were air dried almost as soon as they had left his tear ducts.

Cooper hung suspended from the nylon harness and watched the shades of green jungle flash by under his feet. The river that they had forded appeared at his boot tips as a silver thread. Coop felt a sharp pain coming from his crotch and wiggled his legs to adjust the wide nylon band around his buttocks and better distribute his body weight.

Cooper looked up at the bottom plating on the chopper carrying him, and could see where a number of .51-caliber bullets had scraped and grooved the olive-drab paint. He sighed, thinking about the long flight back to Quang Tri hanging from the helicopter. Coop's mind returned to the extraction site and Lieutenant Bourne, bringing an anguish that was deeper than any bullet could penetrate. He had left a team member alive on the ground—one of the most unforgivable sins a recon man could commit. The lieutenant had waved the chopper away so they would have a chance to escape, but Cooper felt that he should have cut himself free and fallen down to join Bourne. The grief was eased somewhat when Coop's logical side took over. What if he had dropped back down to the ground from the climbing helicopter and broken a leg in the fall? He would have really placed Paul in trouble then. At least the lieutenant had a small chance to escape by himself until they could Brightlight a team back into the area.

Lieutenant Bourne was glad Cooper had heard him call and had dropped his rucksack containing the other half to the secure voice long-range radio and some extra food. Paul didn't know how long it would take for a Brightlight Team to return and extract him; at least he could last for a few extra days now and communicate with the relay site at Hickory.

Single rifle shots echoed through the jungle coming from all around him. The NVA soldiers were getting organized and were sweeping the jungle looking for stray recon men and dead insurgents. Paul checked his CAR-15 and replaced the partially expended magazine with a full one. He analyzed his area map and decided that the safest route for him to take would be northwest. The highway ran basically north and south, and would be very well patrolled for the next week, until the NVA were satisfied that the area was again secure. Traveling east would be the expected direction any stay-behind would take and that area would be the most patrolled. Northwest was the logical avenue to stay out of the NVA search net. Paul set a slow pace for himself, knowing that he would have a long way to go before calling in an extraction team. He did not want to sacrifice any American lives if he didn't have to.

The helicopter hovered above the Quang Tri helipad and lowered the recon team slowly to the ground. The door gunner was leaning out of his open door, directing the pilot over the intercom system. Cooper unhooked his string and dropped down on his knees. The launch-site officer ran under the downdraft coming from the chopper and helped the sergeant regain his feet.

"*The lieutenant is still back there on the ground!*" Cooper almost screamed, "*Get a Brightlight formed . . . I'm going back after him!*"

The officer walked next to Coop toward the operations hut. "Take it easy . . . I'll send a message to headquarters and get a rescue started. . . ."

Cooper eased down against the building, his legs lacking enough blood to support him. The officer ran inside the shack and grabbed his handset.

"Redhopper . . . this is . . . Bluehopper! . . . over."

"Redhopper, send your traffic . . . over."

The launch officer ran his finger down a list of surnames matched next to their code names and stopped when he reached Bourne.

"This is Bluehopper . . . We have a piece of equipment still on a hot extraction site . . . code name Thor . . . I say again . . . code Thor . . . The rest of the equipment is at my location . . . over."

Major Galviston was briefing Mister Michaels in the main operations center when the call from the launch site came over the radio.

"Get RT Coral ready to Brightlight." Galviston automatically took charge of the rescue operation. Michaels stood against the far wall and watched the rescue scenario develop. There wasn't any panic, only an increase in activity as the duty officers began to execute their listed directives and make radio calls to various support functions. Galviston stepped back from the bank of radios and watched his men work.

"What's going on?" Michaels approached Galviston.

"Thor is still on the ground at his team's extraction site. We have to get him out of there soon or he's a dead man." Galviston took the handset from the radio operator and gave the launch officer instructions. The radio operator flipped through his code book and stopped his finger under Lieutenant Bourne's name. The reporter followed with his eyes and read the code name for Paul: Thor.

Lieutenant Bourne stopped next to the roots of a large mahogany tree and shoved Cooper's pack against the trunk. He withdrew his map and plotted his position. Paul had figured that he had traveled at least a thousand meters from the extraction site, but he had actually covered closer to two thousand. He pulled his URC-10 from his pocket as an idea developed in his head. He was still alive and hidden safely in the jungle, and had an excellent chance of continuing his recon mission for a few more days while the area cooled off. Besides, he had an Article 15 waiting for him if he returned to the base camp so soon. The NVA would never suspect that a lone American had stayed behind in the jungle.

Paul gently squeezed the rubber-covered transmitter switch on his hand-held radio. "Foxfire . . . Viper . . . over."

"*Viper!* . . . I was getting worried about you!"

"This is Viper . . . listen closely, this is going to be my last broadcast for awhile . . ." Paul's eyes continuously scanned the underbrush. He felt as if he were yelling into the handset, yet his voice was barely above no sound at all. " . . . call base and tell them not to Brightlight . . . I say again . . . do *not* Brightlight. . . . There are too many NVA down here and we'll lose more ships and people than it's worth . . . I'm safe . . . Do you have a pencil handy?"

"Roger, Viper . . . send your traffic . . ." The FAC pilot held his pencil above the writing pad strapped to his leg.

"Take my birthday: month, year, and day . . . add them together and then add the digits of the sum together . . . that is the time I will send a blind transmission . . . got to run . . . out."

The pilot triggered his mike and spoke to Paul on the ground. "We'll have you covered as long as you're there." He banked his airplane, looking down at the jungle canopy, hoping Paul had been listening. He had. Paul slipped his radio into his side pocket and took a compass reading before heading northwest away from the tree.

Traveling through the jungle without having to worry about taking care of other people was almost a relief to Paul, who took the lives of his people very seriously, almost to a fault. He moved around thick groves of bamboo, always taking the easiest route he could, so that he wouldn't burn up energy he might need if he were discovered by enemy patrols. Paul located a cave area at the base of a long ravine late in the afternoon and stopped to rest. He laid his head back against Cooper's rucksack and allowed his body to recover from the morning's activity and the walk through the jungle. Suddenly he didn't feel very brave. He was alone, in a very hostile jungle where he could vanish without a trace in a matter of minutes. Paul stood and busied himself with his packs to keep from thinking about the fear that was creeping around inside him. The gentle, comforting sound of running water reached his ears. He hefted his canteen and found it almost empty. Paul smelled the uncapped canteen and realized that his body craved water.

The area surrounding him was pocketed with small caves and huge boulders that could afford cover to any number of hostile jungle creatures. Paul picked up his CAR-15 from the pack where he had placed it earlier and walked up the ravine, leaving his rucksacks stashed in a small hole at the base of the ravine. He walked parallel to the ravine wall, looking for a cave that would be large enough to hold all of his gear and that would also have enough room for him to sleep in during the night. Sweat stained his jungle fatigues from the exertion of walking and crawling over the rocks. He spied an opening tucked behind a bunch of chipped boulders and scrambled over to examine the prospective lager site. The cave was perfect. Paul carried a number of large rocks from the lower base of the ravine up to the cave site. He filled in all but a small crawlspace at the entrance of the cave. When he stood back to inspect his work he was happy with the camouflage job he had done. The rocks served two purposes; one was to camouflage the cave entrance, and the second was to give him some protection from attack by night animals while he slept. He smiled and returned back to where he had stashed his gear, making one quick stop at the mountain stream to drink and fill his canteen. He hauled the rucksacks up to the hidden cave after spending ten minutes trying to find it again. He had actually walked fifty meters past the small opening before he had realized his mistake and returned to the site. He was very pleased with his labor, knowing that if he had a hard time finding the opening then any NVA soldiers looking for him would also have difficulty locating him once he was hidden inside. Paul removed his silenced .22-caliber pistol from his pack and the extra box of shells. He knew that if he had a chance encounter with a wild animal, his CAR-15 would make too much noise.

He had found the perfect hiding place in the jungle. Water was close to his cave, along with a high place on the crest of the ravine, from where he could set up the secure voice radio. Paul looked up at the sunlight breaking through the trees and then checked his watch; he had two hours of good light still left in the day and decided to reconnoiter the immediate area surrounding his hidden cave. He started moving in a large circle around the ravine, listening to the sound of the jungle as he slipped past insects that became quiet the instant he violated their boundaries and resumed their conversations with his passing. The jungle almost blended into a single living creature. He listened for the jungle ahead of him to change and become too quiet or too loud. Paul traveled for over an hour before stopping. He figured that he was located at the very northwestern corner of his map sheet. If he kept going in that direction, he would lose the benefit of his detailed map. Paul tugged his canteen out of its case and took a long drink from it. The canteen was still touching his lips when a clear voice reached his ears, followed by an answering deep male voice. A conversation developed between the two men that was calm and didn't reflect any alarm. Paul returned his canteen to its carrying case and snapped the flaps shut. He took his pistol out of its holster and crawled slowly through the jungle. Paul paused and pushed a bunch of dust-covered bushes aside and peered down a narrow mountain trail. He remained flat on his stomach, but slipped forward so that he could look both ways on the hard-packed surface. The trail split ten meters to the north, creating a small delta where three North Vietnamese soldiers sat around a twig cooking fire. Three rifles were stacked in a military tripod five feet from the group. Paul adjusted the front sight on his pistol between the eyes of the enemy soldier who was sitting facing him but looking down at the small cooking pot. The sound coming from the pistol was barely audible. The soldier slumped forward, knocking over the metal-and-bamboo stand that held the cooking rice. The NVA soldier who had been talking turned to see what had caused his comrade's unpredicted act and caught a bullet just above his right ear. The remaining soldier scrambled for his rifle but died with a bullet passing into his cranium from the base of his neck.

Paul slipped along the path, staying next to the thick jungle growth just in case there were more enemy soldiers nearby. He checked the dead for documents and then went over and opened the three rucksacks that had been lined up neatly by the rifles. He removed all of the food, papers, and extra ammunition the NVA had been carrying in their packs. Paul was puzzled when he noticed that one of the packs contained magazines for an American weapon. He looked over at the stacked rifles and noticed for the first time that two of the weapons were Russian SKS rifles and the third an M-16. The American rifle had a hand-painted short-timer's calendar painted on its stock. The American owner had all of the tiny boxes representing days marked off except for the last sixteen. Paul snatched up the three weapons and the pot of cooked rice and melted into the jungle. He stashed the rifles and headed back to his cave carrying the heavy NVA rucksack on one shoulder and his CAR-15 cradled under his right arm. The food in the pot smelled good and he hurried to reach the safety of his hiding place so that he could eat. The dead NVA would be found with their weapons and food missing, which Paul hoped would be blamed on local bandits.

The last glimmer of daylight was flickering through the trees when Paul reached his cave. The rice pot was still warm, and the food tasted good as he filled his mouth using his hand for a spoon. He wolfed down the small pot of fish and rice and wiped his hand clean using his pant leg for a napkin. Paul opened the tie-straps on the rucksack and sorted through the small bundle of papers, finding most of the items to be letters the enemy soldiers had written and were waiting to send back to their homes. Paul tore open the last envelope and removed the color photograph of a woman with two children. The letter was being forwarded to some NVA line soldier, probably fighting in the southern part of Vietnam. Paul shoved the picture back in the envelope and took out a thick folded bundle and opened it. A beautifully hand-drawn map of the surrounding area was revealed in the fading light. The detail on the map was much better than the official military map Paul carried. A trail scaled to the river was drawn leading to an intricate complex of neatly drawn squares Paul stared at the map in the poor light trying to locate a familiar landmark. A trail junction at the very bottom had three names written by it in pencil. He guessed they were the names of the guards at the trail junction. A Vietnamese word was written in the center of each of the squares located in the complex. Paul frowned and tried recalling his Vietnamese. *Phao-bin* was a word he had heard before, and then it dawned on him—artillery. The square represented a storage area for artillery ammunition.

Paul had stumbled on a huge secret NVA ammunition depot.

Jay ran from his hooch over to the operations center after he had heard from one of the other recon team leaders about Paul's being left behind on the ground alive. Major Galviston was standing by the radio shaking his head and talking to Lieutenant Colonel

Clewell.

"Damn it! What in the hell are we going to do about him?"

Clewell rubbed his chin and then answered. "Remember, Galviston . . . the man on the ground calls the shots! If he says that it's too hot to extract him . . . then, damn it, we *wait*!"

"What's going on, sir?" Jay broke into the senior officers' conversation. He knew that they had to be talking about his friend.

"Lieutenant Bourne has just contacted his covering forward air controller and told him not to Brightlight because the area was crawling with NVA with heavy antiaircraft weapons." Galviston shook his head.

"Sir! We *have* to go after him . . . *send me!* I can take my team and insert twenty clicks away and run in!" Jay grabbed the major by his elbow and turned him around. "Sir, we just can't leave him down there alone!"

"Calm down, Loveless. You know the rules—Bourne calls the shots as long as he's in his AO."

"I know all of that bullshit!"

Clewell entered the conversation. "At ease, Lieutenant." He felt as helpless as the young lieutenant standing in front of him clenching his fists. "Let's see what Bourne has to say during his blind broadcast before we do anything else." The commander looked at his deputy. "Galviston, I want all broadcasts going into the Hickory relay site transmitted here."

"Done, sir," Galviston nodded in agreement. "I'll have the communications officer get on it right away."

"Lieutenant Loveless, I want you to monitor the radios tonight in case Bourne needs to improvise a code. You probably know him better than anyone else in camp."

The jungle night was a sheet of total blackness. Paul lay back against his rucksack and stared out of the small opening unable to distinguish anything. He looked at the extremely bright face on his Rolex watch, then tore off a piece of green tape that he always carried wrapped around a portion of his pistol belt and covered the luminous dial with it. The area-studies officer back at CCN had told him that he would have the benefit of a full moon during his patrol. A heavy cloud cover must have slipped in during the early evening hours and blocked out the moonlight temporarily. Paul decided that he would take the secure voice radio to the top of the ravine and risk sending a message back to the Hickory relay site before his preplanned blind radio broadcast. The discovery of the enemy main-supply depot was too important of an item to wait on sending back its exact location.

Paul closed his eyes and the photograph of the North Vietnamese family appeared. He opened his eyes and stared out at the blackness of the cave. His thoughts slipped to all of the enemy soldiers that he had killed. He knew that all of them had families and loved ones; they weren't any different than American soldiers. The killing was really starting to get to Paul. He had loved hunting animals since he had been a small boy but he could feel that he was losing his desire to kill. He would rather just watch wild animals now than track them down and kill them.

Bright moonlight burst through a hole in the dispersing clouds, giving Paul enough light to locate his radio sections and place them all together in his rucksack. He crawled out of the narrow opening and stretched the stiffness out of his sore muscles. Paul checked the ravine very closely before he left the safety of the cave. He was more concerned over running into a hunting tiger than he was about stumbling into a night-moving NVA patrol. The walk to the top of the ravine took him the better part of an hour as he wove his way between the boulders, selecting the best route to the top carrying the heavy backpack. He strung out the heavy copper antenna for the radio and attached the components of the set together. Paul turned the switch on and watched the small lights on the dials emit a soft friendly glow. A rush of static coming through the handset startled Paul and he turned the volume down. He checked the surrounding jungle to see if the noise had alerted anything within hearing distance. He acted out of reflex more than from a need. He pushed the transmitter switch and whispered so softly that he could hardly hear himself.

"Foxfire . . . Viper . . . over . . . Foxfire . . . Viper . . . over . . ."

Static answered his call. He waited five minutes and tried broadcasting again without receiving an answer. He waited.

"Viper . . . Hickory . . . send your traffic . . . over."

The voice startled Paul. He realized that he was operating with a bundle of raw nerves coursing through his body.

"Hickory . . . glad someone is minding the store tonight. . . ."

"Roger, Viper . . . we'll be monitoring all of your assigned pushes from now on."

Jay had fallen asleep with his head resting on top of his folded arms. When Paul's voice coming over the radio's speaker had filled the room, Loveless had almost fallen backward out of his chair. Mister Michaels stepped through the open doorway holding a cup of steaming coffee in his hand. He offered Jay a drink and took a seat next to the recon team leader and listened intently to the broadcast.

"Hickory . . . I have some top-priority traffic for

your higher . . . are you prepared to copy?"

"Send your traffic . . . over."

"Grid 376282 is the center coordinates of a huge NVA ammunition depot. Divert all B-52 missions to that location tonight!" Paul sucked in a lungful of air and continued whispering. "The place is big, so blow up anything within four thousand meters of that grid and you'll be taking out something!"

"Grid 376282? . . . over."

"Good copy . . . I don't know when I can contact you again . . . but thanks for monitoring my frequency . . ." Paul scanned the dark jungle and added, " . . . nice talking to you . . ."

"I have a message to you from Loveless. He said that he knows for sure now that you're a closet leg . . . 'cause you're afraid to ride a STABO rig. . . ."

". . . sure . . . believe that shit!" Paul released the push-to-talk switch and felt the loneliness engulf him.

Jay smiled. The operator out at Hickory had made up the message about being a leg to cheer up Paul. It had worked, both for Paul and for Jay.

Lieutenant Bourne started disassembling his radio as fast as he could. He had spent too much time out in the open and wanted to get back to the security of his cave. The comfort he had felt talking to a friendly voice had only succeeded in accenting his loneliness. He started down the mountain, taking advantage of the downhill slope. The B-52 bombers should be arriving at any time to hit the waiting supply depot. The NVA couldn't do anything to save the huge base, even if they had monitored the broadcast.

Jay picked up the yellow piece of paper from the desk he had used to copy the grid coordinates on and went over to the big wall map to plot the location.

Jay spoke over his shoulder to the newsman. "Would you go over to the room next door and wake Major

Galviston . . . also get Colonel Clewell . . . this is big!"

"Sure . . . Damn! I feel like a soldier!"

Jay glanced from the map to the back of the reporter. "You have a hell of a long way to go before you can claim that!" Jay smiled.

Major Galviston stepped into the command center blinking the sleep from his eyes, followed by Colonel Clewell who was wearing only a pair of fatigue pants.

Galviston spoke, "What's up, Loveless?"

Jay briefed the senior officers on Paul's message and showed them the location of the depot on the map.

"Damn, we've been trying to locate that site for years." Galviston tapped the map sheet with his pencil and added, "We've missed it because our westernmost boundary doesn't extend that far. It's interesting that it falls less than a thousand meters outside our search areas."

Clewell frowned. "I wonder what else is located *just* outside of our operating areas?"

Galviston grasped what the commander was leading up to and hissed out the words, ". . . a double agent?"

"Could be . . ." Clewell shifted his gaze to his deputy. "Let's check it out with our people . . ."

"Leave it to Paul! If anyone could find it, he could!" Jay spoke in jest, but all of the men listening in the room nodded their heads in agreement.

"Damn! He's one hell of a good recon man!" Clewell shook his head. "Get me General Pick's deputy on the line."

Twenty minutes passed.

"Redhopper . . . this is Dragon Six . . . over." General Pick's voice filled the command center after the secure voice light went on next to the speaker set. "Clewell, this is Pick. I've arrived back from Washington early. I've heard rumors that something big is going on in your area of operations."

The secure voice system filled with static and Clewell waited for the system to clear before trying to answer the general's questions.

"General, we've located the largest NVA supply depot of the war. We will need your personal support to divert all of the Air Force's B-52 strikes tonight to the area we have located."

The pause from the general's end of the line lasted at least half a minute.

"Clewell . . . You don't have any idea what perfect timing your discovery is . . . Send the location."

"Grid 3 . . . 7 . . . 6 . . . 2 . . . 8 . . . 2 . . . I say again, 376282. That's located in our Snake area of operations . . . over."

"The North Vietnamese Army has been massing for a major offensive for the past two weeks. If we can hit their ammunition depot and destroy it . . . I'm sure we can have General McWorth's Air Force Support." There was a pause and then the general added, "Which of your teams found the depot?"

"It wasn't a team, General. It was one man . . . Lieutenant Paul Bourne. You might remember him from when you were here last. You decorated him with a DSC."

"Alone? I don't understand . . ."

"Yes, sir, alone. He gave up his extraction rig to a fellow soldier . . ." Clewell spent the next ten minutes explaining to the general exactly what had occurred concerning the lieutenant—from the charges the helicopter pilot had pressed, to the reasons why he had sent the lieutenant out on a mission to wait for the general's return to Vietnam.

"I'm due in Da Nang tomorrow for a meeting with the Corps commander. Meet me at the airport when I land."

"Roger, sir. Do you have any further traffic for this

station?"

"None! Out."

Major Galviston smiled at his boss. They both knew that all kinds of hell was going to break loose when the two general officers met the following day.

Lieutenant Bourne found a comfortable spot on the edge of the ravine above his cave and took a reading from his compass so that he could face the exact direction of the supply depot. He was on much higher ground than the bunkered ammunition center, and if the Air Force bombers made it during the night, he would have a grandstand view of the action.

Paul dozed with his head jerking down and touching his folded-up knees. . . .

The earth-shattering blast from the first two-thousand-pound bomb echoed over Paul's ravine, waking the lieutenant with a jolt from the soft shock wave. Paul slipped behind a boulder as the explosions walked toward his ravine increasing their tempo. The last bomb in the string landed less than five hundred meters from his location. This was the nearest Paul had ever been to a B-52 strike, and the effects of the powerful explosions were awesome. Secondary explosions erupted in the jungle thousands of meters to the west where the depot was hidden under the jungle canopy. The ammunition would continue to explode well into the next day.

"Hickory . . . Foxfire . . . over." The static from the moving aircraft fragmented the broadcast.

"Foxfire . . . Hickory . . . over."

"Foxfire . . . Christ, you won't believe this, but fire is shooting up a thousand feet in the air! . . . I can almost feel the heat coming from the burning ammo. . . . That is one *big* depot down there, and all of it is going up in smoke."

The radio operator located on the radio relay site answered in a calmer voice, "We believe you . . . We can see the fires from here."

Major Galviston listened to the radio relay site operator talking to the forward air controller.

"We've had calls coming in all night long from aircraft pilots who've spotted the explosions. That boy sure has done one hell of a fine job!" Galviston spoke to Michaels and Loveless.

Lieutenant Loveless smiled. His friend had really outdone himself this time. Mister Michaels excused himself from the men standing around the operations room listening to the action over the radio and left the building. He got into his jeep and headed out of the camp gate toward the sprawling Corps Headquarters compound.

"Where's the reporter going?" Galviston nodded toward the exit.

"I guess he's checking in with his wire service downtown. He mentioned last night that he was going to have to submit an outline on his article today." Jay stretched and continued talking to the major. "Sir, I think I'll run over and get some breakfast."

Galviston didn't look up from the map he was studying. "If you don't mind picking me up a couple of bacon'n'eggs sandwiches, I'd appreciate it."

Jay nodded and left the building. He blinked his eyes in the bright natural light of day. The gate guard nodded when Jay flashed his badge and walked down the sand-strewn sidewalk running next to the headquarters building. The mail clerk knocked against the plexiglas window, drawing Jay's attention away from his personal thoughts. The sergeant waved for Jay to come around to the small window through which he dispatched mail to the American team members.

"You've got a bundle of letters today, sir."

"Thanks." Jay held the banded letters in one hand and thumbed rapidly through the pile, looking for anything worth reading right away. Jay looked up at the watching clerk. "Does Paul Bourne have any mail?"

"Just a minute and I'll check." The clerk returned and handed Jay three letters.

Lieutenant Loveless looked at the return addresses on Bourne's letters as he walked to the mess hall. His friend had received a letter from his bank in California and a letter from the Infantry Officers Branch back in Washington. The remaining letter was from an Army nurse in one of the hospitals located in II Corps.

Jay slipped Paul's letters in the side pocket of his fatigues and opened one of his own letters from his hometown steady girl. His mind slipped from war to love-making as he walked toward the mess hall.

Chapter 20

Lieutenant Colonel Clewell sat erect against the seat back in his jeep as he waited for the arrival of General Pick's Lear jet. The Da Nang airfield was busy, as it normally was during the peak arrival period of aircraft bringing in replacements from the States and loading up those soldiers and marines who were completing their tours. The general's aircraft was already forty minutes late. Colonel Clewell wiped the sweat from his forehead with his index finger and flicked it onto the PSP, where it evaporated almost instantly upon contact with the sun-baked steel.

The door to the control tower burst open and an overweight Air Force sergeant called out to the colonel, "Are you Lieutenant Colonel Clewell from the Special Forces unit down the road?"

Clewell nodded his head and left the jeep. He paused to tell his driver to move the vehicle over to the shady side of the tower and wait for him.

"I'm Clewell, Sergeant." He spoke with a tinge of disgust in his voice as he drew close enough to the fat man to see the bulging gut and sweat stains the size of plates under the man's arms. Clewell didn't know why, but a fat man sweating seemed to him as something unmilitary.

"General Pick's aide de camp called and told us to

have you and the Corps commander stand by over at the VIP lounge." The fat sergeant began breathing heavy from trying to talk in the bright sunshine.

"Thanks, Sergeant. You had better get back inside before you get a heat stroke." The sarcasm completely passed over the sergeant's head.

"Yes, sir; it's too hot out here for me!" The sergeant released the door and returned to the comfort of the air-conditioned tower.

Clewell's thoughts returned to Lieutenant Bourne, who was alone and trying to survive in a hostile jungle. The thought of the Air Force sergeant working in the safety of the control tower and Lieutenant Bourne, both drawing exactly the same amount of money for combat pay, brought a smile laced with irony across the combat colonel's weathered face. It really didn't seem fair.

The VIP lounge was furnished with a plush decor accented with carpets and heavy chairs. A full-time bartender worked the Philippine-built mahogany bar.

"May I help you, sir?"

"A glass of orange juice. Heavy on the ice, please." Clewell took a seat next to the window facing the long north-south runway. He could see a jeep bearing a three-star plate pull up in front of the tower below him. The corps commander had arrived almost an hour late. Clewell wondered if the corps commander had talked with General Pick and knew of the delay, or if the lieutenant general had arrived late on purpose, planning on having the senior general wait for him.

Clewell took in a deep breath and adjusted his jacket. He knew that the corps commander would definitely have a piece of his ass over the Bourne incident.

The lounge door swung open and the corps commander strode into the room followed by a pair of brigadier generals and a cluster of colonels. The lieutenant general glanced over at the Green Beret officer and ordered a whiskey and water from the bartender without acknowledging Clewell's presence. The general drank half of the cold drink, then walked slowly up to the colonel, who had remained standing at attention.

"Well . . . Lieutenant Colonel Clewell . . . isn't it?"

"Yes, sir."

"How are things going in the reconnaissance business?"

"Fine, General . . . thank you."

"Thank me?" The corps commander glanced around the room, gaining smiles of support from his staff. "You really should thank me for *not* court-marshalling *you!*" He spun around to face Clewell directly before continuing, "Hell, you can't control that goddamned bunch of hoodlums you call officers . . ."

Clewell's eyes narrowed into slits, but he remained standing at attention and held his tongue.

"Well? Do you have an answer?" the general grinned. "You *know* that I can't stand back and allow a lieutenant to pull a gun on a senior officer . . ."

Clewell cut into the conversation. "Sir, have you heard the other side of the story?"

"How could I?" the general sneered. "Didn't you sneak your lieutenant off on some wild goose chase so I couldn't see him?"

Clewell's heart skipped a beat.

The general continued talking. "Anyway . . . I don't have to talk to him until he's in court. Your lieutenant threatened a senior officer with a gun, who, by the way, has been decorated for bravery in the past. I have heard *some* talk about the pilot refusing to rescue a *suspected* crash-site victim, but the decision to risk the lives of the people on board his aircraft is his to make, as the commander—not your lieutenant's." A slight change in the tone of voice alerted Clewell that the corps commander was verbally maneuvering. "Besides, the captain tells me a very believable story. He states that he was very low on fuel and needed to divert to a Marine base before going after the downed pilot. It sounds to me like your lieutenant was a bit hasty and got carried away with his gun." The general glared at Clewell, daring him to challenge the statement.

Clewell took the challenge.

"Sir, the pilot had the mission to fly supplies out to our relay site, which so happens to be sixty kilometers farther away than the downed pilot's aircraft. If the pilot's story to you is true, he would have crashed from lack of fuel before they would have reached Hickory."

The corps commander glared over at one of his staff colonels, who had taken a seat on the other side of the room by the bar. The colonel had been the one responsible for fabricating the low-fuel story.

General Pick had entered the room unobserved through a private side entrance and had been listening to the corps commander lay into Clewell for the past couple of minutes. He stepped forward into the lighted portion of the lounge and caught the lieutenant general's attention.

"Sir! We failed to see you come in!" A fake smile lighted up the craggy old face of the junior general. "I was just discussing the incident with Clewell."

"I know. I heard you talking . . ." General Pick looked over at the bartender. "A glass of ice water, please." He turned and stared at the drink the corps commander was holding, and frowned. The look that passed between the generals was a reprimand.

General Pick spoke in a low tone. "I would like to talk with you and Clewell . . . alone, if we may?"

The corps commander locked his lips and nodded to his staff. The room emptied quickly, including the bartender. General Pick motioned for the two officers to take seats and then joined them.

"Sir, if I may!" The corps commander was trying to take the offensive and set the tone for the meeting.

"Sure, General—go ahead." Pick raised his eyebrows and leaned back against his chair to listen.

"The morale of my pilots has hit rock bottom after the incident with Lieutenant Bourne. The lieutenant's charge of cowardice against one of my most senior pilots is very serious. I hope you understand that I have three hundred pilots under my command, and I can't let a damn whippersnapper get away with pulling a damn gun on an aircraft commander!" The corps commander hardly stopped to breathe as he rambled on, ". . . We must punish this maverick officer *severely* in order to protect the morale of my troops and maintain discipline! I don't give a damn what in the hell it's going to take, but I demand his court-marshal!" The lieutenant general slapped the tabletop with his open palm to emphasize his stand on the issue. The tactic was a cheap shot that failed to impress the four-star general watching him. Pick realized that the junior general was trying to force him into backing him in front of a very junior field-grade officer.

The corps commander closed his argument, "I want his ass!"

General Pick smiled. A long pause filled the room adding to the silence. Clewell felt very ill at ease sitting between the two very powerful generals. He was well aware that either of them could destroy his career without very much difficulty.

"Well, I agree the action the lieutenant took seemed rather drastic," General Pick reached down into his black leather briefcase and removed a pre-edition copy of *Stars & Stripes*, Vietnam edition, "but have either of you had a chance to read today's edition of the paper?"

Clewell and the lieutenant general looked at each other, neither knowing what General Pick was driving at.

"No, sir," the corps commander answered. Clewell just nodded in the negative.

General Pick placed the open paper in front of the lieutenant general with the headlines upside-down to Clewell. The bold headlines read: LONE LIEUTENANT DESTROYS NVA AMMUNITION DEPOT—STOPS ENEMY WAR EFFORT IN THE SOUTH. A large picture of Paul Bourne covered the rest of the front page.

"Do you know who that lieutenant is, General?" Pick was enjoying playing his trump card.

The corps commander could guess who he was looking at.

"Would you still like to court-marshal him?" Pick stood up and grinned down at the other general. "*I* wouldn't."

Clewell spun the paper around and opened it to the page that described the page-one cover story. It told of Paul's stay-behind tactic.

"How in the hell did the paper get this story!" Clewell's voice reflected his concern. "He's still out there! The NVA will have a copy of this paper by this afternoon! Damn it—this could get Bourne *killed*!"

"*Newsweek* magazine had the story printed nationwide. Mister Michaels feels that the American people need a hero that they can sink their teeth into—and I tend to agree with him, especially after seeing firsthand what the hippie movement is doing to our country." General Pick lowered his voice and added, "In fact, I have to return back to Washington and testify before Congress on the war, and when I return, I want a *complete* packet on Lieutenant Bourne for the Medal of Honor!" General Pick looked at the corps commander with a tinge of malice reflected in his eyes. "We really don't want to court-marshal the biggest American hero to come out of the Vietnam War . . . do we?"

Clewell smiled and turned his head away from the corps commander, who dropped his glare down to the floor.

"I plan on personally tying the Medal of Honor around Lieutenant Bourne's neck when we pull him out of there. The President has given me permission . . ." Pick answered the lieutenant general's question before he had a chance to ask it. The President normally presented all Medals of Honor personally, in the White House. General Pick leaned back in his chair and laced his fingers behind his head. "Clewell, do you know a Mister LeBlonde?"

"Yes, sir. He's one of the better Agency men assigned to the Vietnam office. I've dealt with him a quite a few times and always ended up impressed."

"I tend to agree with you. LeBlonde has an excellent agency network of agents established in the area surrounding Lieutenant Bourne. LeBlonde has ordered his people to link up with Bourne and extract him.

"I hope they're moving fast, sir."

"It's already in progress as we're talking. By the way. . . ." General Pick reached down, opened his briefcase, and removed a piece of blue cardboard with a pair of silver eagles attached, "take off those oak leafs. You're a full colonel as of today. The Department of the Army answered my query concerning your eligibility early this morning, and I wanted to personally pin these on you." The general went over to where Clewell stood and pinned one shiny eagle on his collar, then handed the second eagle to the newly promoted colonel. "Here's one for your beret."

The jeep driver stared at Clewell's beret as the

colonel approached the vehicle. "I didn't know we came here for a promotion ceremony, sir! Congratulations!"

"Just between the two of us, Sergeant . . . neither did I!" Clewell's thoughts flashed back and forth between hundreds of personal thoughts as the jeep pulled through the gates of the airfield and headed back to the Command and Control North compound. He had only had two years in grade as a lieutenant colonel, and hadn't even been expecting to be considered for promotion for at least another year. The new colonel smiled as he thought about his wife and children and how proud they would be. Colonel Clewell forced his thoughts back to business and Lieutenant Bourne.

Three weeks had passed since the enemy ammunition depot had been destroyed. Paul had reconnoitered the area surrounding the depot and found only old signs of enemy activity. The NVA had left in a hurry, abandoning a lot of equipment and some small stores of emergency food supplies. Paul was living off what he could find growing wild in the jungle and some food items left by the NVA soldiers. The pickings were getting very lean. Paul looked down at the torn and filthy camouflage uniform he was wearing and noticed that the ground-in dirt had turned the color of the cloth a medium brown, almost the color of the NVA battle uniform. The camouflage paint had worn off his face and he was feeling tired most of the time, a sure sign of malnutrition. A few days earlier his teeth had begun to ache, and a constant headache throbbed behind his eyes.

Paul opened one of his survival packs and removed a fishing hook and line from the kit. Today he was going to try and catch some fish down by the river. He carried only his combat gear with him as he carefully picked his way down a narrow deer trail. He paused to locate his position on his pocket map, but he had long since walked out of range of the map. He could see the glimmer of open water ahead of him through the trees. He crouched down to crawl under a low overhang of bamboo crossing the trail and froze. A bright green two-foot-long snake hung down over the trail from one of the bamboo stalks. Paul locked his eyes on the bamboo viper that his recon team had been named after and tried skirting around the reptile. There wasn't enough room to slip past the deadly snake without leaving the trail and creating a great deal of noise breaking through the dry bamboo, so Paul used the barrel of his CAR-15 to try and poke the snake off the branch. The reptile opened its mouth and revealed a set of one-inch fangs. Paul stepped back. Tales of bamboo vipers were constantly being told at CCN. The snakes were extremely dangerous to recon team members because of their highly toxic poison and the long fangs the reptile owned that could embed the amber liquid deep into a human muscle, normally in the neck or face of its victim. The snake dropped down on the thick matting of dead bamboo leaves and curled up ready to strike. Paul unholstered his silenced .22-caliber pistol and lined up the front sight bead between the bright yellow eyes. He had been told during his training in the Special Forces School that snake meat was full of protein; he wondered how the snake would taste cold.

The river was the size of a wide stream and was filled with rocks as it cut between a pair of low mountains. Paul found himself a promising looking hole in the riverbed and baited his hook with a small piece of the bright-green snake skin. The first underhand cast brought a quick strike. Paul hauled out a two-pound fish that closely resembled an American rock bass.

The warm sun on the river rocks extracted the tension from Paul's muscles and gave him a pleasant two hours of fishing. The fish he caught would give him the much-needed protein that his body was demanding. All he needed now was some fresh fruit to balance his diet. He smiled as he recalled all the Tarzan movies from his youth, where the ape man would reach up into a tree and pull down hands filled with ripe fruit. The jungle wasn't really like that. You rarely found any ripe fruit hanging from the trees. The monkeys and the birds ate anything before it got half-ripe for human consumption, and the insects would get the fruit that did make it down to the ground. Paul picked up the half-dozen fish he had caught and strung them on a thin vine before walking back to his campsite. He planned on eating his fill and then heading north.

Paul had restrained from calling his relay site for the past eight days because he had had nothing important to report, but he figured that since they might be getting worried about him he would make a short broadcast before he left the ravine ridge. The danger from making broadcasts was getting worse each day because the North Vietnamese were using direction-finding equipment in the area. Paul figured that he could hide for no more than another week before he would need to be extracted.

The raw fish tasted better than the oily flesh from the snake and settled his stomach. Paul carefully buried the remainder of the fish after he had eaten his fill, and then removed all of his equipment from his cave. He was going to take the secure voice radio and the NVA documents that looked important and bury the rest of the items.

He felt a sense of insecurity when he departed the familiar ravine and merged into the dark green underbrush. Paul took his time pushing through the thick jungle, and stopped often until he found a suitable piece of high ground to make a radio broadcast from. The sun was halfway through the afternoon and was starting to send long shadows across the jungle floor when Paul dropped his pack and started assembling his radio. The anticipation of hearing a friendly voice after being alone for so long caused Paul's hands to shake. He turned on the switch and waited an unnecessary couple of minutes for the set to warm up. The static emitting over the earphone was very weak, signaling that the battery was nearly dead. Paul squeezed the transmitter switch and spoke, "Hickory . . . Viper . . . over."

The static resumed. Paul began wondering if he had walked out of the range of the powerful Hickory relay-site transmitter when the radio crackled weakly. "Paul pushed the receiver tightly against his ear and listened.

"Viper . . . Command One . . . Keep your handset keyed so that we can home in on your signal. . . ."

Paul obeyed and keyed the handset. Ten minutes passed and the drone from a large aircraft could be heard high up beyond the thick jungle growth.

Paul called, "Command One . . . Viper . . . over."

No answer. The radio battery had gone dead. Paul dropped the handset to the jungle floor and tore at his pants pocket until he could free his URC-10. He placed the selector switch on the emergency frequency.

"Command One. . . . Viper."

The large aircraft answered almost immediately, "Viper, why are you using this frequency?"

"My secure voice set has lost its power. My URC-10 is all that I have left." Paul looked around at the quiet jungle and sensed danger. "I can't talk long . . . please monitor this freq at all times . . . out."

"Command One . . . We roger your last transmission. . . . We want you to come up on this push every four hours and listen for any traffic that we may have for you . . . out."

Paul disassembled the secure voice radio set and opened the latches that secured the boxes. He used his Randall knife to cut through the wiring and printed circuits. Paul buried the two boxes, scattered some of the critical components around the jungle, and pushed some of the parts back in his pack so that he could hide them along the trail.

A mile away from his broadcast site he stopped and adjusted the straps on his rucksack. The lost weight felt good. Paul recalled the conversation with Command One. The voice had sounded familiar. He stopped and found a hiding place on the jungle floor. He had to take some time to think, and he couldn't concentrate while he traveled in the jungle. When he moved, all of his thoughts were on the jungle and its occupants. Paul leaned back against his pack and thought. The voice coming over the radio was someone he knew—*LeBlonde!*

Mister LeBlonde rested his head back against the soft-cushion chair in the borrowed Air Force Airborne Command Center. The special command and control aircraft was loaded with electronic devices and secret equipment that could simultaneously monitor hundreds of radio channels. The Air Force used the aircraft to control long-range air strikes and flights of fighters that went into North Vietnam. The crew for the C-141 Starlifter was composed of twelve highly trained radio experts and four senior military officers from all of the services who were authorized to make high-level command decisions involving the immediate movement of two ready-action army divisions and over a thousand aircraft. General Pick had given LeBlonde command of the task force, which had been assembled with the sole purpose of getting Lieutenant Bourne out of the NVA-controlled area alive.

LeBlonde threw his handset against the panel of buttons on his radio console. "*Damn it! Piss poor* luck! He had to lose power to his secure voice now!"

Major Galviston and Lieutenant Loveless sat in the seats near the special agent.

LeBlonde glared at Galviston before he spoke. "Why in the hell don't your people carry spare batteries!"

"Sir, our people carry a heavy load as it is when they're inserted. . . . Anyway, who would have thought that he would have survived on the ground alone for a month!"

"Yes, sorry. . . . You're right."

Galviston drummed the tabletop with his fingers and frowned. "We must get him out of there soon. He's been on the ground long enough." Anger flashed across the special agent's face and he continued speaking. "I have already lost the best team of agents we had in the area." LeBlonde shook his head as he thought of the three Montagnards who had been caught earlier in the week by the North Vietnamese while they were trying to infiltrate through the enemy cordon that had been established around the area Paul was operating in. An intercepted NVA radio message had identified the Montagnards as Mauk, Pra-Teup, and Tru. LeBlonde shivered. He knew that for the three men to have given their real names to the North Vietnamese the torture must have been severe.

"Could we send in a Brightlight Team?" Jay spoke to Galviston.

"No . . . the NVA have secured the area surrounding

Bourne and are in the process of tightening the circle. They really want to capture him, and will shoot down anything that even comes close to him," LeBlonde answered Jay. "I'm afraid that the only hope Lieutenant Borne has is in finding a gap in the NVA cordon and slipping through on his own."

The room became very quiet with each of the men slipping into their own private thoughts. Paul's chances of getting out alive were very slim—and getting worse with each passing day.

Lieutenant Bourne was puzzled as to why LeBlonde was getting involved with his mission. The only thing that he could think of was that the Agency was trying to link up one of their special teams to him. Paul thought for a few more minutes and was sure that was what they were trying to do. He knew that he would have to become even more cautious now when he traveled through the jungle, to insure that there would not be any chance meetings where he would be forced to shoot before he had a chance to identify the people. Paul didn't realize it at the time, but the extra level of alertness would soon save his life.

One of the NVA patrols that had been assigned to track down the lone American stopped for a rest break less than a hundred meters from Paul's temporary hiding place. The monkeys gave a warning scream and scampered through the jungle growth above Paul's head. The serendipitous warning forced Paul to alter his course and bypass the large enemy patrol.

Paul had noticed that during the past nine days a larger number of NVA soldiers had entered the area, and instead of traveling very relaxed through the jungle, they were now very alert and moved as combat units. The destruction of the ammunition depot farther to the south wouldn't have been enough to have alerted troops so far to the north. Paul noticed that the enemy soldiers he was seeing were wearing heavy camouflage and crept through the jungle as if they were hunting for someone. He didn't need to guess for whom. Five times during the last week, Paul had heard dogs barking in the distance and had changed his course to avoid them.

Paul had no way of knowing that his picture and a daily story was being run as headline news back in the States and that the *Stars and Stripes* and local newspapers in Vietnam were also running daily stories on him. The NVA received copies of the newspapers being published in South Vietnam almost as soon as senior American officers did, and because of the publicity wanted to either kill or capture Lieutenant Bourne—preferably capture him, so they could use him for propaganda purposes.

The small cave provided Paul with a small sense of security under the jungle canopy, but he realized that his time was running out. He quickly decided that he had to walk out of the NVA-controlled jungle on his own and not ask for help from his headquarters. He knew that they would sacrifice a lot of men to rescue him, which would be too much for him to live with, especially if Coop or Jay were killed trying to save him. Paul flexed his jaw muscles and picked up his nearly empty rucksack. He would walk east until he ran into the nearest American base camp.

The drone from a passing aircraft reminded Paul that it was almost time for his radio message from Command One. He pulled out his URC-10 and held the small walkie-talkie sized radio up next to his ear and listened.

A few minutes passed and then the silence was broken.

"Viper . . . Viper . . . Command One . . . Command One . . . Blind broadcast follows. . . . NVA have established a large cordon around you. . . . We cannot Brightlight. . . . If you make contact . . . turn on your homing device and we'll saturate the area surrounding you . . . We have . . . *bzzzzz. . . . whooss-shhhh. . . ."*

Paul looked at his radio and tapped the case against his leg, but there wasn't anything wrong with the device. The NVA were jamming the broadcast. Paul turned off his radio to keep from draining the battery. He was glad they had decided not to send in a team and sacrifice people trying to get him out, but, being human, Paul felt the fear of being left alone. The NVA were trying in earnest to find where he was hiding, and where before they had ignored thick bamboo patches, they were now taking the time to search.

The olive-drab compass case glimmered from the sweat coming from Paul's palm. He shot an azimuth and continued walking east along his escape route. The thick jungle growth started thinning out and began turning into rolling hills with tall grasses. Paul halted and knelt on one knee when the sparse jungle cover broke on the edge of a large rubber plantation. The trees were neatly spaced in long rows and had small cups attached below series of "V" cuts in the bark. Paul backed into the jungle and turned south to skirt around the open plantation. He walked for almost an hour before he reached an area that was filled with huge boulders and tough shrubs and vines. He climbed carefully along the military crest of the rockpile, looking constantly for hunting cobras, until he found a spot that gave him a commanding view of the plantation and surrounding jungle. The main house of the plantation was at the far corner of the huge field of rubber trees and glimmered white in the hot sunlight. A Frenchman, probably, was the owner of the large plantation and was paying the North Vietnamese taxes so that they would allow him to grow and ship his rubber. Capitalism had a funny way of getting what it wants, even from the most devoted communists, he thought. Paul caught a glimmer of red streaks in the western sky and turned to face the beautiful Vietnamese sunset. Clear bright colors burst out over the robin-egg blue background, sending strips of flaming red and glaring blue over the trees spaced with dashes of yellow. Paul realized that he was watching the most beautiful sunset he had ever witnessed, each color sharp and clear without blending in with the next one. He placed all of his attention on the sunset and forgot about the enemy.

The roar from a large engine brought Paul back to reality. He had been so engrossed with the beauty of the sunset that he had lost his orientation and couldn't place the direction from which the engine had sounded. Paul waited for the machine to crank up again. Five minutes passed; then he heard a clicking sound coming from a starter motor, and a diesel engine started. The noise came from the rubber trees located three hundred meters away from his location. The engine sound was followed by another and another until the quiet sunset was broken as the plantation came alive with the roars of heavy engines idling—and then the sound of tank treads. The NVA had hidden a battalion of tanks on the plantation during the day, to protect them from searching American planes. Paul wondered if he should risk a radio message, knowing that if he used his radio he would have to travel through the jungle during the night.

He decided quickly. "Command One . . . Viper . . . over."

Major Galviston scraped his knuckles against the radio console as he grabbed for the handset in front of his chair.

"Viper . . . Command One . . . come in . . . over."

The rest of the crew in the C-141 came alert when they heard the call. Jay rubbed sleep from his eyes and sat up straight in his chair to listen.

"Viper . . . I've located a large rubber plantation . . ."

Galviston cut in on the broadcast. "Roger . . . I've plotted that location earlier today. . . ."

LeBlonde and Galviston had talked about the large French-owned plantation. LeBlonde's people had been observing the activity around the plantation and knew that they were paying off the NVA to operate in peace. Though the NVA used the plantation occasionally as a staging area, they had never been caught in the act.

"It's filled with NVA tanks . . . Russian-built, and big ones!" Paul paused and caught his breath. "I'd like you guys to get them before they can leave. . . . I'm running . . . out."

The transmission ended.

Paul slid the radio back in his pocket and started moving fast away from the rubber plantation down the backside of the rockpile. The NVA guard saw him first and broke the rhythmical sound of the tank engines with a short burst from his AK-47 assault rifle. Paul felt a flash of searing pain in his left thigh and flipped sideways behind a protruding rock for protection. A siren filled the early evening air followed by the sound of dogs barking on the plantation. Paul was in trouble. He pulled himself around a corner of the rock and saw the NVA soldier walking slowly toward the spot where he had made his original appearance. The NVA soldier had made a fatal mistake. The round from Paul's .22-caliber pistol entered through the man's left eye.

The numbness from the shock of the gunshot wore off within a hundred meters. Pain entered, and took control of his leg from the hip down. Paul stopped and forced air through his clenched teeth, trying to breathe in a counter-rhythm to his pulsating nerves. He took his first-aid packet from his rucksack and opened the dark-green box containing five morphine syringes. He removed two of them and sank the first needle deeply into the thigh muscle of his right leg, and slid the second needle a few inches above the hole in his left leg. The blood flow would soon remove the morphine from his body, but he was hoping that the medication would numb the pain coming from that portion of his body. Paul tied a clean dressing around the gunshot wound and stood to listen to the sounds of barking dogs echoing through the trees. He reached back into his rucksack and felt until he felt a salt shaker. He pulled back the green cloth-tape cover of the top of the shaker and smiled as he sprinkled the white powder around the area where he had stopped to fix his leg. He hobbled away into the jungle, stopping periodically to sprinkle the white, powdered tear gas on the ground. Human eyes couldn't detect the powder, but the extremely sensitive noses of the dogs would find it very fast.

Paul half-walked, half-ran, to put as much distance between the dogs and himself as he could before they reached the tear gas. Time passed without Paul realizing the span. He had to concentrate on controlling the pain in his body and not running into an NVA patrol by accident. In the distance to his rear Paul heard the yips and crys of the dogs when they reached the tear gas and stopped tracking him. He smiled above his pain and then forced himself to listen to the jungle for short periods of time, but the extreme pain would flash across his vision in red streaks when given the smallest opportunity to do so. Paul knew that he had to find a place to rest, even if it meant that his chances of escaping would diminish. He searched the thinning jungle for a hiding place and located a small rise of the ground near a clearing in the jungle. Paul staggered toward the rough piece of open ground and lucked out when he saw a nearby bomb crater half full of water. He slid down the gradual slope and washed his leg and face with the cool liquid. The water felt good, and he chanced drinking directly from the small manmade pond without using water purification tablets.

The short break gave Paul a chance to regain some of his lost strength; enough time to find a secluded spot under a bamboo overhang. Thinking of bamboo vipers and spiders, he crawled into the darkness under the low matting of inner woven branches. Paul stopped crawling and made a pillow for his head using his rucksack. He stretched out on the damp ground and didn't move a muscle for over an hour—until the pain from his wound forced him to sit up and shove another morphine syringe through his pants leg into his thigh. The pain slowly left him, allowing a morphine-induced calm to take over his thought processes. He slid his hand down his pants until his fingers reached the hole in his leg that was located halfway between his knee and hip. He moved his blood-covered hand around to the rear of his leg and slipped it under the bandage to feel the exit hole—it was the same size as the one in front. The NVA had been using armor-piercing ammunition, which was a lucky break for Paul. Regular rounds would have mushroomed, causing a great deal more damage. The pain he was feeling came mostly from the round nicking the bone. He felt like he was suffering a huge charley horse. Paul sighed with relief and lowered his pants so that he could cover the wound with a better bandage. The effort was almost totally exhausting and he slipped into a deep sleep.

The morning rays of sunlight found him feeling

much better and ready to travel once he'd spent a few minutes working the stiffness out of his worn muscles. He limped and used a trimmed tree branch to support him as he slipped through the jungle. He listened to the animals and insects as he wove his way around the big obstacles and thick bamboo patches.

Paul stopped abruptly, almost gagging from the strong smell that assaulted his nostrils. A bamboo pole was tied between two trees above the shallow ditch that made up the homemade latrine. The ditch was nearly filled to the top with human feces, and was covered with a swarm of constantly moving flies. Paul realized that a semi-permanent NVA force was using the latrine on a regular basis because the top layer of feces was still wet. He slipped down into a crouch and searched the nearby jungle. All of his senses were trying to detect any signs of the enemy positions. Paul backtracked the path that led to the latrine and lost the trail when it went over a small rise in the landscape. He quietly skirted upwind from the horrible-smelling hole and walked parallel to the worn path until his eyes detected an enemy bunker with two soldiers sitting on top of it.

Paul froze.

The NVA continued talking to each other as Paul slowly backed away from the fighting position, using the enemy voices to home in on once he was hidden in the jungle. Paul saw an entrance cut into the side of the hill just as he was about to stand upright. A pair of NVA emerged from the man-sized door wearing green uniforms with red collar tabs and pith helmets bearing red stars. Paul lowered himself until his chest was pressing the leaves under him. A group of six NVA soldiers followed the two guards out of the underground bunker. Paul figured from the size of the mound of rocks and dirt that the bunker could take a direct hit from a two-thousand-pound bomb without those hidden inside receiving any damage. The group of North Vietnamese soldiers halted less than thirty feet from Paul's hidden position. One of the older men started talking in a gravelly voice to the others, who were standing at varied positions of attention and respect. Paul figured that the speaker was a very important man. One of the officers facing the man kowtowed and answered him using a very humble tone of voice. Paul risked being detected and turned his head slowly so that he could get a better view. The NVA who had commanded the respect wore a perfectly tailored khaki uniform with two red-and-gold collar tabs. Paul recognized the insignia for a North Vietnamese general.

The dreams Paul had had back at the Marble Mountain base camp of killing an NVA general were now real. Here was his chance, but it wasn't quite the situational terrain that he would have hoped to have for his escape afterward. Minutes passed while the NVA talked, standing out of the bunker in the filtered sunlight. Paul tried to decide if he should take the chance to kill the general or if he should just slip away in the jungle. NVA generals were targets that rarely presented themselves, and killing one of them would be a fantastic coup for his recon unit. The other side of the argument was that he would probably be killed before he could escape the area. Paul ran the chances of his survival through his mind, realizing that surprise and confusion would be on his side for the first couple of minutes—that is, if he weren't hit by a stray round. He reached down and felt his leg. The pain was gone. The two NVA guards were the only ones nearby who had automatic weapons; the officers carried only holstered pistols. Paul's mind drifted back to his leg. Hard running would surely break the wound open again causing him to bleed. He grinned, knowing that his chances of actually walking out of the NVA-held territory were almost nil anyway.

A deeply hidden death wish emerged from the depths of his life force and began battling with his sense of survival while Paul unhooked his last NVA hand grenade from his web gear and pulled the pin. He switched the grenade to his left hand and drew his silenced .22-caliber pistol in his right. Paul took a deep breath and threw the live grenade, at the same shooting the NVA general through the left temple. The general stumbled forward and fell against one of the officers standing open-mouthed in front of him. Surprise at the totally unexpected conduct of the general forced the group of officers to step back into the blast from the hand grenade. The explosion covered the screams coming from the dying NVA officers. Paul retraced his way back around the NVA bunker line and stopped long enough to watch the guards stand to look back toward their headquarters base camp. The guards didn't show any alarm over hearing the explosion from within their base perimeter, probably assuming that a demonstration of some kind was in progress.

Paul moved as fast as he could once he had passed the NVA bunker line. After running for an hour, he stopped long enough to catch his breath and look around at the jungle. The rolling terrain was becoming very familiar. He blinked his eyes and rubbed his head in confusion. He had seen the terrain stretched out in front of him before. He stood and walked forward for a hundred meters, and the jungle opened up to reveal the southern edge of Co Roc Mountain. Paul smiled, and started walking toward the familiar landmark, feeling that he had found an old friend. The excitement from the kill had released enough adrenalin into his bloodstream to keep him going for at least another thousand meters and to the safety of the cliffs fronting the mountain. The pain in his leg was almost unnoticeable and took second place to his excitement. He was almost home.

Mister LeBlonde was shaken awake by one of the radio operators who was on late-night radio watch.

"Sir! Something big is going on!"

"What in the hell are you talking about, Sergeant!"

"Sir! The NVA have broken radio silence and are sending messages in the *clear*!" The seasoned sergeant's voice nearly broke with excitement. "It seems as if someone had an accident with a grenade and killed General Ho Van Duc!"

"The PAVAN Supreme Southern Commander?" LeBlonde shot out of his reclining seat onto his feet and hastened down the narrow aisle to the bank of radios monitoring the NVA military frequencies. LeBlonde stood behind the interpreters and listened to a very upset NVA radio operator talking in rapid Vietnamese. LeBlonde spoke the language fluently and followed the man's story. The NVA radio transmission was stopped in mid-sentence. LeBlonde smiled. Someone had caught the transmission being sent in the clear, and had stopped the message. LeBlonde had heard enough to confirm that General Ho Van Duc and two other junior generals had been killed along with some staff officers by an accidental grenade explosion.

A sergeant paused next to LeBlonde. "Sir, we've picked up some signals from Lieutenant Bourne's homing device. It looks as if he's located in the vicinity of Co Roc Mountain."

"Good! Let's get our aircraft over him. . . ."

Lieutenant Bourne turned on his URC-10. "Command One . . . Viper . . . over."

Jay heard the first call and instinctively grabbed the handset. "This is Command One . . . over."

"Is that you, Jay?"

"Yes, Viper . . . it's me. . . . What in the hell are you doing down there?"

"Well . . . for today's activity report . . ." Paul's voice carried a joking tone, ". . . I think I've zapped an NVA general, and for seconds . . . I've taken a hit in my leg and got to run. . . . I think I'm going to need help getting out of this one . . . good buddy . . ."

LeBlonde leaned over Jay's shoulder and listened. He might have known that with Paul on the ground that the NVA general hadn't had an accident. LeBlonde took the handset from Jay and spoke in a tense voice to the lieutenant.

"Viper. . . . Leave your homing device on . . . The NVA have already located you. . . . We'll use your device to guide in air strikes all around you. . . . We're coming to take you home!"

Mister LeBlonde was wide awake and started directing air strikes from the assets of his task force. LeBlonde was going to bring that boy's body out of there alive—or die himself in the effort.

Chapter 21

Colonel Clewell read the message he held in his shaking hand for the sixth time:

Pick sends
Lieutenant Bourne has become a national hero. Do not allow interviews by the press with any Command and Control North personnel—Break—Congress has approved by special vote a Medal of Honor for Lieutenant Bourne—Break—You will have him extracted immediately and flown to Washington D.C. for the President of the United States to award the medal (I guess I've been outranked)—Break—Good luck—Out.
Pick sends

Clewell dropped the message down on his desk. He wished the brass would allow him to run his own unit. The politicians deciding when to conduct combat operations from their Washington offices had already caused a great many casualties in the Vietnam War. Human lives would be wasted trying to pull Bourne out of the jungle now. Hell, he didn't know what was worse, uninformed hippie doves or uninformed bureaucratic hawks. The colonel's fingers drummed his desktop as he thought on a course of action.

There was a loud knock on the colonel's office door.

“Come in!” Clewell folded the personal message and tucked it in his shirt pocket.

“Sir, we’ve received a message from Command One.” The newly assigned second lieutenant hesitated outside the office door waiting to be invited in. “Major Galviston says that they’re going to extract Lieutenant Bourne.”

“Is the lieutenant in trouble?”

“Yes, sir; he’s wounded and has been running from a large NVA patrol that’s chasing him. A report just came in confirming Lieutenant Bourne’s claim to killing three NVA general officers . . . one of them was General Ho Van Duc.” The lieutenant spoke without force in his voice, not really believing what he was saying to the colonel. He really felt that he was being set up by the other officers in the TOC for some kind of initiation; after all, General Ho Van Duc was the Napoleon of North Vietnam. “Lieutenant Bourne is hiding on Co Rook Mountain.”

“Co Roc?”

“Yes, sir.” The new lieutenant’s face flushed, because the obvious mispronunciation had identified him as a newcomer to Vietnam.

“Thanks, Lieutenant. Have the TOC radioman call General Pick on the secure voice scrambler. I’ll join you in the TOC in a few minutes.” Clewell went over to the hatrack against the far wall and removed his pistol belt and head gear.

“Sir?” The lieutenant paused in the open doorway and looked back at the colonel.

Clewell turned. “Yes?”

“Is this Lieutenant Bourne real?”

Clewell paused and smiled, realizing that the new lieutenant thought that he had been set up for a joke. “Yes . . . and he’s probably the finest recon man in the world!”

"Oh . . . I thought the other officers in the TOC had sent me over here with that message to make a fool out of me."

"Believe me, Lieutenant . . . if you can accomplish a tenth as much as Lieutenant Bourne has done . . . you'll have served your country well!"

Paul moved slowly along the western slope of Co Roc Mountain. The NVA were known to use the mountain as a forward observer's outpost to keep watch on American activity on the Khe Shan plateau. A well-used trail blended in with the natural ridgeline of the mountain leading to the top. Paul crouched down and slowed his pace. He slipped the selector switch on his submachine gun to full automatic. He sensed that the NVA weren't far behind. A cluster of large rocks caught Paul's eye near the top of the mountain's western edge. He changed his course off the trail and slipped up to the strange-looking rock formation. Paul's trained military eye recognized immediately that the rocks had been disturbed by human hands. Voices echoed along the rock tunnel that the wall of boulders concealed from view. Paul squinted and focused his eyes on the rock formation, trying to locate the entrance to the hidden tunnel. The boulders had been strategically placed so they would protect the mouth of the tunnel from bomb blasts. The jungle had been cleared from the entrance in lanes, for well-constructed fields of fire.

Paul slipped over the maze wall and pressed his back up against the rock wall next to the tunnel entrance. He listened to the voices filtering out from the long dark hole. Paul stepped into the darkness and paused to allow his eyes to adjust to the half-light. The tunnel turned immediately to his left and then zigged sharply to the right at a ninety-degree angle, a precaution designed into the outpost to protect the occupants from a bomb blast near the mouth of the cave. Paul placed his hand against the cool wall. It was solid stone, maybe granite, and smooth to the touch. The tunnel had been hewn through solid rock by thousands of hours of hard labor. Sweat broke out on Paul's forehead even though a cool breeze was coming through the tunnel from the direction he was creeping. The tunnel took another sharp turn and then was filled with light. Loud voices bounced against the walls as two of the North Vietnamese soldiers started arguing with each other. Paul had reached the end of the maze. He reached down in the bright half-light and gently shook the thirty-round magazine, insuring that it was securely locked in place and lined up to feed ammo to the weapon's chamber.

Paul stepped into the lighted chamber.

One enemy soldier was lying on a bamboo-framed cot built next to the back wall of the large bunker. A well-built NVA soldier was looking out the observation slit holding a pair of high-powered binoculars to his eyes, and the third North Vietnamese was looking directly at Paul.

The observation post lost its peaceful atmosphere when the enemy soldier scrambled to get his AK-47 off the rack behind him. The rounds from Paul's CAR-15 ricocheted around the stone room, sending sparks flying and screaming their death song. Ten seconds later all of the NVA lay dead. Paul stepped over two of the bodies and looked out of the long, two-foot-high window that had been carved through the face of Co Roc Mountain. He leaned out over the foot-thick ledge and looked down at the river four hundred feet below. The great Khe Shan plateau spread out for miles in front of him, rendering a spectacular view. He could see the friendly smoke from the Lang Vei Special Forces Camp and helicopters the size of small gnats circling in the distance over the Marine base camp at Khe Shan. The NVA soldiers had hewn through a hundred feet of solid rock to build a perfect observation post.

The only exit or entrance was to the east, and was controlled by the NVA. Paul laid his CAR-15 against the wall and dragged the NVA bodies over to the window sill and pushed them out, one at a time. He used a slightly oily rag that he found in the bunker to wipe most of the blood off the walls, and then threw the red cloth out of the window. Paul picked up his weapon and retraced his path back through the tunnel. He didn't want to end up getting trapped inside the observation post like his victims had been.

The jungle hillside was free from any signs of an NVA force. Paul closely scanned the area that surrounded his position. There were three rifle firing positions that had been built to blend with the rocks, and they commanded any approach to the tunnel entrance from the west. Paul noticed that there was a box with a waterproof canvas cover located at each end of the fighting positions. He opened one of the boxes and saw that there was a supply of loaded extra magazines for the enemy AK-47s and five hand grenades neatly lined up on the bottom. Paul grinned a stoic smile when he saw that all of the grenades were American made and still in their cardboard-cylinder shipping containers.

The trail was the only accessible approach to the tunnel entrance, so Paul decided that he would wait at the NVA outpost for extraction. The NVA were well aware of his approximate location, and it would only have been a matter of time until they would have tracked him down. Paul figured his chances for defending himself were much better staying at the well-built outpost then being caught in the open jungle. The NVA builders of the outpost had done their work *too* well. Anyone who held the little fort could defend it against a much larger force. Paul returned to the observation room and quickly assembled all the NVA weapons and ammunition and hauled them back to the tunnel entrance. He returned to the stone room to remove an RPG-7 grenade launcher from its rack on the back wall and to drag a case of RPG rounds to the first NVA fighting position. He put his personal gear by the fighting position that commanded the path leading to the outpost, then spread the NVA weapons out amongst the other fighting locations, with an AK-47 loaded and ready to fire at each. Once everything had been set up exactly the way he wanted it, Paul called the Airborne Command Center.

"Command One . . . Viper . . . over."

"Viper . . . Command One . . . come in . . . over."

"I'm turning on my homing device for three minutes . . . get a fix on my position. . . . This is where I'm going to stay until you come and get me. . . . Tell the boss that I have a rock cave to hide in so he can drop big ones right on my position if he has to . . . over."

"We've locked in on your position . . . be prepared for fast movers. . . . ETA . . . for the first sorties is . . . four minutes . . . over."

"Thanks. . . . You can't get me out of here soon enough!"

Paul's radio broadcast was interrupted by a voice coming from the jungle a hundred meters downhill from his position. A loudspeaker amplified the words spoken in perfect English.

"Lieutenant Bourne . . . We know that you're up there. . . . Surrender to the People's Army and live!"

Paul pushed his radio switch. "The NVA have arrived . . . see ya!"

LeBlonde swiveled in his chair and faced the Air Force colonel. "Get your planes moving!"

Paul peered over the edge of the rock protecting him and saw six NVA soldiers standing out in the open at the edge of the jungle. One of them was holding a white piece of cloth that was tied to a long bamboo pole. Paul smiled and thought the NVA had seen too many American cowboy movies. He picked up the nearest AK-47 and centered the front sight over the NVA soldier's heart, who was standing in the rightmost position in the group.

The loudspeaker broadcast again. *"Don't be a fool, Lieutenant! . . . We have been monitoring your broadcasts. . . . We know that your friends are going to try and rescue you. . . . The People's famous 234th Regiment has surrounded this area. . . . Many Americans will die if you do not surrender. . . . We have antiaircraft guns covering all avenues to this mountain. . . . Bourne! Save your friends' lives and surrender!"*

Paul thought of all the lives that would be lost trying to save just one. He thought what the NVA official had said, one life in exchange for many, made a great deal of sense.

"We will give you medical treatment for your wounds. . . . We respect a hero. . . . As one warrior to another . . . I promise you will be given good treatment. . . ."

Paul squeezed the trigger.

Four of the NVA soldiers smashed down onto the ground, dead. The handheld megaphone bent when it hit a large rock. A voice screamed in anguish up the mountainside, "You *bastard*! We had a white flag!" The voice had an American accent. *"You fucking pig!"*

Paul glanced over the top of his protective rock at the four bodies twitching in the clearing. That was four NVA soldiers he didn't have to worry about later on.

"Surrender! Or we *will* kill you!" The voice speaking had changed from the first one to a clearer American accent. Paul peeked over the edge of his foxhole and saw the new speaker standing next to the enemy bodies. He lowered his weapon sight onto the NVA soldier's chest and fired just as the man jumped behind a pile of vine-covered rocks. Paul missed.

The voice sounded off the neutral rocks. "We will kill you, Bourne!"

A flight of four Phantom jets appeared flying in attack formation in the sky behind Co Roc. The aircraft cleared the top edge of the mountain by less than a hundred feet and dropped their bombs in unison. The scream from the jets' afterburners shook every living thing on the mountain, followed closely with the blast from the bombs and the heat created by the napalm. Paul dropped down in the ditch and crawled on his stomach back to the protection of the tunnel. The American jets made two more passes on the NVA positions and finished with a 20mm gun run. Paul peeked his head out around the corner of the entrance in time to see the last jet bank away toward the east.

"Command One . . . *Damn!* I could have used a *little* warning!" Paul held his URC-10 away from his ringing ear.

"Sorry . . . you didn't answer your radio. . . ."

"I was being serenaded by an NVA welcoming party speaking in English, no less. . . . They want me to surrender. . . . They say they're from the elite 234th Regiment. . . ." Paul saw movement at the edge of the jungle, ". . . gotta go now . . . out."

Lieutenant Bourne leveled the AK-47 he held in his hands and watched the jungle edge for ten minutes before relaxing and sliding back down against the cool stone wall. He was tired and his leg had begun to throb again. He kept glancing up over the wall toward the jungle, expecting an attack. Paul's eyes locked on a huge jungle warrior ant that was walking along the edge of the hewn stone wall surrounding his fighting position on three sides. Paul lowered the warm barrel of his rifle on the ledge and allowed the ant to crawl onto it before he lifted it and lowered the combat ant down to the dirt floor of his foxhole.

"It isn't safe up there, little fella."

The ant wiggled its antennae and turned in a tight circle before selecting a direction to walk in. Bullets bounced off the rocks and boulders surrounding Paul's fighting hole. The NVA were launching a ground assault up the back side of the mountain. Paul ran from position to position, firing the AK-47s at the advancing enemy. A short lull in the attack allowed Paul enough time to push the talk switch on his radio and make a short broadcast.

"Command One. . . . They're attacking!"

LeBlonde's voice came over the radio set. "I hope you can hold them . . . another flight will arrive in two minutes!"

"Try . . . out." Paul's message was cut short. The bullet hitting the rocks near his head sent fragments cutting into his cheek. He reached up and felt the blood, and then became angry. Paul raced along the firing positions, stopping long enough at each to toss a couple of hand grenades at the advancing enemy soldiers. The grenades, coupled with the noise of arriving fighter aircraft, forced the NVA attack to break up.

The Command One aircraft kept a continuous air-ground attack protecting Paul until dusk.

"Viper . . . Command One . . . over."

"Viper. . . ."

"We have to halt the air cover. . . . The Marines are

fighting a pitched battle east of here and need help. . . . Are you ready for extraction?"

"*No!* Too many NVA. . . . See if you can divert a sortie of the big bombers. . . . After they've gone . . . send in a Brightlight Team. . . . I'll be safe from any direct hits in the underground observation post . . . out."

Mister LeBlonde placed his headset down on the narrow counter in front of his radios. A B-52 strike would be the only thing that would keep the NVA units away from Paul until they could slip in a Brightlight Team. The Air Force colonel sitting next to LeBlonde handed the agent a folded slip of paper.

LeBlonde opened the message:

> NEXT B-52 STRIKE IS DUE FROM OKINAWA IN THREE HOURS.

"Send the time coded to Bourne." LeBlonde stood up and walked rapidly down the aisle to the back of the aircraft. He didn't think the NVA would waste the night waiting.

Paul looked down at the luminous dial on his watch: two hours left before the B-52s arrived on the site. The sun had dropped out of the sky, leaving the surrounding jungle black.

The NVA waited.

Paul felt for his weapons, knowing that he was running short of ammunition. He rested the back of his head against the stone and thought. If he stayed in the foxhole until the B-52s came, he might have a chance of surviving until dawn, but then again, the NVA might just launch a more-determined daylight attack or, worse yet, an attack during the night.

Lieutenant Bourne's mind slipped back to his Officer Candidate School days and the words from one of his survival instructors: The best defense is the best offense. He smiled to himself as he thought what that particular instructor was doing right now. Paul crawled up over the edge of the fighting hole carrying only his Randall knife and .22-caliber pistol. He planned on doing some night hunting in the jungle.

"Sir! General Pick is on the line!"

Colonel Clewell picked up the handset and waited.

"Clewell? Pick here."

"Yes, sir; I just wanted to inform you that Mister LeBlonde has already started Bourne's extraction. It seems as though the lieutenant is wounded and has found himself a place to hide in the jungle near Co Roc Mountain."

There was a long pause filled only with soft static coming from the radio.

"Sir? Are you still there?" Clewell adjusted the volume on his radio receiver.

"Yes . . . I was just thinking . . . Clewell—I don't want to lose that boy now!"

"Neither do we, General . . ."

"I know. . . . Is there *anything* I can personally do to help?"

"No, sir, everyone is giving their best. I think you've already been briefed about the Marines making contact with a large NVA force near the border, and they've drawn off a great deal of the support that has been keeping Bourne alive. . . ."

"I know . . . that we can't ignore a thousand men and support just one, but keep me posted on the results of Mister LeBlonde's efforts. I've told my aide to interrupt me anytime."

"Yes, sir."
"Pick . . . out."
The radio went silent.

Lieutenant Bourne crawled forward dragging his left leg. The thick part of the jungle's edge was only a hundred meters away from his fort. It took Paul an hour to get to the cover offered by the jungle. He paused when his outstretched hand touched the jungle growth. Paul tuned his ears for the miniscule sounds coming from the underbrush. He waited. A muffled cough slid along the ground, stopping at Paul's right ear. He pivoted on his stomach and crawled slowly in the direction of the sound's origin.

The NVA soldier's head was silhouetted above the lip of his shallow foxhole. Paul approached the enemy soldier from the rear and sunk the long blade of his Randall deep into the soldier's chest cavity, entering just below the man's voice box. Death came instantly to the soldier. Paul searched the foxhole with his hands and found the man's rifle, but he left it. He was looking for grenades. The second and third soldiers were easy kills as Paul crawled along the NVA defense line from foxhole to foxhole. None of the NVA soldiers were alert—especially the fourth one, who had fallen asleep. All of them had been told that they were hunting a single American soldier, and they were very confident that they would find him hiding under some bamboo in the morning, shaking with fright. Paul capitalized on their foolishness and killed five more enemy soldiers before he realized that he had crawled too far away from his fort and that morning would be lighting up the jungle floor within a matter of hours. Paul crawled faster up the hill leading to his protective fort once he had reached the portion of the NVA defensive line where he had made all the kills. Paul flipped over the low stone wall of his fort and fell down the three feet to the ground. He sensed immediately that something was wrong and noticed that all of his equipment was gone. The NVA had paid him a visit during the night. Paul was glad that he hadn't been home when they had arrived. A noise filtered down the tunnel from the observation post. Paul listened to the soft scraping sound of bare feet slipping over crushed stone that covered the floor of the tunnel. He pressed his back against the stone next to the exit and removed his silenced pistol. Two enemy soldiers dressed in solid black uniforms stepped out from the entrance of the cave carrying all of Paul's personal gear and the three AK-47s.

"Hi!" Paul spoke with a smile on his face.

The NVA soldiers responded too slowly to live. Paul pushed the bodies over the rock wall and listened to them roll down the slope and then stop.

Paul reestablished his defensive position and then turned on his URC-10.

"Viper . . . Command One . . . Command One . . . please come in. . . ." The voice sounded very tired and bored from saying the same thing over and over again for hours.

"Viper . . . over," Paul whispered.

"Where in the hell have you been!" The voice was angry but filled with relief.

"Out hunting. . . ."

"What?"

"I went to visit the NVA lines. . . . They were getting too overconfident and I caught some of them sleeping."

The group of soldiers and airmen who stood around the speaker on the aircraft shook their heads in amazement. Jay crossed his legs on the console and smiled.

"The B-52s were cancelled. . . . We had a night extraction set up for you, but because we couldn't reach you they had to go back and refuel. . . . We'll try again at first light . . . which should be very soon. . . ."

"Roger. . . . I'll leave my URC-10 on so that you can pinpoint my location. . . . Man! I'm ready to come home!"

Paul pushed his rucksack up against the wall and stretched out to relax. He could detect movement better listening in the dark than by trying to see, so he rested his eyes. A slight throb flashed up his leg. Paul dozed, and between the pain from his leg and the night sounds, he rested.

Dawn broke gently over the jungle trees and reached Paul's eyelids. He woke. The jungle was very quiet. He felt hunger and tried to ignore the growling coming from his stomach. Paul kept his eyes on the jungle until the sun was up full in the sky, then he sat back against the wall. He thought, and then started tracing an outline of an American flag in the loose rock dust at his side. He drew the flag waving in a breeze and placed dots in the corner of the flag for stars. Paul waited and drew and thought about the Brightlight Team arriving soon to take him home.

The radio crackled, "Viper . . . Command One. . . ."

"Viper . . . over."

"We're going to prep your area for twenty minutes, and then be prepared for a single ship to come in and pick you up. . . . Oh . . . Cooper wants you to know that he's with the team coming in after you."

"Roger! I feel better already!"

Sergeant Cooper had been listening to the radio with the headset in his helicopter that was circling above the Khe Shan plains waiting for the airstrike to finish. Cooper smiled and felt better. He had been suffering from severe guilt over leaving the lieutenant alone. If anything happened to him while he was trying to get to the lieutenant, at least he would know that he had tried.

Paul started gathering up his gear, but then he caught himself. He didn't need to haul all of that stuff out, just his ass.

The sound of a brassy bugle crashed against the side of the cliff. The unnatural noise scared Paul out of his personal thoughts. He looked over the edge of his defensive position and saw over a hundred charging NVA soldiers with fixed bayonets. He didn't have time to call Command One. Paul grabbed the nearest AK-47 and filled the air with automatic-rifle fire.

The Forward Air Control aircraft circling above Co Roc Mountain banked hard to the right when the pilot saw the charging NVA soldiers.

"Command One! Shit! The NVA are charging! Get those Cobras moving!"

"Roger, out!"

LeBlonde called the gunships that were circling two thousand meters from Co Roc and issued the orders to attack. The Cobra gunships peeled off from their holding patterns one at a time and lined up for the attack. The five helicopters cleared the rim of Co Roc at the same time and opened fire.

Paul heard the roar of the mini-guns, but was too busy shooting to look back over his shoulder. The NVA ranks were being cut to fishbait by the aircraft guns. Paul dropped down on one knee to change magazines in his AK-47, and lowered his head so that he wouldn't catch a stray round.

The thud behind him alerted Paul, and he whirled around to face the threat.

Too slow.

The NVA soldier thrust the two-foot-long bayonet

deep into Paul's chest.

Lieutenant Bourne pulled the trigger on his AK-47 through a reflex action. All of the rounds hit the NVA soldier in the face and right shoulder.

Paul braced himself up against the wall, holding his hand over the bubbling wound. Bright red oxygen-rich blood dripped between his fingers. Paul looked down at the ground and saw the warrior ant looking up at him.

"Well, little fella, it looks like you stuck around for the action. . . ." The pain forced Paul to throw his head back.

The Cobra pilot looked down as he passed over Paul's position less than ten feet above him. The two men's eyes locked on each other for a mini-second and then the chopper banked away.

"Command One. . . . This is Gunfighter. . . . An NVA just ran a bayonet through your lieutenant. . . ."

LeBlonde dropped back in his chair with tears running openly down the hard-lined face. He looked over at Loveless and shook his head.

Paul pulled himself up and reached over for his URC-10.

"Command One . . . Viper. . . ." His voice was tired and weak.

"This is Command One."

The following pause seemed like it lasted forever to the men on the aircraft and all those pilots who were listening in the cockpits of their fighting aircraft. Paul was trying to direct his remaining strength to holding down the push-to-talk switch.

"Jay?. . . . They got me good . . . Jay?"

"Yeah, Paul . . . I'm here . . . go ahead. . . " Jay brushed the tears away. ". . . Hey! You fucking rookie! Don't start talking that shit to me, hear!? Coop is on his way in to get you!"

"Uhhhmmmm. . . ." Pain ran uncontrolled through

the lieutenant's body. "You're right there, Jay. . . . There isn't an NVA *alive* who's got my number . . . *ahhh*. . . ." The gasp of pain transmitted over the radio.

Jay winced. One of the Cobra pilots lifted his black plastic helmet shield and wiped his eyes with the back of his gloved hand. A Marine radio operator monitoring the conversation threw his breakfast can of C-rations against the wall of his bunker in frustration.

"Jay? Man . . . I'm too tired. . . . really too tired. . . . I can't make it to the chopper . . . just want to sleep for awhile. . . ." Paul's scope of vision was narrow, as if he were entering a long dark tunnel.

LeBlonde dropped his head in his hands when he heard Paul begin to ramble. He knew the signs all too well. Paul was dying.

"Paul! Coop's coming! He'll carry you! Hang in there!"

Cooper had been listening over his headset and slid over the steel floor of the helicopter and leaned out to see the edge of the cliff approaching. He was ready to jump to the first sign of the lieutenant. Hate was written on the young man's face. He wanted revenge.

Paul heard the sound of the helicopter far away, not realizing that it was hovering right above him. Paul's vision darkened, but he saw the shape of a man jumping down at him. His vision went black and his body shuddered involuntarily, followed by his bladder releasing its contents.

Cooper hit the rocks hard, forcing his knees to jam against his mouth. The taste of blood caught Coop's attention for an instant, and then he saw Paul lying up against the stone wall.

He stopped.

Lieutenant Bourne's arm was lying extended out on the ground. The index finger on his right hand was touching the ground at the very tip of a flag that had been drawn in the dirt. The grooves in the rock dust that outlined the flag were filled with dark red blood that had run down the lieutenant's arm.

Tears burst from Coop's eyes, and then he acted. He reached down and picked up the paper-light body of his lieutenant. A stinging pain traversed the sergeant's arm, and he blinked the tears away so that he could see. A large warrior ant had sunk its pincers into the flesh of Coop's thumb.

Sergeant Cooper shifted the lieutenant's body and flicked the ant to the ground. The warrior insect landed at the top of the flag's staff and clicked its jaws.

Cooper ran with the body in his arms over to the waiting helicopter.

The pilot pushed the radio switch on his radio. "Command One . . . Gunfighter slick. . . . We have his body and are headed home."

The Airborne Command center was quiet.

Lieutenant Paul Bourne was dead.

Epilogue

Lieutenant Loveless paused outside the locked door to Paul's hooch. Sergeant Cooper stood next to him, looking out over the South China Sea at nothing in particular, just trying to keep his mind off the task confronting him.

Coop looked over at the lieutenant and saw the pained expression on his face. "Sir, I can do this by myself. . . ."

"No, Cooper; I told him that I'd take care of his stuff if anything happened . . . and I will."

The two men entered the plywood-and-tin shack. Paul's cut-offs were lying on his bed. Jay looked up in the rafters and saw the pair of surfboards. He knew then that he couldn't stay, and he walked back out of the hooch.

"Coop . . . go ahead. . . . I just can't . . ." Jay called back over his shoulder.

"No problem, sir; I'll get it together," Coop's voice quavered but held.

Jay walked back to his own hooch and sat on his bed. He leaned his back against the wall and stared at the *Playboy* poster collection covering all of the wall opposite from where he sat. He saw only dim outlines of the beautiful girls as he fought back the tears coating his vision. He had been with Paul for a long time and felt closer to him than he did to his own brothers. War had a way of really binding two people together, sort of like psychological Siamese twins. Jay recalled a friend of his father's, who had served in the Rangers with him during World War II. Whenever the man would call asking for a loan or for help, his father wouldn't hesitate giving him money or finding him a job somewhere. Jay's mother would get very angry and call his father a fool for constantly helping out the drunk, but now Jay understood the bond between his dad and his war buddy.

The stack of mail lying on the window shelf caught his eye and he remembered Paul's letters. Jay sorted through the pile and separated Paul's mail from his own. He stuffed the three letters in the side pocket of his jungle fatigues and walked down to the beach. A strong wind was blowing from the east that felt good against Jay's tired face. He found a quiet spot between two newly formed sand dunes and sat down. The first letter was a bank statement from Paul's bank in California. Jay read the last entry in the column: $18,867.89 in deposits. Paul had saved almost every penny he had earned in Vietnam. He tucked the bank statement under his leg to keep the wind from blowing it away and opened the second letter. It was from a Captain MacReal.

Dear Paul,

I really thought about this a lot before writing to you and decided that you should know. I am six months pregnant. I'll be leaving for the States soon to have the baby. I'm not going to force you into a marriage or any child support. I enjoyed making this baby as much as you did and I don't feel that you're obligated for anything.

I just wanted you to know, and felt you had the

right to know, that you'll be a father soon. You can rest assured that the baby is yours. You are the *only* lover I've had since I came to Vietnam. . . .

Natasha

The letter was short and to the point. Jay read the note three times. Paul was going to be a father! Then the joy over the news left Jay when he realized why he was reading the letter. It was hard for him to accept the fact that Paul was really dead. Loveless folded the letter and slipped it into his shirt pocket.

The third letter began:

A Department of the Army Special Review Board has reviewed your records against those of your peers. It is the decision of the board that your file does not meet the high standards needed to be an army officer.

This decision has been based on your officer efficiency reports with emphasis being placed on the recent report written on your performance by Captain A. D. Hetten.

You will be released from active duty no later than ninety days after receipt of this letter. . . .

The official letter continued, giving details on his separation from the service for reasons of substandard performance. It was too much for Jay to mentally absorb. He stood up and screamed his rage at the ocean.

"Those bastards! Those faceless stupid bastards!"

Sergeant Cooper heard Jay's yelling and ran down the beach toward Loveless, who had dropped down on his knees and was pounding the sand with his fists.

"Sir?"

Jay looked up at the puzzled face of the sergeant and hissed out the words he felt tearing at his throat. "Those bastards have thrown Bourne out of the Army! Can you believe that? For substandard performance, of all things! Can you *believe* that shit!"

Cooper looked puzzled. How could they throw the lieutenant out of the army. He was dead.

"They're going to pay for this fuck up!" A look crossed Jay's face. He knew what would happen if the letter was placed in the right hands, especially if it were given to the newspapers who had been covering the story on Paul's lone adventures.

The officer on duty in the Stovall Building on the outskirts of Washington sat with his feet crossed on the edge of his desk. The half-empty coffee cup he held up to his lips had the insignia of the Chief of Staff of the Army emblazoned on its side along with the dates that the lieutenant colonel had served in that section of the Department of the Army. A young major sitting across from the career lieutenant colonel was reading a copy of the *Washington Post*.

"Colonel, get a load of this headline: LONE GREEN BERET LIEUTENANT DESTROYS NORTH VIETNAMESE AMMUNITION DEPOT—STOPS MAJOR ENEMY OFFENSIVE!"

The lieutenant colonel casually dropped his feet down to the highly polished floor. "It's about time those damn reporters let us have a hero over there!" He started shuffling through some papers cluttering his desk and then, as an afterthought, asked, "Does the article give the lieutenant's name?"

"Yeah . . . I just read it . . . let's see. . . ." The

major paused and ran his finger down the printed lines of the article and stopped. "His name is Lieutenant Bourne . . . Paul Bourne." The major looked up and added. "The article states that Congress has had a special vote and approved a Medal of Honor for him!"

The lieutenant colonel stopped sorting through the stacked papers and looked straight ahead at the wall partition. "Did you say a Lieutenant Paul Bourne?"

"Yes, sir." The major looked over at the senior officer. "Something wrong?"

The lieutenant colonel reached for a list of names on a roster he had Scotch-taped to the side of his filing cabinet. He ran his finger down the alphabetical listing and stopped. *"Holy Shit!"*

The major dropped his newspaper as the lieutenant colonel ran from the room saying, "We've just sent a letter of substandard performance to Lieutenant Bourne!" The colonel stopped just outside the door, ran back to the major's desk, snatched the newspaper from the junior officer's hands—and took off for the commanding general's office.

Colonel Clewell stared out his window while he waited for the sergeant to locate Lieutenant Loveless. Thoughts of Lieutenant Bourne kept waving through his mind. He recalled the first time he had seen the young lieutenant outside of the Nha Trang headquarters. He had been very impressed with the proud bearing the young man had possessed, and the confident grin the kid would give you when he knew that he had performed well. He wished that he could have traded one of the many assholes he knew hiding back in the States for Bourne's life.

A knock on the door disturbed the colonel and brought him back from his personal thoughts. "Come in."

Loveless entered the room and reported to the colonel. Clewell sensed a change in the young lieutenant's attitude but attributed it to Bourne's death.

"Jay, Headquarters has approved your being selected as the escort for Lieutenant Bourne's body."

Loveless looked out the window, failing to show any response to the colonel's words.

Clewell paused and then spoke again, "Lieutenant Loveless, is something wrong?"

Jay's eyes flashed silver sparks when he turned his head from the window and looked at the colonel. Hate formed wrinkles around the lieutenant's eyes. "No, sir! I'm just fine!"

"If you would rather have somebody else. . . ."

"*No, sir!* Paul is my best friend! *I'll* escort him home!"

Clewell stood up. "Tonight . . . the plane will leave for Travis Air Force Base in California and then the . . . uhh . . . body will be flown to the international airport in Los Angeles." The tough Special Forces colonel blinked his eyes and cleared his throat before continuing, "Lieutenant Bourne lived near there before he entered the service, and he stated on his data card that he would like to be cremated and his ashes spread out over the beaches at Malibu." Clewell reached down and picked up a piece of teletype paper. "Also, there will be another casket aboard the aircraft. The soldier is a nominee for the Medal of Honor, a Private First Class O'Toole from the 173d Airborne Brigade." Clewell looked at Loveless. "You'll be responsible for escorting both of the caskets until you reach California, and then a stateside escort will be provided for the paratrooper."

"Who should I give Paul's personal items to, sir?"

"You might run into some difficulty when you reach California. Lieutenant Bourne left a will with Captain

White that left everything he owned to a Captain Natasha MacReal. It seems that she's a nurse working in one of the hospitals here in-country. Do you know her?"

Jay became more attentive with the mentioning of the woman's name. "Yes, sir, but not personally. . . . I know of her."

"Well, we've tried reaching her at the hospital she was working at, but she's left for the States." Clewell looked out of his window over the sand and buildings toward the hidden sea. "I know you and Bourne were close friends and you should know that he's a Medal of Honor Winner. Congress approved his award last week. We were going to present it to him when he was extracted."

Jay's mind backtracked to the letter he had read from the Department of the Army. He stood and placed both of his hands on the edge of the colonel's desk. Anger possessed him when he spoke. "Those fucking bastards! I can't believe those rear-area motherfuckers did that to him!"

Clewell watched the lieutenant and wondered if the young man had cracked under pressure. "Jay? What are you talking about?"

"Talking about? . . . You want to know? . . . All right! I'll tell you!" Jay pulled the Department of the Army's letter out from his side pocket and slid the envelope across the colonel's desk. "That's what I'm talking about!"

Colonel Clewell opened the crumpled envelope and looked up over the edge of his wire-framed glasses at Jay, then read the letter. He couldn't believe what he had read, and he reread the last three paragraphs. "Damn! I can't believe this!"

"*Believe* it, sir!" Jay turned his back on the colonel. ". . .and can you believe the reason was for substandard performance!" Jay turned and took the letter out of the colonel's hands. "I'm going to shove this down their fucking throats!"

Lieutenant Loveless left the colonel's office and went back to his hooch to pack for his trip to the States. He planned how he would use the letter as he threw what few traveling things he had into a well-worn suitcase. Mister Michaels from *Newsweek* would know how to handle the story. Jay was going to make the Army eat a hell of a lot of crow for what they had done to his best friend.

Colonel Clewell sat behind his desk with his fingers pressed together making a tepee. His two index fingers were pressed against his forehead and his thumbs were tucked under his lower lips. He used that position for his hands when he was in deep thought. General Pick had to be notified about the Department of the Army letter. Colonel Clewell knew that no one could take the letter from Loveless, because Bourne had signed an authorization card for his friend to pick up and handle his personal mail. The military was going to suffer a really bad black eye if they didn't move fast. Clewell picked up his telephone and placed a call.

General Pick slammed the door to his office so hard that the frame cracked. The aide de camp who was sitting behind the desk in the attached office jumped to his feet.

The general frowned at the aide and handed him a hastily written message. "Colonel, send this to the Chief of Staff."

Lieutenant Loveless thanked the jeep driver and tapped his knuckles on the hood of the jeep as he hopped out in front of the main air terminal in Da Nang. He looked around at the hundreds of soldiers lying around on the benches and floors of the building, trying to get a few minutes sleep before they left on R & R flights or caught their planes back to the States. Jay wove his way through the crowd to the nearest check-in counter and handed the harried clerk a copy of his special courier orders. She gave him a boarding pass and a flight number. Jay folded the pass slip and pushed it in his rear pocket. He felt like having a cup of coffee, and he pushed his way through the mass of sweating troops to the large snackbar. The lines were wrapped around the room. Jay turned back and went to the boarding gate for his aircraft.

Three military policemen had a soldier standing spread-eagled against the wall. One of the MPs was patting down the man's legs. A suitcase lay open on the inspection counter with the major components for a CAR-15 submachine gun spread out around it. A ten-inch-long clear plastic bag that contained a white powder was being looked at by another one of the MPs. The soldier was a mule trying to smuggle heroin and an automatic weapon back to the States.

Jay shook his head and looked for an empty seat in the rows of benches filling the waiting area. He couldn't find an empty one, so he carried his suitcase to a small open spot near the wall and shoved it up against a pile of duffle bags. A group of army nurses were sitting together near the bank of windows watching the drug bust.

"Look, Natasha! They caught a drug smuggler!" one of the older nurses, a lieutenant colonel spoke to the younger woman sitting down on the bench.

Jay's head snapped around at the sound of the woman's name. The young nurse who was sitting was obviously pregnant. A soldier sitting across from her was leering at the nurse, with his thoughts written clearly on his face. A nurse joined the group carrying a donut box full of paper cups containing coffee and tea.

Jay shoved his way through the crowded waiting room until he reached the nurses. "Excuse me . . . are you Natasha MacReal?"

The pregnant woman looked questioningly up at the young second lieutenant who knew her name. "Yes . . . I am."

"I'm Jay Loveless!"

She didn't respond. He knew her through the letter she had written to Paul, but she had no reason to know who he was. Jay's face turned red. "I mean . . . I was a close friend of Paul Bourne's. . . ." Jay looked down at the cement floor.

"Was?" The word was a whisper slipping from the woman's shocked lips. The nurses surrounding Natasha looked at Jay in shock.

Jay's eyes shifted around the room; it was obvious she hadn't heard of Paul's death. "I'm sorry, Natasha . . . I shouldn't have. . . ." Jay turned to leave.

"Wait. . . ." The deep hurt she had read in Jay's eyes pulled at Natasha's heart. "Tell me what happened . . . please?"

Jay turned to face her again, but this time the tears ran unashamed down his cheeks. "Paul was killed on patrol. . . ."

"Girls . . . please excuse us. . . ." Natasha held her own hurt. She slipped into her protective professional nurse's shell. "Sit down, Jay, and tell me everything that's happened. . . ."

Jay told Natasha the whole story, even the classified portions. He left nothing out. Natasha sat back and listened, holding her hand against her stomach feeling the new life within her. She was very glad that she hadn't had the abortion.

The sedan bearing the four white stars on the bumper tag pulled to an abrupt halt in front of the entrance gate. General Pick and Colonel Clewell exited the car and walked with long strides up to the doors of the terminal. Colonel Clewell paused long enough at the entrance to locate Jay, who sat holding a young nurse in his arms. He tapped the general's arm and pointed to where the pair was sitting by the windows. Soldiers came to attention as the four-star general strode past them, leaving the whole terminal in a state of confusion.

General Pick stopped in front of the lieutenant who was sitting with his back to the crowd. "Lieutenant Loveless?"

Jay looked up from Natasha and saw the general. "Yes, sir," Jay came to attention.

"I'm General Pick. Let's go outside where we can have some privacy to talk." The whole population pressed into the air terminal was staring at them. The two officers left the terminal through the loading gate without being challenged by the guards.

The general stopped outside and turned to face Jay. "Let's get right to the point, Lieutenant. . . . You have a letter that could cause the army a great deal of grief. I want that letter."

The general could see the lieutenant set his jaw in a determined pose.

"Before you answer me, let me assure you that the officers responsible for the letter will pay very dearly for what they have done. . . . Hetten and his cronies are the type of officers that I personally detest!" The general knew that the young lieutenant standing in front of him didn't give a damn about his own career, but he was hoping that the young man had a sense of honor and justice. "Lieutenant Loveless . . . don't punish the *whole* army for the actions of a few bad officers. Think of Lieutenant Bourne. . . . Do you want his image blackened? He's a national hero right now, and there're a lot of reporters back in the States that would love to find something to write about that would change that around. You know how they work . . . anything for a story."

Jay stared deeply into the general's eyes without any fear. He sensed that the general was fair and would keep his word. Jay unbuttoned his khaki shirt and tore the tape away that was holding the letter to his stomach. He handed the plastic-wrapped letter to the general.

"Thanks, son . . . I promise. . . ." The steely general tried to grin but lost the smile somewhere between the thoughts running through his brain. He added, "I sort of liked Bourne myself."

Pick nodded his head at Clewell, who was waiting on the other side of the glass windows. The colonel and the aide de camp joined the general as he strode over the hot tarmac to his waiting Lear jet. He needed to walk in order to release some of the anger that was building up inside of him.

The general paused on the bottom step of his plane and turned to speak to his aide before he boarded the aircraft. "I want Captain Hetten, Sergeant Dryman, and Lieutenant Colonel Bakersun waiting for me in my office when we arrive in Saigon!"

"What was that all about?" Natasha stuck her head through the doorway.

"Come here." Jay held out his arm for Natasha to crawl under. "Let's go over to the aircraft and make sure that Paul is loaded OK."

The loading ramp was attached to the jet's belly and two caskets were waiting on a cart to be loaded. Jay appoached the metal caskets with Natasha at his side. He reached over and lifted an identification tag that was tied on the nearest bronze casket. It read: *PFC Robert O'Toole, 173d Airborne Brigade.*

Jay patted the metal box. "Take care of my buddy on the ride back . . . hear?"

Lieutenant Loveless and Natasha walked slowly up to the rear of the remaining casket. The tag was fluttering in the wind. Natasha caught it and looked down at the words written in bold letters: *Lieutenant Paul Bourne*—and under his name was, hand printed, MEDAL of HONOR WINNER.

GLOSSARY OF TERMS

Airborne Command Center (ACC): Air Force aircraft used to control large operations in the air or on the ground. Aircraft carries advanced electronic and communications systems.

aide de camp: French term. Refers to an officer who is assigned to a general and performs the administrative tasks for the general during travel and social functions.

AK-47: Soviet assault rifle used by most communist countries.

APC: Armored Personnel Carrier. Designed to carry a squad of infantry into battle.

A-Team: The smallest Special Forces operational unit. Used during the Vietnam War to control camps bordering the Cambodian and Laotian countries that remained neutral.

A1E: A World War II vintage fighter bomber aircraft that had a long on-station time and could carry a heavy payload of bombs. The A1Es were a favored aircraft for those troops who were in contact with the enemy and needed air support.

battalion: A formation of soldiers. American: Three companies and numbering around five hundred fighting men. North Vietnamese: Three companies and numbering around three hundred fighting men.

berm: Earth mound that was normally built around an A-Camp in the Delta region to prevent a direct line of fire into the camp.

BOQ: Bachelor Officer's Quarters.

B-4 bag: A gray-colored canvas bag used by paratroopers to pack their parachutes in after a jump. Used by the Air Force to carry personal gear.

Brightlight Team: Code name for a small detachment of heavily armed soldiers who were assigned to rescue another team that was either in heavy contact with the enemy or so decimated that they couldn't extract themselves. Brightlight Teams operated out of Command and Control North (SOG) and were very dangerous missions.

B-Team: A Special Forces unit that is the Headquarters element for three or more A-Teams.

bullboat: A round boat three to six feet across used by Vietnamese fishermen. Craft is very similar to American Indian bull boats.

Charlie: Slang word used for North Vietnamese or Viet Cong.

Chieu-Hoi: I surrender.

Chief-of-Staff: Military duty position. Senior Army officer. (Top four-star general).

claymore mines: Antipersonnel weapon. Placed above the ground and pointed toward the enemy's avenue of attack. Detonation discharges hundreds of steel balls at a high velocity.

click: Slang term for kilometer, one thousand meters.

CO: Commanding officer.

corps: Military unit composed of two or more divisions.

C-rations: Combat rations.

Delta: The southernmost corps or section of South Vietnam. Terrain is very flat and is used for growing rice.

Distinguished Service Cross: America's second highest valor award.

Division: American fighting unit composed normally of three brigades (total: 16,000 soldiers).

FAC: Forward Air Controller. Used by the Air Force to call in and guide fighter aircraft to a target.

gook: Slang word for North Vietnamese.

Hoa-Hoa: Vietnamese religious sect with a strong anticommunist following.

hooch: Slang term for a temporary living space for

soldiers in Vietnam.

K-Bar knife: Fighting blade used mostly by Marines.

LLDB: Lac Luong Dac Biet. South Vietnamese Special Forces.

LOLEX: Low level extraction of supplies from flying aircraft.

LRRP Rations: Long Range Reconnaissance Patrol rations. Dehydrated food packets.

LZ: Helicopter landing zone.

MACV: Military Advisory Command—Vietnam.

mayday: Aircraft emergency call for help.

Medal of Honor: Department of Defense award for valor. The United States' most coveted valor award.

medevac: Medical evacuation.

Mike Force: Three or four companies of highly trained commandos who were used to reinforce Special Forces A-Camps under attack.

Montagnard: Vietnamese "Indians." Tribes located in the high mountain areas of Vietnam and very underdeveloped. Montagnards were looked upon as second-class citizens by the Vietnamese. Montagnards were probably the original settlers of Vietnam.

M-79 grenade launcher: Shoulder-fired single-shot weapon that fired small grenades.

NVA(PAVAN): North Vietnamese Army. People's Army of North Vietnam.

Phantom: American jet fighter F4-E.

POW: Prisoner of war.

Purple Heart: American decoration for receiving wounds while fighting an enemy.

PRC-77: (Scrambler, secure voice radio set) Radio set carried by infantry and recon troops.

PSP: Perforated steel planking. Used originally for making runways, but also used for roof on bunkers and covered with sandbags.

Randall knife: Coveted handmade fighting knife made by the Randall family, Orlando, Florida.

recon: Slang word for reconnaissance.

RF-PF: South Vietnamese Regional Forces and Popular Forces. Used to protect villages. Similar to the National Guard concept.

R & R: Rest and Recuperation. A period of five to seven days' leave for American soldiers to countries surounding Vietnam, such as Australia, Japan, etc.

RT: Reconnaissance Team.

sapper: A highly trained North Vietnamese soldier who was used to infiltrate American compounds and destroy equipment and supplies. Also used as the initial force during an attack on American positions.

scrambler: A device to alter radio transmissions so that they could not be monitored.

SF: Special Forces (Green Berets).

Silver Star: American award for valor (gallantry in action).

SKS: Soviet-made rifle.

SOG: Studies and Observation Group (changed to Augmentation). A top-secret reconnaissance unit. Selected Green Berets were chosen to operate highly trained teams.

Spooky: Code name for a C-130 aircraft mounted with mini-guns.

STABO rig: A device designed by Special Forces soldiers, used to extract a person from heavy jungle where a helicopter could not land.

time (military): 2400 hours = midnight; 0100 = 1AM, 0200 = 2AM, etc.

Viet Cong: South Vietnamese communists.